The Casquette Girls

The Casquette Girls

ALYS ARDEN

SKYSCAPE

SKYSCAPE

Published by Skyscape, New York

www.apub.com

Amazon, the Amazon logo, and Skyscape are trademarks of Amazon.com, Inc., or its affiliates.

ISBN-13: 9781503946545
ISBN-10: 1503946541

Cover illustration by Galen Dara

Cover design by Mark Ecob

Map illustration by Mystic Blue Signs

Printed in the United States of America

To the people of New Orleans—past, present, and future. To the people who inspired the myths and the legends, to the people who continue to tell them, and to the people who continue to believe them.
Which ones are true?
Well, that depends on what you believe in.

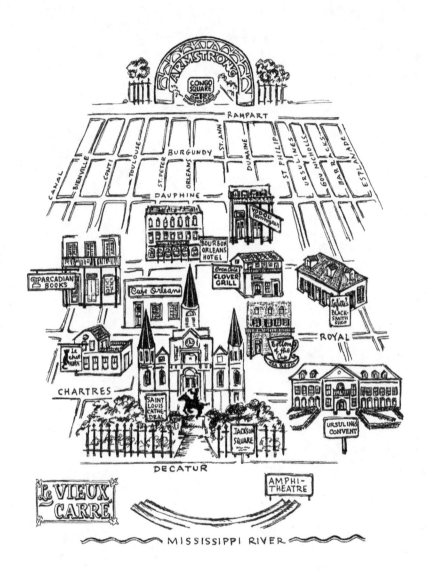

PART 1

The Storm

The city where imagination takes precedence over fact.

William Faulkner

CHAPTER 1

On the Road

October 9th

The day had finally come.

Elation coursed through my head, my chest, my stomach—until the tips of my fingers tingled, as if the sensation were trying to escape the confines of my nervous system.

My father and I were finally on our way home.

Trying not to let the anticipation drive me crazy, I leaned back in the passenger seat and took deep breaths, inhaling the scents of worn black leather and bubble gum. The combination reminded me of sitting in the front seat as a child. I'd always been up for a ride in my father's prized possession because I knew there'd be a sugary pink stick waiting for me in the glove box.

The city wasn't exactly encouraging people to come home yet, but my father had always been a bit of a rebel. This fact, topped with endless nights of me begging and pleading, had finally made those four little words slip out of his mouth: "Okay, let's go home."

As soon as he caved, I fled the Parisian boarding school where my French mother had dumped me while my father and I were "displaced." She didn't tell me good-bye, and I never looked back.

I landed in Miami late last night, and we were on the road by six this morning. I didn't want to give my father the chance to renege.

Ten hours later, we were still purring down the interstate in his 1981 BMW.

But I didn't mind the long drive. In my sixteen years, I'd never been away from my father for that long. I'd never been away from New Orleans for that long either. It felt like years since the mandatory evacuation, but in reality it had only been two months—two months, two days, and nine hours since the Storm had touched ground.

The Storm was the largest hurricane in US history. Scientists were still debating whether it should even be considered a hurricane because it had smashed all previous classification parameters. They didn't even name it. Everyone simply referred to it as "the Storm." Economists were predicting it would end up being the greatest natural disaster in the Western world, and there were even rumors flying around that the federal government was considering constituting the area uninhabitable and not rebuilding the city. That idea was incomprehensible to me.

The media was all over the place about the devastation. We'd heard such conflicting stories there was really no telling what would be awaiting us (or not awaiting us) upon our arrival. Had our home been damaged, flooded, ransacked, robbed—or any combination of those things? Was it now just rotting away? I fiddled with the sun-shaped charm hanging from the silver necklace that nearly reached my waist, wrapping and unwrapping the thin chain around my fingers.

My phone buzzed.

| **Brooke** | 3:42 p.m. | Are you close? Text me as soon as you get home. I want to know everything, ASAP! xoxo. |

I quickly pecked,

| **Adele** | 3:43 p.m. | I will! How's La-La land? <3 |

I didn't exactly have a laundry list of close friends, but Brooke Jones and I had been attached at the hip since the second grade. The Joneses had been stuck in Los Angeles since the evacuation, and Brooke was freaking out on a daily basis because her parents were adjusting to the West Coast lifestyle at an alarming rate. Even the *thought* that her parents might permanently relocate to California made me cringe.

"Waffle House?" my father asked as we sped past the Florida state line into Alabama. He proceeded down the exit ramp before I could respond.

A bell dinged when I opened the door of the infamous southern chain, causing all of the employees to shout a welcome without looking up from what they were doing. My father headed to the bathroom, and I jumped into a booth, grabbing a napkin to wipe pancake-syrup residue off the table.

"I'll be with ya in a second, darlin'," a waitress yelled from across the narrow, shoe box–shaped diner.

Johnny Cash blared on the jukebox, the air reeked of grease, and the fluorescent bulb in the overhead light gave everything a sickly tint. I couldn't help but chuckle, thinking about the stark contrast of this scene to my life just two nights ago: sitting in a café on the Champs-Élysées, eating a crêpe suzettes with my mother. Well, *I'd* been eating a crêpe. She'd never allow herself to eat something as appalling as sugar.

Midchuckle, I caught the gaze of a guy sitting solo in a booth across the aisle, who was slowly stirring a cup of coffee. Our eyes locked. My cheeks started to burn. I grabbed a menu so I could pretend to focus on something and let my long waves of espresso-colored hair fall in front of my face, trying to recall the last time I'd taken a shower. *Ugh.* I'd been in transit for more than twenty-four hours at this point.

I lifted my eyes to find him still looking intensely at me.

He was probably a few years older than me . . . and far too sophisticated to be sitting in this particular establishment among the tall hairdos and flip-flops. His black leather jacket was not the biker kind you might find in any diner in the Deep South—it was softer looking, trendier, possibly custom-made. The jacket, along with his dark, slicked hair, made him appear part James Dean, part Italian *Vogue*. For a split second I forgot where I was, as if stuck in some kind of Paris–Alabama time-continuum hiccup.

When I realized I was staring at him again, I became instantly flustered. His eyes didn't move, but the corners of his mouth slowly spread upward into an innocent smile. Or maybe it was deceptively innocent? Just as my heart began to speed up at the prospect of finding out, my fork slid across the table, flew halfway across the room, and clanked against his ceramic mug.

"Sorry!" I covered my face, mortified, and considered crawling underneath the table. I'd been so caught up in the moment I hadn't even noticed myself flick it.

"Don't worry, honey, I'll bring ya a new one," the waitress yelled.

As if I was worried about the fork. I'd nearly taken out the eye of the hottest guy within a fifty-mile radius. My heart pounded melodramatically.

When I finally mustered the courage to raise my head to catch another glimpse of him, all I saw was his mug on top of a ten-dollar bill. Realizing I'd been hiding my gaze from no one, I became even more embarrassed.

Of course he ran. I am obviously hazardous.

"You okay?" my father asked as he slid into the orange leather booth.

"Yep, the jet lag must have just kicked in," I blurted out, "but I'm super excited for cheesy eggs."

"I thought you hated American cheese?" he asked suspiciously. "You always called it plastic."

"Yeah, well, I guess something becomes more desirable when you can't have it." There were certainly no American-cheese-like products in France.

We ordered and then sat in silence while we waited for our food. My father turned his head to stare out the window. I knew he was too nervous to ask me about Paris, and I was not going to readily volunteer up any information. It was weird to spend your entire life with someone, be suddenly separated for two months, and then reunite. It felt strange that it felt strange being together.

Luckily the food came quickly, and soon he was polishing off a stack of waffles, while I forced myself to choke down eggs smothered in plastic cheese.

"How about I drive for a while?" I asked as we headed back to the car.

"How about I drive and you study?"

"Why should I study? *Technically*, I'm not even enrolled in a school right now."

"You are enrolled in a school right now, Adele . . ."

I unintentionally slammed the passenger door after getting in.

"You are *technically* still enrolled in Notre-Dame International." He pulled out of the deserted parking lot and in his best I-am-serious voice added, "And if we get to New Orleans and find out you can't get into a local school, you're going to be on the first plane back to Paris. Back to school. That was the deal."

"I am *not* going back to Paris." I didn't care what I had previously agreed to. *"Je déteste Notre-Dame International! Je déteste Paris!"* I said in my most dramatic French accent, but I stopped myself before I said something about detesting my mother. Those were words he certainly would've understood. But he had only himself to blame for my speaking French; he was the one who'd forced me to take private lessons since I was five—a year after my mother had skipped town—as if my ability to speak her native language might bring her back.

"I can't believe you shipped me off there in the first place. I belong here, not with rich kids in boarding school. Not with *her.*"

My eyes began to well up. I knew my reaction would upset him, but even the thought of having to go back to Paris made me want to jump out of the moving car and run away.

He didn't know what to do or say next, and soon the old Bimmer filled up with awkward tension. The slightest sign of teen-girl tears made Macalister Le Moyne uncomfortable. My father always tried his best to be paternal, but it never really seemed natural for him, not even after all this time of it being just the two of us.

He patted my hand. "Don't get upset. You know school comes first."

I'd never once heard him say anything bad about my mother, but I could tell he felt relieved that I'd fight to stay in New Orleans with him instead of returning to her in Paris. He was simultaneously terrified and proud that I'd inherited his rebellious streak rather than her need for refinement.

Ever since I could remember, my father lived with a perpetually tired look. He'd inherited the ever-popular bar Le Chat Noir from my grandfather around the same time my mother left us, making him an artist-turned-business-owner and single parent all at once. Since then, he kept mostly nocturnal hours, waking midday to give himself enough time to work on sculptures and furniture in his metal shop before going back to the bar. Now he was unshaven and a bit shaggier than usual, appearing to have aged a few years in the last couple of months, just like all the other displaced citizens of New Orleans.

The Storm had been peculiar, not just because of the suddenness with which it had grown but because its target had been so unexpected. The day before it hit, the Storm was a routine Category 2 hurricane—not something to shrug off but something people knew how to handle—predicted to make landfall somewhere around Galveston, Texas. Eighteen hours prior to hitting land, the hurricane unpredictably changed course and headed straight for New Orleans.

Trying to clear the city with such short notice caused total mayhem. We ended up evacuating to Miami with a few of Dad's bartenders, never dreaming we'd be gone for more than a few days. But before the Storm left the Gulf of Mexico, it tipped the Saffir-Simpson scale, and once it hit land, like most folks upon arrival in New Orleans, it didn't want to leave. We watched in horror as it hovered.

And hovered.

And hovered.

All we could do was stare at the TV and wait for our unwelcome houseguest to take a hint.

That was before the levees broke and turned the city into a fishbowl.

When reality kicked in and we were suddenly unable to return home for an undetermined period, my father decided I would be better off in Paris with my mother than in Miami with a bunch of vagabonds looking for bar work. I wasn't sure if he really believed that or if he'd just cracked under post-Storm pressure; either way, he shipped me off to France as soon as he managed to get in touch with *her*. As far as I knew, that was the first time they'd had contact in the twelve years she'd been gone.

I refused to let the tears fall as I looked out the car window.

I'm not going back to live with her. I won't let it happen. New Orleans is my home.

Even thinking about going back to Paris made me immediately self-conscious. Up until eight weeks ago, I'd always thought of myself as just a normal teenager—not the head-cheerleader type but not the type to be shoved into lockers either. I did pretty well in school but was certainly not in the running for valedictorian. Besides rebellion, I'd also inherited my father's artistic tendencies, but (to my curatorial mother's high-art dismay) I channeled them mostly through designing clothes. Despite all of this, I'd hardly tipped average by Parisian standards. During the last two months, I couldn't have felt more plain, more uncultured, or more passé. My Parisian classmates were like ballerinas in six-inch heels, born to analyze haute couture and recite Baudelaire, making my skinny jeans and DIY dresses seem childish and unsophisticated.

I sighed and attempted to push the French memories out of my consciousness: the sparkling Eiffel Tower, the macarons from Ladurée, and most of all Émile.

My stomach twisted.

I definitely didn't want to think about Émile. Not the way his slight smile always made me wonder what he was thinking. Not his Vespa or 'iz stupid, sexy accent.

Pathetic, Adele. You didn't mean anything to him. He's just your mother's assistant.

The car went over a bump, and I realized trying not to think about Émile was actually making me think about Émile. *Ugh.*

CHAPTER 2
The Final Stretch

An hour later, we detoured from I-10 onto Highway 90 to drive the scenic route along the Gulf of Mexico, or what *used* to be the scenic route. The damage to the Mississippi coastline was insurmountable. I didn't know what to feel, but none of it felt real.

I rolled down my window, twisting and turning in my seat, trying to see everything. Trying to understand how it was possible. Every single one of the behemoth antebellum homes that had lined the beach was gone. Humongous casino barges previously anchored in the Gulf had been slammed onto the other side of the highway, shattered into mountains of neon-colored steel. The souvenir shop with the monstrous shark-mouth entrance, where Dad had taken me and Brooke to buy rubber rafts when we were kids, was gone. The mom-and-pop places, the national franchises, the historic landmarks—all gone.

Am I really ready to handle the havoc wreaked by the Storm at home?

My hair blew around my face as I watched the waves crash over an enormous seaweed-slimed pair of golden arches lying in the sand. I felt like I was floating outside of my body and peering down at the beach from some transcendental reality.

"Damn," my father said coolly, attempting to hide his own shock. "The media's been so focused on Louisiana we didn't hear much about the damage in Mississippi."

"How bad do you think it is in New Orleans?"

He paused for a moment. "I think we should prepare ourselves for the worst." But the tone in his voice sounded more like, *What was I thinking, bringing us back here?*

Fifteen minutes later we had only driven a half mile, trying to avoid the destruction.

"Jesus!" my father whispered under his breath. A gargantuan purple guitar, formerly part of the Hard Rock Casino, was now lying across all lanes of the highway, the handle having crushed a seaside hotel. He threw the car into reverse until he had enough room to whip it around. The desire for the truth about the condition of New Orleans became unbearable as we went back to the interstate.

"What's that?" I asked. We hadn't passed another moving car since Alabama but were now approaching some kind of roadblock.

"Rollers . . ." my father said, taking his foot off the gas.

"An army tank? Really?" The combat vehicle was parked among five police cars with flashing lights. We slowed to a halt, and my father cranked down his window.

"Evening, Officer."

"Evening, sir," said a stocky state trooper. His forearm muscles bulged under his dark skin as he leaned in the window and took a good look at us. "Where y'all headed tonight?"

"Just heading home. Haven't been back since the Storm."

"You got some ID? Only parish residents are allowed back in."

My father fished his license out of his wallet and handed it over.

"And what about you, young lady?"

"She's my *daughter*," my father said, trying not to sound too perturbed. "She doesn't even drive yet."

"It's okay, Dad." I leaned over him and handed the cop my passport.

He carefully examined the documents with a flashlight. "Thank you, Mr. Le Moyne. You can never be too careful in times like this. Are you aware of the mandatory curfew?"

"Yes, sir, nine p.m. lockdown."

It was nearly impossible to imagine a citywide curfew in New Orleans, or anywhere, really. It was supposedly meant to keep people safe while the infrastructure was so poor and crime was so high.

Are they really enforcing it? I wondered.

"If I can offer some unsolicited advice, go straight home and lock all the doors behind you. Assuming you have doors to lock," the cop said, handing back our IDs.

"Thank you, Officer. We'll do just that."

"Oh, and all bridges going over Lake Pontchartrain are out."

They moved the wooden barricades to let us pass, and we drove into the sunset, careful not to go over the speed limit while still within view of the fuzz.

"We're gonna have to take the long route," my father said.

I plugged my phone into the old cigarette lighter and put on a special New Orleans mix I'd made for Émile in an attempt at cultural exchange.

We both settled deeper into our seats.

The familiar tunes made my desire to be home grow more and more intense. I cranked the window handle, letting the humidity roll in, along with that unexplainable presence—the je ne sais quoi of the city. The muggy air hit my face, making me smile with nervous anticipation as I watched the cypress trees go by. They had once been tall enough to hide the swampy marshes, but now they were mostly snapped in half like twigs.

A brassy version of "When the Saints Go Marching In" played next. I'd probably heard the song a thousand times in my life—it was the unofficial anthem of our city—but I didn't think I'd ever paid attention to the lyrics until then. It felt like we were marching in.

My father turned up the volume and sped across the Louisiana state line, the foliage whipping past my window until it was nothing but a blur.

Bienvenue én Louisiane.

The back way, through the Rigolets, was oddly serene. When I looked out toward the setting sun on the lagoon's horizon, it seemed like any other day. The muddy tributaries sparkled. Birds swooped in and out of frame. But once we crossed the parish line, the residential neighborhoods looked more like war zones. My father and I simultaneously reached for the power button to turn off the music, for there was suddenly an overwhelming need for reverence, as if we were passing a funeral procession.

The closer we got to our final destination, the slower we had to drive.

The streets in New Orleans had already been some of the worst in the country, but now there were potholes that could swallow a small car. The massive roots of two-hundred-year-old oak trees had torn through the sidewalks like rippling waves, and the fallen trees now lay lifelessly against houses. Overturned SUVs, boats, broken glass, and mountains of unidentifiable debris caused the roads to appear as if they hadn't been driven on for decades. Nothing seemed to have escaped the fury of the Storm.

When we got to the desolate intersection of St. Claude and Desire, anxiety crept over me. I knew this corner. We weren't that far from my school. I stared hard out the windshield, trying to understand what was out of place, and then horror struck: I was looking at a house the Storm had moved to the opposite side of the street, as if some omnipotent giant's finger had slid it like a toy. By some miracle the house was still standing, but it appeared so fragile that the weight of a resting bird might cause the whole thing to collapse. We bumped in our seats as the car went over the trail of crumbled slab that had smeared across the road.

"Looks like the electricity is still out," my father said, slowing to a halt at an inactive stoplight.

A thin mist had crept in with the approaching twilight, making me wish I hadn't watched *Night of the Living Dead* only a week before (another attempt at cultural exchange with Émile). Concerned that an arm of the living dead might reach in for my face, I quickly cranked up my window and pushed the lock button on the door.

My overactive imagination stopped bombarding me as we continued through the Ninth Ward. Other than the occasional cop car silently patrolling the streets, there wasn't a soul around. We'd known the neighborhood would be bad—it had been getting the most press due to the levee breaches—but nothing could have prepared us for the reality of the destruction. The streets looked as if they'd been bombed out.

It took me several blocks to realize the very distinct line drawn across all the abandoned houses was an indicator of where the standing water had sat for days. The mark of the Storm.

Tears rolled down my face. Everything felt surreal. The scenery seemed familiar, but nothing looked the same.

As the night sky drew in and the last sliver of sun slipped behind the horizon, it became harder to see the horrific details, especially without the aid of electric streetlights. In a weird way, it gave us a little peace—not having to take in all the damage at once.

That peace came to an abrupt halt when my father slammed on the brakes.

Tires screeching, I lurched forward. My seat belt snapped against my chest, and my eyes squeezed shut, awaiting impact. We swerved to a stop, then a loud thud hit the hood of the car.

"Dammit!" my father yelled.

I opened my eyes and pushed his bracing hand from my chest.

"Did you see that?" he asked, spinning around.

"See what?"

"The guy who came out of nowhere . . . who smacked the hood?" He yanked up the emergency brake and opened his door.

"Dad, don't—!"

"Stay in the car," he ordered, slamming the door behind him. "And lock the doors." His voice sounded distant on the other side of the glass.

I unclipped my taut seat belt and felt an immediate release when my lungs were able to fully expand. Instinct brought my fingers to the lock button, but I refused to press it with him outside.

The whole incident replayed in my mind. The screech. The swerve. The aggressive smack to the hood. It hadn't felt like we'd hit something—it'd felt like something had hit *us*.

My fingers tapped nervously on the door handle.

Even though we were only a few minutes from our home, I had the distinct feeling we were trespassing.

"Hello?" my father shouted out into the darkness.

I silenced my strumming fingers and listened for a response.

"Hello? Is anyone there?"

The dead quiet made all the hairs on my arms shoot up. The tingle crawled up my neck to my scalp and clutched the back of my head.

My fingers resumed strumming.

My father's boots clicked against the pavement as he circled the car a couple times. Whoever it was seemed to have disappeared into thin air.

In the beam of the headlights, my father looked back at me and shrugged.

My shoulders mirrored his.

And then we drove away without finding a trace of evidence that anything had even occurred.

The only noises for the remainder of the ride came from beneath the slow-moving tires as the rubber crunched over leaves, sticks, and glass from broken windows.

My heart was pounding with anticipation by the time the car finally edged onto Esplanade Avenue, the border of the Faubourg Marigny and our neighborhood—the Vieux Carré. The historic French Quarter burned to the ground twice in the late eighteenth century. Since then it'd drowned more times than anyone could count and had been a haven for eccentrics and freaks for more than three centuries. It was a place where strange things had been known to happen, but locals had learned not to think twice about every little unexplainable detail; otherwise they'd go mad.

The enormous oak trees bent over both sides of the wide avenue, as if in agreement with the night sky to hide the current state of the gigantic, old homes.

Still, my anxiety levels rose higher with each turn. I wanted to jump out of the car to get a better view. I wanted to cry out, and then I wanted to cry. Instead, I sat perfectly still, was perfectly quiet, and looked straight ahead through the dusty windshield.

"Breathe," said my father.

And I did.

Small flames in the lamps on either side of the front door's wrought iron gate wished us welcome, which meant the gas was working. "Home, sweet home," my father said, pulling in front of the Creole cottage that had been in the Le Moyne family ever since its construction in the mid-eighteenth century. Now, large chunks of salmon-colored paint were missing from the stuccoed exterior, but other than that, things seemed . . . undamaged. Intensely creepy, but undamaged.

"Home, sweet home," I echoed.

Despite cramped legs, neither of us was quick to jump out of the car, and the still-running engine made it feel like we might need to make a great escape. It wasn't just the storm boards covering the hunter-green floor-to-ceiling shutters that made things creepy. It wasn't even the near-total darkness. The most disturbing thing by far was the lack of noise, which normally would've drowned out the car's rumbling engine.

Usually the Big Easy never sleeps. In our part of town in particular, a mere two blocks from the nefarious Bourbon Street, any random night usually boasted a gamut of sounds from people gradually losing their inhibitions: broad-shouldered barkers in suits luring people into gentlemen's clubs, middle-aged women belting out karaoke, frat boys hazing each other, underage teenagers squealing with mischievous delight, over-the-top tour guides shouting out ghost stories, and street musicians pounding jazz out of antique pianos.

Tonight, there was only the hum of our old car. My father cut the engine.

Silence.

The car door opened loudly, and I stood, stretching my legs. Chills crept up my spine when I saw that ours was the only car on the block. The historical commission enforced strict rules over maintaining the building façades, so without the cars, there was little to suggest we were even in modern times. My mind got lost in the fog and the gas lamps and the slate-stoned sidewalks, wondering if this was what the street had looked like three hundred years ago.

Everything was perfectly still, yet the air somehow felt disturbed. "Get a grip," I whispered to myself.

"We're gonna have to leave the car on the street," my father said, pointing to the tree lying in the driveway on the other side of the iron gate.

"Well, I don't think we have to worry about parking violations."

"It's not parking that I'm worried about. It's the record-high crime rates. I need you to be extra careful."

"I know, Dad. You already told me, like, ten times."

"I'm serious, Adele. I will—"

"Dad! Please, don't threaten to send me back to Brigitte's every time you need to emphasize the severity of this situation. I get it. Crime is up. I'll keep my street-smart meter dialed up to level orange—"

"Adele, don't call your mother Brigitte."

Neither of us could really blame the other for the intensity of our moods. We had no idea what the future had in store. Our home and possessions? School? Jobs? Displaced friends and loved ones? The death count was already in the thousands, and tens of thousands were still reported missing. There were too many what-ifs to think about.

"We'll get through this, Dad. We always do." I gave his shoulder a little squeeze and then hopped the steps to hold the gate open.

The heavy bolt clicked as he turned the key in the front door. "Okay, the moment of truth," he said, leaning his shoulder against the old cedar, now swollen in the frame. And with one final shove, the door swung open.

CHAPTER 3

Home, Sweet Home

A wall of warm air hit us when we walked into the foyer. My chest tightened thinking about mold. The dampness lingered, wrapping around my skin as if we had entered a gym locker room. Total darkness. Total silence. But after sixteen years of hearing the pendulum swings of the old grandfather clock, an impression of the sound was burned in my mind. The phantom ticks became louder in my head as we crept into the living room. I flicked the light switch just to be certain. Nothing. We both reached for our phones. That feeling of peculiarity versus familiarity crept over me once again.

My father walked ahead of me with his makeshift flashlight thrust forward and his right arm extended over me in a protective stance. There'd been countless reports of people breaking into homes and squatting in the less flooded neighborhoods.

By the glow of our phones, nothing appeared to be out of place—not that either of us could remember exactly how we had left it.

No signs of water or mold. My father exhaled loudly.

"I'm going to get the hurricane box," I said.

"Adele, wait—"

But I was already halfway through the dormant dining room, the thick, old walls muffling his protest.

Despite the long journey, I felt incredibly alert. My eyes darted back and forth like an animal's as I surveyed each room. Alone in the dark silence, I suddenly became very aware of the beating of my own heart.

Thump, thump.

Thump, thump.

The deeper I moved into the house, the harder it thumped.

Everything seemed okay . . . but I couldn't shake the feeling that something was very wrong.

I stood still in the kitchen. Listening. My hair lifted from my shoulders, sending a wave of shivers down my back. A delicate touch brushed my bare neck, causing me to twist around.

"Who's there?"

A slow creak answered.

I spun toward the noise, dropping my phone. I grabbed it from the floor, and when I rose, my head collided with something soft but solid.

"What the—?" My hair yanked backward.

"Don't touch me!" I yelled, jerking my head.

A sharp hook pierced the skin at the base of my neck. I screamed as the claw ripped all the way up my cheekbone.

Wings flapped frantically in my face, and high-pitched squawks assaulted my ears. Blood smeared from my neck to my face as I tried to keep my ears covered while thrashing wildly in the dark. "Get away!"

"Adele!"

"Dad! Kitchen!" My head jerked backward again as my hair became entangled with the bird's talons, ripping from my scalp, and my arms got scratched up shielding my face.

"Dad!"

Each touch of feathers to my skin sent a wave of shudders down my spine. I fell to my knees, ripping the last of my tangled hair free from the bird's claws.

Tears poured down as I caught my breath.

"Adele! Where are you?"

Glassware fell from the counter, smashing onto the tile floor around me.

"Down here!" I called, crouching into a ball next to a cabinet.

"What the hell?" my father yelled over the ruckus, sliding onto the floor. "Are you okay?" He pulled me close.

His phone illuminated a giant black crow frantically opening and closing its wings, breaking everything it came into contact with.

He helped me up, then swiftly grabbed a broom from behind the refrigerator and shooed the trespasser out the kitchen door. I jumped up and slammed the door behind it.

"Are you hurt?" He held his phone up to my face. My arm covered the wound, but still, his eyes bulged, causing me to look down. Red covered most of my right shoulder.

"It looks worse than it is," I lied, my throat raw from screaming. My face throbbed, but I kept it covered so he'd calm down. "All of this over a bird?" I tried to joke, fighting the tears.

He still had the broom clutched in one hand and his lit phone in the other. I didn't know if it was the anxiety, the weariness, or just how ridiculous we both must have looked, but I started laughing, and soon he did too.

He put the broom down and wrapped his arms around me. "Home, sweet home."

"Never a dull moment." My voice was muffled by his shoulder. I squirmed, trying not to get blood on his shirt. "Wait a second." I raised my head. "That door was open."

"What?"

"The kitchen door . . . I never opened it for the crow to fly out."

He held his phone up to the old brass doorknob. Someone had smashed the lock. He tapped the keypad on his phone three times and brought it to his ear.

"Dammit! No service."

They warned everyone not to come home yet . . .

He gave up on the call, went to the pantry, and lifted out a large cardboard box, putting it on the kitchen counter. I didn't need any light to know it was appropriately labeled "Hurricane Box" in my six-year-old scribble. On the side, written in a range of green Crayola to metallic silver Sharpie, was a list of every hurricane it had been used in, along with the date. We were pretty diligent about keeping it fully stocked because we weren't the type who evacuated every time bad weather brewed in the Atlantic.

He pulled out a robust first aid kit.

I nervously removed my sticky fingers from the wound.

"Dammit, Adele!"

"What?"

"I'm taking you to the hospital."

"Dad, there *aren't* any hospitals."

"Jesus . . ." He hesitated for a second before he managed his manly-dad poker face.

"Dad!" The tears began to well again.

"I'm sorry, baby, it's not that bad." He lied this time. "It's just a lot of blood." He pressed the gauze against my face. "Damn bird."

When the bleeding subsided, he spun the lid off the bottle of rubbing alcohol. My nose scrunched at the chemical smell. "It's gonna burn," he said gently and poured a generous stream of the clear liquid down my face and neck.

My limbs twisted together. I tried not to yelp as the solvent spidered into the wound. He pressed my hand over a fresh piece of gauze.

"Stay here, and I'll check out the rest of the house."

"No, I want to see!" I yelled. But really I didn't want to be left alone.

"Okay, but stay put for two minutes. Keep applying pressure. I'll be right back. I promise."

Something about his exit made me suspicious. I attached the gauze to my skin with some medical tape and dug through the remaining contents of the supply box: a transistor radio, an assortment of non-perishable food items, various kinds of batteries. Voilà. Two flashlights. I flicked them on and off to test the batteries.

When he returned, the beams of light revealed a small black object in his hand. I did a double take. "What is *that*?" I exclaimed in a loud whisper. "You own a gun? Do you even know how to use that thing?"

"Calm down, sweetheart. It was Grandpa's, and it's always been locked up in the safe." He seemed oddly at ease holding the weapon, as if it was something he used on a daily basis. *Who is this guy?*

I placed the second flashlight into his free hand and filed behind him down the hall to his bedroom. He waved his light around to check out the state of his things, while I continued to the back. His bedroom was an old double parlor, separated by sliding wooden doors. The rear room, which led to the courtyard, was his studio. I unlatched the hook and slid open the pocket doors a couple feet.

My brain refused to register what I saw in front of me as I hastily moved my flashlight from one thing to the next.

No.

No.

No.

"I'm so sorry, Dad." I stood frozen, unable to think of anything else to say.

He rushed over, slid the wooden doors completely open, and stepped into the work space.

"Stay here."

Most of my father's lifework was in total disarray, strewn about the large, open room. I focused my light on the rear wall and gasped. My flashlight was shining straight into the back courtyard—a humongous

Greek Revival–style column from a neighboring house had smashed through our exterior brick wall and created a gaping hole at least ten feet tall and seven feet wide. Wind, rain, and Lord knows what else had poured in. I thought of the crow as I slowly approached the hole and wondered if there were any other creatures lurking in the house.

"Adele, stay back! There might be serious structural damage."

Backing away, I picked up two unstretched canvases and tried to separate them, but they had fused together upon drying. I put them down to avoid further wrecking my father's art.

Why couldn't that column have fallen into any other room in the house? Even my own bedroom would have been better. I wondered if any of his paintings or charcoals had survived. A sinking feeling told me, unlikely. At least his main medium was metal . . . Anxiety rushed through my veins, thinking about my own bedroom.

"Come on, Dad, there isn't much we can do tonight." My hand rested on his shoulder as I pulled him away from the acetylene tank he was examining. "We'll get a better look in the morning."

We did a quick run-through of the rest of the house and ended up back in the kitchen. To our relief, everything else appeared unscathed. Including my stuff.

"No squatters or pools of standing water," said my father.

"Just crows and gaping holes."

Dodging broken glass on the floor, he tossed me a bottle of water. "Don't even brush your teeth with water from the sink until the boil-water advisory is lifted." He jammed a kitchen chair under the broken knob, securing the door. "Can you get through the night without electricity?"

"Definitely." I nodded with a jet lag–induced yawn then pulled out my phone, hoping a quick text to Brooke would go through.

Adele	**8:57 p.m.**	Made it home. Able to sleep in the house. Full report tomorrow. xo.

CHAPTER 4

Gris-Gris

October 10th

The engulfing obsidian made me momentarily panic, but as soon as I became conscious of the muggy air around me, I remembered I was home. I waved a hand in front of my face. Nothing. The storm boards on the windows blocked even the slightest crack of light from entering, masking any hints about what time it was. I had agreed to sleep in the living room to appease my father's fear that the back of the house might have structural damage, although I wasn't sure it would have made a difference where we slept if the house did cave in. Now, lying in a heap of blankets and cushions on the floor, I felt better than I had in weeks. Just being home brought on a small smile.

The smile induced a groan. I reached for the bandage on my cheek. The entire right side of my face throbbed when I moved.

"Stupid bird."

Based on how stiff I was, I guessed I'd slept for at least ten hours. My phone told me twelve. *Nice.*

The quick glow from the screen also showed me I was alone. My father was no longer snoring on the love seat. *How did I sleep later than him, especially considering I am on Paris time?*

Curiosity pulled me up and to the front door. I squinted as the morning light poured into the cave-like foyer. Stepping out onto the stoop, I let my forehead rest on the iron gate. The metal was cool. A breeze pricked my skin. *Has the season already turned? Maybe we'll have a cold Halloween . . . ? If we even have Halloween this year.* The only thing harder for me to imagine would be a year without carnival season.

A wave of guilt swept over me. There were tens of thousands of families who had lost everything, including each other, and I was worrying whether all the hours I had put into my costume would be in vain. I pushed the thought away, double-checked the bolt on the gate, and left the door open to maximize the natural light.

The sliding doors separating my father's bedroom and studio were wide open. A squirrel bounced across the room, scavenging through the wreckage. I chased it through the gaping hole and out into the courtyard.

It looked like a tornado had spun through. I guess one kind of had.

Hundreds of sketches, inks, paintings, and brushes littered the studio space. Colorful dried pools of paint, resin, and other chemicals patched the wooden floor. A large oxygen tank had smashed into a wall and cracked the plaster all the way up to the ceiling. Iron patio furniture and a mass of leaves and other garden debris had blown inside. Then there was the culprit: the giant column lying in the middle. *How the hell are we going to move this thing?*

"Zeus, I think you dropped something," I joked halfheartedly. A small smile made my claw wound ache beneath the bandage.

My father was sleeping on an old couch in the corner. My nose turned up, considering how the upholstery had surely been drenched. At least he had bothered to put a blanket down first. He rolled his back to me, revealing a half-drunk bottle of whiskey wedged between the cushion cracks.

"Ugh, Dad . . ." I yanked the bottle free.

He barely stirred.

The only thing that truly seemed to make my father happy was his art. His schedule was erratic because of the bar, so it was hard for him to meet people outside of the nightlife, which he tried to avoid since he was solely responsible for me. Looking around the room again, I decided to let him sleep it off. I pulled an afghan to his shoulders and tiptoed back to the kitchen to sort out more pressing things. Coffee.

Thank God we had a gas stove, and thank God we used a French press—I had to leave the broken kitchen door open to let in light—but no electricity was required for the brew.

As I waited for the grinds to steep, I quietly cleaned up the mess of broken glass and bird feathers, oscillating between guilt and relief that my bedroom had been spared by the Storm. Every one of my things suddenly seemed precious.

Just as the rich smells of coffee 'n' chicory filled the air, in walked my father like a perfectly timed commercial. Only in this version his cheery tone served to overcompensate for his hangover. He broke from rubbing his head to kiss my cheek.

"Morning. It's almost like being a normal person, being awake at this hour."

"I know. I'm so used to your vampire hours." At that moment I realized how much I'd missed him. "It's nice." I wiped down a mug and poured him the first cup. He took a giant swig and nearly choked.

"Jeez, Adele, trying to put more hair on my chest?"

"Gross." My nose wrinkled. "I forgot we wouldn't have milk to steam." Chuckling, I added more hot water to our cups. "What's the plan for today?"

He took another sip before answering. "Find someone to check out the back wall and fix the kitchen door. Sort through what's salvageable in my studio, take photos, and begin the mountain of paperwork to file an insurance claim. Exciting stuff. Oh, then I'll go down to the bar and start the process all over. How 'bout you?"

"The house is like a cave. Can you take down the storm boards first?"

He nodded.

"And set up the generator?"

A yawn interrupted his second nod.

"I'll do an inventory of our food and water and find out which grocers are back in business. Then I have school stuff. And I want to stop by Café Orléans to see if the Michels are back in town—"

"You've obviously had more coffee than me." He drained his cup.

"Oh, and I was thinking I'd move all of my stuff to the room upstairs, but I'll have to clean it out first." Before our quick inspection last night, I hadn't been up there in ages.

"Why would you move your stuff upstairs?"

"So you can move into my bedroom."

"You don't have to do that, sweetheart. I want you to get settled. I can move the studio to the second floor."

"No, it just makes more sense for me to move upstairs. Your studio can be right next to your bedroom, and if you decide to work when you get home from the bar, you won't wake me up going up and down the stairs."

"You're the best." He kissed my forehead. "I'm going to start unboarding the windows."

In a cloud of steam, I stepped out of the dark bathroom and into the dark hallway, hair dripping, candle in hand. After all the hours in transit, the hot shower felt glorious, even if beforehand I had to wait for the brown water to run clear and was subsequently freaked out the entire time because, in the candlelight, I couldn't tell whether it had turned murky again.

When I got to my bedroom, I blew out the candle with a smile—the boards were gone from the ten-foot-high windows. A small win for normalcy.

Everything got a sniff test for mustiness as I dug through my closet. After tossing four different dresses on the floor, I decided everything needed to be washed.

Thanks to *ma grand-mère* (who I'd just met for the first time in Paris), there was certainly no shortage of things to wear in my suitcase. She'd been appalled by the lack of designer names in my wardrobe and had not held back on our shopping spree. I pulled out the simplest thing: a plain black Chanel frock. Walking through the devastated city in a six-hundred-euro dress was deplorable, but there weren't really any better options. At least it lacked embellishments.

I tied the matching silk sash around my waist and dug through my luggage for shoes. I tossed aside ballet flats and dainty booties and went back to my closet for my deep-burgundy Doc Martens—my shit-kickers, as Brooke called them. My feet slipped easily into the molds of the worn boots, making me instantly happy. *Familiarity.*

I rebandaged my wound, grabbed a small blue-fringed bag, keys, and sunglasses, and was out the door.

The shrill of a power tool unscrewing the boards came from the side of the house.

"Dad, I'm going for a walk! Be back soon!"

The drill stopped, and my father's head popped through the side gate. "Please be careful. Cell service is spotty, so text me if you need anything, and be back before lunchtime."

"Uh, okay." My father hadn't told me to be back home by lunch-time since I was about nine years old. In fact, he was rarely awake before lunchtime.

Two blocks later, signs of life began to emerge: a lady walking her dog, a couple of gutter punks kicking a can, an elderly man shouting expletives while taking photos of his property damage.

I turned onto another residential block and came across a shop hidden among the boarded-up homes. A monstrous white SUV was illegally parked on the curb out front. The doors were propped open, and the sign for Vodou Pourvoyeur gently swung in the breeze, making a faint creaking sound. Incense wafted out to the street. I'd never been inside the shop, but I'd referred many tourists from the café where I worked part-time. Now, for no real reason, I found myself crossing the threshold.

Inside, everything was so vivid, colorful, and foreign I couldn't decide what to focus on first. The front room was filled with tourist thrills: make-your-own-Voodoo-doll kits, spell books, premixed bottles labeled "Love Potion #9," vintage Ouija boards, and bright rabbit-foot key chains. To the right was a painting of Marie Laveau affixed atop an altar of flowers, melted candles, and prayer cards. Visitors had adorned it with cigarettes, coins, candies, and a plethora of other small tokens to please the Voodoo Queen of New Orleans.

The earthy smell of incense grew more pungent—floral, with a hint of something sweet, like vanilla. The shop was very long, a former shotgun house, and the deeper I walked, the more exotic the inventory became. Alligator skulls. Necklaces made of cowrie shells, bones, and claws. Statues of Catholic saints carved from wax, wood, and ivory. And a variety of other oddities that appeared to have originated from the local swampland, the Caribbean, or Africa. Both walls of the next room were covered by a sea of rainbow-colored Voodoo dolls decorated with neon feathers, sequins, and Spanish moss. The back of the shop was lit by candles, more reminiscent of an old apothecary.

How have I never been inside this place before?

I stood mesmerized by the floor-to-ceiling shelves of antique books and jars of all shapes and sizes, filled with herbs, powders, salts, and oils. *Indigo. Ylang-Ylang. Wormwood.* I recognized some of the names on the labels, but most completely escaped me.

Two women were near the rear of the room at the wooden counter. Behind the antique register sat an elderly women in a sleeveless white linen dress whose wild gray curls were half tied up into a traditional tignon headdress—it was obvious she'd been a beauty in her time. A tall girl with her back turned to me stood in front of the counter, trying to coax the old woman into eating something from a bowl and was growing increasingly impatient.

My gaze shifted to a shelf displaying an assortment of gemstone-encrusted daggers next to a "Do Not Touch" sign.

"Fine, Gran, don't eat. I'm still not going to the gathering."

Trying to give them some privacy, I focused on the daggers. They looked ancient. I was imagining them having been used in some kind of sacrificial ritual, when suddenly the two nearest my elbow shifted and clattered onto the floor.

The girl dropped the bowl onto the counter and spun around.

"I swear I didn't touch anything!" I mumbled, double-checking the proximity of my arms.

The girl shot me a glare that meant either she was embarrassed to have been overheard or I should leave. Probably both.

"Child," the old woman called out to me. "Child, you need to protect yourself. You need protection."

The girl let out an exasperated sigh.

I brought the fallen daggers to the girl and gently placed them in her hands. "It's okay," I said. "My dad has been super worried about the crime around here too."

The girl looked at me with annoyance and left the daggers on the counter for the old woman to deal with.

To say the girl was stunning was a major understatement. Long, black, pin-straight hair hung past her waist, and her toffee-colored skin was flawless. She towered over my average frame and could have easily passed for early twenties, but judging from the private school uniform and her attitude, she must have been closer to my age. Immediately, I became self-conscious about the giant bandage across my cheek.

"So, your school has reopened?" I asked. The words came out rushed and slightly desperate sounding. "Do you go to school down here?"

"As if. I attend Sacred Heart Preparatory Academy. *Uptown*."

Historically, Americans who had migrated down the Mississippi River settled uptown, away from the wilder and more superstitious European, African, and Caribbean Creoles who ruled downtown.

Sacred Heart Preparatory Academy was the most prestigious all-girls school in the state, possibly the entire South. *The Academy*, as they called it. The campus was only a couple miles away, in the Garden District, but it might as well have been a world away. Supposedly, couples put their progeny on the waiting list as soon as the birth certificates were inked. The school was chock-full of carefully curated pedigrees—a mix of old money and nouveau riche, southern debutantes, daughters of politicians and oil tycoons, and even the offspring of celebrities who made New Orleans their home to escape the limelight of Hollywood.

"So Sacred Heart has reopened?"

"Obviously. In fact, it's better than ever. Holy Cross was decimated, and we graciously took in their student body." Holy Cross was an all-boys school in the Ninth Ward.

The girl was now fully scoping me out. Her blatant gaze started at my feet, where my worn boots got her utter disapproval, and then moved up to my Chanel.

"Nice dress," she muttered, her disapproval fading to befuddlement.

After navigating a Parisian boarding school for the last two months, I was a professional in these kinds of situations. "*Merci beaucoup*, I bought it in Paris. Just got back in town late last night," I said, as if I flew to Paris every Saturday for shopping and croissants. As soon as the words came out of my mouth I wanted to slap myself, but I had her attention now. Her left eyebrow rose, perplexed.

"I'm late." She flipped her hair and grabbed her bag.

"How did your family make out with the Storm?" I tried to change the subject but had maxed out the quota of attention she was willing to allocate to me.

"We don't have problems with storms." She smirked and pivoted out of the room.

The front door slammed shut; I stiffened, a little stunned by her resolute manner.

"Don't worry about Désirée, my dear. She doesn't understand yet."

I turned to the old woman. "Understand what?"

"Her importance in the world," she answered tenderly, as if it were the most obvious thing in the universe.

The comment caught me off guard. My paternal grandmother had died when I was little, and *ma grand-mère* certainly didn't think I had any importance in the world. All she cared about was my French accent and cramming me into smaller and smaller dress sizes.

The old woman began to open and close jars, making meticulous selections. She held one under my nose.

"Lavender, my favorite." I inhaled deeply. "By the way, I'm Adele—"

"Le Moyne," a resonant female voice finished for me.

I turned to find a middle-aged woman standing behind me. She had the same long hair and almond-shaped brown eyes as Désirée, but she exuded authority. With her tailored turquoise dress, navy blazer, and gold bangles, she was more Jackie O than new age Voodoo priestess.

"You're Mac and Gidget's daughter," she said.

"Gidget?" Trying to imagine my mother with a girlish nickname almost made me snicker. Even hearing the Americanized version of her name, Bridget, sounded weird. To me, she was only *Madame Brigitte Dupré*.

"Your mother was—*is* an amazing woman."

"Ugh . . ." I fumbled.

Everyone in the French Quarter knew my father, and most knew me, but very few people knew my mother. She'd lived here for only a few years before her sudden departure more than a decade ago. Or maybe people did know her and just never spoke about her. At least not to me.

"I'm Ana Marie Borges, Désirée's mother, and this is my mother-in-law, Ritha."

The old woman came out from behind the counter.

"Borges? As in Morgan Borges?" I asked.

Ritha smiled in the way only a mother could as she drew close beside me.

"Ow!" I flinched when she plucked a few strands of hair from my head, my scalp still sore from the bird attack.

She quickly retreated behind the counter to her herbs, muttering something indiscernible.

Borges was a household name in Louisiana, with deep roots in the political history of New Orleans, and like most political families, people tended to love or hate them. Morgan Borges had been elected mayor earlier this year. Most of his campaign had revolved around bridging the socioeconomic divide. *It's pretty apparent which side of the divide his daughter stands on.*

"It's nice to see you again, honey," old Ritha said.

Again?

"Take this." She leaned over the counter and curled my fingers around a scratchy fabric pouch. "It's a gris-gris." She had a wide grin and seemed a little kooky. I liked her.

Ana Marie moved directly in front of me and examined my face. Before I could protest, she peeled back the bandage and smeared something from an unmarked jar across my cut. I winced as it tingled.

Overcome with awkwardness from all the matriarchal attention, I searched for purpose by inspecting a basket of herbs at my feet. I grabbed a few bundles.

"Sage," said Ana Marie. "Smart choice. Wards off evil."

"Right . . ." I produced a few dollars, which they refused to accept. "Well, it was nice to meet the both of you."

"Send our regards to your father," said Ana Marie, handing me the unmarked jar of ointment. "It's been far too long."

Is she just being polite? I hoped she meant it.

I exited the shop and paused out front to examine the object that Ritha had slipped me: a small red muslin satchel attached to a long white ribbon. When I pressed my fingers against the fabric pouch, I could feel dried herbs and stones. *And apparently my hair,* I thought, rubbing my scalp. Ritha's warning about protection echoed in my head.

"What's the harm?" I whispered as I tied the ribbon around my neck and hid the gris-gris underneath my dress.

CHAPTER 5

Blue Eyes

Once I left the French Quarter, signs of life went from slim to none. The conditions of houses significantly worsened after I crossed Esplanade Avenue—the change was so sudden it almost seemed purposely engineered. The Faubourg Marigny was a neighborhood where immigrants had originally settled to build homes and chase the American Dream. In more recent years, artists and bohemian types had taken over here because it was cheaper than other parts of the city but still well located. Post-Storm, one could argue whether it was really so well located—in between the Mississippi River and the Industrial Canal.

Pre-Storm, the Faubourg Marigny had been one of the most colorful parts of the city, literally. The cultural diversity of its inhabitants brought a distinct flavor to each one of the old Creole cottages. Chartreuse, orange, magenta—pick any crayon from the box and you could have found it here. Now it felt like I was looking at everything through a dirty gray lens. Rust and mold were the new accent colors, and the neighborhood was more akin to a junkyard: tricycles, hi-tops, ceiling fans, and bunk beds were sprinkled on the lawns. The contents strewn about varied from block to block, but every street looked exactly the same, like it had drowned and then been left out to bake and rot in the Indian summer sun. Flipped cars and boats, some smashed into houses and storefronts, became commonsight. The sidewalk lifted in various places, reminding me of colliding tectonic plates from seventh-grade science.

A cloud of flies swarmed an overturned refrigerator, and an accidental glimpse of the maggot-infested mystery meat spilling out made me gag uncontrollably. I tried to move away quickly, but there were still puddles the size of ponds and no clear paths. I took a giant step, barely avoiding a drowned rat, and said a quiet thank-you for my shit-kickers.

A bad feeling crept up as my school came into view. All the windows of the old converted-factory building were blown out. I approached the nearest one and peered in: a foot of stagnant water still filled the ground level. My heart sank.

The warm, familiar feeling I usually had on campus was replaced with that strange sense of trespassing. A piece of paper inside a plastic sheath was nailed to the front door:

> NEW ORLEANS SCHOOL OF ARTS
> **Closed—Indefinitely**
> Contact the office of the
> School Board Superintendent
> for current status updates.

Despite the official stamp on the paper, there was something so unofficial about the posting that it looked piteous: the handwriting, the nail. For the first time in my life, the lack of bureaucracy made me uncomfortable. School and bureaucracy went hand in hand.

I snapped a photo and texted it to Brooke, adding only a sad face.

NOSA, as the student body called it, was an audition-only arts high school where we were taught that creativity was in *everything*, even in trigonometry, which I struggled to believe. After my audition, my father had sat me down and very seriously explained that the greatest lesson an artist could learn was how to deal with rejection. I think the day I got my acceptance letter was the best day of both our lives.

Now I wondered if this would be it for NOSA.

As I approached the corner where I'd normally see my father's beautiful ballerina sculpture, I braced myself for the possibility that she'd be mangled, vandalized, or missing altogether. He'd donated the sculpture for the school's fortieth anniversary. She was who I'd hidden behind, crying, after Johnnie West robbed me of my *very first kiss* during a scene-study class freshman year. She was the one who'd always listened to my nervous banter before my juried exams. I'd grown attached to seeing her every morning.

"Thank God!"

I nearly skipped when I saw her still midpirouette; her metal tutu, thin as paper, still creating that amazing sense of movement. Even the mask that covered the top half of her face was still intact—a metal version of those traditionally worn during Mardi Gras. She'd always been one of my favorite pieces of my dad's, and now she glimmered bronze against the sad spectrum of gray, almost begging me not to worry. I would have hugged her if she hadn't been smeared in rotting foliage.

At least I'd have some good news for my father—his work withstood the strength of the Storm.

My dad sometimes taught metalsmithing workshops, although not at NOSA; they weren't too keen on allowing students to use blowtorches. Lucky for me, he'd been teaching me the art of harnessing fire since age six, after I snuck into his studio and burned off a pigtail (which gave me a very punk rock haircut for a summer and nearly gave him a stroke). No matter what lengths he took to childproof his work space, I'd always managed to get in and meddle. Teaching me to correctly use the tools was his way of being better safe than sorry.

My eyes teared at the thought of not being able to spend my junior and senior years at NOSA.

Adele, think about how much more other people lost.

I wiped my eyes and started the trek back.

Large orange *X*s had been spray painted directly onto the exteriors of the now-abandoned old homes. I'd seen images of them on TV, but they were so much more upsetting in person. The numbers sprayed into each quadrant of the *X*s indicated when the premises had been searched and how many dead bodies had been found. The dilapidated houses, formerly as vibrant as the Caribbean, encouraged me to flee, but I couldn't help but pause outside one house. Next to the *X*, a rescuer had taken the time to spray out the words:

1 DEAD IN ATTIC

The eeriness that poured out of every broken door and every broken window was suffocating.

Glass crunched under my feet as I walked away—it had come from the shattered window of the black town car parked next to me. There was a man in the driver's seat.

I froze and stammered, "Hello?"

He didn't stir.

I moved to see his face. His neatly groomed blond head was resting in the open window among a scattering of shiny glass fragments—his empty blue eyes looked straight through me.

"Sir? Sir, are you okay?" Southern hospitality took over, even though I knew there was only one explanation for the stillness of his body. I extended my hand toward his neck to check his pulse.

A bird squawked loudly. I yanked my arm back in fright and spun into a full-on sprint, barely aware that my hand had grazed the broken glass.

I ran through the remaining blocks of the Marigny, past Esplanade Avenue, and back into the French Quarter. I kept running until sucking in the humid air became so difficult I had to stop and lean against a brick wall.

Panting, I pulled out my cell phone and tapped the three numbers we were schooled never to dial except in case of a real emergency.

The sound of the busy signal made me burst into tears. How many other people were trying to call 9-1-1 at this exact moment? I'd never seen a dead body before, much less touched one. Now, all I could picture were those blue eyes. I felt his dead skin on my fingers. An asthmatic wheeze came from my throat.

Breathe, Adele.

Tears dripped.

I threw my arms over my head, determined to pull it together. I felt the air pump in and out of my lungs. *Focus on something else.*

But directly across the street, the imposing concrete wall surrounding the Old Ursuline Convent hid anything interesting to look at. My hand throbbed, and I felt liquid dripping down my arm, but before I could inspect it, a rattling noise caught my attention. I held my breath to create perfect silence and heard the noise again.

My throat tightened.

From my vantage point, all I could see were the five attic windows protruding from the slope of the convent roof. On one of them, a shutter had become detached and was hanging loosely, rattling in the wind.

I focused on the shutter as it methodically flapped open and snapped shut. Again. And again. But the man's dead blue eyes had stained my mind. *What happened to him? A car accident?* The rhythm of the knocking wood put me into a meditative state. My tears stopped, and my breathing evened. The claps gradually became louder, drawing my focus back to the window. Something seemed off.

A rusty smell pinched my nostrils, and only then did I realize the cut in my palm was bleeding profusely. I untied the sash from around my waist and wrapped it tightly around my hand. *Back less than a day and I already have two injuries. Dad is going to freak.* I silently mourned the death of the Chanel as the blood soaked through it.

Sweat dripped down my back. *Gross.* I tugged my dress and wiped the tears from my face with the back of my bandaged hand, all the while watching the attic window. The heat was incredible, rippling down my torso, almost feverish. *Is it wrong to pray for a cool front?* I wondered, staring at the convent. *Maybe just a little breeze?*

The shutter snapped back shut—and then I realized what was off.

I stood perfectly still. There was no breeze. The air was dead. *Is someone pushing the shutter from the inside?* It snapped open again, as if demanding my attention. *No, the glass window behind it is shut.*

My pulse picked up.

I squinted as the shutter flapped open and shut again, and I thought I saw a flash of movement behind the pane. *What the hell?* I blinked the remaining water from my eyelids.

When I looked back up, the shutter swung open.

Faint clinking sounds came from the convent courtyard, like metal raindrops hitting the pavement. Curious, I crossed the street and approached the convent's wrought iron gate, trying to keep my eyes on the dark window behind the shutter.

Through the iron bars, the overgrown garden looked as if it had been abandoned years ago, but then again, that was how most of the city looked at present. I reached for the ornate handle, but the fixture turned downward before I touched it. The loud clank made me jump back, and the gate creaked open just enough to let me through.

A little voice inside my head pleaded with me to bail, but instinct led me through the maze of dead hedges as if I'd been there a hundred times before. My eyes went back to the window and refused to look away. As I drew closer, the wooden shutter continued to open and close—slowly and precisely. Once I was directly underneath, I could see the nails popping out of the adjoining shutter. I glanced at my feet. The ground was covered in long black carpenter nails—clearly the work of a blacksmith, not a modern machine. *Was it really necessary to use so many nails to secure the shutters?* A tiny raindrop hit my face.

The shutter flapped twice more. Faster and faster. It was slowly pulling itself off the building. Only a single stake in the center hinge kept it from falling, but it too protruded as if being pulled by some invisible force. The cut on my hand throbbed; the blood had soaked completely through the sash.

A clap of thunder made my pulse race, but still my feet wouldn't carry me away. I stood motionless, neck craned, watching the shutter wrench itself free until it was suspended by just the very tip of the stake.

For a brief moment, the world seemed to freeze.

Then gravity prevailed.

My arms flew over my head as the dangling shutter crashed three stories to the ground—just a few inches from my feet.

The speed with which the sky became dark felt wholly unnatural. Bigger droplets of rain began to fall. Too stunned to move, I tried to make sense of what had just happened.

Suddenly, the remaining wooden shutter slammed open, and the windowpane blew outward in an explosion of showering glass. I fell to the ground, curling into a tight ball, shielding my face as a whoosh of wind whipped around me and a loud whistle faded into what sounded like sardonic laughter.

And then there was absolute silence.

This is not happening right now. This is a dream.

With my tense arms still wrapped around my head, I peeked out with one eye. The thick iron stake that had held the shutter rolled along the cement toward my face, as if pulled by magnetic force. It stopped right before it touched my nose.

I quickly sat up and grabbed it. The metal felt strangely powerful in my hand, a giant nail twice the width of my palm.

I looked around—even though my eyes told me I was alone, my gut told me I wasn't. Every ounce of my being screamed, *Get out!* Now I really was trespassing, and on the private grounds of the archdiocese.

Another crack of thunder made me scramble to my feet and bolt back through the garden.

The iron gate banged shut behind me, just as the chapel bells clanged.

CHAPTER 6

Staked

I sprinted the remaining six blocks home and slammed the front gate behind me, pausing on the stoop to catch my breath. I grasped one of the slick, wet bars and looked both ways down the street.

No one. Nothing.

Safe behind the iron gate, my pulse mellowed, but then I remembered there was a giant hole in the back of our house—not exactly high security.

Rain dripped from my dress and weighed down my Docs as I stormed to my room. I kicked off the boots and flopped onto my bed, not caring when my hair soaked the pillow.

What the hell just happened?

The stake was still clutched tightly in my right hand. I loosened my grip, allowing blood to flow back to my fingers, and then turned the piece of iron over and over, examining it, but there was nothing to give me a clue.

Blue eyes. Dead, blue eyes. Why were his eyes still so blue? He showed no signs of decay, but the Storm hit over two months ago. My hands began to shake. I set the stake down on the bed as I tried to recall the scene in exact detail.

The black sedan seemed undamaged, except for the smashed driver's-side window. Gray suit, blond hair, blue eyes. My breathing picked up. What if the man hadn't actually been dead and I'd neglected to help him?

No, he had no pulse. He could *not* have still been alive. And yet, he certainly couldn't have died two months ago. *Did I discover a man who'd just died?*

I sat up quickly, knocking the stake off the bed. My heart pumped faster as I tapped 9-1-1 a second time.

No signal.

I dialed four more times until I finally heard ringing.

"Hello."

"Hello! I need to report a murder!"

"You have reached the New Orleans Police Department's automated hotline. If you're calling to report a missing person, please visit our website at www.nopd.gov. If you're calling to report a crime or another emergency, please stay on the line."

"You've got to be kidding! Who in this city has Internet right now?"

An instrumental version of "Mardi Gras Mambo" started playing. Then a gentle scraping sound came from the ground next to my bed. I glanced down.

"What the . . . ?"

The stake was standing upright on its point. I blinked several times. As the hold music droned on, the stake slowly started to turn, grinding itself into the floorboard.

"To report a dead body, press one. To report a dead animal, press two. To report a non-Storm-related violent crime, press three."

I pressed the number three without looking.

"Please state the nature of your call. You can use phrases like, 'My house has been robbed.'"

"Um, I'd like to report a crime. A dead body, possibly a murder—"

"Thank you for calling the NOPD. Who am I speaking with?" asked a despondent female voice.

The stake stopped turning.

"Hi, my name is Adele Le Moyne." My tongue garbled the words.

"Miss Le Moyne, what's your location?"

"Burgundy S—but the body's on Chartres Street around Franklin—"

"There is a separate line to report Storm victims, Miss Le Moyne—"

"He's not a Storm victim! I mean . . . his eyes were still normal, so he couldn't have been dead for that long, right?"

"Calm down. Slow down. Did you witness any acts of violence?"

"No, I was just walking and found him in a black town car on the side of the street, about forty minutes ago. I tried to call earlier, but the line was busy." Talking about the corpse brought the reality of post-Storm New Orleans to a whole new level. My father and I had been driving down that street less than twenty-four hours ago.

"And you have reason to believe this was a homicide?"

"Yes. I mean, I don't know. It didn't look like he'd been in a car accident . . . His driver's-side window was smashed in."

"Did you see any other distinctive wounds or unusual markings?"

A splinter of wood cracked—the stake was twisting itself into the floor again.

"Um, no, but I was only there for a minute before I ran away."

"Okay, Ms. Le Moyne, any other details you'd like to report?"

"No, I don't think so."

"All right, we'll send a unit over to investigate. I just need your contact information; an officer will reach out to you for an official statement."

I gave her my info and hung up the phone.

"What the heck?" I tugged the stake out of the floor. It felt hot.

I flung it into the nightstand as if it had some contagious disease, slammed the drawer, and fell back onto the mattress with an incredulous head shake.

"I'm losing my mind."

When I woke, the sheets were damp. I was unsure whether it was from the rain-soaked clothes I'd fallen asleep in or from the layer of sweat coating me thanks to the humidity and lack of air-conditioning. My face throbbed from when I'd accidentally rolled over on it, and my left palm ached. The silk sash wrapped around my hand was now encrusted with dried blood. I pushed it over enough to reveal my watch.

"Nine o'clock?" I groaned. "Ugh, jet lag." That was four a.m. Paris time. Immediately, those dead blue eyes popped into my mind. Memories of the nonsensical events at the Ursuline Convent attic followed.

I suddenly wanted something to do—anything to avoid the vivid memories. There was still the daunting task of moving my entire life's contents upstairs to the attic. *Perfect.*

First, I retrieved the first aid kit. The alcohol stung, but the cut on my hand wasn't that bad; the blood had made it seem far worse. I wrapped it tightly, applying some of the ointment Ana Marie had given me, and wondered where my father was, out past curfew.

The staircase led to an attic my great-grandparents had converted. I could count the number of times I'd been upstairs on one hand; the ground level had always been plenty big enough for me and my father.

I pushed the simple wooden door, and it swung open.

The air on the other side was thin and stale. A flip of the light switch got me nothing. *Ugh. Maybe Dad didn't connect the attic breakers to the generator?* I slowly scanned the unkempt bedroom with my flashlight as I stepped over sacks of Mardi Gras beads from years past, crates of bulk art supplies, and a box of winter clothes I would soon pull down for the two months a year that allowed for wool blends.

In the darkness, the room was unassuming, the furniture covered up with drop cloths. I bumped into a tall, slender object and pulled off the sheet, revealing a lamp. When I toggled the switch, muted light shone through the yellowing linen shade.

"Success!" I removed the lamp shade to amplify the light. "Good enough for tonight."

The room was actually quite large, covering the width of the downstairs. The ceiling sloped at various heights, and four dormer windows protruded over the front of the house. There was a fireplace and two doors on opposite walls.

The first door revealed a small room, about ten feet by ten feet. I flicked my flashlight around for a few seconds. Mountains of stuff were piled up to the ceiling. My elbow bumped a stack, sending a tower of books tumbling. I shut the door, hiding the mess.

"A task for another day," I said, moving on to door number two.

A single bulb flickered on when I pulled the long ball 'n' chain dangling from the ceiling, revealing a pedestal sink, over which hung an oval mirror covered so thick with dust I struggled to see the small smile spread across my face—the task of cleaning everything out suddenly didn't seem so arduous if the end result meant having my own bathroom.

With slight trepidation, I opened the glass door of a tall, narrow cabinet—even though I had a rightful claim, it still felt like I was digging through someone else's things. Stacks of towels long past their prime. A heavy silver hairbrush. And an assortment of vintage cosmetics. I ogled a collection of perfume bottles made of multicolored, unlabeled glass.

I picked one up, disrupting the long-settled dust, which, in turn, disrupted my sinuses and caused me to sneeze three times. The only word on the rose-colored bottle was "Paris."

Who did you all belong to? You're way too old to have belonged to my mother.

The little objects begged me to make them shiny again.

First, I pulled out the rotting linens. They were far from salvageable, but my affinity for fabric made me poke through them anyway. A misplaced square of lace lay among the tattered terry cloth. The dry-rotted Chantilly fell apart at my touch, revealing a round piece of silver. It was too big to be an old coin. One side of the medallion had an ornate border but was otherwise rough, as if something had broken off and left behind a scar in the metal. There was something familiar about the shape—an eight-pointed star. The other side was flat and smooth. Blank. It looked sad. Unfinished, like a canvas someone had given up on.

More upset by the loss of the old textiles, I slipped the medallion into my pocket and sighed at the tragic state of the disintegrated loops of lace. But after another minute of mourning the fabric, I started a trash pile, telling myself I couldn't get attached to every inch of vintage something or other I found while cleaning.

The smell of bleach permeated the air as I wrung the mop into the sink. My fingers ached from scrubbing. I caught a glimpse of my watch: more than two hours had passed—and I had only finished the bathroom.

Break time.

The air in the lamp-lit bedroom wasn't much better. I struck a wooden match and nearly dropped it when the flame leaped higher than expected. *How old are these matches?* The smell of sulfur singed the air. I held one of the Voodoo shop's sage bundles over the flame, unsure whether it would help or hinder the dusty and now chemical-filled air.

At least the room will be free of evil spirits.

The dust began to tickle the back of my throat, making me cough.

I left the smoking herbs in a glass dish on the fireplace mantel and, with some force, managed to wriggle open one of the windows. In the darkness, there was nothing to look at save the moon, but I rested my elbows on the sill and breathed in some of the cooler, cleaner air.

No tourists, no screaming drag queens, no horse hooves clacking down the street, the perfect still of the night was something I'd never get used to. Not in New Orleans. The quiet freaked me out.

My mind drifted back to the Ursuline Convent. The shutter. The nails. The stake. I could almost feel the swoosh of energy that had moved past me after the shutter burst open and the glass rained down in sparkling shards.

A trapped breath escaped.

It is a miracle I walked away unscathed.

I leaned out the window and tugged at the shutters, which were almost exactly like the ones at the convent. Neither of them budged. They were fastened securely open—I was not sure what else I expected to happen. With my upper body still hanging outside, I noticed a silhouette perched on our neighbor's balcony: a large black crow. Its head turned to the side, the crow stared at me. I yanked myself back in and slammed the window shut, banging my head in the process.

"Dammit!"

Touching the bandage on my face, I looked through the glass spitefully, but only the moon stared back at me. *Come on, Adele, it's just a stupid bird.*

I shoved the window open again and turned back around, determined to resume cleaning.

"Adele—"

"Dad!" My hands fell to my knees, my pulse exploding. "Are you trying to scare me to death?"

"I'm sorry, sweetheart. I called your name when I walked through the front door." He pulled me up. "What's wrong?"

I hesitated as the day's events sped through my head. There was no real need to tell him about the dead body. It would only make him worry and might even result in attempts at stricter parenting, an experiment in which I did not want to be a test subject. And there was no rational way to explain the bizarre events in the convent courtyard. The raining nails. The stake. I felt insane just thinking about them.

"Nothing's wrong. You just startled me. How was your day?"

"Okay, all things considered. No leads on finding someone to fix the wall. The supply-and-demand ratio for labor is already way out of whack. It's gonna be mayhem when the masses return."

"And the bar?"

"Looks like it got a couple inches of water, just enough to damage anything that was resting on the floor, drywall, etc."

"*Oof.* That's good? I guess?"

"Yeah, it could have been a lot worse, I suppose. The smell was the worst part, but I managed to drag out most of the rank furniture. Did you make it to school?"

"Uh, no." I braced myself for the onslaught of guilt after lying to my father, but I didn't want to open that can of worms tonight. I moved my bandaged hand behind my back.

"What's that smell in here?"

"It's sage. Oh, I ran into an old friend of yours . . . and Mom's. She sends her regards."

His left eyebrow raised into a question mark.

"Ana Marie Borges."

"Where'd you run into Ana Marie?"

"In their shop. That place is so cool! I can't believe you've never taken me there before."

"What were you doing in Vodou Pourvoyeur?"

"Nothing, really. I moseyed in because it was actually open."

He looked a little more uncomfortable than usual.

"It was kinda weird," I added.

"How so?" he asked.

"Just, they kinda acted like they knew me."

"Ana Marie and Morgan have a daughter about your age."

"Désirée. We met. She's *delightful*."

He laughed. "Well, I'm sure she's grown up wanting for nothing."

"That's an understatement."

"Let me guess, the Storm went easy on their shop?"

"To quote Désirée, the Borges 'don't have problems with storms.' Oh, I have some more sage if you want to bring a bundle to the bar."

He gave me a funny look.

"You know, for the rank smell?"

"Right. You should go to bed. It's late."

I looked down at my watch. "It's after midnight? Whoa, where have you been all night, Dad?"

"I told you, at the bar—"

"But what about the curfew?"

"It's not like I was out loitering or looting, Adele. People have lives. People have families to support! Damn curfew."

"Jeez, sorry I asked."

"And that doesn't give you permission to be out past curfew."

"All *right*."

He moved to the window and pushed it shut.

"I took an epic nap," I said. "So I'm not really tired."

He picked up the bucket of dirty mop water. I sighed, switched off the light, and followed him down the stairs to my bedroom door.

"Try to sleep. It's the only way you'll get back on Central Time." He kissed my cheek. "Good night."

"G'night."

I kicked off my flip-flops and stripped off my T-shirt, finding the gris-gris necklace Ritha had given me stuck to my chest. Something about the casual way my father had spoken about the Borges struck me as odd.

I peeled the gris-gris from my skin but decided it could stay.

CHAPTER 7

Ciao, bella

October 11th

I leaned so close to the vanity mirror, my nose nearly touched it. The natural light poured through the open curtains, directly onto the cheek I was examining. Like magic, the crow's slash had stopped hurting overnight. *What's in that ointment?* Regardless, there was a disgusting scab forming from the base of my neck almost to my eye. *Thank God the crow didn't tear another inch. I could've been blinded in one eye.* The scab was gross, but at least now I could lose the bandage. My hand dressing was downgraded to a couple of large Band-Aids.

In better news, listening to my father and not staying up all night meant signs of life were slowly coming back to my face. No more bloodshot eyes, and the puffy, dark circles from switching time zones had mostly faded.

———

After showering, I slathered on an assortment of fancy French crèmes my mother had stocked my dorm room with. *She must be doing something right, to stay so young looking.* As I breathed in the lavender moisturizer, I wondered if she used the same scent. Too lazy to do much else, I ripped a brush through my tangles, spritzed in some leave-in conditioner, and hoped my mop of brown waves would dry in a decent manner.

Black leggings. Gray T-shirt. Shit-kickers. Long chain with the sun charm.

It was unsettling that my old routine felt only vaguely familiar. *When will things start to feel normal again?*

My brush handle spun, knocking something off the vanity that hit the floor with a clank. It was the silver medallion I'd found in the disintegrated lace. In the morning light, I could now see there was something underneath the impression of the burned star. Initials. I breathed heavily on the silver and rubbed it with my towel, vowing to clean it properly later in my father's studio.

The letters *ASG* had been etched in a sweeping calligraphy that matched the ornate border.

I flipped it over to see if I'd missed anything else last night. Blank. Then I found myself slipping it onto the silver chain next to the sun charm. My collar slouched off one shoulder, revealing the gris-gris ribbon.

Who was ASG?

My father looked depressed, blindly dumping stuff into a large garbage can. I stood in his doorway, holding my second café au (powdered) lait, wondering whether I should stay and help him.

"Morning," I said.

"Hey, baby." He walked over and took a hard look at my injured cheek.

I looked around the room as he moved my chin around and decided that having to unexpectedly throw away piles of your own work was something an artist would want to do alone. "I'm gonna go for a walk, check out the grocery situation, and swing by Café Orléans. I didn't get a chance yesterday."

"All right, let's go for a run when you get back, before it gets too hot?"

"Ugh, sure." It had been weeks since I'd done any real physical activity.

"That's the spirit, honey."

I smiled and left the coffee for him on his workbench.

In the foyer, I stopped to grab my bag, but before I could reach my keys, they shot up into my palm.

I stopped short.

Instinctively, I looked around to see if anyone else had just witnessed the strange occurrence.

Breathe.

My eyes slipped shut as phantom ticks from the grandfather clock pounded in my chest. I racked my brain for a reasonable explanation, but nothing came to mind. I felt strangely at odds, like my subconscious was trying to fight back—fighting the part of me that was desperately trying to suppress yesterday's memories as if they were a bad dream.

"Oh, good call," my father said, coming up behind me. He kissed my cheek good-bye before skipping up the stairs.

"On what?"

"On winding up the clock," he yelled down.

"But I didn't . . ."

When I turned around, the pendulum was swinging in the grand-father clock. The ticktocks were no longer phantom. For a moment I stared at the second hand swiftly ticking around the circle. My fingers tightened into a fist around my keys. The metal felt warm.

". . . but I didn't touch the clock," I whispered.

Trying not to go into a full-on panic attack, I dropped the keys into my bag and did what any reasonable person would do: ignored it and hustled out the door.

My nervousness transferred from my shoulders down to my feet, which carried me down the block at a nonsouthern pace. I misjudged the hop onto the curb and stumbled.

"Adele? You okay?" Felix Palermo yelled, witnessing my spastic moment. *He sure has good eyesight for someone pushing eighty.* The old man was hunched over a broom, next to a pile of window shards. I hurried across the street, eager for the distraction.

"Hi, Mr. Felix!"

"If it isn't little Miss Addie Le Moyne."

Behind him, a couple of younger guys I didn't recognize exited the little corner store, carrying a moldy refrigerator. Palermo's Italian Delicatessen was not in good shape, but I tried not to let the shock show on my face.

The guys dropped the fridge near the curb and quickly retreated back into the deli.

"When did y'all get back?" I asked, giving the old man a hug.

"We snuck back a few days ago, but it wasn't till yesterday I found a couple boys to help us start haulin' out the trash. They're staying in the top-floor apartment, trading labor for rent. If ya ask me, I'm getting the better end of the deal—the apartment doesn't even have electricity. But they're over from the motherland, lookin' for some missing relatives, so they've got bigger problems."

"We're running a generator," I said. "I don't think anyone in the Quarter has electricity yet."

"We got a few feet of water. It poured in the storefront window where an old Chevy pushed through. It's still beyond me how the boys managed to get the car out last night. Must be nice being young. Looters trashed the place." He sighed. "I suppose I can't really blame them. People need to eat. This hurricane, Addie, I don't know. I've been through Betsy and Camille and at least a couple dozen more, but something's just not right."

I understood what he meant. Something felt off. I'd tried to convince myself it was just a mix of being away for so long combined with shock, but I couldn't shake the feeling that something else was different. Something had changed.

He gestured to the store. "You go in there and take anything you and your pop need. That is, if there's anything left."

"I can't just *take* stuff—"

"Adele, you go salvage anything you can. And don't you worry about it. I'm filin' an insurance claim tomorrow. *Capisce?*" He gave me an exaggerated wink.

"*Capisce.*" I smiled and walked toward the entrance.

"And be careful in there, Adele! It's a goddamn mess."

I yelled, "Okay," over my shoulder and stopped at the entrance. The enormous retro letters that spelled out the store's name, usually lit up in red, white, and green, had come loose. "PAL" still seemed secure, but "ERMO'S" now hung at a dangerous ninety-degree angle. I hurried underneath. The whole city was starting to feel like one giant booby trap.

Flies buzzed around mounds of brown-colored mush that used to be fruit but now reeked like rotten grass. I covered my nose and mouth to mask the smell, in an attempt to control my twitching stomach muscles, but then hurried to the other side of the store, extra careful not to step on anything that would require a tetanus shot after.

Sauntering down the remaining aisles, I assessed my options, scared of anything not preserved in glass, aluminum, or a vacuum-sealed bag. Most of the nonperishables had already been cleared out. I grabbed a can of steel-cut oats as if it were gold and then a couple sacks of red beans 'n' rice. *Will bigger supermarket chains look like this too—empty shelves with rotting inventory? Will we have to ration these oats? Surely the government will intervene if it comes to that . . . right?*

I scooped up two cans of tomato soup. The empty shelf space gave me a view to the other side of the room, where the guys were ripping commercial freezers from the wall. Neither seemed to be breaking a sweat.

Impressive.

One had light blond hair, and the other's was nearly black, but there was something very similar about them. *They must be brothers,* I thought, watching them from between the jars of pepper jelly and dusty cans of minestrone. Even their movements were synced; each carried out the manual labor with a strange amount of grace. Over from the motherland? Mr. Felix must have meant Italy . . . Their slickly styled hair seemed very Italian to me. Flashbacks to my European days suddenly made me feel very underdressed.

The dark-haired guy was closest to me, but all I could see was the back of his head. He wore dark jeans and a black leather jacket, and even from behind, he seemed more focused on the task at hand than the blond, who appeared bored, his thin lips in a near pout.

The blond looked to be in his midtwenties. The cuffs of his pale-blue denim jeans were turned up, and a pair of tan leather suspenders that buttoned onto his waistband, making them look old-timey, stretched over his shoulders. He had the most perfect skin I'd ever seen, but his aquiline features combined with his lackadaisical demeanor made him come across as some kind of naughty prince.

"How long do we have to do this, Brother?" he asked.

"Until we've acclimated. Or until everyone is reunited, I suppose." The dark-haired brother's English had only a hint of a foreign accent, while the blond's was much thicker.

"I assumed finding everyone would require some brute force, but this wasn't exactly what I had in mind," the blond said as he jerked the refrigeration system from the wall.

"Stop whining. Like you couldn't do this in your sleep."

"Don't mention sleep around me."

His brother softly chuckled.

My chest stung. *How could you sleep if you were missing loved ones?*

Suddenly the blond's tone became serious. "We have to find Giovanna . . . I can't stop thinking about what might have happened to her—"

"Gabriel, she hasn't been seen since . . . You need to prepare yourself for the idea—"

"We *will* find her, Brother. I don't care what it takes."

Out of nowhere, the cans of minestrone betrayed me by flying off the shelf onto the floor in a series of loud crashes. I watched in horror as a can rolled all the way over to the boot of the blond.

"Well, whom do we have here?" he asked, overjoyed to have a distraction from the labor.

I was mortified, caught spying on a private conversation. And not just any conversation, but one between two beautiful foreigners. *What were the odds . . . at Palermo's of all places?* I tried to walk casually to the other side of the shelf, as if I were just doing the daily shopping.

"Hi, I'm Adele."

"Adele?" The blond looked at me with an eagerness that made me slightly uncomfortable. From my hiding spot, I hadn't realized how tall they were, both over six feet.

"Yeah, Adele Le Moyne." My attempt to offer a hand failed because I was holding too many things, so I resorted to a half nod, half curtsy. Blood rose in my cheeks.

"*Buongiorno, Adele.* I am Gabe . . ." The blond's light-green eyes sparkled against the grim backdrop of the store. "And this is my youngest brother, Niccolò."

Niccolò nodded at me and then casually leaned against the wall with one foot up, his hands stuffed deep into his pockets. It was like he was watching his brother watch me.

"*Bienvenue.* Nice to meet you both." *Is a welcome appropriate under these circumstances?*

"The pleasure is entirely ours," Gabe said, looking down at me with a dramatic smile. The outline of his well-defined chest was easy to see through his fitted white T-shirt, which he'd somehow managed not to dirty at all.

I scrambled to think of something to say. "Mr. Felix said you're over from Europe. Italy?" I placed my bags on the ground.

"*Sì,* we are looking for our family. We have three missing in action, including our sister. Maybe you know them?"

There was something about the way he asked that reminded me of a mafioso casually inquiring about his next victim. My knowledge of the Mafia, of course, came only from watching *The Godfather* movies repeatedly with my father.

As I listened to Gabe describe their missing relatives, I couldn't help but notice Niccolò's gaze shift to me. He had the same light-green eyes as Gabe, only his made me think of a cat preparing to pounce on a toy. My fingers went to the chain around my neck as my eyes flicked to his—never for more than a few seconds at a time. He was just as attractive as his brother but with more of a James Dean vibe about him.

Wait, do I know this guy?

I blushed when I realized there was no way I could have met a guy *this* attractive and then simply forgotten about him.

His lips moved into a slight smile, as if he knew I was trying to figure it out.

Then I noticed the silence. Gabe had stopped talking and was looking at me, obviously expecting me to answer a question.

"I'm sorry," I stuttered. "What's the name?"

"Me-di-ci," he repeated.

"Leave her alone, Gabriel." Niccolò finally spoke. "She doesn't know anything." The softness of his voice surprised me.

"It's okay," I squeaked, dropping the chain. The charms bounced against my stomach as I turned back to Gabe. "I'm sorry, I was paying attention. I just . . . got distracted." I tried not to smile, knowing Niccolò was still looking at me. "I don't know any Medici. I'm sorry," I repeated, desperately wishing I knew something, anything, about their family. "Three people. Your sister? That's horrible."

Gabe let out an exasperated sigh. "Don't worry, little lamb, we won't rest until we find them." He walked across the room and stood right outside the doorway, staring down the street like a posted guard.

"What happened to your face?" Niccolò asked.

"Um, a bird attacked me." I was not thrilled for the attention to switch focus to my giant scab. "I know, random."

"What kind of bird?" he probed in a serious tone. I had a hunch it was only a slight variation from his natural disposition.

"A crow . . . I think. It was really dark in the kitchen."

"A crow? In your home?"

He seemed to mull over the idea as he slowly approached me.

My mouth moved, but I no longer heard the words coming out . . . something about how great the city was under different circumstances. My brain ping-ponged between wondering where I knew him from and wondering whether I should stay and continue embarrassing myself with my pathetic attempts at conversation. Unfortunately, he said nothing to interrupt my rambling as he moved closer, although his focus was so attentive on my wounded cheek, I questioned whether he was even listening.

He stopped directly in front of me. "It is an amazing city. Luckily we've been here before."

My throat tightened. "Oh good."

He was so close I could smell him over the lingering stench of putrid produce: leather and soap. The scent reminded me of Émile. Probably because Émile was one of my few points of reference when it came to male scents.

He raised his hand to my face, and I prayed I wasn't showing any outward signs that my knees were about to buckle. Careful not to touch the wound, his fingertips grazed my cheek, sending chills into my hairline. Surely he must have noticed.

He took a deep breath and whispered, "Lavender."

His hand swept along my neck as he delicately picked up the thin silver chain, following the tightly woven links all the way down to the two charms dangling at my waist. He brought the medallion up to his face, pulling me even closer. I strained to keep my balance and not bob into him as he flipped it over, keenly examining both sides. My gaze nervously wandered out the window to the broken Palermo's sign hanging over the door, where Gabe was still standing sentry.

"Pretty necklace. Where did you get it?"

We were standing so close I could barely breathe. I tried to turn sounds into words, but nothing came out of my mouth easily, for a change.

"My dad—"

A loud screech of scraping metal interrupted us. "Look out!" I screamed to Gabe.

The latter half of the massive sign tore free and plummeted toward him. My arms shot around my head, and I ducked, anticipating the crash . . . but a few beats of silence went by instead.

What the hell?

I cautiously opened my eyes to find them each holding one end of the broken neon namesake. The sign was so old it must have been extraordinarily heavy, but they rested it on the floor as if it were a kitten. They both brushed their hands and turned to me with a look of bewilderment plus a hint of suspicion. Which was strange, because that's exactly how I was looking at them.

"Are you okay?" I asked, hurrying over.

"You saved me," Gabe said.

"No . . ." I balked.

"Your warning . . . I am forever in your debt." Gabe gallantly kissed my hand. Niccolò remained stoic.

The metal screeched again.

I looked up just in time to see the lonely letter *L* dropping from above us.

Before I could blink, Gabe jumped up and knocked it aside. Niccolò jerked my arm, pulling me out of the way as it crashed onto the slate sidewalk in an explosion of glass and plastic.

Air wheezed from my throat. Gabe looked me straight in the eyes and smiled.

"I guess you're even now," Niccolò said.

They both just silently stared at me, seemingly undisturbed. Rampant insecurity took over. I wasn't sure what to do or say next, so I fled back for my bags and gathered up my loot. Their gazes continued to burn through me—whether with disbelief, admiration, or scorn, I had no idea.

Trying to be nonchalant on the way out, I grabbed a bottle of rubbing alcohol, a large box of salt, and a couple boxes of baking soda.

"Well, it was nice to meet you both."

"Until we meet again," said Gabe. *"Arrivederci."*

"And welcome to the neighborhood." I looked at Niccolò. "I wish it were under better circumstances."

"Me too." The corner of his mouth crooked. *"Ciao, bella."*

CHAPTER 8

Bisous, bisous

Completely frazzled, I took off in the wrong direction. Luckily, I'd only covered one block before I came to my senses and detoured onto Bourbon Street.

Usually at this hour, employees would be receiving truckloads of inventory and hosing out the proof of last night's vices from barroom floors. Usually I had to hold my breath because of the rank, aromatic meld of stale beer, ashtrays, bleach, and garbage baking in the end-of-summer heat. But this morning that was not necessary. Today there was only one man in view, and he wasn't hosing. He was just leaning against the entranceway of the Court of Two Sisters, smoking a cigarette, shaking his head.

I looped onto Orleans Avenue and sped up, partly out of excitement and partly because my bags of nonperishables were getting heavy.

This particular block, where Café Orléans was located, was one of my favorite streets in the city—I loved its duality. At the far end was one of the loudest blocks of Bourbon, home of the infamous hand grenade: a toxic-green melon cocktail served in a plastic yard glass shaped like an explosive device and touted as the world's most powerful drink. The opposite end of the short block dead-ended in St. Anthony's Garden, the back courtyard of the St. Louis Cathedral. New Orleans, like this street block, was a place of contradictions. Especially in the French Quarter, you could never guess what you'd find.

Seeing the wooden sign for Café Orléans hanging from its chains caused a rush of excitement to fill my chest—I'd helped Sébastien climb up and take it down before his family evacuated, so they must have returned.

I stood in the doorway and watched as the four of them bustled about.

Sébastien Michel and his twin sister, Jeanne, were the closest things to siblings I had. Their grandparents, natives of France, had raised them since they were nine, after their parents, who had apparently been big-time archeologists, both died when something went wrong during an excavation. Mémé and Pépé Michel had been like surrogate parents to me too, ever since my mother left. Because they had a French-speaking household, my father wouldn't allow anyone else to babysit me when I was a child. It was his version of language immersion/torturing me. French wasn't widely spoken in New Orleans anymore, so it wasn't particularly useful, but he did it because it was supposedly important to my mother. He always seemed sad when he reminded me of that, so I never fought him on it.

Mémé and Pépé were wiping down the furniture with something that smelled like pine. Jeanne was tugging on her wheat-blond hair while meticulously recording inventory on a clipboard, and Sébastien was lugging in a giant sack of coffee beans from the back alley.

I tried to put my bags down gently, but the weight of the canned goods made a clank. Everyone paused and turned their heads in unison.

"Adele!" cried the twins, cueing everyone to hustle over and make a fuss. French, English, everyone talking over each other—after spending so much time alone recently, it felt like a party.

Jeanne threw her arms around me. "*Comment était Paris?* I want to know everything!"

"*Misérable,*" I replied. "*Tout le monde parle français à Paris!*"

She laughed. "Well, it's a good thing you have such a brilliant French tutor! Wow, your accent is better than mine now! *Très impressionnant.*"

When I was nine, my father decided immersion wasn't enough and started paying Jeanne to teach me things like grammar.

"*J'en doute.* I *seriously* doubt it." I couldn't imagine ever being better than Jeanne at anything. The twins were only four years older than me, but she was about to finish her PhD in biochemistry, was dating a surgical resident, and had the confidence of a beauty queen—all of this before she was legally able to drink. *Maybe that's what happens when you get to skip the formidable high school years?* Yes, the twins were both supergeniuses. All the elite universities had offered them spots during the evacuation, but they refused to go anywhere without Mémé and Pépé. I loved how tight-knit they all were.

Sébastien leaned forward to gently kiss both of my cheeks. "*Salut, Adele, bienvenue.*" His voice was quiet, but I could tell he was just as excited as his sister. He pushed his black-rimmed glasses closer to the aquamarine eyes that were identical to his sister's. "What happened to your face?"

I sighed. "It's an embarrassing story involving a bird. How long have you guys been back?" I felt kind of bad. I'd been so wrapped up in trying to navigate the heinous waters of Parisian boarding school I'd done a crummy job keeping in touch with the people I cared about the most.

"We just got back from Cambridge yesterday." Jeanne pulled my arm and whisked me down to a café table. "I thought being displaced would be terrible, Adele, but MIT was *so* amazing. I got to work with—"

"*We,*" Sébastien corrected. "*We* got to work with three different Nobel laureates."

"And they even put Mémé and Pépé up in this adorable little colonial house. It was so beautiful, all the xanthophylls, carotenoids, and anthocyanins—"

"She's referring to the different colors of the changing leaves," Sébastien translated. "They actually have four seasons in Massachusetts."

I gave him my all-too-familiar *thank-you-for-explaining-her-craziness* look.

"But thank goodness we were able to leave before winter," their grandmother interjected from across the room. "They got thirty inches of snow in one blizzard last year! Can you imagine? These old bones do not shovel snow."

"Adele! I can't believe I forgot to ask—" Jeanne's usual scrutinizing eyes grew wide with concern. "*Ta mère?* What was she like?"

Everyone else pretended to go back to work as I scrambled to figure out what to say about my mother.

All the way across the Atlantic, I'd imagined one hundred different scenarios for our joyful reunion, wherein she would tell me a complicated, heartbreaking story explaining how she'd been forced to abandon me and my father and how she'd lived in agony ever since. In some versions I cried, in others I yelled, and in most we ended up drinking tea next to a fireplace and talking for hours.

But any pathetic fantasies I'd entertained about finally rebuilding a relationship with my mother burst upon arrival in Paris, when the only person who came to greet me at *Aéroport de Paris–Charles de Gaulle* was her driver, Paul-Louis, who took me directly to boarding school. There was no trace of her cold-blooded heart other than a small bottle of champagne in the car with a beautiful card:

> *Bienvenue à Paris, mon amour.*
> *Bisous,*
> *Brigitte*

It was probably the standard greeting she used for all of her acquaintances arriving at the airport. Not that I was surprised by my mother's epic fail. I'd just thought maybe with the Storm and all she might have suddenly started caring that I was alive. There'd been a basket of luxurious French beauty products and boxes and boxes of Chanel dresses waiting for me in my dorm room, but I had to wait another week before even hearing from Brigitte. I was in full-on rage mode by the time our first meeting occurred.

"What was she like?" I repeated, reminding myself not to say anything too bad, considering the twins' own mother was dead. "I wouldn't really know. I saw her three times over the course of two months. We had approximately seventeen interactions, if you include voice mail, text, and e-mail. I did, however, see *ma grand-mère* a few times. She was appalled by my French but bought me racks of fancy clothes to make up for it."

"To make up for being appalled or to make up for your appalling French?"

"Hmm. *Je ne sais pas*, both, maybe?" Everyone laughed. "Whatever." I forced a smile and tried not to roll my eyes. "I'm over it."

"I'm sure her intentions were good, Adele," Mémé said loudly in French from across the room. "And now you're back home where you belong, safe and sound."

I smiled back at her and, for a moment, pretended she really was *ma grand-mère*.

"So, are you coming back to work?" asked Jeanne, wagging her eyebrows.

"Oui, s'il te plaît, oui!"

"Thank God," she said, looking at her grandparents. "I *need* to get back to my lab."

"So do I!" chimed Sébastien from behind the counter.

"No problem. NOSA is closed indefinitely, so I've got nothing but time . . ."

"I don't see your papa letting that stand for too long," said Mémé without turning from the window she was spritzing.

"Oui, oui. He says I have to go back to my *mother's* if I can't get into a school pronto."

"We'll homeschool you before we let that happen, right, Bastien?"

Jeanne and I both looked up at him with big eyes.

He walked over, leaned on the back of my chair, and looked at his sister. "Why do I see that turning into *me* tutoring Adele in *all* of her subjects while you conveniently get stuck at school?"

I flicked his arm as hard as I could.

"Ouch! You know I'm kidding!"

He was right, though. Jeanne didn't have the attention span to tutor me in subjects as elementary as precalculus and physics. At this point, I was more her practice partner with French than her tutee.

"Don't worry, *mon chou*," Sébastien said. "We won't let your dad send you back to Paris. Whatever you need—"

"Precal!"

"You cover my shift tomorrow, and I will teach you everything I know about function derivatives."

"Deal."

"No, cover my shift tomorrow afternoon!" Jeanne yelled, grabbing my arm.

"Too late," he said.

"I'll cover both of your shifts. I have to get into a school first, before I can attend one. And for the record, I don't need to know *everything* you know about function derivatives, just enough to get, like, a B."

"Slacker," they said simultaneously.

I was so excited to be back in action I kissed all of their cheeks good-bye before skipping out the door. *"À demain!"*

"Dad?" I yelled, entering the house through the broken kitchen door. "Dad, are you home?" I tried yelling a little louder; sometimes he wore protective earphones if he was using loud equipment in his studio.

"In the living room, Adele," he responded, his voice beckoning me.

My hand froze as I dropped my heavy bags on the kitchen counter. We *never* used the living room. It was reserved for formal circumstances, like Christmas morning or the occasional spot of tea with a wealthy patron of the arts who was viewing my dad's work.

As I walked down the hallway, I heard a second, vaguely familiar male voice talking about the curfew and then the electronic beep of a walkie-talkie. I stopped short in the doorway.

Oh shit.

My father was sitting on the couch, tapping his foot, and Officer Terry Matthews was sitting in a wing-back chair, sipping coffee from the strawberry-shaped mug I'd scored at a thrift store last year.

"Hi, Officer Matthews." My voice reached an unusual octave. I sat on the couch next to my father but directed all of my attention toward the man in uniform.

"Actually, Adele, it's detective now; just got the promotion this morning," he said sheepishly.

The New Orleans Police Department lost a lot of officers to the Storm . . . meaning many fled with the evacuees and then stayed in greener pastures. I had to give credit to the ones who stayed behind to defend the city and its inhabitants.

"Adele, Detective Matthews is here to follow up on the police report you filed yesterday. Remember, the dead body you found?" My father's tone indicated that I had some serious explaining to do once the detective left.

"Congratulations on the promotion!" I smiled as innocently as I could.

"Thank you, young lady. What happened to your face?"

I quickly told him the story about the bird.

"Well, no need to worry. You're looking more like your mama every day."

Whenever I met people who actually knew my mother, they were never able to resist mentioning how we could be twins. Even though Brigitte and I did share an uncanny resemblance, it grated on my nerves. I tried not to let my jaw clench as I asked how his family was.

"The kids are in Houston right now with their mom. We're waiting on a timeline from our insurance agent . . ."

Just when I hoped he might ramble for a while, he stopped and asked, "So, what's this business about a body you reported?"

"Well . . ."

"Don't be afraid to mention every tiny detail. What may seem insignificant to you might be a clue to the trained mind." He flipped open a small pad.

"Right." I could see the protocol running through his head as he clicked the pen. I guessed his promotion had been unexpected.

I avoided my father's gaze as I recounted my run-in with the blue-eyed corpse.

". . . and where were you coming from?"

Cringing, I debated whether telling the truth about this next bit was critical. Lying to a cop didn't seem like a good idea. I sighed.

"I was coming from NOSA. I went to see if there was any information about school reopening."

I refused to look my father's way but was certain there were wisps of smoke coming out of his ears. *I knew I shouldn't have lied last night, Paris threats or not.*

"And he was dead upon arrival?"

Dead.

My mind wandered back to the street scene. "His blue eyes just stared at me . . . like he was horrified." My own eyes began to sting as I waited for the next question. I quickly wiped them and then felt my dad's hand on my back.

"So, I'm going to take that as a yes?"

I nodded, and the detective handed me a folded handkerchief from his pocket.

"Were there any visible signs of violence? A wound? Blood?"

"No . . . but I didn't hang around for very long."

"Did you see any other people, any other witnesses?"

"Just him."

"And this was around eleven a.m.?"

"Yeah, right before it started raining. I got soaked. I tried to call the police right away, but the line was busy, so I kept calling when I got home."

"And you went straight home from the crime scene?"

I contemplated telling him about the shutter incident, but an image of me being dragged to Charity Hospital in a straightjacket popped into my head.

"Yes, I went straight home."

"Did you witness anything else that might be strange, unusual, or bring further evidence to the case?"

"No, that's it."

"Well, thanks for calling in the body, Adele. The longer these things sit in the heat, the more evidence we lose." There was something too complacent about the way he said "these things." *How many dead bodies has he seen in the last couple of months?*

"Has there been other news about the case?" I asked.

"These things are complicated, but we're ruling it as a homicide for now . . ."

Great, my dad is definitely going to put a lock on my door.

"It's crazy out there. This is the twelfth body we've found in the past three days, most of them in the last twenty-four hours."

"What?" my father yelled.

That does seem excessive, even for New Orleans.

"All left the same—"

"Have you identified him yet?" I interrupted before my father decided never to let me out of the house again.

"We don't have any suspects yet. The crime scenes have been completely clean, but—" He stopped himself, probably realizing he was giving away more information than he should.

"No, I mean the dead man."

"Oh, Jarod O'Connell. He had a local driver's license. We haven't been able to find any family yet, so we don't know much else." He downed the last sip from the strawberry and stood up. "Thanks for the coffee, Mac. I'll keep you posted about the curfew. I understand it's gonna cramp your biz when people get back into town."

"Much obliged." Dad gruffly shook his hand, and we followed our guest to the front steps. My father put his hand on my shoulder, as if I might take off running down the street.

Detective Matthews cranked the engine of the unmarked Crown Vic, rolled down the passenger window, and yelled out, "Oh, and Mac, I'll file a report about your kitchen break-in. It's always better to have everything on record."

"Thanks, Terry, I appreciate it. Stop by the bar soon."

"Bye, Officer Matthews—I mean, *Detective* Matthews," I called.

"Not sure I'll ever get used to that," he said with a goofy expression.

We waved as the car pulled away and then stood in silence for a few seconds. I braced myself for one of my father's painfully awkward lectures.

"Dammit, Adele."

Here it comes.

Instead he went silent again. I didn't know if he was pausing for emphasis or taking a moment to suppress his temper, but it confused me, and my father rarely confused me. *Maybe being apart for so long is throwing off my game?*

"Go put on your running shoes."

"What?"

"Go get changed. We're going for a run before it gets too hot. Remember?"

"Um, okay." I was no longer in any position to argue.

CHAPTER 9

Run, Run, Run

I was both curious and mildly disconcerted that my father was just ignoring the fact that I'd lied to him. I mean, he was so tense about the crime in the city I couldn't imagine him just letting it slide. Each second it took me to lace up my running shoes and loop my hair into a ponytail built my dread of the upcoming interrogation. I traded my silver chain for a house key on a knotted shoestring and hurried through the front door to get it over with.

He was already waiting outside, rolling his ankles. I bent over next to him and became temporarily woozy as the blood rushed to my head and the stretch moved up my hamstrings.

"When's the last time you ran?" he asked.

"Uh, I think I ran twice in Paris, in the very beginning."

"That's not much to keep your lungs in shape, Adele."

When I was a kid, I developed juvenile asthma, right around the time my mother left. Even though the doctor told him the attacks were anxiety based, my father became obsessed over the health of my lungs. I hadn't had a panic attack since the seventh grade, but he still kept the house stocked with inhalers, and we used to run together three mornings a week before school.

"I ran every day in Miami," he continued.

Good for you.

Normally, I would have said it, but something about this trite conversation warned me to proceed with caution, so I held back on the sarcasm. "My dad, the fitness buff—who'd have known?"

He did his best not to crack a smile. "Well, what else was I supposed to do without you around to bug me all the time?" He tossed me his second bottle of water and took off jogging.

So we're joking now? My father could never stay mad at me for long, but this was a record. Something else was brewing.

"Wait up!"

"Catch up!"

"Oh, this is going to be loads of fun."

The quick sprint left me panting. I took his right side; my father was adamant about the man's position always being on the street side. He seriously watched too many Mafia movies.

We jogged in silence through Jackson Square, up the cement stairs of the amphitheater, and over the two sets of nonfunctioning tracks (one for the train and the other for the streetcar), finally arriving at the riverfront, otherwise known as the Moonwalk.

The Toulouse Street Wharf was annihilated. Pieces of it bobbed on the river, along with a mass of other buoyant debris, and heaps of floating trash occupied the large, empty space where the SS *Natchez* had been docked since the early 1800s.

Just as my breathing began to even out, he broke the silence. "Up or down?"

"Up." And that was the end of our conversation for several more minutes.

The murky Mississippi was calm. I pretended the paddleboat was just out on the river, lazily taking mint julep–drinking tourists on leisurely rides. The absence of the old riverboat was another reason the city now felt so eerily silent. If I concentrated hard enough, I could hear the steam shooting out of the whistling calliope—I'd heard that pipe organ at 11:00 a.m. and 2:00 p.m., like clockwork, almost every day of my life. My eyes burned, and I had to tell myself not to cry over a missing riverboat. *Pathetic.*

"I heard the *Natchez* is docked somewhere in Baton Rouge," my father informed me, as if he knew it was bothering me.

"Oh good." I sucked in a breath of air, and then we were back to silence. The muscles in my legs eased, and side by side, we fell into a steady rhythm. I spaced out for a while.

We passed the open-air French Market, which was now a ghost town, and crossed the border into the Faubourg Marigny. When we approached NOSA, just a few blocks from where I'd found the body, my father said, "So, we need to talk about school."

I picked up the pace. He followed suit.

"Dad, I am not going back to Paris just because I found a dead body and didn't tell you. I'm sorry I lied about going down to school. I was just scared you were going to freak out and try to send me back to live with Brigitte!"

"Adele—I'm not sending you back to Paris . . . Not yet, at least. Although, you have one more encounter with a dead person and I will quickly change my mind."

My brow momentarily unfurled.

"I got a call from your guidance counselor. NOSA is in line for the city-state-fed-whatever government to allocate funds for rebuilding, so who knows when they will reopen."

My chest tightened. I could already see where this was leading: my father was going to try to send me away again.

"In the meantime, students have been placed in arts high schools around the country, including the Chicago School for Visual Arts and some place in Florida. A couple even went to New York City."

I could've undoubtedly listed the students who'd gone to NYC. I had many Broadway-bound classmates working night and day to become triple threats.

"She told me about a program you might be interested in, a high school that agreed to autoadmit a few displaced Storm kids. They have a textiles program; you'd get to meet real designers and work with real fashion labels."

I jogged faster. His longer stride easily kept up.

"And where's this dream school located?" I mumbled.

He took a deep breath. "It's in California. Los Angeles."

My eyes welled up.

"I already talked to the Joneses, and they would love to have you stay with them."

The tears began to drip. *I shouldn't be upset.* There were thousands of kids crammed into schools in Baton Rouge and Houston, without books, friends, or routines . . . But I couldn't help it; I'd just gotten home, and I didn't want to leave.

"Sounds like a cool opportunity, Dad," I choked out.

He stopped running. As did I, gasping at the ground.

"Then why are you crying?" He sucked in a couple breaths of air.

I did everything I could to hold in the tears, which made the words come out in a near scream. "Why do you keep trying to get rid of me?"

"Sweetheart, that is ludicrous. I am not trying to get *rid* of you. How can you even say that? I just don't want you to miss out on any opportunities because of the Storm. You have to be in school, so I figured you'd like this much better than going back to your mother's, although I wish you'd consider that option."

I scowled.

"You'll be with Brooke, and you can come home for Christmas."

It was a perfectly rational justification, but I still didn't want to hear it. I stayed hunched over my knees, unable to look up at him.

"I don't care about school, Dad. I am *not* leaving New Orleans again."

He put his hand on my shoulder. "I thought you might feel that way . . . and I may have a happy medium. Do you want the good news or the bad news first?"

I smeared away the tears with the back of my hand. *Is my father actually executing a classic bait and switch?* I filed a mental note to use the tactic on him in the future.

He continued with caution. "So, I made some arrangements."

My back shot straight up. "Some *arrangements?*" The last time my father had "made some arrangements," I ended up on a plane, flying across the Atlantic, only four hours later.

"If you want to stay in New Orleans . . . then Sacred Heart Preparatory Academy has agreed to permit you a seat."

He must be confused.

"Surely you don't mean *the* Sacred Heart? As in uptown? As in Désirée *Borges's* Academy?"

"The one and only."

"They agreed to permit me a seat? What does that even mean?"

"It means they're taking in three displaced students per grade, and they agreed to offer you one of the slots, starting as soon as they can get all of your records together."

"So, I'm a charity case?"

"Well, it's not exactly charity."

"Dad, there's not a chance in hell we can afford something like that."

"Don't curse, Adele!"

"Don't be evasive!"

"Well . . ." He looked behind me, up at the sky. "Your mother made a call."

"*What?* Since when does Brigitte get to take part in making decisions about my life?"

"Well, I'm sure your *mother* didn't make the call," he said, trying to get me to laugh. "I'm sure she had her assistant do it."

But the thought of Émile helping my mother plan my little high school life only made my jaw clench.

I started jogging again, back the way we came. *Do not overreact.*

He quickly caught up. "Adele, if you want to stay in New Orleans, then you are going to Sacred Heart, because I know you'll be safe there—and that's final. Take it or leave it. It's your choice."

"So my choices are imprisonment in my own personal hell of cotillion balls or banishment to the land of Barbie dolls?"

"Well, there is a third choice," he said with a curt smile.

I looked at him with a glimmer of hope. After all, he'd said there was good news too.

"You can always go back to Paris with your mother." He laughed and took off running.

"Ugh, I hate you!" I yelled, chasing him back down the river.

"Don't be so melodramatic," he yelled back. "Whatever you choose, it's just temporary."

I had less than two years of high school left, but at the rate aid was coming to the city, "temporary" might as well have been "forever."

He slowed his pace until we were back together.

"So, what part was supposed to be the *good* news?"

"Well . . . in order to keep your status at NOSA, you'll have to continue your mentorship training, so you only have to attend Sacred Heart for half the day."

At NOSA, we spent the mornings doing regular classes, like biology and literature, and then spent the afternoons doing intensive workshop-style training in our focus area. I'd spent my sophomore year apprenticing with the head seamstress at the University of New Orleans's theatre department, working on the school's spring production of *A Midsummer Night's Dream*. I was dying to show her my Halloween costume. I'd spent every weekend in Paris working my fingers to blisters, hand-stitching embellishments. The haute couture master classes had been the highlight of my trip. Not to mention they were how I met Émile. Those were the only times my mother parted with her assistant—so he could escort me between my dormitory and the classes every Saturday and Sunday. On week two, we had moved from her car to the back of his Vespa. On week three, he was lying to her about what time my class ended.

"Does that mean I get to work at UNO again?" This situation was starting to appear slightly more tolerable.

"Not exactly. Actually, NOSA is making this exception just for you, sweetheart, since Sacred Heart isn't an art school."

"Why? I don't understand."

"On account of you knowing an amazing local artist willing to mentor you. One of the best in the city, if you ask me." His lips pressed into a smile, waiting for a reaction. I tried my best to remain poised, but my words became short as I struggled to run, breathe, and speak at the same time.

"You. Want me to go . . . to Sacred Heart Prep. And then spend every afternoon apprenticing with you in the metal shop?"

"Jeez, do you have to put me in the same category with your disdain for prep school?"

"That's not what I meant, Dad." A seagull squawked as it dipped low to investigate a pile of floating wreckage. "I'm supposed to be apprenticing in fashion. What would we work on together?" I tried my best not to sound as though there was nothing he could teach me.

"What do you mean? There's tons of cool stuff we could do. You could create a jewelry line. We could focus on your fashion illustrations, which you and I both know need serious work so you can put together a decent portfolio."

That stung a little, but he was right.

"You've been talking for ages about wanting to learn how to make your own hardware for your pieces."

He'd obviously been thinking about this a lot. His pitch was start-ing to sound pretty convincing.

"We could do chainmaille or something really high concept."

My mind raced with possibilities as he rattled off more and more ideas.

"Dad, stop!" I couldn't keep the giant grin from spreading across my face. "You had me at chainmaille."

His shoulders relaxed, and I saw the excitement in his eyes. "Really? You'd choose Sacred Heart and me over Brooke and a real atelier?"

I really, really wanted to be with my best friend, but how could I leave this place? There was so much to do, to rebuild. It was utterly overwhelming. My father put his arm around me and pulled me close. I concentrated on my feet so I didn't stumble in his running embrace.

"Gross, you're sweaty, Dad."

"So are you!" He squirted water in my face. Sometimes he really was a child.

"All right, now that that's settled, can we go home?" I said, letting the water run down my neck. It actually felt pretty good; the noon sun was in full blaze.

"Home? We're just getting warmed up."

"Warmed up! Maybe you are, but not all of us vacationed in Miami for the last two months," I teased. "My legs are like jelly. I'm going home." I veered onto Esplanade Avenue as he continued down the river.

"Going to let your old man show you up?" he yelled over his shoulder. *"Oui!"*

"And don't think I forgot about you lying to my face yesterday."

"Yeah, yeah, yeah . . ." There was now too much distance between us to yell back and forth. *What's he going to do? Ground me?* The whole city was already on lockdown. None of my friends were back. There was no Internet and barely any cell phone reception.

I slowed down to pace myself for the remaining ten blocks home. *Did I really just agree to go to the* Academy? Images of Catholic school-girl uniforms, sweet sixteens, and hundreds of cookie-cutter copies of

Désirée Borges popped into my head. I cut across the neutral ground onto Chartres Street and began to count down the blocks when an unfamiliar sight caught my attention.

People. There were three of them standing in the middle of the road on the next block.

A shrunken old lady leaning on a cane was looking up, her hand shielding her eyes from the sun. Behind her were two goth guys who appeared to be either elated or scowling; between the makeup and facial piercings it was hard to tell. As I approached them, I realized they were standing outside the cement wall behind the Ursuline Convent, in almost the exact spot where yesterday's crying fit had begun. I suddenly had a sinking feeling that I knew what they were all looking at.

The taller goth, with the twelve-inch bleached spikes, was Theis, the boyfriend of one of my favorite coffee-shop regulars. He was contorting himself into various positions to snap photos with his phone. His aperture led my gaze straight to the attic window.

It looked just as I had left it yesterday: glass blown out and one shutter missing. The remaining shutter now swayed, although today there was a decent breeze pushing it back and forth. Anxiety pricked my stomach, warning me not to incriminate myself. For what crime, exactly, I had no clue.

"They definitely escaped," Theis said dryly to his shorter, Manic-Panic, green-haired companion.

I ducked my head as I jogged past them, but the old lady turned to me anyway. "I guess even all those nails from the Vatican couldn't hold a candle to the power of the Storm."

I had no idea what she was talking about, but I craned my neck back to her, nodded, and mumbled, "Mother Nature."

"You got it, baby. Lord, help us."

I picked up my pace.

The crazies are sure out in full force this morning, I thought, shaking my head. *What did Theis mean, "escaped"?*

CHAPTER 10

Lady Stardust

Focus on something, Adele. Anything.

By the time I dragged my luggage upstairs, I felt like I'd had a total body workout, but whenever I rested for more than a minute, my mind bounced back and forth between the convent and Sacred Heart, until I felt like I was going to explode.

Finish cleaning.

I stood in my new attic bedroom with my hands on my hips, trying to figure out where to start. The afternoon sun illuminated the dust, making everything sparkle in a weird, whimsical way, and the sheeted furniture cast oddly shaped shadows on the walls, reminding me of a modern art exhibit. I snapped a few photos, then held my breath and pulled off the first sheet, sending dust sparkles everywhere.

Whoa, an upright piano. Maybe everything isn't just old junk.

I tore off the rest of the sheets like a kid on Christmas morning. A rocking chair. A beautifully carved vanity with a trifolding mirror. A rose-colored chaise, and a large oak wardrobe. The perfect little setup from the past. In the middle of the room was a large bed with four ornate brass posts that would have held a delicate canopy once, but from which now hung a couple of limp drop cloths. Without thinking, I yanked them off and plopped down onto the plastic-covered mattress.

My gaze settled on the last drop-cloth sculpture. It was an incredibly odd shape. *Tuba?* I jumped up and ripped off the cover, revealing a phonograph.

"Cool."

The case over the turntable had been sealed tight, so it wasn't even that dusty when I opened it. "Do you still work?"

I raced down to my father's studio and then, breathing heavily, ran back up the stairs with an armful of randomly selected records: the soundtrack to *Jesus Christ Superstar*, a classic Louis Armstrong, a Led Zeppelin, and a David Bowie. I carefully looked over the cardboard case protecting *The Rise and Fall of Ziggy Stardust and the Spiders from Mars*. I didn't know much about David Bowie, but something about the bright gas lamp on the cover attracted me like a fly. *Will these records even work on this old machine?* I wondered, gently pulling the vinyl from the sleeve. I placed it on the turntable and moved the needle.

My fingers searched for a power switch. *You're an idiot, Adele.* I reached for the hand crank, but I couldn't get it to budge. *Mental note: get the WD-40 from Dad's studio.*

I gave the phonograph a little pep talk and exerted some force on the handle.

It gradually started to turn.

The record spun, and the music began playing, all without the power of electricity. "Just like magic," I whispered.

The glam-rock beats sounded raw and scratchy coming from the large flower-shaped cone, and the slow start of the opening song crept over me with the grip of a soon-to-be obsession. I spritzed dusting cleanser with the downbeats of the tune and wiped the rag over the piano as if I were performing onstage. By the time the next track began, I'd moved on to the vanity mirror and decided that I loved Bowie.

When the third track began to crescendo, my fingers picked an air guitar, but just as I started to shred, the music cut off and the room became completely still. I caught sight of my frozen pose in the mirror and quickly dropped the imaginary instrument.

I glanced at the phonograph, hoping I hadn't broken it. Blaming the spiders from Mars, I forced myself to keep cleaning, but it wasn't the same. Even though we'd only just been introduced, I was already having *Ziggy Stardust* withdrawal.

"Ugh, the crank!" I said, having a second mini revelation over the machine's need for manual power.

Finish the mirror first . . .

Without even the slightest ambient street noise coming in through the open windows, the swooshes from my rag seemed loud. I worked faster, eager to get back into David Bowie's spaceship, but then a wave of tingles jettisoning down my spine made me freeze midscrub.

A faint rattle came from behind me.

I strained to listen. *It's just the old pipes.* The rattling sounded way too close to be coming from behind a wall.

Scrubbing again, my nerves began to frazzle, but I refused to look back, feeling safety in not knowing the truth. The noise grew louder and louder, chipping at my curiosity like an ice pick. Chip. Chip.

Breathe.

Without moving my head, I raised my eyes to the mirror and blinked a couple of times at the reflection. Across the room, the metal hand crank was aggressively jerking, causing the entire music box to shake. I spun around, dropping the rag.

As I gaped at the machine, the handle slowly began to turn itself and the music started up again, just as if it had never stopped.

"What the . . . ?"

Am I losing my mind? I forced myself to go back to cleaning. *Some kind of Storm-induced post-traumatic stress disorder?*

The next time the volume died, the sound of my pounding heartbeat was interrupted again by creaking metal. I knew what was making the noises, but my brain could not adjust to the idea.

Creak. Creak.

Breathe.

Once again, Bowie's voice warbled back to full volume, and the room was back to feeling like a 1970s rock opera.

I exhaled loudly, swooshing the rag around the bucket of soapy water, racking my brain for a logical explanation, but I didn't land on anything scientific. *Maybe it's a ghost?* A lost spirit who really, really wanted to listen to *Ziggy Stardust?* I couldn't blame it. *Wait, do I even believe in ghosts?*

The volume died again.

Annoyed by the start-and-stop, I whipped around—the metal handle spun so quickly the album hardly skipped a beat—and David Bowie's voice parachuted in to keep me from going into panic mode.

I had no idea whether I was dreaming, awake, crazy, or sane, but as the *B*-side repeated, I began to relax, and my thoughts moved from a recently grayed-out New Orleans to an explosion of color in Mr. Bowie's fantastical world.

I hadn't realized that I was full-on rocking out with the mop until my father appeared and twirled me around.

"There is absolutely no denying you are my daughter," he yelled over the music. I was loving it too much to be embarrassed.

He grabbed the shadeless floor lamp and belted out the "Lady Stardust" lyrics, doing his best David Bowie impression. I burst out laughing.

"Oh my God, Dad, stop. You're ridiculous."

He sang even louder.

The more I laughed, the more dramatic he became. I hadn't seen him act this silly since I was a kid. Maybe we were both going loopy.

He slid across the piano bench and banged out the chords on the long-dormant instrument.

His ridiculousness escalated until I was doubled over with tears pouring down my cheeks. I couldn't remember the last time I'd laughed so hard. My ribs hurt. My cheeks hurt. And I was gasping for air.

That's when I discovered a really good laugh could change everything.

He jumped up from the piano bench just in time for the last verse, spun me around a few times, and then slowly rocked me back and forth. As the song finished, so did the crank, and the music stopped.

"Everything's going to be all right, Adele." He kissed the top of my head. "I promise."

I willed myself to believe him, but when I opened my eyes, I saw the metal crank vibrating, as if it were trying to figure out what I wanted it to do. And then, even stranger, I felt myself commanding it to stay still.

CHAPTER 11

Absinthe vs. Wheatgrass

Dancing turned into a dinner date. My father cooked a bland feast of plain red beans 'n' rice, all the while loudly playing *Hunky Dory* to further my Bowie indoctrination, and I took on the gag-inducing task of cleaning out the fridge. It was funny experiencing such a domestic scene in our home. Usually we just sort of coexisted, sharing the occasional cup of coffee and discussion about art when our schedules overlapped.

After dinner, he hurried off to Le Chat Noir, and I was left alone, trying to change the overhead lightbulb in the attic. Even standing on my toes on top of the piano bench with my arms fully extended, I wasn't close to reaching it.

"You're way taller in your mind than in actuality, Adele." I sighed to myself.

Fetching the ladder wasn't an appealing task after hauling all of my clothing, books, sewing paraphernalia, and sixteen years' worth of God only knows what else up the stairs, but, unless a bottle of potion labeled "Drink Me" suddenly appeared and made me grow, there were no other options. Then, as I had one foot out the door, a ridiculous idea entered my mind. I stepped back onto the bench, looked up at the old bulb, and imagined it turning.

Nothing happened.

"This is insane," I said, before realizing that talking to myself only confirmed the statement. But then it happened:

The bulb shook a little.

My heart skipped.

I had this feeling that it *wanted* to move.

Focus. Who knows when the lightbulb was last touched? Maybe it's stuck. I concentrated explicitly on the metal ridges of the bulb's base, picturing them moving in a slow, counterclockwise motion.

"Come on, you can do it!"

It budged a millimeter. This time, instead of fearful, I felt exhilarated.

"That's it. Slow and steady."

I watched in amazement as the bulb slowly unscrewed itself and then plopped into my cupped palms.

My hand shook as I pulled the new bulb from its box and extended it upward. When my arm reached its full length, the bulb left my hand, gracefully floated up to the fixture, and turned itself into place. My shoulders tingled with excitement as the base of the bulb was swallowed and the bright light popped on.

"And then there was light," I whispered, looking around, almost fearful someone had witnessed me bend the laws of nature.

My pocket vibrated before I could further freak out.

"Please, please, please tell me you are moving to L.A.!" Brooke screamed into the phone before I could even say hello.

"Oh my God, it's so weird here without you! How's Los Angeles? How are your parents?"

"Oh no, girlfriend. Don't think I'm letting you off the hook that easily. Are you moving to L.A. or what?"

"Well . . ."

"What? Nooooo! I already cleared out half of my closet for you. I mean, it's not like I really have any stuff, so it wasn't that hard, but still. Adele, this school is uh-mazing. Last year they worked with Rodarte, Chanel, and *Project Runway*."

I tried to pay attention as she rattled on about the fashion program, but I was stuck on how casually she'd mentioned having no stuff. In New Orleans, Brooke Jones cleaning out half her closet would've been a major feat.

"The program sounds cool."

"Cool? Adele, it's *Chanel*, as in the empire built by Coco Chanel, your idol—"

"I know! It's just that . . . everything's so messed up here. I don't really know how to explain it. I just can't abandon the city. I mean . . . not that I think y'all abandoned the city. We just had something to come home to . . ."

She didn't say anything.

I slipped off my shoes, climbed into my freshly made bed, and snuggled into the quilt. "So . . . have your parents been back? Has anyone been to your house?"

She remained silent, which was usually impossible for Brooke, so I knew she was crying, which was also unusual for her. I was the crier between the two of us.

I didn't know what to say, so I just waited.

"We don't know anything for sure, but there's not much hope— the whole Tremé was obliterated. Dad's going home next week to see if anything's salvageable and to speak with our insurance agent. The settlement's already turned into a battle. I begged him to let me go with him, but he refused." She paused again. "He says there's nothing left for us there."

I knew it was selfish of me, but I couldn't imagine spending the rest of high school without Brooke. And I couldn't imagine Mr. Jones actually feeling that way. Alphonse Jones was—*is* a part of this city. His horns could be heard on most of the major records that had come out of the Big Easy in the last couple decades.

A giant lump formed in my throat. There was no way I'd be able to get words out. *Do not cry, Adele.*

"I'm sure it will only be temporary," I said. "No one's back yet, I swear. Seriously, the streets are empty. It's *so* quiet."

"Quiet?"

"Yeah . . . it's creepy."

There was another long pause and a wet sniffle on the other end.

"Enough of this mopey stuff," said Brooke. "We haven't talked in like two months . . . Tell me a story. *Bonjour*, how was Paris? And don't say anything about it being lame, or I will jump through this phone and smack you!"

Classic Brooke. This was why I loved her.

"Well, Paris was . . ." I struggled to describe the raw magnificence of the city. "Paris is amazing. It's Paris." Giddiness rushed over me as I curled deeper under the covers. "It's so hard to describe without sounding like a sappy cliché."

"I already know you're a sappy cliché, so we're all good."

"'There are only two places in the world where we can live happy: at home and in Paris.'"

"Whoa, that's deep, Adele."

"*Oui*, but I can't take credit; it's Hemingway."

Émile had turned me on to Hemingway, yelling in a fiery fit, "How iz it possible zhat you've never read 'emingway? 'E's even American!" Mortified, I'd spent the rest of my stay devouring all the Hemingway I could get my hands on.

"Again, in your own words, please."

"Hmm . . . Paris has this joie de vivre that devours you. Kind of like NOLA, but times a hundred. Your feelings are heightened just by walking down the street. If you're happy, you want to dance. If you're sad, you want to weep openly in the street."

"And if you want to *love* . . . ?"

"God, shut up! Do you ever think about anything but guys, Brooke?"

"Uh-huh . . . sore subject, much? Go on, but don't think I'm going to let you keep the Émile saga a secret forever."

That was a conversation I was dreading. Brooke had probably made a hundred friends in California. I really didn't want to report that the *one* pseudofriend I'd made was also on my mother's payroll. It was exponentially harder to focus now that I was thinking about Émile again. I dug deep for words.

"Paris . . . there are so many emotional things on every street corner—a café where a poor Toulouse-Lautrec used to drink absinthe, a scene from a Baudelaire sonnet, a street Marie Antoinette once rode down, a corner where a revolution sparked. Hugo, Sartre, Piaf, and not to mention Coco—the list is endless! Everyone says you fall in love with Paris, but sometimes I had this burning jealousy of her." I paused to take a breath, astonished by how much I'd been suppressing over the last couple of months, burying anything good that had happened in Paris out of fear I wouldn't want to return home to help rebuild.

"And?"

"And what?"

"And tell me about the boy!"

"Hello, it's your turn! What's L.A. like?"

"Mmm hmmm . . ."

"I mean, besides celebrities and wheatgrass shots?" I pushed.

"Fine. It's not New Orleans, but I get why people like it here. The weather is perfect—like, always perfect. From the Santa Monica Pier, you can listen to the ocean and see mountains in the background at the same time."

"Wow, mountains?" I laughed. "I've never seen a mountain in real life."

"Yeah, the nature here is out of control. It's the polar opposite of home. Everything is clean; no one smokes—well, not cigarettes, at least. Everyone is beautiful, and everyone is always on, from their hair to their clothes to their cars—like they need to be magazine-ready at any given moment." She paused. "The hardest part is my mom. She's upset about the Storm, but she just seems so happy here. She's totally back in her element. We were here for like a day before she was offered this high-powered PR position at Capitol Records, and my dad's been getting all these gigs and recording sessions. She thinks it might be his big chance to 'break out of the New Orleans scene,' whatever that means."

Brooke always joked that she got the best of both worlds from her parents, and I tended to agree. Her mother was a California girl more akin to a Russian supermodel, and her father was born and raised in the Faubourg Tremé, a historic African American community with a rich lineage of prolific brass musicians. Brooke's gene pool gave her a totally unique look and a voice that could silence a stadium. No surprise, she focused on music at NOSA. There was no doubt in my mind she would become a famous singer one day.

"Adele, I'm gonna freak if I have to stay here!"

"Don't worry. If your parents end up staying, you can come and live with us when NOSA reopens." I didn't tell her how bad a shape our school was in.

"Wait a second, if you aren't coming to L.A. and NOSA isn't reopening for a while, why isn't Mac sending you back to Paris?"

The *other* inevitable question I had been dreading.

"Apparently, Sacred Heart Prep is permitting me a seat." I moved the phone away from my ear.

"What?! Oh, good one, Adele."

"Yeah . . . I'm not joking."

"What? What does that even mean, *permitting you a seat*?"

"That's exactly what I asked." I explained the situation as best as I could, realizing how few details I actually knew. As soon as Brooke started ranting about prissy girls and Catholic school uniforms, my fingers began nervously twisting my hair. I joked, "Next thing you know, my picture is going to appear in the society column of the *Times-Picayune*."

"Okay, spill it. What are you hiding? Did you do it with him?"

"Jeez, Brooke, we didn't do it!" My face burned red through the phone. For some reason it was hard to tell her it wasn't even *close* to anything like that. "I'm not hiding anything."

Well, not about Émile, just about my apparent newfound ability to move things with my mind. I wanted to tell her, but it was the only thing harder to talk about than Émile. "I just don't really know what to say about him."

"But you *like* him?"

"No. I don't know. We just spent a lot of time together."

"And . . . ?"

"And, he's very hot and very French." I left out the part about me still checking my phone four thousand times a day to see if he'd messaged me.

"What exactly is the problem?"

"He's very much my mother's assistant! And twenty-three! And confusing. Kind of the bad boy, but always knew how to cheer me up, even with everything going on." I didn't know how to explain that he always made me feel like he had some unfair advantage, like he'd read an operating manual on me before we met. "It was almost like he was too perfect."

"Oh my God, Adele! Can't you ever just let something good happen to you without sabotaging it?"

"See?! This is why I didn't want to talk about him! He was fascinated with my banal existence but never really revealed anything about himself." I'd always felt like he'd had some ulterior motive for trying to pry information out of me, like spying for my mother. How could I explain to Brooke, without seeming crazy, that every time I'd let him get closer, a million tiny warning bells had exploded throughout my body, telling me to run?

A sigh came from the other end of the line. "You seriously have abandonment issues, Adele."

My eyes rolled in return. "What does it matter now? He's in Paris. With my *mother*."

"Have you heard from him since you left?"

"Nope."

"Jerk. Have you heard from her?"

"Nope."

"Double-jerk."

"I'm starting to feel like it was all in my head, like I just read into it too much—"

"Adele, are you still there?"

"Yeah, can you hear me?"

"Are you there?"

I hung up and tried to call her back, but the call wouldn't connect. I couldn't say the idea of ending the Émile conversation broke my heart. I pecked a text and prayed it would go through.

Adele	**11:09 p.m.**	Call dropped. Can't reconnect. Reception here is abysmal. Talk mañana! xoxo.

It was after eleven. Dad was out past curfew again.

Trying not to worry, I aggressively fluffed my pillow.

Before the Storm, there wasn't a waking hour in which Brooke and I hadn't communicated in some way, shape, or form. Now, we'd barely spoken since I left Miami two months ago and put a nine-hour time difference between us. My heart told me Brooke would stay in L.A., and I hated that idea.

Soon, I felt myself drifting off to sleep as I lay there staring at the ceiling, thinking about the little things that were slipping away. Things I'd taken for granted before the Storm. But I couldn't muster my lead-like muscles to get up and turn off the light. The long chain dangling down from the ceiling fan started swaying back and forth.

Tension spread through my body until I was stiff as a board.

The chain slowly gained momentum until it swung in a circular pattern. I was so tired it was difficult to focus on the blur. I imagined a forceful pulling motion.

Click.

Darkness.

Breathe.

CHAPTER 12

The Truth

October 12th

My fingers tapped the kitchen counter, waiting for the pot of water to boil. My eyes kept moving to the clock on the wall.

It wasn't even seven a.m. yet—residual effects of jet lag. Before the Storm, I'd certainly never gotten excited about waking up early for work, but now I was just eager for life to return to normal. My eagerness, however, was no match for my muscles, every inch of which was sore.

I groaned as I bent over to stretch. My legs immediately started to shake. "Thirty more seconds," I whispered and began to replay my afternoon with *Ziggy Stardust* to distract myself from the pain. I barely made it to the half-minute marker before my torso flung up. The head rush made the magic music box incident seem even more surreal. It wasn't just the keys, and the lightbulb, and the phonograph—*everything* was different now. And it all felt like a dream.

"There's a logical explanation for all of this. You just have to figure it out." I extended my arm across the counter toward the box of oatmeal and imagined it coming to my hand.

Nothing happened. I felt like a clown.

"Ugh, boil already!" I snapped at the pot.

The fire under the pot seemed to pulse bigger.

Maybe I am going crazy after all?

But then the water began to gently bubble, and I became more excited about breakfast. "Finally . . ."

When the oats formed a hot mush, I sprinkled cinnamon and sugar on top, wishing we had milk. I grabbed the nondairy creamer and then stopped myself. *Too disgusting.* Without looking, I reached for the cutlery drawer, but before I could grasp the handle, it shot open and crashed into my hip. My yelp faded as a spoon jumped out of the drawer and landed in my hand.

My heart felt like it was going to pound out of my chest. I unclenched my fingers from around the utensil, and it vibrated in my palm. On a whim, I popped the spoon into the air; it dove into my oatmeal and stirred in the auburn swirls. A smile slipped out as the scent of cinnamon danced around the kitchen, reminding me of what our home used to feel like.

Lived in.

Without air-conditioning, there was no discernible difference in the temperature when I walked out of my very own steaming bathroom. It was an odd feeling. My father usually kept the house freezing because it got so hot in his studio with all of his torches.

My phone told me there was zero cellular service at present. Lamenting the loss of the Internet, I pushed the plug of an old-school boom box into an electrical socket and was immediately assaulted by voices at varying levels of hysteria. I stopped twisting the dial when I heard a woman with a more grounded tone replying to the DJ.

"The real question is, why isn't anyone talking about the fact that people are still dying around here? Are we all really this desensitized to death? And what is Morgan Borges really doing about the crime? The mayor's curfew doesn't seem to be helping anything; it's making the empty streets easy target zones for predators!"

Evidently, the early hour wasn't keeping people from going at it. I sat at the vanity and attempted to put moisturizer around the scabbing on my face, but I was already beginning to sweat. *Don't even think of complaining about the lack of air-conditioning. At least you have a home, unlike Brooke's family.*

"Thanks for calling in, ma'am. Do we have our next caller on the line?"

"Hello? Hello? Am I on the air?"

"Yes, ma'am, you are live on the air."

"Oh good, my name's Nora Murphy. My boyfriend is missing, and I wanted to ask whether anyone out there has seen Jaro—"

"Excuse me, ma'am, this is just a morning radio show," the DJ said with care, "but I can give you our hotline number to report missing Storm victims—"

"He's not a missing Storm victim! We've been back from Memphis for over a week. Two days ago, he went out to try to find groceries, and he hasn't been back since." She broke down in sobs. "The cops just tell me he probably bailed on the situation, on New Orleans . . . he never would have!"

"Do you hear that, folks? Something is going on in this city. Fourteen people reported dead and countless reported missing this week."

The woman's sobs became hysterical.

"Ma'am, please stay on the line; we'll collect your information and do whatever we can to help."

I squirted a cloud of mousse into my palms and rubbed it through my quickly drying waves. Without even trying, a flick of my mind twisted the tuner dial.

"Recent figures show that only about twenty-five thousand inhabitants of Orleans Parish have returned. Electricity has been fully restored in Baton Rouge, but there is no timeline yet for Orleans, Jefferson, Saint Charles, or the surrounding parishes. We have reports that all gas stations in Orleans Parish are wiped clean, so make sure to fill up outside the city limits. There's still no news on when any of the major supermarkets will reopen."

I put one leg into a pair of jeans, but then, suffocated by the denim, kicked them off and dug through the mountain of clothes on the bed until I found a lilac cotton sundress I had made at the beginning of the summer. It had a large sash that tied into a bow in the back—a tad dressy for work, but at least my legs and back would be free to breathe. I slipped on black Converse sneakers to tone it down.

Three commercials came on in a row, each one with different attorneys claiming they could help get your insurance settlement. When I couldn't get the radio to turn off on its own, I sprang from my seat and snapped the plastic power button before I could hear the empty promise of another lawyer.

Desperate to be out of the hot attic room, I headed toward the door, but then a thought made me turn around. *Souvenirs!* I went back to my suitcase and pulled out a T-shirt—a small velvet sack I didn't recognize came flying out with it.

"What the . . . ?"

Opening the drawstrings revealed a matching velvet box with a tiny, folded note. *Could it possibly be from Émile?* I paused, wondering whether to open the box or the note first, and then feverishly unfolded the stationery. My heart fluttered, pushing my lagging brain to translate the handwritten French faster.

Dearest Adele,
Even though your visit was short, I hope you were able to
find joy in the streets of Paris, in the way I do every day.
Enclosed you'll find a ring that has been in your father's
family for many generations, and now it belongs to you.
    I do long for the day when we can be friends.
    Bisous,
    Brigitte

I was stunned.

Oh Jesus. What if this is her passive way of returning her wedding ring to my father? I popped the box open, and a wave of relief washed over me. It contained a ring of an entirely different sort. Its style was unlike anything I'd ever seen: an opaline stone was nested in a thick silver medallion, like a giant pearl in an oyster shell, encircled by an intricately engraved border.

I slammed the box down on the vanity. *Friends? She didn't even say good-bye! How did she slip the ring into my suitcase?* I'd only stayed at her house—my grandmother's estate—for one night before my early morning flight home. I hadn't even seen her that morning; the only things that had awaited me were a basket of brioche and her driver to whisk me to the airport.

My subconscious gnawed at me.

Are you really upset to find a note from her? Or just disappointed that it wasn't from Émile? Ugh.

I slipped on my standard silver chain and roughly knotted my hair into a loose bun on top of my head. "He's not your boyfriend. Don't let this ruin the morning."

As I approached Café Orléans, I realized how much the outdoor tables, with their heart-shaped chairs, resembled any quaint corner of the Faubourg Montmartre in Paris. Usually I could smell the coffee beans half a block away. Today, not even close. I could, however, hear Chet Baker floating through the open doors, which meant Sébastien must have opened up. Jeanne usually blared Beethoven concertos.

It was sad but not surprising to see the place devoid of customers.

This hour of the morning was usually the café's peak time due to the overlap of the day-job crowd heading to work and the service crowd retiring from the graveyard shift. This morning there was only one guy, nineteen if I had to guess, sitting by himself at the corner table in the front window, sketching on a pad of paper. Messy, dirty-blond hair hung in his face, and large headphones hugged his ears.

"Sébastien?" I yelled. *"Tu es là?"*

I must have startled the customer, because he appeared a little shocked when he looked up from his pad. As soon as I smiled, his wide eyes went back to his pencil.

A head of perfectly combed and gelled hair popped up from underneath the counter. *"Bonjour!"*

"Oh my God!"

"Désolé!" Sébastien said, laughing. "I didn't mean to scare you."

"Shouldn't you be behind a microscope, Mr. Neuroscientist?"

"Haha." He blushed and pushed his glasses up his nose. "Mémé's been on the phone with our insurance agent for the last two hours, so I told her I would come downstairs and open up." If asked, he could rattle off ten different international scientists as heroes, but I knew his grandparents came first. Sébastien was well aware he'd never be where he was today if Pépé hadn't worked on a ship running coffee beans from Central America for all those years until he had enough money to open the roasters.

I joined him behind the wooden counter, where the espresso machine was laid out in a million pieces.

"I wanted to make sure there was no mold on any of the parts . . ."

I scavenged elsewhere for caffeine. Usually, we kept several different industrial-sized vats brewed at once. Today there was only one lonely pot of standard coffee 'n' chicory. I poured myself a cup.

"No milk, eh?" I asked.

"*Non*. No dairy. Nothing fresh, really." He nodded to the empty pastry case.

"I wonder how long it'll be before things go back to normal."

"I have a feeling we'll be redefining what constitutes normal." Always the pragmatist.

I stirred in a spoonful of nondairy creamer.

"Oh!" I pulled three boxes of macarons from my bag. "I brought something for *la famille*."

"*Ladurée?*" He kissed my cheeks, tore open a box, and stuffed one of the pistachio confectionaries in his mouth. "*Merci, Adele.*"

"Anything for you." I sipped the light-brown coffee, trying not to cringe from the taste of the fake milk. "So, where should I start?"

He gave me an apologetic look as he eyed the pile of cleaning supplies in the corner.

"Don't worry," I told him. "I'm a professional at this point."

Two hours later, I had finished the mopping and the dusting and was at the front of the store, staring at the giant jars on the floor-to-ceiling shelves.

"Are you sure we have to dump *all* the beans?" I asked Sébastien.

"The Department of Health says yes. All consumables have to be tossed."

"It seems a bit ridiculous to be throwing away food under these circumstances."

"*Oui,* but we can't take a chance with bacteria. Can you even imagine what's floating around in the water right now? Everything from fecal—"

"Got it! Tossing!" I yelled, pouring a five-gallon jar of Sumatra into the garbage can. Then I poured another. And another. By the time I got through the third shelf, my biceps shook as I lifted the jars over the garbage. Just as it became difficult not to complain, a booming voice filled the room.

"*Ma chérie!* You're back!"

"Ren!" I jumped down to greet my favorite customer.

His giant arms squeezed me in a bear hug, lifting me into the air.

"Ren . . . crushing ribs . . . can't breathe."

He gently dropped me to the ground. "Sorry about that. It's just been so long."

"It has." I smiled, having forgotten the magnitude of the man's hugs.

René Simoneaux was what people call "a character." He was born and raised somewhere south of New Orleans in the bayou, but he'd been a permanent fixture of the French Quarter for as long as I could remember. At six feet seven inches, Ren was a pale-skinned giant. Black curls rippled down his back and he had a Cajun accent thick as caramel. With his collection of white peasant shirts, red velvet jackets (in winter), black leather pants (year-round), and boots with shiny brass buckles (also year-round), he reminded me of a model from the cover of a cheesy romance novel. The women on his tours fawned over him, never guessing he went home and curled up next to Theis, the guy taking pics at the convent yesterday, a pasty Scandinavian DJ who also had fangs that had been surgically implanted by a dentist or, as I'd once heard him say, by a fangsmith.

"I have something for you, Ren!" I scooted behind the counter and rummaged through my bag.

"For *moi?*"

I pulled out a large white T-shirt with black gothic script that read, "*Equipe* Edward!"

"Adele, how many times do I have to tell you?" he said in a very serious tone. "Vampires do *not* sparkle."

"Okay, fine." I pretended to pout. "I'll give it to someone else."

"No, you will not!" He yanked the T-shirt out of my reach. "Sparkles or not, I am *still* Team Edward." We both laughed, and he hugged me again.

"*Ça va?* How was Paris?"

"I hated being away for so long."

"At least you were back in the mother ship."

"I know. That's what everyone keeps saying . . . *J'adore Paris!*"

I poured him a coffee, slid over the powdered milk, and told him the ten-minute version of my French adventures. "And you? Where did you guys end up?"

"Theis and I drove to Austin with Madame Delphine, thinking we'd be there for only a couple days." Madame Delphine was their white Persian cat. "But once the media frenzy turned into a circus act, we kept driving through New Mexico and into the Grand Canyon. We camped there for a couple of weeks. When things still looked grim, we drove north and stayed with friends in San Francisco. Just got back yesterday."

"Back yesterday and already working?"

Every morning, starting at Café Orléans, Ren led crowds of tourists through the trials and tribulations of the streets of "Naw'lins." There was also a special evening version of the tour, which he touted by promising to spill the secrets hidden in the dark crannies of the Quarter. The odds of even a single tourist being in town right now were slim to none, but he'd still showed up at the rendezvous point, just in case. Admirable.

"I've done enough waiting around in the last two months to last a lifetime," Ren replied.

But for the next hour, waiting was exactly what Ren would do—no one else came through the door. I cleaned until I could barely lift my arms and then took my place on the stool behind the counter. It was sad to see Ren, who was normally polished to perfection, with droopy bags under his eyes and rumpled clothes.

"Ren, tell me a story, *s'il te plaît*." It was a request I usually reserved for slow August afternoons, when people stayed inside to hide from the heat.

"Hmm . . ." He carefully twirled the end of his waxed mustache. "Do you know the story of the Carter brothers?"

I shook my head and leaned on the counter. I could tell that even though Sébastien was meticulously putting the espresso machine back together, he too was listening.

Ren walked to the middle of the café and brought his fingers to a point. His flair for the dramatic always led me to question how much truth there was to his stories, but their accuracy didn't really matter because his entertainment value was ace.

"The year was 1930. Huey Long was two years into his infamous reign as the governor of Louisiana. The country was still recovering from World War I, and the stock market had crashed less than a year prior. With the breakneck decline in foreign trade, warehouses on the Port of New Orleans emptied, and activity on the docks hushed. Times were hard all throughout the city, and the French Quarter was in dire straits. The buildings were in deplorable condition, many of the historic establishments had been temporarily closed or abandoned, and the Prohibition had created a swell of illegal underground activity. Debauchery ran rampant, even more than usual." He paused to give me a theatric wink.

I rested my head on my hands to get comfortable. He was just warming up.

"John and Wayne Carter were brothers who lived just around the corner from here on Saint Ann and Royal. Other than the charm that was expected of southern gentlemen, they appeared to be just your average men with labor jobs down by the river.

"One cool autumn afternoon, while the Carter brothers were down at the docks, a nine-year-old girl escaped from their house and ran all the way to the police station on Rampart. Her face was gaunt, her eyes were sunken in, and her hair was thin where patches had fallen out. At first glance, she appeared sickly but uninjured. That was until she held out her arms, palms up. The authorities thought her wounds were a botched suicide attempt, but upon further examination, they discovered the cuts had been made in a very precise way—with the skill of a surgeon—as if to drain her blood slowly over time. The little girl was in such a state of shock she was unable to tell her tale, but she kept repeating the words 'help them' over and over again. When the policemen raided the brothers' three-story house, they found—"

"Ahem," a female voice interrupted. "Is anyone here actually working?" The voice belonged to Désirée Borges.

When did she walk in? I'd never even seen her in the café before, but, as far as I knew, we were the only coffee shop in the neighborhood open for business. If you could call it that.

"I'd like a nonfat, vanilla granita. Extra whip."

I stared at her, puzzled she thought we could accommodate such a request.

"Please?" she added, trying to get me to hustle.

"Um . . . We can't make granitas right now. We're barely operational."

"Fine, I'll just have a sugar-free vanilla iced coffee. Soy milk."

"We don't have iced coffee or—"

"It's still summer! Why are you open if you don't have iced coffee?"

I considered mentioning my new Sacred Heart status in hopes that knowing someone as lowly as me would be attending her school might cause her head to explode, thus ending the conversation, but Sébastien intervened.

"Apologies. Between conserving the generator and the mandatory boil-water advisory, we aren't serving anything cold." Far more diplomatic than I'd have been. "And what would iced coffee be without ice?"

"Oh, then I'll just take whatever's caffeinated." She obnoxiously batted her eyelashes. I had to keep myself from making gagging noises. Of course, Sébastien was completely oblivious to her flirtation.

Hoping she wouldn't stay, I poured her coffee into a paper cup, splashed in some sugar-free vanilla syrup, and slid it across the counter with a smile as fake as hers. *How the hell am I going to survive Sacred Heart?*

Her heels clicking on the pavement outside cued Ren to reclaim the stage. This time, Sébastien stopped fiddling with the machine and leaned on the counter next to me.

"*Procéder,*" I said.

Ren pretended to ponder. "Where was I?"

"The policemen were just getting to the home of the Carter brothers," Sébastien reminded him.

"*Oui, oui, merci beaucoup.* The policemen waited for John and Wayne Carter to return from work and ambushed them inside their own home. Even though the brothers should have been exhausted after their day of manual labor, it still took over a dozen men to hold them down. When they raided the three-story house, they found seven other people held captive, all with their wrists sliced open. Most of the victims praised God for the miracle of being rescued, but those who had been there for more than a few days begged for death. They screamed that they would never be able to escape the Carter brothers or all the horror they had witnessed.

"The victims claimed that every night, when John and Wayne arrived home from work, the brothers would slice open their captives' flesh and drink the blood directly from their pierced veins.

"The cops found only two dead bodies, but the survivors claimed to have witnessed at least six others come through the front door and never leave. They said that once a victim's blood had been completely drained, the Carter brothers would dispose of the body by shoving it through a trash chute into a bath of acid below. No traces of these bodies were ever found.

"As you can imagine, there was a media frenzy after the arrests. The Carter brothers photographed well and were charming enough to gain a surprising swell of sympathizers—but despite their charisma and good looks, the sadistic killers were sentenced to be hanged. Postexecution, their bodies were laid to rest in St. Louis Cemetery, No. 1.

"Now, here's where it gets interesting . . ."

Sébastien and I exchanged looks.

"I'm sure you know that if you live or, more specifically, die in New Orleans, you might end up buried in an oven tomb, since the high water table makes earth inhumation difficult. You'll spend your eternal slumber in something that not only looks like an oven but literally roasts you, like a slow cooker. In times when the body count outnumbered the tombs available, resting bodies got exactly one year to roast in peace—not a day more, not a day less. Then the crypt keepers would push the crumbling remains to the back and slip in a fresh corpse.

"When the Carter brothers' remains were scheduled to be pushed to the back, the crypt keeper found the tomb empty of bone fragments. No burial clothes. Shoes. There was not a trace of John or Wayne Carter ever having been laid to rest."

Ren drew a deep breath, allowing his audience a moment to ponder the strangeness of his story.

"In all the decades since, no one's been able to explain how the two corpses simply vanished without a trace. The mystery is all that remains."

He took a dramatic bow.

I clapped loudly, and Sébastien joined me before returning to the espresso machine with a smile on his face.

Ren took another bow. Despite the meager audience and the events of the last couple of months, nothing had affected his ability to tell a story.

"John and Wayne?" came an unfamiliar voice from the corner. The sketcher was still there. "As in John Wayne? Do people in this town believe this crap?" His headphones were still on, but he must have turned his music off and listened in on the story.

I scowled, annoyed by his blatant skepticism, but the questions didn't faze Ren in the slightest. On the contrary, the naysaying seemed to enliven him. There was nothing Ren loved more than a debate about the supernatural.

"Oh, people in this town believe far crazier things, young man. But you are probably correct that the brothers were living under false names. Even so, that's who they claimed to be, so that's how the story goes."

"Blood drinkers?" the guy asked, pushing his hair behind his ears. "And do people in this town believe in vampires?"

"The truth is relative," Ren answered, being purposefully vague.

The scientist in the room interjected. "A logical truth is a statement that is true in *all* possible worlds. As opposed to a fact, which is true only in this world, as it has historically unfolded."

I groaned. Sébastien made my brain hurt.

"Don't bring logic into a discussion about the truth, my boy!" Ren yelled.

Sébastien raised one eyebrow but knew arguing would be an exercise in futility.

Ren looked back at the sketcher. "The truth depends on what you believe in."

The guy closed his sketch pad, slid his pencil over his ear, and looked straight at Ren. "I believe if I ever came across a vampire, I would stake it." He gathered up his things.

"Them are fighting words, son!"

"You have no idea," he mumbled, walking out the door.

The three of us looked at each other with blank expressions and then burst out laughing.

"Testy young fellow!" said Ren.

Suppressing giggles, I apologized on behalf of the sketcher.

"Miss Le Moyne, if you remember only one thing I have ever taught you, let it be this: You can never please everyone. As an artist, if your work doesn't inflame at least part of the audience, then you might as well call it quits and sell insurance. And that goes for you too, *Dr.* Michel. The world needs more boundary pushers, not more boundary creators."

"Haha. I'll keep that in mind when I'm defending my thesis," Sébastien replied.

Ren nudged my elbow and motioned toward the corner table. "Anyway, he was cute."

"Yeah, Adele," Sébastien teased. "Maybe the two of you could go vampire hunting together."

CHAPTER 13

The Unexpected Muse

October 19th

Seven days went by with nearly the exact same routine. I woke up to a silent house, showered, listened to the radio while getting ready, and then went to Café Orléans.

The thrill of going back to work quickly wore thin—there was barely anything to serve and hardly anyone to serve it to. I never saw more than a handful of customers a day, most of whom were cops or government recovery workers. Sébastien had returned to his lab rats. I hadn't seen Jeanne; she was practically sleeping in her lab. Pépé spent most of his time at the roasters, and Mémé spent most of her time upstairs on the phone with insurance agents, lawyers, and vendors. There wasn't really a point in opening the coffee shop, but it gave us hope that one day things would return to normal.

———

After I finished the post-Storm cleaning, there was nothing to do but watch the clock tick away the remaining days of my plaid skirt–free life. My prep school anxiety grew so intense I began feeling sick. I attempted every persuasive argument I could think of to get out of going to school, but my father, whom I'd barely seen all week, wasn't budging.

Every day, he disappeared, driving out of the city to find groceries or gasoline for the generator or construction supplies. Between the broken infrastructure and the scarcity of goods, this endeavor sometimes took the entire afternoon. Then he went straight to the bar "to get things in order," not to return until after I was asleep. Always after curfew.

We hadn't been able to find anyone to fix the wall, but my father had managed to get a government-issued blue tarp. The blue plastic patches were becoming a frequent sight all around the city—a marker of someone who'd returned home. My father said at least his studio was finally well ventilated. He joked, but I knew he was desperate to get the wall fixed, especially since the crime in the city was out of control (three more dead bodies had been found). Every day, I worried more and more that he would send me back to my mother.

But the physical destruction didn't hold a candle to the mental damage the Storm was doing to the city's inhabitants. For me, the worst part of the aftermath was the guilt. I felt guilty I'd survived when so many others hadn't. I felt guilty that we still had our home. I felt guilty that our most frustrating problem was finding gasoline for the generator. Bouncing between the guilt and trying not to feel sorry for myself was maddening.

The lack of interaction with people forced me into an even deeper state of introversion than usual. At times, I felt like an empty shell of myself, staring blankly at things I was supposed to recognize. Everyone else appeared zombielike as well, but the solidarity only brought temporary comfort. It was as if we had all gone to war together.

I had two distractions from the dystopia that was real life. The first was Arcadian, the used bookshop next door to the café. Even though they hadn't reopened yet, Mr. Mauer let me borrow books like he always had. I helped him clean, and together we mourned several trash cans' worth of pages that had drenched 'n' dried, but seventeen feet of water had poured into the neighborhood where he lived, so the ruined books were the least of his problems.

Maybe the solitude was a good thing, since I was becoming a walking hazard, leading me to my second great distraction—tinkering with my new, er, talent.

I attempted to use it only when no one was around and only after I'd reached the peak of absolute boredom with everything else. I don't know whether this was because it scared the hell out of me or I was hoarding it, like saving the last bite of my favorite food on the plate until everything else was gone. A cherished treasure that gave me something to do when I felt like I was on the brink of solitude-induced insanity. Sometimes it worked, and sometimes it didn't, but the random, freak occurrences were making me a frazzled wreck.

Yesterday, at the café, I'd been in such a deep Émile daydream that I hadn't realized I was stirring my Americano with a floating spoon—at least, not until Ren walked in and it clanked down onto the rim of the cup.

Note to self: be more discreet.

Regardless, Ren was the highlight of my days. He came into the café every morning and patiently waited, just in case people showed up for a tour. No one ever came, although he mentioned that two or three customers were trickling in for his nightly ghost tour.

The only other people I consistently saw were the uniform-clad mayor's daughter and the naysaying vampire hater, whose name I'd learned was Isaac. I still wasn't sure why Désirée came downtown every morning just to turn around and go back uptown for school, but we had gained her patronage. Isaac always came in around ten and stayed for at least two hours, always with headphones on and sketchbook in hand. Besides his name, the only other piece of information I had garnered was that he was from New York City, which was apparently superior to New Orleans in every way and which possibly explained his too-cool-for-school attitude. I had grown immensely curious as to why he was in town—the city being far from tourist friendly. Other than ordering his coffee (plain black, not that we had much else to offer), the only time he ever spoke was to complain about something.

His condescending air was the reason I had initially disliked him. The reason I *continued* to dislike him was that whenever I broke from my book, I caught him looking at me. He'd lower his gaze when our eyes met, but I had a sneaking suspicion he was sketching me, which made me extremely self-conscious. And extremely annoyed. And even more trapped in this bizarre reality. It wasn't like I could ask him to stop without seeming totally presumptuous. I didn't have any real evidence that he was actually doing it, but each day I caught him glancing at me more and more frequently, and each day playing the role of unexpected muse made me loathe his presence. I desperately wanted to catch a glimpse of his sketchbook and vindicate my suspicion. Luckily, I had a lot of time on my hands to plot.

The only good news was that the heat had finally broken, and the dreadfully long, un-air-conditioned summer was over. But the electricity in the fall air, which I usually loved, now only amplified the feeling that each day was a ticking time bomb.

CHAPTER 14

T-Minus One

October 20th

"Why don't you guys just have plain New York coffee?" Isaac asked, pushing the tips of his dirty-blond hair out of his face. An assortment of colorful hemp bracelets covered his left wrist along with a military-looking watch, and the sleeves of his dirty gray T-shirt hiked up just enough to reveal that his biceps weren't as tanned as his forearms. As soon as his shoulders relaxed, his hair fell back in his face. He pushed it behind his ears again as if on autopilot.

Today was really no different from the last eight; only today I was having trouble suppressing the urge to drop-kick him as he asked for a refill.

"Oh, I know where you can get some plain New York coffee," I said. His big brown eyes lit up.

"In *New York*. I'm sure they would looove to have you back."

He started laughing. "Are you sure you're from around here? Aren't southern girls supposed to be hospitable?"

I wanted to jump across the counter and strangle him. Instead of getting angry, he was actually being congenial for the first time. *Is this how New Yorkers are? Be mean to them, and they like you back?*

"So, where *are* you from?" he asked.

I was still a little taken aback by his nonobligatory chatter.

"I'm from around the corner." I knew exactly where this conversation was going. I'd had it a hundred times with tourists over the years, but it had never truly annoyed me until the question came from him.

"You were born around the corner?"

"Well, technically, I was born in a hospital a couple of miles away, but I was raised my whole life, minus the last two months, around the corner from here."

"You don't sound southern," he replied in his usual know-it-all tone.

Films and TV shows almost always got the New Orleans dialect wrong, further perpetuating the incorrect assumption that we all have a twang. It was a pet peeve of all native New Orleanians. Even though Isaac was correct—my accent did sound nearly identical to his—I scowled, not wanting to be disassociated from my hometown, especially not now.

"Are you some kind of expert on southern dialects?"

"Uh, no. I just thought—"

"You just thought we'd all sound like Scarlett O'Hara?"

"I guess. I don't know . . . You seem to really love this place."

"Well, yeah. It's messed up right now, but you're an idiot if you can't see why I love this place."

His smile cocked. *I call him an idiot and he smiles?*

"Maybe you could show me around sometime? Take me to see some of the things that were so great?"

"*Are* so great. The city isn't dead!"

"Right . . . I guess I've only seen the dead parts."

He was not helping his cause.

"So how about it?"

Is this some coy way of asking me out? And like that, my defensiveness flipped into nervousness. I slammed his coffee mug down, sloshing the contents over the rim. "Sorry, I don't have time. Too busy trying to keep things from dying."

"Fine, sorry I asked."

He went back to his table, jammed his headphones on, and started furiously moving his pen.

Great, now he's probably turning me into a monster.

I cranked some classical music, hoping to scare him off, then picked up the loaner copy of Franz Kafka's *The Metamorphosis* from the small stack of books I kept handy on the counter. The deceptively thin paperback was the only book on the Sacred Heart reading list I hadn't already read. I sighed, shuffled the pages to my bookmark, and read the next three sentences.

Then I read the same three sentences again.

And again.

Despite not retaining much, I turned the page, trying to prompt my brain into a reading rhythm.

Read.

Read.

Read.

My eyes kept moving from the page to the two lonely nickels sitting in the tip jar—they begged me to play with them.

Unlike my reading progress, it took only a little mental focus before the coins were dancing around the jar to the Tchaikovsky overture blaring in the background. Careful not to let them clink on the glass and bring attention to what I was doing, I smiled as a dime did a swan dive to join the pirouetting nickels. The motion was hypnotizing.

When the song ended, I glanced up and saw Isaac staring at me from his table. The coins clanked back to the base of the jar. *There's no way he could have seen the tiny coins from across the room, right?* This time his gaze didn't break away as quickly as usual. My cheeks flushed, and I ducked under the counter to have a moment to myself.

Ugh. Focus your energy on something productive, or you're going to end up doing something stupid.

I took a deep breath while I searched for a less dramatic song on the radio and then grabbed a small black notebook from my bag. When I stood back up, his gaze had returned to the felt tip of his marker. I day-dreamed that the marker floated from his hand and inked a mustache across his upper lip. Thank God it didn't actually happen, but trying to contain the giggle made me snort.

He looked up. My hand flew to my head to hide my smile as I flipped open the notebook.

Trying my best to ignore him, I drew a line down the middle of a new page. On the left side I listed all the items I'd tried to move but couldn't: box of oatmeal, ceramic bowl, sponge, tennis shoe, bag of coffee beans, single coffee bean, toilet paper, broom, towel, stick of gum, book.

There must be some kind of pattern.

I forced myself not to chew on the pen while I recalled more items.

A chill swept up my arms, making the hairs stand up. Without looking up from the notebook, I tugged the short sleeves of my coffee-stained V-neck and rubbed my arms, my fingers landing on the thin gris-gris ribbon.

"Your cut is getting better—"

I slammed the notebook shut, jumping an inch off the stool. The voice had come from lips just a few inches from my forehead. Niccolò Medici, the *Italiano*.

"*Scusa,*" he said softly, trying not to laugh. "I didn't mean to scare you."

"No worries." I attempted to resume my casual position on the counter, but it now felt awkward. He was still staring at my face. My hand went over the claw mark, which was now a scab-free, pinkish-purple raised line from the base of my neck to my cheekbone. He pushed my fingers away and softly touched the tender mark. His touch was cool on my warm skin; he must have been working outside this morning. Our eyes locked. I tried not to let my nervousness transfer from my pulse to my cheek to his fingertips. He did not need to know how intimidated I was by the close proximity of his ridiculous good looks.

But it was too late. Niccolò shifted back.

"Absurdist fiction?" he asked, picking up the tattered paperback. "So, you are into Kafka?" His accent slightly dragged the first vowel in the author's name.

My brain begged me not to lie. It had barely retained part one of the German novella.

"Well, I'm reading it for school. The jury's still out on whether I'm into it or not." My brain thanked me, but then I immediately wanted to choke myself to stop the next words from flying out. "But generally I like the absurd."

He laughed. "Me too." His forehead briefly scrunched, probably because he was trying to figure out whether I was alluding to Ionesco or just trying to be abstract. So was I.

He continued. "Although, I've learned to appreciate when things are simple, more straightforward." He leaned on the counter, his hands nearly touching mine. I had no clue whether we were still talking about literature. I nodded, even though "simple" was not the vibe I got from him. Something about him exuded cryptic—and for some twisted reason I was attracted to the confusion. Like wasabi-flavored ice cream.

Before I could respond, Isaac butted in with his empty mug. I quickly refilled it.

He gave Niccolò a hard stare before going back to his seat, and with that, our moment was over. I sighed internally. "Can I get you something?"

"No, I'm good."

"Are you sure?" I didn't want him to leave. "I know we aren't in Rome, but I can pull a pretty decent shot of espresso."

"No, *grazie*. I just came to see you."

"Oh." My stomach did a backflip.

"And I wanted a break from work," he added, "and from my brother."

"Gabe seems pretty full-on."

He let out a deep laugh and leaned back down on the counter. "That is a drastic understatement." His lips pressed into a tight smile. Then, as if beckoned, his older brother walked through the door.

"*Bella*, my heroine! We meet again."

My eyes widened as I suddenly wondered if I'd actually caused the Palermo's sign to fall, nearly crushing him.

He kissed my hand in a dramatic fashion, which I assumed was his norm.

Gabriel Medici was the type of guy who commanded the attention of a room simply by walking in and being beautiful. It was strange to think about a man being beautiful, but it really was the most fitting word to describe the blond—well, both of them, really, but Gabe had the unabashed personality to go along with it.

"Why do you look so sad, *bella*?" he asked, raising my arm over the empty pastry case and guiding me around the counter. "A beautiful woman should never look so sad." He spun me around just as a Louis Armstrong and Billie Holiday duet started. No big surprise Gabe was as good at dancing as he was at posing. He led me around the floor in perfect time with the music, turning me at all the appropriate moments. It was totally over the top, but I couldn't say I didn't enjoy the attention, especially since he was doing it right in front of Isaac, which for some reason delighted me.

Gabe seemed to pick up on this and further taunted Isaac by bending me into a low dip directly in front of his table. I shot the northerner a look that meant, *Take note*, as Gabe held the pose for another measure.

Isaac must have gotten the hint, because he grabbed his stuff and huffed out the door.

When my attention turned back to my partner, his eyes were stuck on my chest. My face flushed the color of a Creole tomato. Instead of attempting to hide his overt behavior, he looked up at me with an inquisitive expression and then looked back down at my chest.

That's when I realized he was just looking at my necklace. The medallion had slipped out of my V-neck. *Innocent enough, I suppose.* He pulled me up with such excitement my feet couldn't keep up with the spin. I stumbled toward the door, where I careened into Désirée Borges. My momentum knocked us both over, because, of course, she was wearing six-inch heels. She was cursing my name before we even hit the ground.

She knows my name?

In a flash, Niccolò put himself between me and Désirée's whip of venomous lashes. As he helped me up, Gabe extended his hand to Désirée, and we all witnessed her slanderous rage dwindle to silence as her gaze went from his fingers to his face. I tried to contain it, but watching Gabe's mere presence shut her up, I couldn't help letting out a quiet giggle.

"Please accept my apology, *signorina*. I am entirely at fault." He helped her up with one fell swoop.

She looked from Gabe to me and then to Niccolò as she adjusted the micro-miniskirt over her perfect stems. She seemed rendered speechless by the idea of *me* fraternizing with *them*. I couldn't say I blamed her.

"No harm, no foul," she finally managed.

I walked back behind the counter to get a better view of whatever was about to unfold.

"Adele, aren't you going to introduce me to your friends?"

She knows my name? "Friends" was a bit of a stretch, but there was no way I was going to let an opportunity like this pass me by. "Désirée

Borges, meet Gabe and Niccolò Medici. They're over from Italy, looking for some missing relatives and staying with the Palermos."

"That's so terrible," she said. I couldn't help but wonder if she cared at all or just wanted to jump Gabe. "Anyway, it's nice to meet you."

"The pleasure is entirely ours," Gabe said as he kissed her hand.

Niccolò looked my way and rolled his eyes. I got the impression this was something he'd heard a thousand times before. Another quiet giggle escaped my lips.

"We're not staying with the Palermos anymore," he said to me. "We managed to get our own place around the corner."

"So, how do you ladies know each other?" Gabe asked Désirée.

The look in her eyes showed she was falling fast. "Well . . . um . . . our parents . . ."

I intercepted. "We don't actually know each other that well." She appeared grateful to no longer be on the spot but alarmed I might blow the fact that we weren't BFFs. "But we're going to be spending a lot of time together soon."

Her eyebrows slanted with suspicion.

"Because we'll be attending the same school as of tomorrow, right?" I flashed her a beaming smile.

Her eyes bugged out. "Right," she said through gritted teeth.

I guess she hadn't heard I was the Academy's newest recruit.

"*Eccellente!*" Gabe said. "Adele is my absolute favorite person in New Orleans. Promise me you'll take good care of her."

"Really?" Désirée asked, flabbergasted.

I owed Gabe for this. *Big time.*

"*Sì,* she saved my life, but that's another story for another day."

"I promise," she said. "And you can tell me the whole story . . . another *night.*"

While she continued to flirt relentlessly, I realized Niccolò had disappeared. My disappointment surprised me, but I couldn't blame him for wanting to bail on the nauseating display of high school flirtation. I wished I could have.

I made Désirée her sugar-free vanilla coffee so I didn't have to watch every move as she threw herself at the elder Medici. When I slid the cup across the counter, she happily grabbed it and seductively sucked on the straw, ogling Gabe.

Vomit.

"Burgundy, right?" she asked as she flipped her hair and sashayed to the door. The question was directed at me.

"Huh?"

"You live on Burgundy Street, right? Tomorrow morning. Seven sharp. Bring coffee." Before committing to the exit, she turned back and winked at Gabe. He returned a small wave.

I was stunned. *Did Désirée Borges really just offer me a ride to school?*

Gabe leaned on the counter, posing again, and turned to me. "Well, she seems like trouble."

"*Sì,* she scares me."

We both laughed, and then he looked me straight in the eyes. "She's nothing you can't handle, Adele."

"I don't know . . . she might cast a spell on me."

"A spell?"

"Her family owns the Voodoo shop around the corner."

"*Pfft . . .*" He paused, as if thinking. "Like I said, nothing you can't handle." He winked, and it somehow felt genuine, like he had finally stopped performing.

"*Grazie,* Gabriel."

CHAPTER 15
Walk of Shame

October 21st

Cleaning out my new room was a constant treasure hunt, always ending with something beautiful and vintage. I'd been excited when I first found the little brass clock hidden among the junk in the closet, but now, as I lay in the dark, the ticking felt like the prelude to my execution. I imagined myself smashing the alarm clock against the wall.

Breathe.

Most of the night had been spent like this—suffering first-day jitters for the third time in one semester. It wasn't humane. My mind time-warped to Paris, reminding me how pathetic I'd felt lying in my dorm room, terrified of the sun rising. I'd been so jealous of my roommate, who lay peacefully asleep while my pulse raced. But Paris was different: over there, everyone had just cause to prejudge me. I was the foreigner invading their land of wealth and glamour. Feeling like a foreigner in my hometown was so much worse.

5:12 a.m.

I rolled over, groaning. The cute, little alarm clock went flying into the wall.

"Shit!" I sat up. All three lamps snapped on.

I hope it's not broken. I looked at the clock lying on the floor and then over at the corner where a small pile of things I'd destroyed over the last week had accumulated. This parlor trick—ability, whatever you call it—was out of control and one more reason I had new-school anxiety.

Now that my nerves were fired up, I conceded to the day's events. Standing. Stretching. Forcing my skin to embrace the chill in the air.

Legs shaved, skin moisturized, and hair tamed, I pressed the power button on the boom box, not caring that it was too loud for six in the morning. I didn't care if it woke my father; he had no reason to be out all night given the curfew. Plus, as far as I was concerned, me having to go to the Academy was entirely his fault.

"Add one more tally to the dead-body count," the DJ said, and I turned to look at the speaker. "The NOPD still doesn't have anything to say about these recently reported crimes." Then he went on about the lack of aid from the federal government.

Ugh. Listening to people rant about our demise wasn't going to help my anxiety. Without moving, I spun the tuner knob to the next station, but it was just more people shouting at each other, as was the next station and the next. I spun the knob until the shouting was drowned out by a boy band crooning about how beautiful I was. I walked to the full-length mirror for a self-assessment:

A little skinnier than usual . . . easily attributed to my meager diet of oatmeal, canned soup, and coffee. I hadn't eaten a piece of meat or a vegetable since my transatlantic meal on the plane, if that even counted as real food. Hanging loose, my waves fell several inches past my shoulders now, much longer than they had been at the beginning of summer—before the Storm, when life was normal. Back when Brooke and I were still planning out our junior and senior years.

I moved to the metal garment rack usually reserved for in-progress designs. Now there were just two hangers: on one hung layers of tulle covered in hand-stitched beading, and on the other hung various layers of blue, white, and gray. Three months ago I would've had trouble guessing which one was my Halloween costume.

We can't buy milk or find someone to fix our wall, but Sacred Heart has managed to get me monogrammed uniforms.

I shimmied into the scratchy polyester skirt and buttoned up the collared shirt. Over went the navy blue cardigan with *ALM* embroidered over my heart.

I'd never worn a uniform in my life. Even my boarding school in Paris didn't require one, hence the multiple shopping sprees with *ma grand-mère*. On the bright side, the uniform should make it easier to blend in. Taking cues from an old Britney Spears video, I pulled on a pair of white kneesocks and laced up the saddle Oxfords. Hmmm . . . I actually kind of liked the contrasting black-and-white leather shoes.

No amount of concealer dabbing was going to cover the dark circles under my eyes, nor had my prayers been answered about my battle wound miraculously fading overnight. My hand shook as I swept powder over the hideous pink line on my cheek. Today, the scar looked ten times longer and thicker than it had yesterday. *It's not a scar,* I told myself. *It's going to heal.* I forced myself to put the makeup brush down so it didn't end up looking worse.

Two layers of black mascara. Light-pink lip gloss. Silver chain. I knotted my hair up into a messy bun on top of my head and started to feel more like myself.

I tucked the gris-gris underneath my shirt. *Am I even allowed to wear jewelry?* I picked up the little velvet box, trying to suppress the angst that rose whenever I thought about my mother. *It's an heirloom from Dad's side.*

I popped the box open.

Light caught the milky, iridescent stone as I slid the ring onto my middle finger. The metal was warm against my skin. *What era is it from?* I suddenly found myself silently thanking my mother. Maybe it was the pop music (though I never would have admitted it) or the residual effects from the warm bath, but I felt a bit better. *Maybe I'll actually make friends? Maybe I'll forget about Émile* . . . I drew the navy-blue tie under my collar and snapped it into an *X*.

When I went back to the mirror, I waved my hand just to make sure the reflection belonged to me and then messaged a photo to Brooke so she could get a good laugh upon waking—maybe it would get her to call me back. I hadn't heard from her since our initial call, despite there no longer being an ocean and several time zones between us. She was probably mad at me for not moving to L.A., or maybe she had adjusted to her new life and already forgotten about me.

I tossed my notebook, Kafka, and some pens into a black canvas tote bag and felt unusually light not being weighed down with art supplies. My keys flew from across the room and fell gently into my palm. That was it. There was nothing else I could do to procrastinate. The day was officially starting. I slipped out the front door to hold up my end of the carpool deal. Coffee.

Small flames flickering in the gas lamps on houses led the way through the low-hanging fog, not that I needed them. I could do the walk to Café Orléans in my sleep. Regardless, it felt strange to be out in the dark after being cooped up every night since we'd been home. A glance at my watch assured me the sun would soon make an appearance. The silence, however, continued to freak me out—no bars closing up, no drunken idiots yelling, no garbage trucks disposing of last night's glut. My familiarity with the route was lost.

Chills invaded my body like a virus, giving me the sense that I wasn't alone. I pulled my cardigan closed and hustled down the last two blocks. Faster. Then to a near jog. By the time I fumbled the keys into the café door and shoved it closed behind me, paranoia had engulfed me.

Calm down. You're just nervous about school.

I twisted the key into the lock and dropped my stuff on the floor and went straight to the giant wall of now mostly empty jars. While I contemplated the only two types of fresh beans we had in stock, the gas lamp's soft light flooding in through the window flickered, as if temporarily obstructed.

A quick glance showed nothing suspicious outside.

I lifted the jar of dark-roasted Kenyan beans, but another break in the light made my heart freeze. The brass dead bolt snapped into the locked position. I walked to the large bay window and scanned the street in both directions. No one, not even a rat.

I hurried through the process of measuring, grinding, and filtering the beans, and then the machine hummed on, leaving me with nothing to do but wait for the coffee to drip.

I glanced out the window repeatedly.

It wasn't until the first rays of morning sun peeked underneath the door and the delicious scent of freshly brewed dark roast filled the air that the knot in my stomach began to untangle.

Wait, what if Désirée doesn't turn up? What if she only offered the ride to score brownie points with Gabe?

My stomach went back to knots. I glugged sugar-free vanilla syrup into one of the cups, as if getting Désirée's coffee order correct might give me some kind of good juju, and then proceeded out the front door. Between my bag and the two warm cups, my hands were full. I willed my keys out of my cardigan pocket and into the lock.

"*Voilà!*" The door locked, and the keys dropped back into my sweater. "*Merci beaucoup.*"

Each heel click of my brand-new saddle Oxfords seemed to echo louder and louder down the desolate street. My pace quickened as the thought of Désirée arriving early and leaving without me chewed at my nerves.

One block later, I suddenly wasn't so sure whether the clicking on the pavement was coming from my shoes alone.

I glanced behind me.

No one.

But as I continued to walk, the sounds seemed a little sharp for my flats. I stopped short to convince myself it was in my head, but the staccato click lasted an extra step.

I started walking again. Faster.

The second set of steps followed suit, no longer trying to hide under the cover of mine. The rising sun forced me to squint. Lost in my escalating hysteria, my pace quickened to a run.

I turned the corner and smacked right into a tall, hooded figure. I fell backward, dropping everything, but before I hit the ground, his arm swept underneath my back, and he aggressively yanked me into his chest to keep me from falling. My arms reflexively shot around his shoulders.

I regained my balance and tried to back away, but his arms enclosed me, trapping me in the awkward embrace. "Let me g—"

"Shhh!"

All I could see was the blinding dawn over his shoulder. Again, I tried to break away. "Get off—"

"Shhh!" He hissed again, shaking me hard.

In the silence, I realized he was listening.

Like a hunter.

The sharp clicking of heels against cement was still approaching. Fear radiated from every part of my being, but then his intense interest in the person following me brought an unexplainable sense of relief.

I craned my neck sideways and caught the silhouette of a woman with a hooded cloak passing us on the other side of the street. She turned back and flashed a twisted smile, like she meant to taunt him. He growled so low I could barely hear it, but I felt the vibrations in his chest. For a sick split second, I hoped he might drop me and go after her, but then his grip tightened once more. His fingers dug into my rib cage, making me wince.

Then the sounds of her clicking heels faded into total silence.

We were alone.

My fingers clutched the back of his leather jacket so tightly I began to shake.

I couldn't breathe. He didn't stir.

"*Scusa,*" he whispered. His soft words ricocheted off my neck. I forced myself to suck in air, my lungs pushing against his chest. The breath brought in a vaguely familiar scent: leather and soap. His head shifted toward me. "Are you okay?"

All I could do was nod as Niccolò's face showed from underneath the hoodie he was wearing under his jacket.

He finally let me go . . . but not completely. His cold fingers paused at the back of my neck, making chills radiate throughout my entire body.

The way he stared down at me blankly made my voice squeak. "Fancy running into you here."

A memory. Or déjà vu. Or something flashed in my head, too fast for me to catch it. Again, I had an overwhelming feeling that I knew him from somewhere before we were introduced.

He inched closer, until our bodies were practically touching again.

My heart pounded with an aggression I'd never felt before. *Is he actually going to kiss me?* The closer he got, the more peculiar his eyes appeared, almost as if he were in some kind of trance. His expression seemed uneasy, and him being uneasy made me uneasy.

My voice shook. "Have you had any luck finding your family?"

His shoulders tightened. He pressed his incredibly red lips together until they became white. I immediately regretted asking. He would have mentioned good news.

"I shouldn't have brought it up. I'm sorry . . ."

He opened his mouth to reply, but before a word could come out, he snapped it shut again.

"Are you okay?" I asked.

He nodded. The bright morning light washed out his pale face.

"Your mouth . . . I think it's bleeding?"

His jaw clenched. *Am I making* him *nervous?* Beneath his pinched lips, his tongue circled over his teeth. *Unlikely. He probably just doesn't want to admit he's hurt?* He looked like he was struggling not to implode.

"Um, are you sure you're okay?" I raised my hand to his jawline, but he swatted it away and quickly licked his lips.

"You're *bleeding.*" I stood on my toes to investigate. "What happened?"

This time when my hand touched his face, he covered it with his own. I trembled, unsure whether I was terrified or excited by his touch. His head lowered closer to mine.

A loud squawk broke the silence.

He blinked. His gaze slid over to the crow flapping on top of a street sign. The moment, our moment, whatever it was, was over.

He stared at the bird for a long beat, again like a hunter. "Do you think that is your crow? The one who attacked you?"

"Ha. Who knows?"

He forgot to snap his mouth closed—the lines of his gums were stained with blood. When his attention turned back to me, I was staring.

"I bit my tongue, and it won't stop bleeding," he mumbled. "It's not a big deal." Reaching down, he picked up the one cup of coffee that, by some miracle, had not been destroyed in the tumble.

Lights flashed, followed by a prolonged honk.

"Do you want a ride or not?" Désirée yelled from the driver's window. She'd followed through after all.

"That's my ride. I have to—"

But he was gone. As was the crow. It was just me with the single cup of coffee in hand.

My hands trembled as I wiped the drips off the cup with my sweater's cuff. I stepped over a giant java puddle, praying the surviving coffee was the one with the vanilla.

"Was that who I think it was?" Désirée asked as soon as I opened the door.

"Uh, Niccolò?" I handed her the cup of coffee.

She looked at me with one eyebrow raised as I climbed into the giant SUV.

"What?"

"Oh, don't look at me with those doe eyes, sister. Parting ways with one of the hottest guys on this side of town before seven o'clock in the morning?" A wicked smile spread across her face. "I just might have underestimated you, little Miss Adele Le Moyne."

My face burned. "It's not what you're thinking, if that's what you're thinking."

"Riiiight." She tapped her perfectly manicured nails on the steering wheel.

"Well, I'm sure you're going to believe whatever you want," I snapped. The speed in which I slipped back into Parisian boarding school mode startled me, but my defenses were sky high after the bizarre run-in.

"Hmm." Her mouth crooked. "Maybe I really did underestimate you." She put the car into drive. "Whatever. I really don't care if the two of you were having an early-morning romp."

I caught sight of my reflection in the window—a small smile fought my lips. Just the idea that Désirée thought I stood a chance with Niccolò boosted my ego. But it also made me wonder why he'd been out so early. *Did I bust him on a walk of shame? Ugh.*

It was certainly plausible. In the city's current state, what else was there to do before sunrise? Nothing was open that early. He was certainly hot enough to have met someone so quickly. A droplet of jealousy bubbled. *What the hell, Adele? You don't even know this guy.*

"What's the deal with his brother?" Désirée asked. "Does Gabe have a girlfriend?"

As happy as I was for the conversation to move from me to her, I worried I didn't have enough intel on Gabe to satisfy. "I don't really know."

Her brow creased.

"I mean, I doubt it. He and Niccolò have only been here about a week." I crossed my fingers I hadn't just dismissed some girl in Italy waiting for Gabe to come home.

Her expression relaxed, and she turned on the radio. "I'm going to take Claiborne."

"Traffic?"

"There's no traffic, Adele. No one is back in the city. They've cleared most of Claiborne, so it's faster. How do you not know this? Don't you drive?"

"No, I was in Paris for my sixteenth birthday." I refrained from telling her I didn't even have a learner's permit.

"Don't you ever leave downtown?"

"Not really."

When we pulled onto Claiborne, I quickly understood what she meant. The multilane avenue was almost completely empty. Despite it being rush hour, we were one of only a handful of cars on the road.

"Jesus, is that . . . ?"

"Yep, the waterline."

Everything we drove past—an abandoned supermarket, a dilapidated bank, a gym, a hamburger chain, a Laundromat, a pizza joint, a housing project—everything had the same distinct mark of the Storm left on it: the waterline. As we moved from block to block, the five-foot-high line continued alongside us.

Neither of us said another word for the duration of the ten-minute ride.

When we turned down Napoleon Avenue, the houses became bigger, the cars fancier. Even the plants seemed greener. It was like we had entered another world.

No matter how many times I went uptown, its beauty never escaped me. Even in the aftermath of the Storm, St. Charles looked like a scene from an oil painting. Giant oak trees created a canopy over the long avenue of historic mansions, further preserving the exclusivity.

Most of the damage on this side of town had been from the wind tossing cars around or ripping roofs off, and since St. Charles sat atop a natural levee, there'd been less flooding. More people had been able to return home. Uptown being far livelier than downtown was a weird role reversal—the lack of damage to the Lower Garden District shocked me almost as much as seeing the areas of the city that were destroyed. I was overjoyed for these residents, but it was frustrating that the people with the most money seemed to have experienced the least amount of damage, although I'd have to bury that thought if I wanted to survive my junior year at the Academy.

Désirée easily maneuvered the sprawling SUV into the school parking lot and cut the engine.

"So, do you have any advice for me?" I asked.

"You only need to remember one thing to survive at Sacred Heart," she said without looking my way. "Stay away from Annabelle Lee Drake."

"Who is Annabelle Lee Drake?"

"My bestie." Her fake tone was back to accompany her fake smile. It was as if she had switched on her uptown persona. She grabbed her bag and exited the car, slamming the door behind her.

As soon as I shut my door, a beep signaled the activated alarm. I took it as a sign that I was now on my own. My heart sank a little, but what had I expected? That Désirée Borges and I would walk onto campus, arms locked, as she shouted introductions to all her friends? I took another peek at my reflection in the car window and tried to wipe the terrified expression off my face.

"Here goes nothing," I whispered and followed the gaggles of uniformed teenagers toward the large iron gate that surrounded the campus, protecting the city's finest youth from the proletariat.

CHAPTER 16
Uptown Girls

There was no denying that the school grounds were magnificent. The Greek Revival estate had a connected wing on each side and a white balcony that wrapped around the entire second floor. A large crucifix with a green patina sat atop the cupola on the roof. Every window shined. Workers bustled about, busy getting the courtyard landscaping back to its pre-Storm state.

As I walked through the giant iron archway that spelled out "S A C R É C Œ U R" I remembered riding up the hill on the back of Émile's Vespa to the original *Sacré Cœur* in Paris. From atop the steps, we had watched the sun set over the city. The view from the hilltop basilica had been worth the trip to Paris in itself.

Despite the symbolic pair of hearts sculpted every few feet into the concrete base of the Academy, I had a feeling this Sacred Heart wasn't going to be as romantic.

Wandering into the main building, I tried not to gawk at the other students. The halls were full of the kind of beauty only money could buy: glistening teeth, shiny coifs, sparkly jewelry on French-manicured fingernails, and these were only the obvious details. Hair extensions, nose jobs, and even breast implants enhanced some of the more permanently modified minors.

I pulled down my bun so my hair fell over my wound.

The hallway buzzed with energy. I wondered whether it had always been this lively or whether the recent integration of Holy Cross's all-male student body had anything to do with it. I tried to muster enough courage to approach a group of students that looked my age but chickened out as soon as they looked at me. *Pathetic.* Instead, I walked over to a lonely-looking tween whose nose was buried in a book.

"Excuse me, can you tell me where the administration office is?"

Her face lit up as she pointed me in the right direction and then looked a little sad when I thanked her and walked away.

Please don't let that be me in a week. I looked at my watch and hustled through the office door.

"Miss Le Moyne, I presume?" asked the white-haired secretary.

"Yes. Hi, I'm Adele—"

"Here's your schedule," she said. "They're waiting for you inside."

I pocketed the small card and paused in front of the closed oak doors; she motioned for me to go in. As I exhaled loudly the doorknob began to turn on its own. I frantically grabbed it and looked back at the secretary to make sure she hadn't seen. Luckily, she was hunched over, cleaning her glasses on her blouse.

Principal Campbell's office had a classic feel: navy-blue brocade drapes, walls of books, and lots of framed accolades. A middle-aged woman in a red skirt-suit and reading glasses, with a tight ashy-blond French twist, stood behind a large, wooden desk that had been waxed until shiny. She looked more like a high-powered CEO than a high school principal. Across from her sat two other students: a boy with skin as dark as cocoa beans and a closely shaved head, who looked even less excited to be there than I was, and a short, buxom blonde with perfectly coiled curls, who appeared to have been born ready for this meeting.

I felt a moment of relief when I realized I wasn't going to be alone in this endeavor. *Maybe we can band together as newcomers? I might actually be able to survive this place in a group of three.*

All six eyes followed me. I snuck a glance at the clock on the wall. I was still two minutes early, which, at the Academy, apparently meant I was late.

"Please take a seat, Miss Le Moyne."

I moved quickly to the empty chair next to the boy. He was rubbing his head as if he expected something more to be there. It must have been a new cut.

Three fat files sat on Principal Campbell's desk. I stared at the manila folder with my name on it. *What about my life could possibly fill a two-inch-thick file?*

"Dixie Hunter, Tyrelle Laurent, and Adele Le Moyne, you are the three *displaced* students who were carefully selected to join the junior class of Sacred Heart Preparatory Academy. Holy Cross in your case, Tyrelle." There was something about her voice that said we were not actually welcome—like someone had forced her to invite us to her party. Only two of us picked up on it: Tyrelle adjusted his tie and slouched to one side in his chair. I was pretty sure I could see a tattoo under the edge of his cuff. This was someone I could get along with. Dixie, on the other hand, smiled cheek to cheek as if she had just won the lottery.

"I hope you understand what a stupendous opportunity you've been given, as we almost *never* accept transfer students." Principal Campbell slowly took her seat. "You have a lot of catching up to do. Sacred Heart Preparatory Academy holds the utmost standards when it comes to both academic performance and grooming virtuous young adults, and it is imperative that this standard is upheld both on campus and *off.*"

Do not fidget, I repeated in my head as she continued talking up the school. But I was completely uncomfortable, both physically and mentally. I had to concentrate just to sit up straight.

She only glanced my way once, rarely taking her eyes off Tyrelle. Her gaze kept dropping to his chest. I couldn't see that he was doing anything offensive, but I was too scared to move my head to get a better look. She said something in Latin, and I made sure to nod as affirmation of my attention.

"Adele, we're thrilled to have you transfer from Notre-Dame International in Paris," she said in French.

I blinked, trying to keep my eyes from rolling at the pretentious mention of Notre-Dame, where I had attended school for only two months.

"We'll expect great things from such a worldly artist."

Worldly artist? These people really do choose to believe whatever they want. "Um, I'll try not to disappoint."

Dixie and Tyrelle both looked at me, equally unimpressed. I responded with an awkward smile.

"I think I speak for the three of us," Dixie said in a heavy Texas twang, "when I say we're honored to be here and can't wait to get involved with the Academy." She sounded like a perfectly rehearsed debutante. There was a long pause as she looked over to me and Tyrelle, as if it was our turn to suck up. Neither of us obliged.

Principal Campbell handed us each a thick handbook of the school's policies and values, which we had to sign and date before she cut us loose into the sea of teenage piranhas.

"Well, I'm the token kid from the hood," Tyrelle said as we stood outside the office, examining our schedules. "How'd the two of you end up here?"

Now I could see the outline of a large gold chain underneath Tyrelle's white button-down shirt and tie. I patted the hidden gris-gris against my chest.

"I have no idea how I ended up here," I said. "I don't even recognize my own life right now."

"There are no tokens at the Academy." Dixie enlightened us. "We all paid our way in, fair and square."

"What's fair and square about paying your way into something?" I asked.

She looked at me as if I had spoken Chinese and then turned back to Tyrelle. "My family just moved here from Dallas. My father owns the third-largest construction company in the South, and he says this place is a gold mine. Lots of things around here need reconstructing."

I was speechless. I certainly hadn't bought Dixie's sickly sweet southern-girl act in the principal's office, but I couldn't understand how *anyone* could be so crass about the city's fragile post-Storm condition. Sadly, I suspected it wouldn't be my last encounter with carpetbaggers moving to New Orleans to exploit the current state of affairs.

Dixie got no response from either of us, so she turned her back with a swirl of her skirt and flounced down the hall.

"And then there were two," I said, watching her walk away with the misguided confidence of a teen beauty queen. I turned to Tyrelle. "What class do you have next?"

He looked me up and down for a few seconds, as if trying to figure out whether or not to trust me. I guess I didn't meet his criteria, because he plugged in his earbuds and walked off, shaking his head in disgust.

Zero for two. If I couldn't even befriend the two other *transfer* students, how would I ever win over the natives? The bell rang loudly.

Lockers slammed. The hands of couples tore apart, and cliques scattered like flocks of startled birds. I double-checked my schedule while the crowd thinned. I didn't even need to look up from the card to know heads were turning as they passed me. Like Principal Campbell had said, transfer students were rare. Like unicorns.

Great. My first period was AP English, the senior-level class they had stuck me in since, coming from art school, I was ahead in humanities credits—as if I needed one more reason to stick out.

I looked up, searching for a room number just as I passed two extrapreppy guys, one of whose hand lingered for a second too long on the small of the other's back before he took off to class. The remaining guy, a tanned blond, must have caught my smile, because he stopped directly in front of me.

"Are you lost?"

There was something about his polished tone that demanded my silence about what I had just witnessed. Not in a threatening way, but in a way that silently begged the question, *Are you cool? Can we trust each other?*

I smiled, letting him know that his secret was safe with me. "Yeah, actually, could you tell me where to find classroom 317?"

He extended his hand, and I surrendered my schedule.

"It's in the east wing." He gestured for me to follow.

I adjusted the bag on my shoulder and prepared to hustle, but he seemed utterly unconcerned about getting to class on time. We strolled.

"If you just explain where it is, I'm sure I can find it." I peered at my schedule like it was a hostage between his fingers.

"Thurston." He held out his other hand. "Thurston Gregory Van der Veer III. And you are?"

"*Enchanté.* Adele Le Moyne, NOSA transfer student," I answered with a firm shake.

Maybe it was his perfect diction or the way his perfectly straight back made him appear as if he'd had equestrian training since he was a toddler. Whatever it was, I felt like a total mismatch walking beside him. The instant rubbernecking by the few students left in the hall reinforced my feelings.

"So, when did they merge Holy Cross?" I asked, following him up two flights of stairs. Holy Cross was even closer to the levee breaches than NOSA.

"About two weeks ago."

"Sorry about your school."

"Luckily only a fraction of each school's student body has returned, so this campus is not too overcrowded, *yet*. But I'm ready to get out of here." He examined the rest of my schedule as we sauntered down the third-floor hall. "You're a junior? In AP English? Only the best at the Academy, eh?"

Do I sense sarcasm?

Before I could answer, we arrived in front of the door marked 317.

"Well, thanks for showing—"

He opened the door, holding it for me. "I apologize for our tardiness, Sister Cecilia. I found Miss Le Moyne wandering the hallways, lost."

"Wait, you're—?"

"How chivalrous of you, Thurston," the teacher replied with annoyance. "Oh yes, Le Moyne, the junior."

I felt my face turn red as all the ears in the class perked up at the mention of the lowly word.

"You can take the empty seat right here in the front row."

"Who's she?" someone whispered.

"I don't know, but I'm texting Annabelle."

"Me too."

Annabelle?

I sank into my seat, already regretting walking into the room with Thurston Gregory Van der Veer III. The one advantage to sitting in the front row was that if I didn't turn my head, I couldn't see the gossip, glares, or other snide gestures. Adversely, my back felt exposed for anyone to stab, which escalated my paranoia.

"Before his metamorphosis," said Sister Cecilia, "Gregor is alienated from his job, his family, his humanity, and even his own body. This is evident when he barely notices his transformation . . ."

How could someone barely notice he had turned into a giant bug?

As hard as I tried to pay attention to the lecture on guilt complexes, I couldn't stop thinking about Niccolò. I could still feel the imprints where his hands had held me. And I couldn't get the image of his bloody mouth out of my head. *More importantly, was I being followed before I bumped into him? Who was the woman?*

In precal, I chose a seat in the middle of the classroom, not wanting to insult the bubbly teacher by going straight to the back row. But arriving early didn't make my assimilation any easier. I doodled, trying not to watch as five girls entered the classroom together.

A gorgeous girl with thick auburn hair and creamy skin walked a beat ahead of the rest. I sensed all eyes following her from the doorway across the room. Dixie Hunter followed directly behind her, talking excitedly. Jealousy plagued me—two and a half hours into the day, and Dixie was already hobnobbing with the inner circle? Had this chick arrived with some kind of secret popularity manual? Désirée trailed behind them, texting, uninterested in whatever Dixie was babbling about.

I sat up straight. *Will Désirée actually acknowledge me in front of her friends?*

I wouldn't have to wait long to find out—the redhead walked straight to my desk. The group followed suit, crowding over me like a pack of hyenas. Dixie and I were the only ones who seemed surprised by their pit stop.

None of them said a word. They just looked me up and down. Désirée rolled her eyes in boredom and took her seat.

I stood up to feel less like their prey.

"Nice bag," Dixie said in a sweet voice wrapped in bitchy sarcasm.

All eyes went to the black canvas tote hanging on the back of my seat. The girls standing around me were all carrying leather ranging from Vuitton to Hermès. I instantly regretted not unpacking the Chanel bag *ma grand-mère* had bought me in Paris.

No expensive bag is going to make you one of these princesses, Adele.

The redhead touched the canvas, examining the bag's only marking—a barely noticeable, hand-painted fleur-de-lis.

"It's from this season's *Mode à Paris*," she said, shooting Dixie a look of disapproval, and for the second time that day I saw confusion sweep Dixie's face.

"That's Fashion Week in Paris," Désirée translated.

"How'd you come across one?" asked the redhead.

"I went to the Comme des Garçons show," I replied as if it weren't a big deal, even though it had been the most exciting twenty minutes of my life. I didn't feel the need to tell her I'd actually PA'd the show or that the stage manager had swiped the swag bag for me as a thank-you for the abuse I suffered during the twenty-two straight hours of manual labor I'd contributed free of charge.

The redhead looked impressed, but the moment was fleeting; I saw her beginning to mull over the question of whether or not I was a threat.

"She just got back from Paris a couple of weeks ago," Désirée said, throwing me a bone.

"Bienvenue au Sacré Cœur," said the redhead, *"Je m'appelle Annabelle Lee Drake."* She smiled and went to her seat before I had a chance to respond.

Dixie was in a total state of shock at how quickly the tables had turned. I couldn't help myself and gave her a tiny *don't mess with me* look, which Désirée caught—she cracked a smile, which felt like a major feat, considering the only other time I'd seen her smile was around Gabe.

As they all walked to their seats, Désirée looked straight at me with an expression that said, *Don't say I didn't warn you about Annabelle Lee.*

"That's the transfer who was hanging all over Thurston this morning."

I turned around to find a girl pointing at me. *Hanging all over Thurston? We barely exchanged fifty words!* My pen shot off my desk, clearing the students to my right before hitting Désirée's Vuitton.

Giggles erupted from behind me.

"Sorry!" I said as a pimple-faced boy handed it back to me. *Thank God it was capped.*

I turned to apologize to Désirée, ready for her wrath, but she looked at me with squinty inquisition rather than her usual stink eye.

I slunk down in my seat.

CHAPTER 17

Fight What You Know

As soon as the bell rang, I practically skipped off campus, extra elated for my mentoring session since it meant missing the terror that was the lunchtime cafeteria. But I came to a halt when I got to the street—I hadn't thought about getting home from school—the St. Charles Streetcar line wasn't close to operational. I contemplated calling my father, but I was curious about how the rest of this side of town had weathered the Storm and decided walking three miles wouldn't kill me.

Walking through town wearing the Catholic-school uniform made everything feel even more surreal. Having survived my first day at Sacred Heart only exacerbated the weirdness. The fact that it hadn't been *that* bad made me nervous, like the calm before the storm. I plugged in my headphones, floated my phone from my pocket to my hand, and searched for happy music. By the time I reached the desolate streets of the mostly abandoned Warehouse District, I'd already forgotten about the catty girls.

It was easy to identify which residents had returned. The garbage-collection service hadn't started back up, so the occupied buildings had mounds of trash on their curbs. Dismantled storm boards, fallen trees, uprooted shrubs, piles of ruined drywall, moldy furniture, and boxes and boxes of books, clothes, and toys beyond salvageable—all stacked up in hill-shaped heaps twice my height. The pop music couldn't hold a candle to the sullen atmosphere as I passed by one blighted building after another.

When I arrived at our house, I found that our own trash mountain had grown considerably since I'd left that morning. Several discarded jars of dried paint told me my father must have been cleaning out his studio. I pulled a thick bundle of canvases from the pile and unrolled the top layer. It was a sketch of the Mardi Gras–masked ballerina sculpture. She always had a certain sadness to her—like she was dancing a tragic scene—but now water had dripped down the canvas and the charcoal had dried in streaks, making the drawing itself appear to be weeping.

It made my own eyes well. My father had always been so attached to his ballerina; seeing him let a sketch of her go into a giant pile of garbage was not something I could deal with. I rolled the canvases back up and ran up to my bedroom to stash them, not wanting him to argue with me about reclaiming them.

"Dad?" I yelled as I bounced back down the stairs.

Music poured from his studio. I opened the door to find a shirtless guy ripping down the remaining plaster from the damaged wall. His back was to me—thank God—so he didn't catch me hovering at the door in surprise. Splatters of dried paint covered his ratty jeans, and his dirty-blond hair was just long enough to fit into a tiny ponytail.

He swung a sledgehammer toward the top of the wall, stretching his back. Just as I became fixated on the way his muscles moved with the motion, my father shouted my name from another room, and he turned around—

"What are *you* doing here?" I yelled, hearing the shock in my own voice.

The corners of Isaac's mouth turned up, and I crossed my arms in an aggressive stance.

"What are *you* doing here?" he echoed.

"I live here!" I wasn't sure if I was more shocked at finding Isaac in my house or at the tone of his upper body. Either way, I was at a loss for words.

"Nice uniform. I didn't take you for the Catholic schoolgirl type." He laughed. "I can't believe *you're* Mac's daughter."

What the hell? Isaac's on a first name basis with my father?

"You expect me to believe this is just a coincidence?"

He held up his hands in innocence, although he didn't really seem that surprised to see me. My father walked in from the hallway with two stools from the kitchen. "Isaac, keep your shirt on in front of my daughter, please."

"Sure thing, Mr. Le Moyne—"

"I told you, call me Mac."

Isaac grabbed a dirty white T-shirt and stretched it over his shoulders. It was impossible not to sneak another glance at his chest as I grabbed my father's wrist and pulled him into a corner. "What is he doing here?" I hissed.

"I finally found someone to repair the wall! His name's Isaac Thompson. He's down from New York City with his pop, working with Habitat for Humanity to rebuild houses. It gets better: we're doing a barter. He's helping me fix the wall in exchange for some art lessons."

"Wait, what?" I felt like I was on another planet. *Isaac's been rebuilding houses?*

"He wants art lessons, and I figured since we're going to be working on your NOSA mentorship every day, it might be nice for you to have a partner in crime." He smiled. "What's wrong, sweetheart? Do you know this boy?"

"Apparently not," I answered, still trying to process this Dr. Jekyll side of Isaac, who put down the measuring tape and looked at me.

Insecurity erupted.

I ran upstairs to change, cursing the stupid school uniform on my way, and came back down in jeans and an old Quintron concert tee. My father had cleared off his workbench to simulate a classroom, and Isaac was sweeping up wall crumbles. I took a seat on one of the kitchen stools, trying to hide my disbelief that I was about to start my apprenticeship with my father and *him*.

When Isaac finished sweeping, he leaned on the table next to me and looked me straight in the eyes. "Do you want me to leave?" The vulnerability in his voice hit me unexpectedly.

"Whatever . . . this day couldn't possibly get any more random."

"Famous last words," he said and pulled his stool right next to mine.

A smile twitched my lips. His usual smug attitude had been replaced with . . . something else. I was glad my father could get the wall fixed, but I wasn't buying Isaac's innocent act just yet.

My gaze crept back to him, and my face immediately flushed. He was staring at me. At my face. The cut. Just as I prepared to answer the question for the fiftieth time, he looked away without asking me about it. I breathed a sigh of relief.

My father stood before us in full metalsmith safety gear: boots, rubber apron, giant gloves, and helmet. I'd seen him dressed like this thousands of times, but now it seemed utterly ridiculous. I had to suppress giggles as he droned on for fifteen minutes about the importance of safety when working with chemicals and fire.

"I can't believe you're willingly subjecting yourself to this," I whispered to Isaac without moving my head to look at him.

"Whatever, Mac is so cool," he whispered back.

I rolled my eyes and smiled.

"Okay, let's move on," my father instructed. He seemed a bit nervous. "Take out your sketch pads."

"What?" I asked. "Why? Aren't we going to work with metal?"

"We will. Later."

"Later? After all that?"

His eyes pleaded with me to cut him some slack.

I dashed upstairs again to get my supplies. Upon my return, Isaac's sketchbook was lying on the table in front of him, and I practically had to sit on my hands to keep myself from throwing his pad across the room.

Maybe his Dr. Jekyll/Mr. Hyde condition is contagious?

I'd never met anyone who stirred such polarizing feelings in me, besides maybe my mother.

My father put one of his sculptures on the table—a two-foot-tall prototype of the ballerina at NOSA.

"I'm going to give you fifteen minutes to draw this figure." He set an egg timer. "I want you to think about proportion and depth perception. Try to draw it as close to scale as you can."

I gazed at the figure and then back down at the blank page. I'd only drawn three lines before my father came over and changed the position of the pencil in my hand.

"It feels awkward now," he said, "but once you get used to it, you'll have more control."

He repositioned Isaac's pencil too, which made me feel better, and then sat down across from us with his own sketch pad.

When the timer buzzed, my father put down his pad, but neither Isaac nor I did. Out of the corner of my eye, I could see that my dad had not only sketched the entire figure but had already moved on to shading it. Isaac had finished a line sketch. I was stuck on the feet.

"Pencils down. Don't worry if you aren't finished. I probably should've given you a bowl of fruit, but there isn't a piece of produce within fifty miles of this place." He stood behind me and looked over my shoulder. "Nice job for a first try, especially given the time constraint. You need to work on proportion. See how your dancer is elongated?"

"Commentary on the emaciated state of ballerinas?" Isaac joked.

I shot him a dirty look. Just because I let him stay did *not* mean I was interested in his critique.

My father moved on to Isaac's pad.

"Nice job with the form, especially the slight arch of the back. Capturing movement is one of the hardest parts of drawing."

I tried not to get into a competitive mind-set, but I was definitely annoyed that Isaac was already head of the class. As I listened to my father give him more advanced tips, my attention diverted to the pile of drawing tools on the table. I could swear the pile was *moving*.

An X-ACTO knife was vibrating, causing the pile of charcoal pencils to shake. I blinked a couple of times, and the knife bounced with the rhythm.

I slapped the tool down on the table and reached for its safety cap, causing both my dad and Isaac to look up at me. I smiled, and they went back to the critique.

The knife continued to vibrate on the table. Even capped, the little blade made me nervous. I rested a book on top of it.

"Are you okay, sweetheart?" my father asked with a quizzical look.

"Mmm hmmm."

The knife rolled out from under the book and onto the floor.

Out of sight, out of mind.

"Okay, we're going to repeat the exercise." My father turned the statue upside down and leaned it in between two stacks of books so she stood on her head. "This time I want you to try to forget this is a ballerina. Forget you know she's a woman and that she's wearing a tutu. Forget she's wearing a mask. I want you to look at the object like a newborn baby would. Draw what you see: a series of lines and curves, groups of shadows and highlights. Try to draw each line exactly as you see it, and replicate each area of negative space as it relates to the boundaries that create it."

"Why are we doing this, Dad?" I asked, genuinely interested in the process.

"Our minds are trained to call on experiences we already know. Since you know you're drawing a ballerina, your memory informs you what a ballerina should look like. Turning the statue upside down will help you to draw what you *see* instead of what you *know*. Fight your intuition, and draw what feels instinctual. Fight what you know to be true."

After staring for a couple of minutes, my mind eventually let go of the image of the upside-down ballerina, and I began to draw lines and shadows as if it was natural. When the timer went off, we both put down our pencils and eagerly flipped our pads around. I expected to see a crazy tangle of graphite, but, to my surprise, a ballerina was staring back at me—feet and all.

"Whoa."

"This is crazy," said Isaac.

I looked over at his two sketches. The second was nearly perfect. "Nice job."

"You both did a nice job," my father said. "Sometimes, being an artist is about forgetting the constructs society has been instilling in you since birth."

"Oh my God, Dad, you sound like . . ."

"What?"

"You sound like an actual teacher."

He laughed. "Is that so shocking?"

"Well, yeah, kind of . . . It's just that teachers are old and bald, and you are . . . I don't know, not that."

"What are you saying? You think I'm cool?"

"Not exactly—"

"On that note, I'm going to quit while I'm ahead. That's it for the day."

"Thanks, Mac. That was awesome."

Did he mean that, or was he just sucking up? One day back in prep school had me questioning everyone's motives.

My dad turned the miniature statue upright and asked, "So, Isaac, how long have you been in town?"

"We arrived from New York about twenty-four hours before the Storm hit, since my pop's consulting for the feds on the trauma rescue—"

"How exactly did you get into town so close to the Storm hitting?" I asked.

"They flew us into Keesler Air Force Base in Mississippi, where the National Guard transferred us to a chopper along with some other military first responders. It was pretty surreal. We thought we'd be here for a couple of weeks, but you know how the story goes."

Isaac was a first responder? Seriously?

"So, how do you like New Orleans, despite everything?" my father asked.

"Well, to be honest, sir, I haven't really seen much of the city. I have to be on-site by four thirty. Plus, the curfew."

"That's very admirable, son."

"Thanks. I'd really like to see the city, though. It seems like a pretty special place."

I struggled not to snap my pencil in half. I could see where this was going.

"Well, I'm sure Adele wouldn't mind showing you around. Right, sweetheart?"

"Dad!"

"What? You know so much about the city from all of those books you read, and you can explain how everything is supposed to look. How it will be again, once everything is rebuilt—"

"I would love that," Isaac said, trying again to look innocent.

Trickster, I thought, fuming.

"Okay, you want to see the town?" I asked sweetly. "Meet me in front of the cathedral at seven."

"It's a date," he replied, with a look of concern over my sudden shift in mood.

"It's not a date," my father corrected. "Don't make me change my mind."

"I mean, not a *date* date—"

"If she's not back by curfew, I can assure you, there will never be another nondate. Is that clear?"

"You've got room to talk," I muttered.

"What was that, sweetheart—?"

"Yes, sir!" Isaac said. "You don't have to worry."

"I'm serious, Isaac. I get that you're from New York City, but crime's different here. If I hear she leaves your sight, it will be the last time you hang out."

"Dad!"

"No problem, sir. I completely understand, Mr. Le Moyne—I mean, Mac."

"*I'll* make sure I'm back by curfew, not Isaac," I snapped. "Don't talk about me as if I'm not here!"

"I'll see you at seven in front of the cathedral," Isaac said, trying not to smile as he packed up his things.

CHAPTER 18

Downtown Boys

Yawning, I turned off the alarm on my phone. My eyes drooped. I hadn't meant to fall asleep, but after my restless night, I could have easily slept through till tomorrow. Just as my lids slipped back shut, "Moonage Daydream" cranked out of the scratchy cone at full volume.

"All right! I'm up!" I yelled at the phonograph. If I was late meeting Isaac, my grand plan wouldn't work out.

I forced myself out of bed and into a black sweaterdress, sheer turquoise tights, and black ankle booties. I quickly reapplied the day's makeup, stealing a few seconds to add a little smoky eyeliner. If we ran into my father, I hoped it'd make him sweat. Maybe he'd think twice next time before inadvertently playing matchmaker. His behavior surprised me. Normally, he did anything he could to keep boys away. Especially boys with long hair and attitudes. Maybe he was concerned by how much time I'd been spending by myself since the Storm? *Unlikely.* Maybe he just wanted me to have a bodyguard? *More likely.*

Spritz of perfume. Chain. Ring. Gris-gris.

Accessorized, I reknotted the loose bun on top of my head and skipped out the door just as "Lady Stardust" wound down.

The sun was setting over Jackson Square, which felt creepy without the fortune-tellers, artists, and street performers who usually littered the pedestrian streets late into the night. Isaac was sitting on the steps of the gated park in front of the cathedral. I was surprised but happy to see a few other people standing around the old town square. When the click of my heels against the slate came within earshot, he looked up. "Hey." The relief in his voice didn't escape me.

"Did you think I wasn't going to show?"

"No, but I guess I kind of deserve to be stood up."

"Yeah, don't ever pull anything like that again."

"Just say yes the next time I ask you out and I won't have to."

Before I could fire back, he quickly added, "I'm sorry, I'm sorry. I don't want to fight on our first date."

"It's not a date, remember?"

"Call it whatever you want. I'm just glad I managed to get you here."

I swallowed my smile.

"*Ma bébé!*" a booming voice yelled—exactly the man I wanted to see. "To what do I owe this pleasure?"

I turned around, straight into a crushing hug. "Ren . . . ribs . . . can't breathe."

His eyes were fixed on Isaac before he even set me down. "Hmm, curious . . ."

"Ren, Isaac wants to learn about the great city of *La Nouvelle-Orléans*, so I thought, what better way for him to get to know the city than on your walking tour?"

"I see. *Oui, oui. Bienvenue.*" He looked Isaac up and down, as if assessing his likelihood of heckling.

Isaac leaned close to me and lowered his voice: "Nice one."

I tried my best to contain my grin from growing extra wide.

"*Laissez les bons temps rouler!*" Ren yelled, accepting the challenge.

Isaac looked to me. "Are you gonna give me a clue?"

I laughed. "Let the good times roll."

"Gather round, everyone," Ren called out to the few people lingering in the square. "So glad you all decided to brave the nightfall. I'm sad to say this tour is gonna be cut a little short thanks to the parish-wide curfew, but don't worry, you'll still get all the tales, because we won't be making any pit stops for drinks. Unfortunately, everything is closed. Everything legal, that is, er—" He cut himself off when he saw the inquisitive look on my face. "But please feel free to partake in your own libations, if you brought 'em." He lifted his coat to reveal his flask. "It is perfectly legal to drink here on the streets of *La Nouvelle-Orléans.*"

The tour hadn't even begun, and people were already enthralled by Ren. "I wonder if he dresses like that all the time?" one of them whispered.

I chuckled. Ren was in full gear tonight, somewhere in between the gentleman-pirate Jean Lafitte and the vampire-prince Lestat.

A brief round of introductions told us that five out of the eight other people on the tour were recovery workers from various organizations, and one couple was in town to help relatives clean out their house. The last, a blond woman, offered no real information about herself. Her hair, which flowed in beautiful, wild waves, was so bright it glowed white, and despite the temperature she wore a skintight tank top and a gauzy pink skirt that blew when the breeze picked up.

How is she not freezing?

I looked at Isaac, who was just in a white T-shirt. "Aren't you cold?"

"No, I'm from New York . . ."

"Right, how could I have forgotten?"

The woman looked at me; her lips pursed daringly. Chills swept up my spine. I turned away and crossed my arms.

"Oh, are you cold?" he asked.

"No, I'm fine." I dropped my arms to appear more convincing.

Ren went around the group, collecting money. When he got to us, Isaac pulled out two twenty-dollar bills.

"I can get my own ticket."

"No, I got it. You wouldn't even be here if it wasn't for me," he insisted, but I shook my head. I didn't want to owe Isaac anything.

"Like I'd ever take your money, *ma chérie*," Ren said to me. "But I'll gladly take yours." He plucked one of the bills from between Isaac's fingers.

"I promise I'll be on my best behavior," he reassured Ren.

"Son, I love trouble. Don't change your ways on account of me."

"I'm not changing them on account of you." Isaac glanced at me.

"Interesting," Ren murmured, looking back and forth between us, "very interesting."

My eyes dropped to the ground.

"Time to start, folks!" Ren yelled to the group and then beckoned us to follow him down Pirate's Alley.

The flames in the gas lamps created the perfect ambiance for a ghost tour, and the bells in the steeple clanged as if they were part of his act. He stopped halfway down the alley and, after an attention-commanding pause, proceeded to tell us the story of how the infamous alley got its name.

As he spoke, the echo of heels on slate became louder. I turned to see the silhouette of a girl hurrying down the alley toward me.

Is that Désirée Borges?

Isaac's back stiffened. "You know her?"

"Sort of."

"Sorry, I'm late," she grumbled to Ren, pulling cash from her wallet, but he shook his hand, motioning for her not to interrupt. She merged into the group next to me. I couldn't tell whether she was annoyed or relieved to see someone she knew. Especially since that someone was me.

"What are you doing here?" I whispered.

"My dad forced me." She sounded annoyed. "You know, help boost tourism, support local businesses, blah, blah, blah."

"Hmm. I'm still surprised you came."

"I have a plan, and it doesn't involve staying." She pulled her phone from her blazer pocket.

"In that case"—Ren snapped the twenty from her hand— *"Bienvenue, shay."* Even with the interruption, he didn't skip a beat. "Listen up, folks, there are two alleyways on either side of the Saint Louis Cathedral: one is named after a pirate and the other for a priest. Scientists from all around the world flock to one of them and claim it has one of the highest records of concentrated paranormal activity on the planet. Can you guess which?"

Everyone laughed.

"Of course, we New Orleanians do not need gadgets and gizmos to record noises and auras in order to know when we're in a nexus of supernatural activity." He looked directly at the blond woman as he carefully articulated the last sentence. Her shoulders straightened, and her face lit up. She loved it.

"This way!" He walked us around the church, where an illuminated statue of Jesus cast a fifty-foot shadow on the back of the cathedral. *I guess the church thought Jesus deserved a generator?*

Like everyone else, Isaac was hanging on to Ren's every word. I forced back a smile, watching him.

"*Psst.* Adele, come take a picture of me in front of the statue, but wait until some other people are behind me so it proves I was on the tour."

"Come on, Désirée, it's rude. I don't want to distract Ren."

"Oh please, that statue of Jesus could start twerkin' and Ren wouldn't break character."

She had a point. Plus, I wanted her to pick me up for school tomorrow. I sighed and grabbed her phone. "Get close to the light so I don't have to use the flash." I hurried to frame the shot as the group walked behind her.

As she held her extrafake grin and I snapped a few pics, I felt Isaac's gaze shift to me—watching me like a hawk, just like my father had requested. I returned her phone and walked back to him as Ren began describing the ghost of Julie, who haunted the Bottom of the Cup Tearoom.

"Nothing like the ghost of a scorned lover," I whispered to Isaac. He smiled quickly, staring at the roof of the building where Julie had frozen to death.

We walked the rest of the block to the corner of St. Ann and Royal Street. The moon shone over the corner building like a spotlight for just us. The dark-green floor-to-ceiling shutters were latched closed, and wrought iron balconies wrapped around the second and third floors of the maroon three-story residence.

"John and Wayne Carter were brothers who seemed to be just your average men—"

The woman with the long, blond hair let out a loud cackle and then quickly tried to calm herself. *"Pardon moi,"* she said, and squeaked out another giggle.

Désirée mouthed the word "nutcase" to me. I suppressed a laugh and turned back to Isaac, who was staring hard at the woman. Remembering this particular story, I became nervous that his inner naysayer might make an appearance, so I dropped to the back of the group; luckily, he fell back with me.

"By the way, you look really nice tonight," he leaned in and whispered, his breath tickling my ear.

The compliment caught me off guard. "You look, uh, clean," I joked.

"Haha. Some of us have to get our hands dirty while others go to fancy schools."

"That's not fai—"

Hands from behind wrapped around my eyes, interrupting.

"*Piacere!* What's going on here? Did our invitations to the *festa* get lost in the mail?"

I didn't tell him there was no way Niccolò would say something so cheesy, which left only one Italiano to suspect. He kissed both of my cheeks and then moved out of the way so his brother could do the same.

"Ciao," Niccolò said, looking almost bashful.

His shyness rubbed off on me. "Twice in one day," I barely managed to get out.

"The tour has already begun," said Ren.

Isaac smirked.

The blond woman stared intensely at Niccolò. The way he stared back at her—it was like they were silently daring each other. *Maybe she is the reason for Niccolò's early-morning stroll?*

Ugh. I tried to convince myself that what Niccolò Medici was doing at dawn was none of my business.

Her stern expression faltered when Gabe smiled at her with a hint of glee. It was painfully obvious they all knew each other.

"Are you sure you can't take just two more?" Gabe asked, approaching Ren with a couple of crisp bills. "We're very generous tippers," he added, looking him straight in the eyes.

And with that, Ren changed his mind: "I've always had a hard time saying no to a handsome foreigner."

From my peripheral vision, I saw Isaac scowl.

Bashfulness gone, Niccolò touched my face. "Your wound is finally healing." He kept one eye on Isaac, as if he were some kind of abusive boyfriend—which wasn't fair and certainly didn't go unnoticed by Isaac.

"So little time, so much to see!" Ren yelled, scooping his arm toward Bourbon Street.

"So, Dee," I asked as Isaac grabbed my arm and pulled me along with the group, "are you still leaving, or do you need more pictures?"

Désirée must have also noticed the bizarre exchange with the blonde earlier, because she looked directly at her, as if rising to the challenge. "Oh, I'm definitely going to need more pictures." And then she wrapped her arm around Gabe and snapped a selfie. They looked like a pair of supermodels.

"Most people know the Vieux Carré, or French Quarter, is the oldest neighborhood in New Orleans, settled by the French in 1718, but what most *don't* know is that the majority of the buildings around us are not actually French. Two great fires in the eighteenth century destroyed nearly everything in the Quarter.

"Spain occupied the city at the time when the old square was rebuilt, so most of the buildings standing before you were constructed by the Spanish. There are only four original French structures remaining"—Ren looked straight at me and Désirée—"a Voodoo shop, a Creole cottage on Burgundy Street, the Ursuline Convent, and this former brothel."

I'd known our house was an original French cottage (there was even a plaque on the outside from the historic registry), but I had no idea it was one of only *four*.

"Wow, I can't believe I'm working on one of those places," Isaac whispered, nudging me. "Cool."

"You might be thinking it's curious that these four buildings survived all of these years, through the fires and the storms. *Is it a coincidence?* After all, what do a convent, a brothel, a Creole cottage, and a Voodoo shop have in common? Of course, it wouldn't have been a Voodoo shop back then . . ."

"Back then, that sort of thing wasn't legal," Désirée finished.

"That's correct, Mademoiselle Borges. Back then any shop selling magic fixin's would've appeared to be just a shop where certain items might have come with a little lagniappe. But you'd know more about that than lil ole me."

Désirée rolled her eyes as his accent thickened for the tourists.

"This way, people, *allons-y!*" He hurried us along toward the house of New Orleans's most famous murderess, Madame Delphine LaLaurie.

I started to move forward with the group, but a tug at my dress made me pause and turn back.

"Hey," Niccolò said, his hand lingering on my arm. "I just want to apologize for this morning." The sound of his soft voice brought me back to our tangled embrace.

"For what?"

"For acting so weird. The truth is, my brother and I were out drinking, and we got into a little scuffle with some guys who were being foolish. I didn't want you to think I was that kind of guy."

"What kind of guy?" I wrapped my arms around myself.

"Are you cold?"

"N—"

Before I could answer, he stripped off his black leather jacket and swept it around my shoulders.

"*Grazie*. Someone hit you?"

But it was Gabe who answered for him, joining the conversation out of nowhere. "Oh, Adele, don't worry about Nicco . . . You should have seen the other guy. Out stone-cold." He tousled his brother's hair, and Niccolò quickly swatted his hands away.

"Why would someone hit you?" I asked. It was hard to imagine. Niccolò seemed like the quiet guy in the corner. Gabe, on the other hand, I could totally see instigating a brawl.

"I could think of a couple reasons . . ." Isaac had reappeared with Désirée in tow, and I could see Mr. Hyde coming out to play.

Niccolò's jaw tightened.

"So much for your best behavior," I mumbled, giving Isaac a look.

"Save it for the frat house, boys." Désirée put her arm around me and walked us back toward the crowd. "Don't look back. Pretend you don't care."

"I *don't* care."

"Riiight."

"She's beautiful *and* unforgiving," Gabe yelled. "My favorite combination."

I felt Désirée's entire body smile, not that it showed on her face.

Gabe caught up, breaking us apart. With his arms around each of our shoulders, we hurried to catch up with the rest of the tour. Désirée let out a genuine giggle.

We had missed nearly the entire story of *le Comte de Saint-Germain*. Something to do with a residence on the corner of Royal and Ursuline.

"And the next two tales bring us to the end of the tour."

When I looked up, we were standing directly behind the old Ursuline Convent. My heart began to knock against my chest.

Gabe looked down at me as if he could hear the pounding. I moved from underneath his arm to the familiar gate.

This time when the chills rushed up my spine, I also broke out into a sweat. I tightened Niccolò's jacket around my shoulders—the attic window I'd witnessed explode was now completely bricked up, preventing even the moonbeams from coming and going.

Ren leaped onto the hood of a previously drowned car and paused for dramatic effect as he prepared himself for *la grande finale*.

"New Orleans came to be thanks to the real crème de la crème of Parisian society: the thieves, the crooks, and the murderers. That's right, folks, New Orleans started as a penal colony. These fine founding citizens were convicts from la Bastille who'd been granted pardons by the king in exchange for building *la grande capitale* of New France. So, early on, the city was a cesspool of scoundrels and scalawags, which means not much has changed since." He winked and then took an exaggerated sip from his flask.

"These unruly Frenchmen survived hurricanes, indigenous swamp creatures, and the cannibalistic ways of certain native tribes, but how could a population of only men evolve into the society meant for such a fine city? They demanded, pleaded, and begged the king to send over women! Being a reasonable man, the king emptied the female correction houses and raked the streets for spare ladies of the night, who were then shipped to New France like a platter of beignets, though not nearly as sweet.

"Now, King Louis XIV was on a mission for *La Nouvelle-Orléans* to be *le Paris* of the New World. Propaganda was launched across France to arouse adventurous men to seek their fortunes in this new land of opportunity. In response, a new class of Frenchmen made the grueling journey across the Atlantic Ocean—only to find a giant swampland full of mosquitos, alligators, and serpents.

"Of course, it wasn't long before they too demanded the king send ladies! Having already rid the French streets of excess undesirables, King Louis scavenged hundreds of virtuous young women from convents and orphanages to send to these opportunity seekers. He gave the girls small dowries and sent them on their merry way to marry the colonists and propagate the burgeoning city. The small chests, or cassettes, given to the women to hold their wedding dresses looked very similar to caskets and earned the girls the title *les filles aux cassettes* or simply 'the casquette girls,' as the locals say."

"What does this have to do with the Ursuline Convent?" I asked, barely hearing the words come out of my mouth.

"Yes, mademoiselle, the nuns! Now, for as much of this city's soul as is built on Vodun folkways, Native American spirits, and everything in between, the Catholics also dutifully staked their claim into the soggy soil of *La Nouvelle-Orléans*. And there is no better example of that sense of duty than the sisters from the Order of Saint Ursula.

"The Ursuline nuns came from France to open *L'Hôpital des Pauvres de la Charité*, or Charity, as the locals now know it. But the Ursuline nuns' real mission was education, not hospitals! Before crossing the Atlantic, they'd made a deal with the bishop: they'd gladly make the perilous journey to a bayou country full of savages and pirates and tend to the sick, if—and only if—they were also allowed to open a school. And so they did on the property that stands before you, a school that served only girls—*all* girls, regardless of race, color, or social class.

"It's said that it was the Ursuline sisters who took in the casquette girls when each shipload docked in the French Quarter. They stored their cassettes in the convent attic for safekeeping, and then housed, educated, and chaperoned them until each was married off.

"But as things go in New Orleans, scandal struck when the first marriage proposal was accepted . . . When the sisters fetched the girl's cassette, they discovered, to everyone's dismay, that it was empty! No dowry from the king. No wedding dress. Nothin' but cobwebs. Every cassette in their care had been emptied."

Ren switched to an unidentifiable Eastern European accent.

"Legend has it the casquette girls had smuggled *les vampires* across the ocean in those casket boxes, and these vampires had been sleeping in the attic during the day and running amok at night, feeding on anyone they fancied. New Orleans was the perfect cover. Between the crime and the disease, death rates were already astronomical. Who would bat an eye when another dead body turned up? Who was going to notice another missing ex-con or prostitute?"

I began to wrap and unwrap my chain around my fingers.

Blue eyes. Dead, blue eyes.

Ren looked around the silent crowd. "And that's the story of how the vampires came to New Orleans. To America."

"Riveting," said Gabe, looking at the blond woman, who seemed oddly somber.

"So what's the deal with that attic window?" I blurted.

The group turned to see who had spoken.

"I'm so glad you asked, m'lady. If you walk around the French Quarter, you'll find that every set of attic windows is permanently latched open. Can anybody guess why?"

"Because of the heat," Niccolò answered dryly.

"Exactly correct, my fair-faced friend! It gets hotter than hell here in southern Louisiana, and in the early eighteenth century there was no central air. Since heat rises, the attics were the hottest rooms in these Creole cottages, and they were also where the children often slept. The shutters on the attic windows were kept permanently latched open out of fear they'd swing shut in the middle of the night, leaving the dreaming youngsters to cook to death.

"However, the attic windows of the Ursuline Convent are all latched *shut*. Legend says that one thousand nails were sent from the papacy in Rome, blessed by the Pope himself. And that while the monsters slept, the Ursulines nailed up the shutters completely to protect their convent and the citizens of New Orleans from the attic's deviant denizens."

The blonde's eyes lit up with excitement. "Ha! Like za Catholic Church could imprison a clan of vampires!" she said with conviction.

Is her accent French?

Désirée walked to the convent's gate and peered through the iron posts. "I agree with blondie. It sounds like there was more going on here than the work of the Lord."

"Well, honey," Ren said, "you know that in the Big Easy, there's always more than meets the eye."

He gave us a minute to take it all in.

A history of strange or unusual happenstances flooded my head. My pulse began to race as I thought about every shadow, every creak, every unexplainable occurrence in my life I'd never given a second thought to before. Désirée also seemed to be processing something buried in her subconscious. *Maybe she's thinking the same thing?* After all, we were the only two of the group who'd been born in this town, where the debate between fact and fiction is grayer than the newspaper it's read from.

"As you can see, a shutter is missing from one of the windows. I have it on good authority that it fell only a week ago . . . and yet somehow, even in this time of chaos, the archdiocese managed to brick up the window right away. Whatever could cause such urgency when there are people to feed, houses to rebuild?" Ren slowly scanned the crowd. "I don't know the answers. I just tell the stories."

Violent chills spread throughout my entire body until my teeth chattered uncontrollably. The gate rattled in the breeze.

Breathe.

"Hey, are you okay?" Isaac asked. "You look even paler than usual."

I nodded, unable to move my eyes from the attic window.

"You're trembling." He put his arm around me.

On the verge of a claustrophobic fit, I stepped away, following Ren to the church adjacent to the convent, where he continued:

"A different version of the story simply claims that vampires live in the attic and are able to move through the convent windows at night. Barely more than a decade ago, that rumor inspired a college-aged couple from California to come to town with the brilliant plan to make a documentary on our extracurricular nightlife. They set up their cameras, camped out in front of Saint Mary's, and waited . . .

"The next morning, their bodies were discovered . . . drained of eighty percent of their blood. On their tapes, nothing but static. There was no evidence of—"

"I heard it was a woman who killed that couple," said the blonde.

Niccolò moved to my side, and Ren hurried along with the story, speaking directly to her. "There were a few *unreliable* witnesses who claimed to have seen a young brunette bent over the bodies." His gaze shifted to me. "But there was never enough evidence to hold any suspects for more than a night."

He carried on with his story, but the memory of the methodical banging of the shutter clogged my ears. It got louder and louder and faster and—

A sharp whistle brought me back to the present.

Everyone around me was clapping enthusiastically, cheering for Ren as he took deep bows. The tour was over. I put my hands together in appreciation and forced a smile. *It's only a stupid story, Adele. Chill out.*

The blonde turned to Gabe with an expression that could only mean she was looking for trouble. "Surely there is something to get into tonight? It is still *La Nouvelle-Orléans*, after all. How much could it really have changed?"

Definitely a French accent. Definitely trouble.

"I am in wholehearted agreement, *signorina*," said Gabe.

Niccolò looked at her and then at me. "How are you getting home?"

"Uh, walking; I live arou—"

"I'll walk you."

"That won't be necessary," Isaac said, stepping in between us.

This time it was Niccolò who smirked, almost beckoning a challenge, which in turn made Gabe grin from ear to ear.

My eyes rolled at the ripple of testosterone. "Ren, will you walk me home?"

"At your service, mademoiselle."

Isaac shot me an exasperated look, unable to fulfill the promise he'd made to my father about not letting me out of his sight.

Gabe offered his hand to Désirée, but Isaac walked in front of it. "I got it," he snapped, not giving her a chance to disagree, which I thought was kind of hilarious.

As Isaac pulled Désirée away, she turned back to me. "See you at seven tomorrow, Adele. And try not to be late." She gave Niccolò an obnoxious look of approval, which *everyone* noticed.

My cheeks burned like they were harboring fireballs.

"*Merci beaucoup*, and good night, folks!" Ren yelled with satisfaction. "*Au revoir*, boys. *À la prochaine!*" He spun me in the direction of my house, linking his arm through mine.

"Ciao," I yelled over my shoulder to Niccolò, Gabe . . . , and the blonde.

CHAPTER 19

La fille à la cassette

"Oh, to be young again and have so many gentleman callers fawning all over me," Ren said with an exaggerated southern accent.

"No one is fawning over me." I laughed. "I have even less of a life post-Storm than I had pre-Storm, which I didn't think was possible."

"Oh, child, you're growing into quite the ingénue, aren't you?"

I ignored the comment. "Can I ask you something, Ren?" Nervousness flooded from my stomach all the way to my shoulders, making them tingle. "How much of that *stuff* do you believe?"

"There you go, changing the subject. That means you *are* sweet on one of them. Which is it? I'm gonna guess the Yankee. You two bicker too much to actually dislike each other."

"Ren!"

"So, it's the foreign fox?"

"Stop! I'm serious. It's important!"

"*D'accord, d'accord.* How much of that *stuff* do I believe?" He twisted the end of his mustache. "Well, I believe bits and pieces of it all. Legends are legends for a reason; they don't just appear out of thin air. But over the years, they morph. They evolve to serve a purpose of the time."

"But what about the stories you just told? The Carter brothers, the casquette girls, the filmmakers . . ."

"You mean the vampire stories?"

"Oui."

"In the words of the great Monsieur Baudelaire, 'The finest trick of the devil is to persuade you that he does not exist.'"

I began to twist the ring around my finger.

"Why so serious, darlin'? What's the mat—?"

"I-think-I-opened-the-attic-window-at-the-Ursuline-Convent," I garbled.

He looked at me blankly for a moment. "Why on earth would you think that, *bébé?*"

"It was right when we got back into town. I had just discovered a dead body and cut my hand, and his blue eyes were just staring at me, and I ran. When I stopped in front of the convent to catch my breath, the shutter started flapping, only there was no wind—"

He put his hand on my shoulder and pulled me into a narrow alleyway. "Breathe, darlin'."

"I didn't mean to trespass. It was like the window pulled me in, and before I knew it, I was in the courtyard. I didn't touch anything, I swear—the shutter flapped itself until it came crashing down! The window shattered, and . . ."

"And?"

The last words rushed out of my subconscious in a shrill whisper. *"And something flew out!"* I froze, admitting to myself for the first time what had happened that morning: *something* had come out of that window. I *knew* it.

He looked at me with a serious but sympathetic expression. "What flew out? Some kind of monster?"

"Well, no . . . maybe . . . I don't know! It was raining, and it all happened so fast, and my hand was bleeding all over the place—I didn't see anything, but I swear I *heard* something, Ren. And I *felt* it."

The fear that flicked in his eyes made me instantly regret telling him. "You don't *really* think there were vampires trapped in the attic, do you?" I asked.

"Calm down, *bébé*. There's no way you opened that window. Stop worrying your pretty little head." His acting skills were no longer as convincing, but I appreciated him trying to comfort me. "I'm sorry if the story spooked you."

"How are you so certain I didn't open it?"

"Well, the story has more holes than a New Orleans road. Besides, it's not just the blessed nails from the Vatican you'd have to get past: It's been said that what really keeps the vampires trapped inside the attic is something much more magical. A spell. Or a curse, depending on how you look at it. Naturally, the church quickly quelled that rumor, but, unless those nuns had some other miraculous gifts from God, that theory makes the most sense to me. This is the only thing I can tell you for certain: there is no way you could've accidentally undone the spell of another. I may not be a shaman, but anyone who knows about magic will tell you that only the original caster of a spell can undo it."

He smoothed my hair.

That seemed plausible to me. I didn't know anything about binding or unbinding spells, but I desperately wanted to grasp onto anything that proved I hadn't unleashed a drove of bloodsucking killers into the city I loved so much.

"Adele, you were traumatized: the city's a ruin, you'd just discovered a corpse, and it was pouring rain. Besides, it looks like you have men lining up at the door to protect you." He winked, attempting to lighten the mood, but I was hardly paying attention—my mind was rewinding all of the weird things that had happened since the Storm.

"Ren, can I ask you one more thing?"

"*Oui*, of course."

The two copper gas lanterns over our heads began to creak back and forth.

"Do you really believe in magic? Like, *really*?"

"*Oui, bébé*. Moving pictures and flying machines both seemed like magic at one time. It's not a huge leap to believe that what seems irrational or magical now will be commonplace in the future. I believe everyone has magical powers. However, only certain people—the ones who are open to it—can tap into the true capacity of the mind and push the current brink of human thought. Some are called geniuses, some are called prophets, others are called witches."

"So, if someone's not open to magic, they could prevent supernatural things from happening?"

He chuckled. "If only it were that easy, *bébé*. Sometimes magic finds us; we don't find it. And once it does, it's nearly impossible to close ourselves off to it. It'd be like trying to forget how to read or speak or walk. Usually people who unlock magic within themselves don't understand their importance in the world."

I frowned. *Hadn't I heard that before?*

"Just remember, everything happens for a reason. *D'accord?*"

"Okay."

"Anything else?"

I paused, debating whether I should tell him about my recent bout of telekinesis. Instinct pinched my lips and shook my head.

Luckily, he let it rest and linked our arms back together.

When we got to my front door, he kissed my head instead of giving me one of his bear hugs. "*Lâche pas la patate, bébé,*" he said. "You'll figure it out, whatever it is. That I can guarantee."

"*Merci beaucoup.*"

"*Bonne nuit.* Sweet dreams." He waited for me to slip inside and lock the door.

Through the peephole, I watched him walk down the street—that's when I noticed the crow perched on top of the street sign, staring in my direction. I stumbled backward into a small table, having to grasp the overhanging mirror as it nearly slid off the wall.

"Dad?" I called out into the dark house as I straightened it back in place.

Only the pendulum swings of the old clock answered. *He must be at the bar.* At least he wouldn't know I'd arrived ten minutes past curfew.

A million thoughts spiraled as I lay on my bed, arms crossed, staring at the lamplight. *You've got to relax, Adele—*

Like that's going to happen.

The phonograph cranked on, but the glam-rock beats just made me more restless.

I didn't want to believe I'd released a bunch of monsters into the city . . . monsters who'd been trapped in a convent attic for three hundred years and who were probably really pissed off about it. I *really* didn't want to believe that.

My fingers strummed my stomach, and my feet rocked back and forth, moving faster and faster. Then a loud crack exploded.

"Shit!" I sat up in the sudden darkness, clutching my chest.

The lightbulb spontaneously combusted.

Breathe.

As I sucked in air, a little flame slowly grew from a vanilla-scented candle on the fireplace mantel.

This is not happening.

This is not happening.

A second flame ignited from a neighboring candle.

"This is happening."

I jumped up from the bed, flipped on the overhead light, and looked around the room, wishing there was a witness to tell me I wasn't going crazy. When my gaze landed on the closet, the brass handle turned, and the door creaked open a few inches.

I swallowed a lump in my throat. *At this rate, I'm going to have a heart attack before my seventeenth birthday.*

But instead of giving in to the fear, I yelled out to no one, "*C'est parfait!* A good cleaning project is exactly what I need!" And then I walked straight toward the little room. I waved my hand through the air, and the door swung open.

A yank on the rotting cord hanging from the ceiling bulb shed dust-dimmed light in the tiny room. I fought the urge to sneeze.

Piece by piece, I brought everything into my bedroom: I stacked piles of books ranging from poetry to medicine along the wall, trashed piles of disintegrating linens, and moved a box of old vinyls to the phonograph. I consciously focused on each task, refusing to let the idea of vampires running around the city raid my thoughts.

An hour later, the last thing to go was a large, antique steamer trunk decorated with tags from all around the world. In theory it should have been easy to move because it stood upright on wheels, but it weighed a ton and the metal parts badly needed oil. I pulled the beast of a trunk with all of my strength. It moved an inch, and I slid down to the dirty floor, exhausted.

From the ground, I could see that the wheels were thick with rust. *"Fight what you know to be true."* I concentrated, visualizing a turning motion, until the wheels squeaked loudly and began to move. As the large chest slowly wheeled itself into the bedroom, I realized I'd actually managed to distract myself for another half hour. Of course, as soon as this realization hit, the vampires rushed my mind with a vengeance.

I grabbed the broom.

Once the wooden floor of the closet was swept, I aggressively repeated the process with the mop, only stopping when one of the strings snagged a nail. I bent over to free it, but the nail refused to let go.

"Whatever." Yawning, I jerked the mop, ripping the string from its head.

As I reached up for the light cord, I felt my chain sliding off my neck. "No!" I yelped, grabbing for the medallion, but it clanked to the floor.

I worried the chain had broken—it had just come unfastened. I held my hand out to retrieve the sun charm and the medallion, and they leaped into my hand, along with the nail that had snagged the mop string. It was a long, black, handmade carpenter's nail, like the ones at the convent.

I restrung the necklace, making sure the fastener was secure, and reached back for the light.

Again, I felt the slink of metal down my neck. I slapped my chest, again, not fast enough. The necklace clanked back to the floor.

"What the . . . ?"

For the second time, I reached out and gained another nail from the floorboard along with the medallion. I dropped the nail to the floor, but it leaped right back up to my palm.

"What the hell?"

All the nails in the two floorboards beneath me were vibrating. The rest of the floor seemed normal—it was just this spot.

My heart rattled in my chest as I knelt down over the shaking nails. Instinctively, I raised my hand over the boards. The nails slowly wiggled themselves out and rose to the palm of my hand.

The wood was so degraded I could easily squeeze my fingers in between the planks and shake them until they loosened enough for me to pry one free. And then another. I hastily cast the floorboards aside and peered into the dark hole, like a child about to discover a treasure. But I didn't find anything at all.

I slipped my hand into the small space and felt around. Nothing but cool metal, like the inside of a safe.

The lightbulb overhead flickered. My pulse climbed.

I hurried back for the vanilla candle, setting it inside the hole to take another look.

Nothing. I sighed.

As I stared at the flame in frustration, the candle trembled and the metal floor underneath it warped. *"Fight what you know to be true."* I held my hand over the metal, and the surface rippled. At first there was just a slight tingle in my shoulders, but then the energy traveled down my arms like a current, until my whole body began to shudder. My fingers burned. I cried out, *"Fight what you know to be true!"* And just as I was about to rip my hand away, the metal floor parted in a circular wall of waves.

The candle fell into the lower compartment, but illuminated something else before it flamed out. Without thinking, I thrust my hand into the hole and grabbed it. As soon as I jerked my arm back out, the waves collapsed.

I pounded on the metal surface, dumbfounded. It was warm but solid. I raised an eyebrow at the leather-bound object in my hand and scurried back to my bed. *All that trouble for a book?*

But it wasn't just a book. It was a very old lock-and-key diary. The antique metal lock made the dense diary even heavier, and the hand-stitched leather binding and thick paper made me believe it must have been expensive in its time.

How old is this thing?

The edges of the pages were mismatched and browned, but the diary had been so perfectly preserved in the secret compartment it was difficult to guess its age.

I imagined the metalwork unlocking—and the tiny latch snapped open.

Adrenaline coursed through my veins as I carefully opened the cover of the unlocked treasure. A folded square of paper had been pressed between the cover and the first page.

Careful not to destroy the old stationery, I unfolded the handwritten French letter.

5th February 1728

Dearest Adeline,

It is my greatest desire to be able to make this voyage with you to La Nouvelle-Orléans, *as the adventures in which you have accompanied me are the fondest memories a father could ever hope for. But, alas, there are urgent matters that I must attend to first oceans away.*

Make me a promise that you will record every single detail in this diary that was made especially for you. When we meet again, I will read and reread every word, one hundred times until your memories are my memories.

I know that you will set up the Saint-Germain estate perfectly, and I will be there before you can even miss me. You are wise beyond your years, my sweet Adeline, but please, I implore you, take every precaution on this journey.

Remember everything I have taught you. Trust no one.

With all my love and affection,
Papa

My fingers went to the medallion around my neck. *Adeline. The Saint-Germain estate? ASG? This is ASG's diary?*

I fanned through the pages, and my heart fluttered as I caught sight of a phrase among the motion. I flipped the pages back, frantically scanning for the words I knew I'd seen. And then, there they were, staring back at me.

> *You will never believe what the locals call the orphan girls. The townspeople have given them the funniest name, "les filles aux cassettes."*

"Les filles aux cassettes?" I whispered. "The girls with the cassettes . . . the casquette girls?"

> *Although, I shouldn't speak of them as if they are a group separate from myself. I may have boarded the ship under different circumstances, but after numerous events that have bound us together, I consider them to be my sisters.*

The ring around my finger suddenly felt warm. I slipped it off, tossing it lightly into the air and reaching to catch it. Midair, the silver disc, with its spherical, milky stone, dislodged from the setting, and both pieces fell gently back into my hand.

Dammit! Whatever . . . Dad can fix it.

But then the ASG medallion, still hanging from my chain, floated into my other hand. Unable to decide which one to focus on, my eyes flicked back and forth between them. Then they started to float off my hands so slowly I hardly realized it.

Breathe.

I wanted to shut my eyes, but I forced them to stay wide open. The two silver medallions rose higher and higher; my heart pounded harder and harder. And then they stopped midair right in my sight line, at the perfect angle to see the details.

How did I not notice this before?

They both had the exact same delicately engraved border. With a snap they clamped back-to-back as if magnetized. A golden flicker chased the edges, magically welding them together into one thick medallion. It slowly turned in the air, allowing me time to examine it. The design no longer looked incomplete—one side had the stone, and the other side had the imprint of the star and the initials ASG.

According to my mother, the ring had belonged to my father's family. Did that mean ASG was . . . one of my *ancestors*?

Ren's voice boomed in my head: ". . . only the original caster of a spell can undo it."

"Who were you, Adeline Saint-Germain?" I whispered.

PART 2
The Coven

Carriage, take me with you! Ship, steal me away from here!

Take me far, far away. Here the mud is made of our tears!

Charles Baudelaire

CHAPTER 20

Je t'aime Paris

(Translated from French.)

3rd March 1728

So, the journey has begun, Papa. We have been aboard the SS *Gironde*, under the command of Captain Vauberci, for seven days now, although we have only completed three days' worth of our journey due to rough weather. Being trapped inside the private cabin makes me feel like a giant stuck inside a doll's house. I found this extraordinary gift you hid in my hatbox, and I will do my best to fill the diary each day, with the hopes that eventually the pages will become worthy of the ink. Although, I admit to finding the request odd. If your desire to be part of this journey was so strong you wish for the details of every passing moment to be recorded, then why did you not accompany me instead of disappearing to the Orient three weeks ago? The mystery surrounding your actions has me ever so curious.

So now, here I sit, with only paper and ink to keep me company. I believe the story begins the night before we left Paris . . .

The moment you told me you were sending me away, I began reading everything I could find about this new foreign land across the Atlantic. The king's court advertises this New France as the pinnacle of modern society—all the luxuries of Paris but full of endless possibilities for people to make new lives, new investments, and new riches. It is said a man can start over in New France and that his past can be erased and he can be whomever he wants to be. I wonder if this is the same for a woman? It is this prospect that keeps me from jumping over the ship's edge on this wretched journey.

It is still so early in the king's exploration there is not much information in circulation, so I spoke with as many people as I could, including some sailors who were in town between journeys. (I kindly remind you it was you who forced me into this position.)

Curiously, the tales of the seamen did not confirm the king's proclamations of bountiful luxuries and opportunities. The more inebriated sailors even called the stories "lies" and the adverts "propaganda." Some of the sailors' news had allegedly come from the church—from a group of nuns of the Order of Saint Ursula who are setting up a hospital in *la Louisianne*. It turns out, Father, that some of the nuns from this same order are traveling on this very ship with me! (Do not fret; I have not forgotten your warning never to trust anyone on this journey, not even those who walk in the eyes of the Lord.) The sailors also said the land of *la Louisianne* is full of drifters, prostitutes, and criminals—ex-convicts the king has pardoned in exchange for building the grand city of *La Nouvelle-Orléans*. I heard stories of all kinds, but no two were the same, except for the tales of the hot and humid weather.

And this is why, the day before my departure, I found myself in the tailor's shop, picking out a light silk for a new cloak. I knew my traveling garments would serve well aboard the ship in the cold ocean winds, but what upon arrival? I had heard tales of men and women stripping off layers of clothing due to madness brought on by the sun! I confess this idea made me even more excited to travel across the ocean.

Louis draped the fabric over my shoulders and then pinned and snipped. The task took longer than necessary because of his insatiable need to gossip, but I didn't mind. I was going to miss his friendship. He asked me a hundred questions about my pending journey, and I was just telling him that he was welcome to take my place aboard the SS *Gironde* when in walked a very debonair man. Louis became excitable, which could only mean one thing: the gentleman's purse was full.

To his credit, Louis did not leave my side (I am sure your position as count had something to do with it), despite seeming absolutely mesmerized by the man. And the man was indeed hypnotizing: his dark hair was held perfectly in place under a top hat, which matched his suit made of fine velvet, and he had the kind of green eyes that are impossible not to notice. It really is unfair when a man has the sort of eyes that sparkle. While Louis tended to me, the man waited patiently; he had a smile like an innocent boy's, but a chill on my arms warned me the innocence was deceptive. Even so, it would be false to say I was not intrigued when we finally began to converse.

He said to me, "What good fortune I have running into you, Mademoiselle Saint-Germain."

To which I replied, "Dear sir, it is impossible I could have forgotten your face, which means we have not met, and it is hardly fair that you know my name while I have not yet learned yours."

Our apparent acquaintance sent Louis into a tizzy. He ran off to retrieve a pair of shears, or so he claimed. I suspect he was trying to give us a moment of privacy.

The moment we were alone, the stranger looked deeply into my eyes and told me: "But we have met, mademoiselle. It was during carnival season last winter. I was a guest of Mademoiselle Jeanne-Françoise Quinault at a masquerade ball at your father's estate."

Is that not ridiculous, Father? As if there has been a person in our own home in my sixteen years whom I don't remember, masquerade ball or not! The very idea is absurd. When I didn't agree, he repeated the statement. I can hardly explain it, but it was as if he was trying to will me into believing we had met before. I laughed, and the man appeared frustrated, so I played along.

"You will have to forgive me, sir, and tell me your name a second time."

He quickly composed himself, as if he realized he would have to deploy a different tactic to get what he desired. *"Jean-Antoine Cartier, enchanté."*

When he kissed my right hand, my left instinctively curled at my side.

There wasn't a part of me that believed for one second his name was actually Jean-Antoine Cartier. It's not that he seemed insincere. Au contraire, he had an extremely calm and inviting aura, but there was something about him that fired up all of my senses. He was a man who knew exactly what he was doing. In the spirit of the game, I asked him where he was from.

"Now, that is a very long story," he told me.

I warn you, Papa, you are not going to like the next part of this tale, but you are not exactly in the position to reprimand me, so I will speak openly about it, as we always do in the flesh. Despite our distance, it will comfort you to know as I put these words on paper I can feel you chastising me for my actions.

He said to me, "I realize it is forward of me to ask, with your father abroad, but would you care to accompany me this evening to the salon at the home of Mademoiselle Quinault?"

I had wanted to go to that very gathering but had given up on the idea without you to chaperone, Father.

His eyes were just as inviting as his words, but it was only when he made his next statement that I really had to concentrate on keeping my brow straight. "I have been to New France three times already," he said. "Twice to the great city of Montréal and once to the site of *La Nouvelle-Orléans.*"

Not that I needed more reason other than simply to quell my boredom, but a mysterious, handsome man who knew the exact way to capture my attention piqued my curiosity, and this tease solidified my decision. His offer was the perfect invitation for mischief on my last night in Paris. I promise I was not looking for a scandal, Papa, but really, how could I say no to someone who might satisfy my need for information on the land I would be traveling to in just one day's time? A land which not even you have been to yet . . .

So, that evening, Monsieur Cartier's carriage picked me up.

When we arrived at the salon together, the looks of surprise on the other guests' faces were alone worth the trip. Many of the women looked at me with contempt because I was on the arm of such a handsome man, but mostly they were all just desperately curious as to why the daughter of *le Comte de Saint-Germain* would be traveling to New France.

Do not worry. I did not tell them the reason was mysterious even to me or that you were forcing me to go—nor did I mention that in doing so, you seemed to be under duress. I simply told them I was bored with Paris and that you were sending me to marvel over your new investment in the New World. Of course, they drew their own conclusions. I overheard their little comments as we walked by.

"I heard the Count is shipping her off to Tuscany."

"Well, I heard he is locking her up in a lunatic asylum in London."

"No, no, you both have it wrong. He is shipping her off to a Catholic nunnery in *La Nouvelle-Orléans* because she is so unwieldy."

"Oh, what I wouldn't pay to know who her mother is."

"Either way, he should have married. What else could he possibly have expected to happen? Raising a daughter on his own, letting her run completely wild?"

"I've heard the Count doesn't like women—"

"Well, I've heard he just doesn't like sex—"

"I've heard he just didn't like you . . ."

As they laughed, I smiled and pretended to be so smitten by Monsieur Cartier's words that I couldn't possibly hear anything they were saying, just as you taught me to do in such situations.

Once we made it through the parlor of leeches, the lady of the house whisked me away from Jean-Antoine's arm and whispered in my ear, "Child, I am so glad you made it."

I greeted her with affection and apologized for not sending notice.

"Leave it to Mademoiselle Saint-Germain to show up with the most beautiful man in Paris when she couldn't show up with the craziest man in France."

Blood invaded my cheeks. "My holiday to New France was supposed to be a secret, but it appears all of Paris knows."

"Well, my dear, you know secrets travel fast in Paris. It is not gossip you must worry about, only the days when you are not worth gossiping about."

Her words made me smile, as did the boisterous call from one of your favorite, and rather drunk, budding playwrights.

"Adeline Saint-Germain! If I send a manuscript with you, can you ensure it is the first comedy performed in *La Nouvelle-Orléans*?"

To which I replied, "In *La Nouvelle-Orléans*, your name will be bigger than Molière!"

Everyone laughed. I smiled, and before I could finish scanning the room, Monsieur Cartier was gently guiding me by the elbow through the crowd to a settee in a far corner.

"Mademoiselle," he said and offered me a glass of bubbling wine (it's becoming all the rage), which I gladly accepted after successfully navigating the blockade of Parisian aristocracy.

He began telling me about his adventures, and not long after, I found myself clinging to his every word. This surprised me, having witnessed men telling their tales, shouting their dramas, or drunkenly sobbing their poems since the day of my birth, thanks to your constant need to entertain, Father. I tried not to fiddle with the medallion strung around my neck, but I couldn't keep my hands still and didn't want to have an unfortunate accident with an airborne utensil.

Time flew by, and the sparkling wine never stopped. He confirmed the stories of endless opportunity: "For those who can survive the weather," he joked, "the air is always wet, as if the clouds are about to burst." He spoke of the beautiful homes the planters are building and how *la Louisianne* is not like any of the puritan British regions of the New Colonies.

"How could it be," he said. "After all, it's French."

There was no arrogance to his tone, so typical of Parisian intelligentsia, nor the abhorrent self-loathing of the artists they surround themselves with. He clearly knew I had been raised in the parlor rooms of some of the greatest salons in Paris, yet he was not intimidated in the slightest. And he seemed to take no notice of the other women in the room, who were all plotting their next moves to speak with him. He paid such close attention to my face that at times I couldn't help but feel like I was a caged canary and he a cat.

I had been utterly bored and lonely from the moment you left, and he was so charming—I soaked up his company. It all just felt too romantic, too perfect. His descriptions of the foreign land made it sound beautiful and exotic, and he also spoke of the endless opportunity in New France for the right kind of people—people who are resourceful.

"And you, mademoiselle," he said, "strike me as an extremely resourceful woman. You will love it there."

As the night went on, the more we drank and the more I prodded him for information, the more the stories moved in a darker direction. He told me of serpents and of rats the size of my arm and of flying bugs that pinch all over your skin in the night. He warned me that the streets were dangerous and told me strange tales about the native people and cannibals and young virgins being kidnapped! He spoke of enslaved Africans casting curses on their owners. I was enthralled by his experiences and jealous of his ability to live life as he so freely desired. His stories drew me so close at times I had to refrain from curling up into his lap.

Although he was full of information about his travels, anytime I queried him about his family, he managed to deflect. I kindly returned the gesture. But the more elusive one of us became, the deeper the other dug.

"You will find me to be a very patient man, Mademoiselle Saint-Germain," he said, in a way that I found quite coy.

"A quality not usually found in a man so young, Monsieur Cartier."

"I must confess, despite my age, I feel I have lived many lives. I have had so many trips, so many adventures—and fortunately, because of my age, I have so many yet to come."

Now, this is the most peculiar part of the story, Papa, and I know I already confessed to drinking perhaps too deeply of the wine, but I can assure you I tell this next account exactly as it happened.

We left the salon in his carriage, where I asked him to tell me the darkest encounter he had ever witnessed in *La Nouvelle-Orléans*. Suddenly, he grabbed both of my arms with great excitement and begged me not to go. His reaction left me completely confounded.

"You don't understand," he insisted. "It is dangerous. It is not safe for someone like you."

"Someone like me?"

"Someone . . . so beautiful. Someone so pure."

I laughed. "Dear Monsieur Cartier, I believe you have me mixed up with some other ingénue. I am certainly not as innocent as I look."

"You mock me . . ."

"Of course I mock you. You are speaking nonsense!"

"I could travel with you—there will be pirates on the water, looking to plunder and pillage. You might not even make it across the ocean! It might sound like nonsense, but I am absolutely serious."

"Serious? We leave for the coast tomorrow. The ship sets sail in a week! How would you even get a ticket?"

"I don't need a ticket. You could sneak me on board in your luggage." I stopped laughing when he grabbed my hands and held them tight. "I won't let anything happen to you; I give you my word."

His persona had seemed so demure all night—this behavior rendered me speechless. Now I could feel his strength through his grip. His power surprised me, and his cool touch excited me. I thought he might attempt to break the silence by kissing me, but instead, he looked intently into my eyes. "You will invite me to come with you, and you will allow me to stay inside your trunk, and you will tell no one we are traveling together."

Utterly flabbergasted, I stared blankly at him with bated breath. He didn't stir, nor did I as we bumped along in the carriage.

I held still until I could no longer contain myself, then I began to giggle uncontrollably. He huffed and puffed in frustration. Again, it seemed as if he had thought he could will me into doing whatever he wanted. I laughed until I was gasping for air and then leaned into his chest and took a deep breath.

His back stiffened, and he asked, "What, pray tell, are you doing?"

I took another deep inhale of his coat. "Monsieur Cartier, I am trying to figure out if you smoked an opium pipe while I wasn't looking."

"Adeline, you know I didn't leave your sight all night."

"That is true, but I cannot think of anything else that would make you say something so absurd."

He gazed upon my smile, bewildered and a bit sullen, as the carriage approached our house.

"Well, Monsieur Jean-Antoine Cartier, I do thank you for escorting me to the salon, and I do regret having only met you on my last night in Paris."

He helped me out of the carriage and bid me farewell before stepping back in. "It is not possible we will not see each other again, Mademoiselle Saint-Germain. That I can promise you. I bid you *au revoir*, till we meet again in *La Nouvelle-Orléans*."

"I cannot believe this is my last night. I believe my heart will always be here. *Je t'aime, Paris*."

He leaned out of the window and kissed both of my cheeks. "And Paris loves you."

Absorbed by his words, I smiled and waved as his coachman prepared to leave, but then he pulled my attention to him one last time:

"Mademoiselle Saint-Germain, do tell your father I called, *s'il vous plaît*."

His smile turned devilish as the carriage took off with a jolt, leaving behind only the echoes of hooves against the cobblestones.

CHAPTER 21

Macarons, Milk, and Metal

October 23rd

"Our city drowned two months and three weeks ago, and now the world's moving on without us."

The words of the ranting DJ became impossible to ignore. I broke from translating the diary and snapped the radio off. Even though I didn't want to hear it, the DJ was right: As fresher headlines popped up elsewhere, the national media started leaving town, and slowly the world had stopped paying attention. We'd been left to fend for ourselves on the eroding banks of the gulf, of the river, of time.

Time had always passed slowly in the South, but now it was like the Storm had hit the pause button, and we were frozen between frames. The pace of life had gone from slow to barely existent.

Progress stalled as local, state, and federal government agencies fought over control of funds and power. The longer things stalled, the more people blamed each other, and the more people blamed each other, the less rebuilding happened. We were quickly moving out of the we're-all-in-this-together phase and into bitterness, resentment, and outrage. Most of us were still at the mercy of the defunct power grid. We were still living under the mandatory curfew, and we were still eating scrounged canned goods. Of course, my father and I were far better off than the hundreds of thousands who were still displaced, not to mention those who hadn't survived. The body count continued to rise—both from the Storm and from the murder rate.

Thoughts of death forced everything else to escape to the back of my mind, except, of course, the supernatural questions that had plagued me even more since the night of our tour. The shutter. The attic. *The legend.* The dead blue eyes felt permanently stained behind my eyelids. *Could all the recent murders really just be a coincidence?* The alternative was so silly it stayed safely tucked away inside my head. But the longer the truth eluded me, the more torturous every hour of every day became, until eventually I was drifting along in an incessant dream-state. In this dream-state I believed *vampires could exist.*

Believing this fundamentally changed the way I looked at everything. It must be how people felt when they found God—processing everything after that moment in a brand-new way.

I had no proof of their existence, just this feeling, like the puzzle pieces of my brain had suddenly snapped into place. The only point of comparison I had was the Santa Claus discovery. I had only been seven years old, but I could still remember that exact moment when it all suddenly made sense—the cookies, the presents, the reindeer—it was this very distinct moment of clarity. I'd rushed to my father and demanded evidence as to how a fat man could come through our chimney. He immediately went into crisis mode, stuck between the adult thing to do and the parental thing to do. When I threatened to drag Jeanne and Sébastien, the eleven-year-old future scientists, into the discussion, he caved and told me the truth.

We hadn't had any secrets since. In retrospect, I think he was relieved not to have to keep up the fantasy any longer.

Even as a kid, I'd felt so silly knowing I'd believed the hoax when the truth had been so obvious.

I'd needed proof then. And that's what I needed now.

I had to find evidence that would weave this dream-state, in which vampires *could* exist, with the reality that taught me the idea was fiction. This time, I couldn't rely on my father or the twins to confirm my hypothesis. They'd think I was crazy. When I thought about it, I felt crazy.

Am I crazy?

When I asked myself too many questions, everything began to unravel. A little voice inside my head warned me to let it go, but that was no longer an option—it felt powerful to know something no one else knew. However, with no idea where to start, I felt like Alice chasing the White Rabbit's shadow, fumbling around in the dark for the hole, for the fall, for the proof of Wonderland's existence.

In this chase, the rabbit morphed into Adeline Saint-Germain, whom I'd become instantaneously obsessed with. Chasing her shadow. Her ghost. Neither her necklace nor her diary was ever more than an arm's length away. My attachment to these artifacts was different from the love I usually had for all things vintage. I had an inexplicable, overwhelming need to protect them. I didn't even show the diary to my father. *What if he asks me where I found it?* I worried constantly that anything abnormal might result in a one-way ticket back to Paris.

Unfortunately, thanks to Franz Kafka and a mountain of other "so you can catch up with the other Sacred Heart students" homework, plus my mentorship, I was swamped. But still, I fell asleep each night translating the pages. The ornate handwriting, faded antique ink, and eighteenth-century French made the translation process drag, but I continued obsessively nonetheless, hanging on to every word, romanticizing Adeline's *grande aventure*.

———

I felt myself becoming more and more withdrawn, which wasn't difficult given no one at school spoke to me except for Thurston Van der Veer, who turned out to be Annabelle Lee's boyfriend. Yes, boyfriend. *Gay or straight or whatever—didn't he know other girls were not allowed to speak to Annabelle Lee Drake's boyfriend?*

This, of course, made me a massive target with Annabelle's clique.

The worst part was that although I could feel the hate emanating from Annabelle Lee (and so could everyone else), she was always sweet as pie to me, even though the fake tone in her voice sent a signal to all those within earshot that I was not to be welcomed, spoken to, assisted, or even looked at until she decided what to do with me. She was a shark, constantly circling, just waiting for the right time to attack. No one wanted to be near the shark bait. With good reason.

As far as I could tell, there were only two people who didn't bow down to her authority. The first was her bestie. Don't get me wrong, Désirée was deeply woven into the social order of the student population, but her general attitude of disdain seemed to trump everything, including Annabelle's dictatorship. I guess that's what happens when you're born with everything or when your father's the mayor. Or maybe it's just what happens when you're that beautiful—rules no longer apply to you.

Ugh.

Everything about high school seemed so trite now. I pretended not to care.

The only person who outright refused to bow down to Annabelle or any social hierarchy in the school was Tyrelle Laurent, unlike Dixie Hunter, who, every day, made it apparent how ready and willing she was to do whatever was necessary to earn a permanent place in Annabelle's throng. I did everything I could to try to win Tyrelle over—my next step was to cook up the dusty box of brownie mix in our pantry (with no milk or eggs) and beg. The grapevine told me he was the son of one of the most famous rappers ever to come out of New Orleans or all of the Dirty South. His father had been in more scuffles with the law than could be counted on two hands, and one of his brothers was currently serving time for an infraction involving a gun. So everyone steered totally clear of him, as if he were suddenly going to pop a cap. Tyrelle seemed to like it that way, but I was pretty sure the only thing he was popping was the curve in our physics class.

I tried to keep a low profile, but sometimes my parlor trick made that impossible. On multiple occasions, I hadn't been able to keep my locker from slamming open, and once it nearly clocked the head of a burly lacrosse player whose locker was on my left. He thought I was flirting and said something idiotic like, "So, you like it rough?"

Tyrelle, whose locker was on my right, had laughed (at the locker slamming the lacrosse player, not at the lacrosse player sexually harassing me). I wanted to punch them both, but I was so nervous, wondering whether Tyrelle had seen what really happened, that I just ran away.

The angrier I became at Annabelle Lee Drake, the more impossible it became to control my abilities—until today.

I was at Café Orléans—just me and my textbooks, which were strewn about the counter, along with a half dozen papers where I'd tried six times to solve the same equation, getting a different answer each time. It was hard to focus because all I wanted to do was translate more of Adeline's diary.

That counts as studying for my French midterm, right?
Before I could answer myself, my phone buzzed.

Pépé   4:30 p.m.   Préparer un pot frais de
                                     chicorée.

"Yes, sir, a fresh pot of chicory, coming up!" I smiled, still not used to getting messages from him. Before the Storm, he'd refused to learn how to use his phone for anything more than talking, but these days in

New Orleans, it was the only form of communication that worked on a semiregular basis.

I hope that means he's coming by.

I dumped out the nearly-full pot I had brewed this morning, which had thickened, sitting on the burner all day.

"Tout va bien?" came a voice from the door.

"Bastien!" When I turned, I found a look of concern on his face. I was so excited to see a familiar face I ran around the corner to give him a hug.

"Is everything okay?" he asked again.

"Yeah . . . of course. Unless you are talking about my precal." I pointed to the pile of chicken scratch as I walked behind the counter. He barely looked at it for ten seconds before he grabbed a pen and marked it up. "You need to use the expanding binomial theorem."

"I know! That's what I was doing . . ."

"Is that what this is?"

"All six times—"

"Tout va bien?" Jeanne yelled, hardly in the door.

"What's with you two? Everything's fine."

She held her phone up to her brother, and then he held up his. They both had the same message from Pépé, asking them to come to the café right away.

"All I got was a message about making coffee," I said, holding up my phone.

"What the heck? I just ruined an entire batch of . . ."

"All of her experiments are time sensitive," Sébastien explained as she rattled off a string of six-syllable chemicals.

The back door to the courtyard opened.

"Is Bertrand here yet?" Mémé asked.

"No," all three of us replied.

"Is everything okay?" Sébastien asked her.

"Everything's fine. He said he had a surprise. He wouldn't even tell *me*! I hope it's good news from our insurance agent about the roasters."

Me too. The roasters was just a couple blocks from one of the levee breaches in the Ninth Ward. Standing water had been inside for weeks.

They all began to speculate, while I ground the coffee beans, their voices rising and falling with the timing of the grinder. I added a scoop of chicory, and just as I turned the machine on, in walked Pépé.

"*Parfait!* You're all here!" he said with absolute seriousness. Everyone stopped in silence. Both of his hands were behind his back, and he was trying not to smile. He spoke slowly in French, for peak dramatic tension. "Me and a couple of the boys were out driving, trying to find some building materials, and we drove past this farmer, sitting in the back of his truck with an ice chest—"

"Is that what I think it is?" I yelped, moving my head to try to see behind his back.

"*Oui, mon chou!*" he yelled, thrusting the two bags forward. It was easy to see through the white plastic grocery bags, and in each were three glass quarts . . . of milk.

"Oh my God!" I yelled, running around the counter. I gave him a hug before taking the bags from him.

"Café au lait for everyone!" Mémé yelled.

"You pulled me away from school for milk?" said Jeanne.

"Okay, none for you!" I said.

"*Non!*" she yelled, playfully grabbing my ponytail as I went back behind the counter.

"You had me worried that something was wrong, Pépé," Sébastien said, taking a seat at a table with his grandfather.

"Me too," his sister added, taking a seat on Pépé's other side.

"You two are too serious," he told them in French. We all laughed as he continued to poke fun at them.

Mémé set five cups with saucers on the counter, filled them halfway with coffee, and then left them there for me to finish. She joined them at the table while I steamed the milk into creamy white foam. After I filled the first cup, I couldn't wait any longer. I put down the metal steaming pot, grabbed the mug, and brought it to my lips. The first sip burned my tongue, but I didn't care. I greedily took another. The mixture tasted like a robust jazz trill. Familiar and soothing and provocative all at once. It tasted like New Orleans.

I quickly filled the remaining mugs, and Sébastien helped me carry them to the table.

"Is this even pasteurized—?" asked Jeanne.

"Oh, shush!" her grandmother answered.

"All I'm saying is that I have antibiotics back at school if anyone gets infected by salmonella . . . or E. coli . . . or listeria—"

"Just enjoy it," Pépé yelled, laughing. We all knew this was her way of enjoying it. I savored every sip as I sat listening to them talk, and in that moment I didn't care if I died from dysentery.

"One more thing!" Mémé said. She pulled a familiar green box from her bag. "I've been saving mine for a special occasion!"

"Amour paradisiaque!" Jeanne yelled, taking the box of macarons I'd brought from Paris.

"I want the pistachio!" Sébastien tried to grab the box from her, but she was too quick.

The French delicacies crunched when they shouldn't have crunched but never tasted better. It wasn't long before they were all gone, along with the pot of coffee and the first quart of milk.

Mémé helped me clear the table. As I washed the dishes in the sink behind the counter, she squeezed her fragile arms around me. "You know, you can come up and visit while I am doing paperwork, anytime you'd like."

"I know. *Merci beaucoup*," I said. She kissed my cheeks before heading upstairs with Pépé.

"We're going to be the cat's meow around here," I said, crouching to look at the remaining quarts of milk in the minifridge under the counter. When I got no response, I looked up. Sébastien was examining something on the counter with a perplexed look.

"What are these lists?" he asked.

He was reading a page in my journal, which I'd accidentally left open—my documentation of everything I'd either succeeded or failed at moving telekinetically.

"Ugh . . ." I coyly tried to turn the tables. "What do you think the lists are?"

Jeanne peeked over his shoulder and took a look for herself. "A list of objects that contain metals and a list of . . . random junk."

I ripped the notebook back and scoured the lists. *I am an idiot.*

But I was too excited to be down on myself about the oversight. "How do you do that?!"

"Do what?"

"Nothing. Never mind."

"What are the lists for?"

"Um . . ."

Maybe I should just tell them? But, with no evidence to support my claims, the scientists in them would fret over my lunatic hypothesis connecting the convent attic and the current murder spree. Of course, I did have one piece of proof that something in my life was awry, but I wasn't willing to reveal that just yet.

"It's just something for my physics lab . . . materials, magnetism."

"In a high school–level physics class?" Jeanne asked. "I thought that school was supposed to be the best. *Sheesh.*"

My answer must have been decent enough, because they didn't ask any more questions, and they both stuck around, helping me prep for my precal midterm until curfew.

Needless to say, apprenticing with my father in the metal shop was about to become a lot more interesting.

But until then, it was just me and Adeline and the Atlantic Ocean.

CHAPTER 22

Bon voyage

(Translated from French.)

10th March 1728

One would think, stuck aboard a ship with no one other than nuns and orphans, I would be writing nonstop simply out of boredom, but alas, somehow the time slips. The good news is I have gotten my sea legs, as the sailors say, so now it is easier to write without feeling dizzy from the constant push and pull of the ocean's grip. The weather has been tumultuous, with rain pounding down on our vessel both night and day, but finally the sun is shining, and one of the sailors has secured my parasol on the deck to help shield me from both the blazing rays and the ocean's spray.

As the sailors hustle around me, pushing the ship to her limits to make up for lost time, I sit in solitude, recording this adventure, wondering where in the world you are, and praying that writing to you will distract me from the ever-present cabin fever. Father, I do trust you have a good reason for sending me to *La Nouvelle-Orléans*; however, I wish you would have given more careful consideration to your choice of chaperones for me. One would have thought my nursemaid of sixteen years would have been a better choice rather than Monsieur and Madame DuFrense, who still seem like strangers.

I have had one good conversation with Claude DuFrense, who seems to be pleasant enough: he explained to me the layout of the town whilst describing the real estate plans you have invested in together. His fervor for the endless investment opportunity is infectious; however, his wife is less than thrilled to be "ripped away from the heart of the world." The much-younger Martine DuFrense, whose rosy cheeks and honey-colored curls best match the elaborate costumes of the theatre stages she was used to in France, has made it abundantly clear that, having left the grand opera companies of Paris, her life is now over. Claude promises to build her the grandest opera house in all the world, and being reminded of this momentarily raises her spirits, but most of the time she stays locked up in their cabin, sinking further into depression.

I hope that once the weather permits a bit of socializing on the deck, Martine and I can be friends. Almost none of the other passengers will speak to me—everyone knows I am the daughter of a count. Besides the DuFrenses, this leaves me with only Captain Vauberci and the Reverend Mother Superior Marie Lorient. I will try not to harp on this now and will instead give you the details you requested, no matter how banal I consider them.

Every morning is the same: breakfast with Claude, Martine, and the captain, which consists mostly of a little bread and hard cheese. We are also given dried figs and a lump of sugar each for our tea, which riddles me with guilt as the orphans, who get none, sit near us at one long table.

If I have counted correctly, on board there are twenty-six teenage girls, all being sent to *La Nouvelle-Orléans* at the request of the king, and six sisters of the Order of Saint Ursula, who are looking after them and who will board and school them until they are all married off to

French settlers in the new colony. All of the passengers are stacked in bunks of six to a room, except for three orphans who, for some reason, were given their own cabin. Of course, I have my own *première classe* cabin, as do the DuFrenses.

I hope over time the usual societal hierarchies can be abandoned, even if only temporarily, while we are trapped aboard this ship; otherwise I might have to throw myself overboard to avoid dying of boredom. As things stand now, I end up spending most of my time talking about our destination with the crewmen, who have no problem speaking out of social order—as long as the captain is out of earshot.

17th March 1728

My sincerest apologies for not writing, but the task of reliving the boring days by writing them down is even worse than living them. My health has been good, but some of the orphans have suffered from seasickness. The poor things sometimes look so pale and can do nothing but lie in their cabins suffering from light-headedness and fevered dreams. Other than a couple of screams in the middle of the night from these sickly girls, there really has been nothing to report.

Despite the seasickness and only having the slightest amenities, there is a strong sense of camaraderie amongst the orphans. Every day I grow more jealous of them. The orphans have each other, the DuFrenses have each other, and the nuns have each other—even the crewmen have each other. I try not to wallow in my own misery because, as you know, being emotional makes it more difficult for me to control myself.

Captain Vauberci senses my loneliness and sometimes invites me to sit next to him while he uses foreign instruments to study the stars and keep us on track. He tells me stories as he drinks spirits in between shouting commands at the crew. I often wonder if his kindness is just out of obligation because of the fame your name carries, Father. Either way, he is the only companion I have. If only the society ladies could see me now, sitting alone with the drunk, middle-aged captain. It would be gossip enough to keep them entertained all season.

23rd March 1728

As my loneliness continues to grow, there are three girls in particular whose bond drives me mad with jealousy. They are sisters—triplets, in fact, with the exact same fair skin and blond hair so bright it shimmers white like the moon. They don't get the same special treatment my ticket affords, but they are the ones I previously mentioned who have their own cabin to share, despite being with the "King's Daughters," as I have heard the orphans called by the crew.

These triplets have a sense of spirit that seems to transcend societal constraints, yet they still do not speak to me. I cannot understand why not, and this is what drives me mad! I long to talk, to laugh, to sing, to dance, but more than anything, I long to know these sisters, and yet every time I approach them, they stop their excitable whispers. They don't look at the ground when I pass, like the other girls do; they look at me with suspicion, as if trying to figure out whether or not to trust me—a feeling I am all too accustomed to from hobnobbing with the Parisian aristocracy. Sometimes at night I pass a dormitory cabin and hear them singing to entertain or comfort the other girls, and last night I caught them on deck, dancing under the light of the moon! They looked like goddesses, with their hair loose and wild and their night-gowns fluttering in the nautical breeze. They danced and giggled, utterly unconcerned that their bare feet were exposed to the elements! I have never wanted anything more than to join them, but fear of rejection kept me in the shadows, alone in my misery.

Each day, I find myself becoming more and more withdrawn, Papa.

This is absurd! If I can survive sixteen years of the scandal and rumors that come with being the daughter of *le Comte de Saint-Germain*, then I can certainly befriend these sisters. Tonight, I will devise a plan.

24th March 1728

At breakfast, I snuck my lump of sugar and dried figs into a fold of my dress, along with a seashell given to me by a sailor, and left these small tokens, wrapped in a hair ribbon, on the pillow that had been monogrammed with the letter *C*, which I assumed stood for the sister I've heard called Cosette, whose astute behavior leads me to believe is the eldest of the three.

27th March 1728

After three days of leaving small treats to no avail, I returned to my cabin to find the hair ribbons tied to my doorknob. I hope this is a sign that things are progressing favorably.

28th March 1728

Today was the most eventful evening since leaving Paris, Papa! I was feeling restless after another sluggish day, and even though we are not supposed to leave our cabins after dark, I threw my cloak over my sleeping gown and slipped into the narrow path of light created by the beams of the crescent moon.

On deck, nightfall had unveiled a sky of a million stars. The crashing waves disturbed the silent night, and the cold spray enlivened my senses. The closer I got to the far end of the ship, the louder I heard the beautiful sounds of song. I hurried to find the source.

At the end of the stern, I saw the backs of Cosette, Minette, and Lisette—the triplets. They were sitting with their feet dangling over the water, seemingly without fear of being washed overboard, singing "Au Clair de la Lune," a lullaby learned by all French children. The melody blended with the waves in a delicate harmony, as if the ocean herself knew the tune. The sailors sat perched like stone gargoyles at their night posts, so comforted by the lullaby that they allowed the girls to continue rather than sending them back to bed.

Careful not to disturb them, I sat next to Cosette, and after a breath I joined the verse. They looked at me for a moment, and then we continued the lullaby together, looking back toward the hidden horizon. Happiness overwhelmed me as I searched for the line where the real stars ended and their reflections on the black waves began. I closed my eyes and became lost in the motion of the boat.

At some point during the song, everything became as it should. We knew that our voices blended together were stronger than each was on its own. It was a feeling of kinship I had never felt before, a feeling of great power.

Soaking wet, we continued to sing for another hour, through our chattering teeth. I thought nothing could ruin that moment of perfect serenity, until a bloodcurdling scream tore through the SS *Gironde*.

Instantly the four of us, along with several of the lullaby-hazed seamen, took off running toward the scream. By the time we reached the dormitory corridor, there were already half a dozen sailors with swords in hand, ready to battle any intruder who may have stowed away.

Inside one of the cabins, a nun cradled an orphan whilst another held up a lantern to the girl's ghostly face; a third began shooing the men out of the room. Sweat fell from the girl's forehead, and blood was smeared down her chest. Minette took her hand and called out her name, but despite her chest rising and falling, nothing made her respond.

Cosette tried to coax an explanation from the other girls in the room, but they had all been asleep.

As one of the nuns cleaned the wound, it was deduced that the sick girl must have suffered a fevered nightmare, due to seasickness, and scratched herself in her sleep. Nevertheless, the captain stationed a sailor to guard the door.

Alas, as I write, I see shadows passing through the hallway light that shines under my door. I must now extinguish my flame, as we are not allowed to use candles or lanterns in our rooms, not that I have either.

1st April 1728

The injured girl, Sophie, keeps a temperature too high to wake from. Cosette has been sneaking into her room with a pulp made from herbs she steals from the kitchen. She applies the mixture to the girl's wound, which she seems to have developed a mild obsession with. I find this to be a tad gruesome.

Other girls continue to suffer from seasickness, especially in the mornings, but the symptoms usually dissipate by lunchtime. Nothing more out of the ordinary has happened. I spend my days either on my own or with the DuFrenses, and my nights with my three new companions.

7th April 1728

Sophie continues to live without waking. The nuns pray over her every morning and evening, but I am beginning to fear the worst.

Martine DuFrense does not approve of my spending so much time with the triplets, but their friendship keeps me from the brink of insanity whilst aboard this ship. We read to each other, play cards, or make up silly games to pass the time. Sometimes we gossip—we suspect one of the orphans is having an affair with a sailor! Lisette, or Lise as she prefers to be called, claims to have seen his silhouette sneaking into the girl's room in the middle of the night.

If they are caught, I'm not sure whom they should fear the most: the captain or the mother superior, who has a kind face but whom I sometimes think is the one who truly rules the SS *Gironde*. I hate to laugh at the misfortunes of others, but at this point, the entertainment of it all would be grand.

In regard to entertainment, it is a pity to have aboard this ship a well-known opera singer and three sisters talented enough to have sung for the king of France yet spend the days and nights without performances. It is my new mission to arrange one for everyone on the boat. I believe it will do wonders for Martine's spirit.

That's correct, Papa, I said the triplets attended French court! Like me, the triplets are sixteen years of age, and they too lost their mother early on, but even worse, they also lost their father and were made wards of the state at the age of seven. At thirteen, they ran away from the orphanage to join a traveling theatre troupe, which eventually received an invitation to perform at the palace. The king loved the audition but especially loved the triplets, and so the whole troupe was invited to become a regular act in his court, and soon they were entertaining the French elite during the royal soirées. Lise told me Cosette is such a talented pianist that the queen herself arranged for private lessons, which caused quite a scandal with the tenured court musicians.

Papa, for the first time in my life, I wish I had accepted more invitations to the palace—it's quite crazy to think I could have possibly seen a performance! Never in a million years would I have guessed I would meet girls aboard this ship who were able to trade stories about members of French society. But these sisters know far more than any socialite, for they have witnessed so many events, so many parties, so many nights of debauchery.

"I don't understand," I told them one late afternoon while Lisette finished braiding my hair. "How did you end up on this ship? Why would you ever want to leave your troupe?"

Their heads tilted like dominoes, as if to silently agree on how much information to share, and then Lise admitted with a sigh, "There was a scandal at the palace."

Minette clarified, "Well, not really a scandal, because nothing actually happened."

"It was a *rumor*," said Cosette, but then Lise explained, "You see, many of the ladies at court envied Cosette. Everyone was jealous of her beauty and her talent."

Cosette blushed deeply. "They were jealous of *all* of us. We are identical, remember?"

Her sisters giggled, and then, without a twinge of jealousy, Lise said, "It's true that we look the same, but you are modest, Sister, for it is you whom every man is drawn to."

Cosette peered out the tiny, round window. "Yes, I caused our demise."

"Oh, don't be so theatrical," said Minette. "You know that is not what she meant."

I understood. All three look identical at first glance, but their personalities are in such stark contrast that once you spend time around them, they begin to appear as different as the sun, moon, and stars. Lisette is cheery and optimistic, which makes her seem younger; Minette is bookish and shy, which makes her seem delicate; and Cosette is utterly fearless both with her actions and her tongue (yet somehow everything comes out of her mouth in flowery song). It is easy to see how any man would vow to follow her to the end of the Earth. I could imagine the ladies in court, whose riches make them bitter and plump, hating any girl with Cosette's magnetism.

"Well, it doesn't matter now," Cosette said. "Once a few of the ladies got it into their heads that we were to be removed from court, it was only a matter of time."

"We're lucky we got out with our heads," said Lisette.

"What do you mean?" I asked, for that seemed a little extreme, even for the French.

Minette pulled me next to her on the bed. "Those women did everything they could to have us removed. They went to work digging up our past. You see, Adeline, we had been traveling with our troupe under the name of *Les Sœurs d'Or*."

"Because of your golden hair?"

"Precisely. But when the women of court discovered our birth name was really Monvoisin—"

"Monvoisin?" I interjected. "But certainly no relation to *La Voisin*?" I asked the question assuming that the answer would be a firm *no*, but you'll never guess what came out of Cosette's mouth, Papa!

"Yes, sweet Adeline," she whispered. "We are the granddaughters of Catherine Deshayes Monvoisin, 'the Great Poisoner'—or so they called her when they burned her alive!"

Upon learning this news, I couldn't help but sit back with a little smile on my face, for I am not one to be easily shocked by scandal, yet this was the last thing I ever expected to hear from these innocent girls. Upon reflection, I knew there was a reason I was so attracted to them from the moment we stepped on board this ship.

Minette continued the story: "When the women of court discovered our birth name, suddenly one of the servants turned up dead, and when the court doctor announced the cause of death was poison, someone conveniently announced our relation to La Voisin and accused us of murder! They demanded we be sent to the guillotine, but luckily for us the king's mistress understood what was going on and begged him to show mercy to us. The king consented, and so we found ourselves being smuggled out of the palace, each of us with a cassette containing a wedding dress and dowry, to join the girls being sent to marry the townsmen in *La Nouvelle-Orléans*."

"Lucky us," said Cosette.

Knowing the triplets are descendants of Catherine Deshayes Monvoisin and, therefore, connected to *l'affaire des poisons*—the greatest scandal in the history of French court—only makes me sympathize even more with their plight and feel closer to them.

Living with the reputation of those who came before us is just one more thing we share in common.

10th April 1728

I knew deep within my soul it was bound to happen, that our secrets were bound to become intertwined. Tonight was the night, Papa!

Despite the late hour, I was in the Monvoisin sisters' cabin. Minette was teaching me how to mend my skirt, and Cosette was writing in her diary, when Lise burst through the door.

"He's here! He's here!" she yelled, but then she clammed up, realizing her sisters weren't alone.

"Who is here?" Minette asked.

The question was not permissive enough for Lise. Cosette wrapped an arm around her sister's shoulder and sat her on the bed next to me. Minette dropped to the floor in front of us, took her sister's hand, and asked in a hushed voice, "Are you trying to say what I think you—"

"*Oui!* He's here. The man from the dock is here, on this boat."

"What man from the dock?" I asked, trying not to become agitated by the sudden cryptic air.

"Shh!" all three of them hissed at once.

"What man from the dock?" I whispered, my curiosity now fully piqued, but again, Lise looked to her sisters, unsure whether or not to divulge the answer.

The idea of having secrets between us broke my heart. I knew the possible implications of revealing myself to them—you have warned me of the consequences ever since I was a child—but my shoulders felt like they were growing flaming wings as they continued to debate my trustworthiness in hushed voices.

I sprang off the bed. "I cannot stand for there to be any secrets between us!" My voice shook, as I knew what I was about to do, although deep down inside, I trusted the triplets completely.

As I raised my arm to a small iron candelabrum on the wall, my heart pounded so hard it felt like my chest might rip open. I had never showed my magic to anyone other than you, Papa. But before I could think about it any longer, my wrist flicked, and the iron fixture tore from the wall and flew into my hand. With the triplets watching, the rush was indescribable: quite possibly more exhilarating than even the first time I moved an object with my mind.

The room became perfectly silent as I grasped the dusty piece of metal.

I had originally planned on stopping there, but their lack of judgment encouraged my showmanship. I cupped the waxless candelabrum, and almost instantly, the light shining between the cracks of my fingers glowed so warm I had to move my hand, exposing the flame to the wide-eyed girls.

"Now you know my secret." Despite my racing pulse, the words came out clear and calm.

I watched the reflection from the fire flicker in Cosette's golden-brown eyes. As her smile grew, I knew things would never be the same . . . Nor would I ever again be alone with my secret.

CHAPTER 23

A Whirlwind Romance

October 24th

All night I had dreamed of fire, and now it was all I could think about as my father droned in the background about the art of lost-wax casting. *Adeline could produce a flame from thin air . . .*

"Don't rush," he was saying. "Precision is key. The more you learn to control your movements, the better you'll be able to control the outcome of the piece."

Two brass candlesticks he'd made before the Storm, now left in a pile of metal objects awaiting polishing, kept grabbing my attention.

"Ha. I thought *control* was for the scientists," Isaac joked.

"There's a fine line between art and science when it comes to working with metal, and blurring of the two dates all the way back to the Bronze Age . . . Take out your wax sculptures."

I peeked at Isaac's piece. Even in the cobalt wax, the perfectly sculpted feather looked real—he must have spent hours scraping out each little hairline wisp. For someone with such an abrasive personality, he certainly had a delicate hand when it came to his art. It was going to look amazing once it was cast in silver: this lesson's metal of choice.

My fingers were still raw from accidentally scraping my skin with the metal files while carving my wax star. I'd become obsessive over the symmetry of the eight points, wanting the little lines to match up perfectly like patchwork. Next to Isaac's piece, it looked basic, but I wanted to replace the missing star on ASG's necklace, Adeline's necklace.

My necklace.

I rubbed my thumb over the rough impression the original star had left behind on the medallion.

I'll do something more complicated next time, I reassured myself, placing my little wax sculpture over it. A perfect fit. I envisioned what the silver version would look like after I cast it, and then came to a realization that made my breath cut short.

"I am such an idiot," I whispered.

"What?" asked Isaac, looking up from his carving tools.

"Nothing," I snapped. I smiled to make up for the tone. "Just talking to myself."

"Right." He raised one eyebrow and went back to his feather.

I grabbed my phone and quickly banged out a text to Brooke, who still hadn't returned any of my messages since our call.

Adele	3:30 p.m.	Random Q: do you still have the star charm I gave you a couple of years ago? Is it with you in L.A.?

When we were thirteen, I'd found a star-shaped charm in an old cigar box, along with a bunch of other buttons, loose stones, and metal scraps that had collected in my dad's studio over the decades. *An eight-pointed star charm,* if my memory served me correctly. I'd fallen in love with it instantly. My father taught me how to polish it, and I didn't take it off all summer. Not until freshman year started and Brooke was chosen to sing "The Star-Spangled Banner" before a Saints game. It was the only time I'd ever seen her nervous before a performance. She was terrified. I took the charm off, wrapped it around her neck, and told her she was going to be a star one day. She killed it onstage and claimed the star as her good-luck charm. Afterward, knowing I'd given away my prized possession, my father surprised me with the sun charm currently hanging around my chain. I liked it even better and had probably worn it every day since.

Surely she took the star with her to Los Angeles? I texted her again:

Adele	**3:36 p.m.**	It's kind of important. Just want to know if it's here in the city. If not, maybe you could mail it back to me? I know you don't need luck anymore (not that you ever did).

What else could I say? "I'm looking for clues about the vampires I accidentally released from a convent" seemed slightly out of the question, although it may have elicited a quicker response.

Ten minutes later, my phone buzzed.

Brooke	**3:46 p.m.**	Is this a joke?

Adele	**3:47 p.m.**	No... it's kind of complicated. Do you have it? My dad is teaching me to cast, so I can make you a better one, completely made by moi!

| Brooke | 3:48 p.m. | Just b/c I've been busy, you want your necklace back? Doesn't sound complicated to me. |

| Brooke | 3:48 p.m. | And how can you say I don't need luck anymore? Have you suddenly forgotten about everything that happened to me in the last 3 months? |

| Brooke | 3:48 p.m. | Whatever... |

| Adele | 3:49 p.m. | Maybe it would sound more complicated if you ever returned my calls!? There's a lot of crazy shit going on down here! You aren't the only person going through a lot these days. |

| Brooke | 3:51 p.m. | I'd know what's going on if you had moved to L.A.!!!!!! |

| Adele | 3:52 p.m. | Thanks for understanding... Can you just tell me if you have the charm? |

Brooke	**3:53 p.m.**	I didn't bring it. Have fun digging around in what's left of our house. I'm sure one of your new friends at THE ACADEMY would love an old piece of tarnished silver.

I slammed my phone down.

"Are you sure you're okay?" Isaac asked.

"Fine." I tried to contort my scowl into a convincing smile.

In the past, fighting with Brooke would have brought me to tears, but this was actually some semblance of good news: she hadn't taken the charm out west. I gave myself a reality check—the likelihood of finding something so teeny in her house was slim to none. But who knows? It was certainly worth a try.

"Dad, we're almost done here, right? Brooke needs me to go over to her house and look for something."

"Yes, but I have to go to work after this."

"So?"

"I can't take you."

"Take me?" Brooke's house was a fifteen-minute walk, tops, and an even quicker bike ride. I'd probably done it a thousand times. "Dad, I don't need you to come with me."

"Adele, I don't want you going out that far by yourself. It's going to be dark soon."

"Far? It's not far!"

"That's final. I don't want you going into the Tremé by yourself."

"What? That's ridic—"

"In fact, I don't want you leaving the French Quarter by yourself. Besides, the Joneses' house might have structural damage."

"Dad . . ."

"I can take her," Isaac volunteered. "We won't go inside the house if the conditions are too bad."

"Don't *do* that!" I yelled at him.

"Do what?"

"Don't talk about me as if I'm not here! It's *you*. I can take *you*." The carving tools on the table started to tremble.

Breathe.

Thank God they were both too distracted by my outburst to notice.

"I'm sorry, Adele, I can escort *you* on your errand, if you'll allow me the privilege." He smiled at me in a way that was not meant to antagonize, so I tried not to take it that way.

Dead, blue eyes flashed in my mind.

"Merci beaucoup," I said through gritted teeth, knowing this was my only chance of charm-hunting today. I couldn't pass up an opportunity to find a missing puzzle piece.

"We'll be back before curfew, Mac—"

"Be back before sundown."

"Uh, okay, sir."

"Fine with me," I said with more bite than necessary. "There's no point in staying after dark, given there's no electricity." *What was my father's obsession with getting the bar in order?* Nothing indicated the curfew was going to be lifted any time soon.

"Here, take the car." My father tossed his keys to Isaac. "It will be quicker and safer."

WHAT? My father is letting Isaac take his car out?

"Now I really feel like I'm on another planet," I said under my breath.

A huge grin spread over Isaac's face. "Thanks, Mac! You have nothing to worry about."

"You'll have my daughter and my car. I have everything to worry about."

Almost blushing, Isaac skirted out of the room to change into a cleaner set of clothes. My eyes went to the ceiling.

"I'm sorry, sweetheart. I know this isn't easy, but it's just the way it has to be right now. Things will go back to normal eventually." He kissed the top of my head.

Normal? I thought, watching him hurry off to work. *What does that even mean anymore? Flying keys. Exploding lightbulbs. Coexisting with a bunch of severely undernourished vampires?* Things were never going to be *normal* again.

Waiting for Isaac, I eyed his sketchbook on the table, then seized the opportunity. "This is a total invasion of privacy, Adele," I whispered, flipping it open.

There was the sketch of his feather. I turned the page. More feathers of all shapes and sizes—some beautiful, others dark with severe lines and shading. I flipped through a few more pages and stopped, letting the book fall open on the table.

There I was, staring back at myself.

Or was it me?

The girl in the portrait faintly shared my facial features, but her hair was longer and swept up in an intricate style, and she wore a gown more likely to be found in Marie Antoinette's wardrobe than mine. On the next page, there she was again, and again, and again. I stopped when I landed on a sketch of the girl holding out a candlestick. There was no wax candle in the holder, and yet there was a bright flame, causing her face to glow.

"What the hell, Isaac?" I whispered.

"What the hell *what?*"

I slammed the book shut and spun around.

"Obsessed with feathers, much?" I squeaked.

He gave me a strange look and stuffed the sketchbook into his knapsack.

The Faubourg Tremé bordered the northern perimeter of the Quarter, so the ride was quick but nonetheless awkward. Surely Isaac knew I'd been snooping, but he didn't seem angry. In fact, he seemed a bit sheepish, which was exactly how I felt. In a way, we were both guilty of the same thing: we'd both been caught spying on the other.

To fill the silence, he gave me a progress report on the back wall of the studio. I listened overattentively as I directed him to the Joneses', but he stopped midsentence when we crossed North Rampart Street into the Tremé.

I mentally prepared myself as the conditions gradually got worse—I did *not* want to appear weak in front of him. Isaac was used to seeing this level of devastation every day.

We had no choice but to park three blocks away. Isaac looked nervous about leaving my father's baby out of sight with looters still running amok, but I took off, giving him no choice other than to catch up.

Glass crunched underneath our feet, a sound I was getting used to. Even though the sun was still up, the street felt gloomy. We walked past a house that'd been torn in half by a fallen oak tree and another whose façade had been smashed by a truck.

My nervous excitement about finding the charm fizzled as I walked up the porch steps of Brooke's house, which was painted a robin's egg color that used to rival Tiffany's. Now the residence, like all the others on the block, looked as if it had been abandoned seventy years ago. The screen door was missing, and the porch was not much more than a pile of tinder. The waterline cleared my head by several feet, and the now-familiar *X* had been spray-painted on the exterior in black and orange. Fortunately, it was filled with zeros.

My fingers were raw from filing away at my sculpture, but still I wrestled with the spare set of keys in the front door—only when they nearly bled did I step aside and let Isaac bully it open. Immediately, my hand jerked over my nose.

I gagged on the overwhelming sour stench of rot as I forced myself to walk inside.

Hundreds of thousands of tiny black specks of mold had spread up the walls, all the way to the high ceilings, like an attacking virus. My body shuddered as I tried to keep my stomach muscles from jerking.

Isaac produced a bandanna from his pocket. "It's not a fix, but it should help." He struggled not to cough as he tied the fabric loosely over my nose. He did a good job hiding it, but I caught his abs twitching.

"I'll be fine," he said.

I breathed slowly through the fabric—the first breath into the cloth smelled musky, like him, but that was it. Nothing would mask the smell of the Storm here in the Tremé. Not for a long time.

Tears welled as I looked around.

Every single thing the Joneses owned had been destroyed. The furniture was scattered upside down, chunks of drywall vomited from the walls, and the fan hung dangerously low from the living-room ceiling. Nearly the entire ground level had been submerged. Only the attic might have stayed dry, which was why so many people had died in them during the Storm—seeking refuge in the driest place in the house only to become trapped.

Trying not to cough, I made a beeline to the back, Isaac trailing close behind.

When we got to Brooke's room, the shock was paralyzing—in junior high I'd probably spent just as much time in this bedroom as I had in my own. I blinked away the tears.

Isaac's hand touched the small of my back as he moved around me. He picked up Brooke's desk, set it upright, and then retrieved the chair from across the room and set it in place on its remaining three legs. It would all have to be thrown out, but I understood why he was doing it—it felt disrespectful *not* to.

He moved to her giant dresser, which had toppled to the ground. I ran to help him lift it.

Once we got it standing, I took a deep breath through the bandanna. My chest shuddered, trying to contain the emotions.

"Are you okay?" he asked.

I nodded, despite being utterly overwhelmed. I didn't volunteer any information, and he took the hint.

"Good luck," he said. "I'll go check out the rest of the house. Just yell if you need me, okay?"

I nodded, taking another deep breath through the fabric, thankful for both the handkerchief and the privacy.

Focus, Adele.

I tried not to get emotional as I started scavenging, but every single Storm-soaked stuffed animal brought me closer to a panic attack. Again, my heart shook inside my chest. I was in such a daze it took me another moment to realize the medallion was actually shaking underneath my shirt. It felt warm against my skin. Unnaturally warm. I pulled it out.

"I could really use some help right about now, Adeline."

The warmth crept through my hands and up my arms until a current of energy bolted through my shoulders, making me gasp.

"What the . . . ?"

The medallion floated up on the chain and then moved to the right, pointing like a compass to a mountain of moldy fly-infested clothes.

I choked, trying not to gag, as the medallion pulled me toward the pile, which appeared to be shaking also. Beneath the pile, the edge of a familiar black leather case poked out.

Brooke left her box? She always brought it on evacuations. I guessed everyone had taken less stuff this time; after all, we'd evacuated just the weekend before for what turned out to be a false alarm.

As I pulled the old trumpet case out, her ruined clothes, damp with mildew, spilled onto me. I swatted them off, nearly throwing up at the smell, and moved the case back to the other side of the room. I knew it well: it had originally contained her father's very first trumpet, an instrument he'd once been forced to hock in his harder, younger years and which he'd been able to buy back after his first gig at Tipitina's, where he had to perform with a borrowed horn.

The family had mounted the trumpet over the piano in the den, but Brooke refused to allow the case to be thrown out. She used it to store her most precious things.

I opened the now-warped leather box and let out a delighted yelp. Its contents were dry.

"Thank God." I breathed a sigh of relief for Brooke.

Even though I could have guessed most of its contents, rifling through her treasures still felt wrong. My fingers moved quickly: her NOSA acceptance letter, a dozen notes from Darius Luella—her eighth-grade crush—blue talent show ribbons, photos of the two of us where magazine cutouts of pop stars had been glued next to us. And there it was, knotted on a strand of black leather: the good-luck charm, Adeline's eight-pointed star.

This has to be it. I ripped it off the leather cord and placed it onto the impression left behind on the medallion. With a quick jerk, the star twisted itself so all eight points lined up with the setting. A wisp of sparks traced the edges of the star, welding it into place. I'm not sure what I'd expected to happen next, but nothing else did.

"Come on . . . !"

I flipped it over and over, trying to understand what I was missing. "Ugh." I banged the case closed.

"Isaac?" I yelled, case in hand, stepping into the den.

The windows were blown out. Guiltily grateful, I stuck my head outside and sucked in a big breath of air. When I turned back around, I accidentally sent a clarinet piece rolling across the once-beautiful wooden floor, which was now warped like a roller coaster. I put down the trumpet case and stood, frozen, staring at the graveyard of brass. A twisted tuba. A discolored trombone. A piano that had sprouted weeds. The room contained enough musical instruments to supply a small orchestra, or at least a couple of Second Lines—all heartbreakingly broken now. The golden records, awards, and other recording paraphernalia that had once decorated the walls were now wrecked. Thousands of pieces of sheet music were strewn about the room. Most had dried into crisp leaves, while others had pulped into giant lumps of papier-mâché. Most of the melodies and lyrics had washed away from the papers, but I hoped they were still stuck in the head of Alphonse Jones and not lost forever.

No wonder he said there was nothing left for them here.

I struggled not to completely break down. *How could I have fought with Brooke? How could I have acted like such a brat?*

Then I realized Isaac was standing next to me. My throat clenched when I tried to talk, and the bandanna slipped down to my neck.

The sympathy in his eyes made it even harder to contain the emotion. My bottom lip started to quiver. But before the first tear could escape, he leaned in and kissed me.

My heart rate soared as he lingered for a second.

Hardly breaking away, he whispered, "Breathe," and slowly brushed the hair from my face. I nodded and inhaled, my eyes barely able to meet his, but then my hand moved to his face as if I no longer had control over it. His arm snaked around my waist, pulling me closer. His touch made me forget about all the bad things. My nose brushed his, but then I paused, intimidated by my own behavior. He moved the last couple of inches to meet my lips.

My eyes closed. I couldn't think about anything else as he kissed me—as I kissed him back. I couldn't hear anything else, smell anything else. Only him.

For a moment, I felt like I was floating, like we were floating.

I pulled him closer.

A whimper escaped my throat. Followed by a pang of self-consciousness. Then a scream from a voice in the back of my head: *What are you doing?*

My body tensed. It was only for a fraction of a second, but he pulled back.

Suddenly we were back on solid ground, back to reality. I opened my eyes, a little terrified to face him. I wanted to slap myself for giving in to him, and then I wanted to slap Isaac for taking advantage of such a vulnerable situation. Yet, I was desperate to pull him close and go back to that moment where I'd felt nothing. That moment where all of the pain went away.

"I'm sorry," he said, flustered. "You just looked so sad. I didn't know what to do."

I couldn't keep my eyes from growing wide. Nor could I get words to come out of my mouth. *I don't even like Isaac—not like that. Right? Then why is it taking every ounce of my strength not to close the distance between us?*

I took a step backward. A protective reflex I immediately regretted when I saw how the small move stung him.

Right then, I wanted nothing more than to feel his strong arms around me again.

What's wrong with me?

My entire being ached for comfort.

Do not cry, Adele.

Then I cracked.

Tears began to drip from my eyes. He moved toward me, and I didn't have the will to take another step back. I knew in that moment I might do something I'd regret later. A squeak of protest came out of my mouth, but he calmly shushed me and moved his bandanna to wipe the tears from my cheeks. New tears welled. I nervously followed his mouth, preparing to give in to him. Once more my eyes slipped shut, but this time he pulled me into his chest and whispered soothingly into my ear. With my face hidden, I couldn't stop crying. He wrapped his arms around me even tighter.

In his unlikely embrace, I cried even harder for Brooke, Klara, and Alphonse Jones. I cried for their neighbors. I cried for all the displaced people of New Orleans. I cried for the man with the blue eyes and for all the others who had died. I cried for myself, because I had no idea what I was supposed to do about it.

Pressed together, there we stood until I ran out of tears.

I began to feel light-headed. Again, like I was floating.

A breeze brought my mind back to the present. *A breeze?* I blinked twice, and when the last of the tears dissolved, I gasped.

Hundreds of pieces of paper were floating in the air around us, slowly spinning in a clockwise turn. We were standing in the middle of a slow-motion cyclone.

Only, we weren't standing at all.

We were levitating four feet from the ground, in a whirlwind of faded music. My heart plummeted with vertigo; my arms circled tightly around his neck.

"What the . . . Am I doing this?"

His expression was perfectly serene, as he looked down at me and then up at the ruined leaves of paper dancing through the air around us in a symphony of rustles.

I could feel his heart begin to race when he barely managed to whisper:

"No, I'm doing this."

"It's . . . beautiful."

In the car, neither of us spoke another word about either incident.

When I felt him steal a glance, I looked out the window. My stomach clenched into a knot. It was just a desperate act of loneliness. *Right?*

My eyes fell to his hand on the stick shift. I suddenly had this desire to crawl under his arm and tell him all of my secrets. I understood how Adeline must have felt with Cosette and the Monvoisin sisters. I wanted to show him these tricks I had no explanation for.

Instead, I just sat there, clutching Brooke's trumpet case, overwrought by what his good-night parting expectation might be.

When we pulled up to the house, I jumped out before he could even cut the engine. He scurried around the hood of the car.

"Adele, I'm really sorry about before."

"Don't wo—" I started to say, but was cut off by another male voice, causing us both to stop in our tracks.

"Apologizing?" Niccolò said, emerging from my stoop. "Tsk, tsk, tsk."

"Hey!" I was a little too overenthusiastic about the interruption. "I was wondering when you would show up."

"Ciao, *bella*," he said quietly and kissed my cheeks, which were now burning.

I turned back to Isaac—the words just flew out of my mouth: "Thanks again for the ride and for making sure the roof didn't fall on my head. See you later." I caught the stunned look on his face as my attention returned to Niccolò with an embarrassing quickness, but I really didn't want to be around the two of them together.

"Hang on a minute," I told Niccolò. "I'll be right back."

When I returned from the house a minute later, with Niccolò's jacket, Isaac was, of course, still there, leaning against the car. Dr. Jekyll was gone for the night.

"I'm so sorry," I said to Niccolò, handing over his leather jacket, which I may have worn on a couple of extra occasions. "I was so caught up in Ren's theatrics that night I completely forgot I was wearing it."

"*Nessun problema, bella.* It gave me an excuse to come see you."

Isaac made no effort to hide his contempt for the soft-spoken Italian as he walked over and placed my father's keys into my hand.

"Adele . . . how is your face healing?" Niccolò asked, looking dead-on at Isaac.

It was the second time he'd mentioned the wound but directed the comment at Isaac instead of me.

"I told you. It was a bir—"

But then the absurdity of it all came crashing together. The night of the tour I hadn't understood why his question had sounded like a threat, but now . . .

The cut on my face, the feathers, the wind, the levitating.

The crow.

No.

CHAPTER 24

Stockholm Syndrome

(Translated from French.)

10th April 1728 (cont.)

I find myself lying awake, still thinking about tonight's events, and so, I have nearly perfected the floating flame. It gently hovers overhead while I write to you from bed, contemplating the evening.

Secrets are a peculiar thing, Papa. They cause scandal and distrust. Time after time, I have seen secrets tear people apart. But sharing this secret brought us together in such a way that I know I will never doubt our friendship. I trust Cosette, Minette, and Lisette Monvoisin with my life.

After my little reveal, Lise told us she had seen a man going into sleeping-cabin number seven. "The same man we met on our last night in Paris," she said. "The one who asked Cosette about her dowry cassette from the king, and who appeared at the dock the morning of our departure."

My head nearly spun at the familiarity of her story, but when I asked about this man, Lise described him as garish, boisterous, and blond—quite the opposite of my salon escort, Cartier. Regardless, the parts of their tale identical to mine were certainly enough to cause alarm.

According to their story, on their final night in Paris, as soon as the last curtain hit the stage floor, they were whisked off to a brothel by the Seine. The king's mistress had arranged their stay, knowing no one would find them in such a place. Their voyage was supposed to have been of the utmost secrecy—their safety depended on it—but somehow a man there knew of their plans. After first inquiring about purchasing a night with the girls, to which they gave him a very firm *no*, he offered to accompany them on their voyage and to protect them from the dangers of the New World, which the sisters laughed off as absurd, just as I had when Cartier made a similar proposal.

Cosette told me, "The strangest part of our conversation was not his question, but the way he looked at me when he asked if we would stow him aboard in my cassette. It was as if he were trying to play some kind of mind trick. That was when Minette realized who he was—"

"Rather, *what* he was," corrected Minette.

"I do not understand," I said. "What was he?"

"A *strigoi*," she answered.

"A child of the night," whispered Lise.

"*Un vampyre*," said Cosette.

Nervous laughter escaped my lips, but then their silent stares made my heart seize. Not at the notion of the existence of vampires, but at the notion of such a predator being aboard this ship with us, thousands and thousands of leagues from land.

11th April 1728

Could it really be true, Papa? Could such creatures exist? Lurking in the shadows of the world, hiding under the blankets of children's tales and in the pamphlets of overzealous theologians? It wasn't the first time I had heard the term *vampyre*. In the last year, it had often been whispered, debated, in the late-night hours of the Parisian salons. Is the notion really so far-fetched, knowing the secrets that our family keeps? Every moment on board the ship has become heightened. Every creak, every shadow piques my curiosity, which is extraordinarily unnerving, given that the constant bob of the ocean causes everything to shift all day and all night long.

And so, I struggled not to fall asleep in my porridge this morning. That was until an empty chair at the orphans' table caused Cosette to spring out the doorway. I followed suit, despite Martine DuFrense's colorful remarks about my table manners.

In sleeping-cabin number seven, we found the missing girl, pale as a ghost, shivering, and too nauseous to get out of bed. It was easy to see why her bunk-mates had dismissed her symptoms as seasickness.

Cosette removed a scarf from around the girl's neck and found two puncture wounds, already nearly healed. Although the girl claimed to have no recollection of how the wounds came to be, she nervously yanked the scarf back and tied it in place.

Cosette and I ran back to her sisters.

"It's as we suspected," she told them. "He's on board the ship and has been coming out to feed under the cover of darkness."

12th April 1728

The orphan girl Sophie has died. She never woke from her unconscious state and finally stopped breathing last night. We have had our first casualty, and thus can no longer just wait in a defensive position to be preyed upon like helpless animals! But what can we do to stop an invisible monster who leaves no evidence behind other than his victims?

13th April 1728

This morning, a crewman was found dead at his night post, with no visible wounds. A rag was tied around his neck, but I found no reason to remove the fabric and spread panic. The crew wasted no time preparing his body, along with Sophie's, for burial at sea, and we paused from the voyage to sing songs as their toes were tipped overboard.

Now, I am finding it difficult to sleep, for whenever I close my eyes, I see our monster.

14th April 1728

I am afraid I have only more bad news. Monsieur DuFrense seems to have awoken with the "seasickness" symptoms. He has only a slight fever, so I hope he will make a full recovery.

The monster is becoming more arrogant regarding when and where he feeds. He takes members of the crew from the deck, and girls even go missing for periods of time in the middle of the day. No one seems to notice, or is it that the power of the monster extends past the physical and plays a role in silencing the passengers of the SS *Gironde*? Whether this is strictly with fear or by some other supernatural means, I've yet to discover. It is now more critical than ever for us to execute some sort of quiet retaliation. And, as if these two pieces of news weren't bad enough, a ship of corsairs was spotted. The crewmen are keeping a careful watch on the pirate ship, while we keep a careful watch on the moves of our nocturnal enemy.

15th April 1728

I have never been so thankful to have these blank pages on which to report the thoughts I dare not say aloud! Dare I report the night was amazing, Papa? That he was amazing! Night after night we have waited, hiding behind doors, behind barrels, and in piles of rope. Tonight, Cosette lost her patience and moved from her hiding spot, sauntering across the deck. It took only a minute before his silhouette drew from the shadows. The creature moved closer to her, causing the three of us to pop up. In an instant, he ran across the deck and then straight up the sail like a spider, leaping across the masts, higher and higher, and then he stopped, almost midleap, and slowly twisted in our direction, nothing more than a shadowy figure against the moon.

When we refused to back away, he leaped to the crow's nest with such delicate ease the sailor on watch did not even notice: a sailor whose only duty was to be on the lookout for danger! The monster perched on the wooden bucket that held the poor seaman and simply looked down at us. We had chased him directly to his next victim! Without saying anything, we understood his message: either we let him down without giving him away, or there would be another burial at sea. He was giving us the choice.

I was infuriated to have come so close only to have to back away now! I was tempted to shoot a flame at the monster, but the move would have been far too risky—it might have destroyed the vampire, but it would certainly have killed the watchman too. Was taking the life of one man to save the life of another something I could live with? To save the lives of many? I hope never to know the answer. We carefully backed away until the sailor, his predator, and the crow's nest were all out of sight. But still the questions lurk in the back of my mind and have caused me another sleepless night.

The tired seaman returned unharmed from his post this morning, and you can imagine his shock when I nearly knocked him over with affection.

22nd April 1728

Claude DuFrense's condition continues to worsen, and his wife has become understandably hysterical. Cosette gives me herbs, which I brew into Martine's tea to calm her long enough to sleep.

To make matters worse, the corsair ship has now been flanking our vessel for two days, and we can only surmise they are foe rather than friend. The captain is taking the necessary precautions in case there is an attack.

As the sailors prepare the cannons, they swap tales of pirates traveling the open sea in search of booty and a wild romp. The nuns spend the hours calming the other girls, but Cosette, Minette, Lisette, and I have all been too preoccupied with our dark passengers to worry about pirates.

Yes, *passengers*. Two more girls in cabins on opposite sides of the ship have awoken with the "seasickness" symptoms, leading us to believe there is more than one vampire stowed away. Cosette swears she saw a female running across the deck last night. *A female!* Can you imagine? Or maybe these are things so well-known to you that my reactions seem silly to you, Father? Exactly how many have stowed away, we have no idea, but the number of victims climbs each night, meaning the monsters are growing stronger. Why they feel the need to grow stronger with such haste keeps me up tonight, Papa. I can only hope it is not because they sense our desire for retaliation.

Now I must try to sleep, for the dawn will bring the confrontation with the pirates.

24th April 1728

So much has happened, so much has changed, I can hardly believe it has only been two days since I last wrote to you, Papa. As I write now from the squalor of my new dwelling, I can still hardly believe what happened . . .

The morning of the attack—before the sun had a chance to rise—everyone on the ship made preparations for combat, by order of the captain. The crew armed themselves with steel, and the nuns armed themselves with rosary beads between their fingers. The captain did everything he could to create the illusion that we were a force to be reckoned with—the king's daughters were forced to dress as men to make our crew appear larger. I wonder what would have happened if the pirates had known from the start that the cargo on the SS *Gironde* was just a few dozen virgin girls rather than a hundred chests filled with emeralds. Would they have turned away, or would they have come faster?

If the captain was nervous as the mysterious ship inched closer, he revealed no signs to us. Nor did his first mate or the rest of the crew. Once the enemy closed the distance, I was ordered below deck with the DuFrenses. It was not long before I grew embittered, trapped inside with the hysterical Martine and the barely lucid Claude.

What happened next is a blur; even now, it is difficult to keep my fingers from heating the quill as I try to record the story, but I will aim for accuracy:

We heard a loud bang; the boat shook, and that was enough suspense for me. I tore through the hallway as more shots were exchanged. Smoke was already filling the narrow passage, making it hard to see and difficult to breathe. I made it out onto the deck to discover we had raised the white flag in surrender. Now it was just a matter of time before they would invade the ship.

With their hair still hidden beneath borrowed sailor hats, the girls held each other, weeping, while the nuns continued to pray, but it was not God who was going to save us.

As the sun fell toward the horizon, the corsair lowered a small dory full of pirates. An undercurrent of terror rippled through the SS *Gironde* as the men rowed closer. Every metal object quaked as I paced past.

The dory contained twelve men, if you could call them men. They clambered onto our ship, using hooks and ropes, and landed on the deck with hoots and snarls. Their long, wild hair was tangled with scraps of rag, and they wore mismatched ensembles of sailor's slops and once-fine threads now tattered and salt stained. I had never seen anything like them, and I think the sight of our group gave them equal shock.

Mumbling in an indecipherable English dialect, one stepped forward from the pack with a curled lip that revealed a few rotting teeth. He hopped to Lise in a way that suggested he was drunk or insane. He got so close to her face their noses very nearly touched.

We watched in horror as he tore off her cap. "What've we got 'ere?" he asked, making her whimper as her bright-blond locks fell loose.

A sickening grin spread over his face, and then he buried his nose into the crook of her neck, inhaling deeply, ready to lap her up like a starved dog. Growls of excitement came from his mates, making the other orphans recoil. Captain Vauberci drew his sword but found four blades touching his throat. I was so outraged I shook violently, but Cosette managed to remain cool.

"Pardonnez-moi, monsieur," she beckoned in a voice as soothing as Aphrodite's, coaxing the pirate away from her sister. Both relief and guilt washed over Lise's face as the pirate walked toward the hexing triplet with his pelvis thrust forward—his imminent death being the furthest thing from his mind as he scratched his crotch with great élan.

Coercion—this is Cosette's specialty. She can speak or sing or sometimes simply stare at someone, and that is all it takes for them to fall under her spell. When he reached her, the despicable pirate grabbed her bosom—in broad daylight! Again, this appalling display brought our crew's hands to the hilts of their swords, but despite being assaulted by his fondling hands, Cosette calmed our men with one reassuring look. She wanted to prevent a battle, not start one. Even as he ripped open her shirt, still no metal was drawn. The pirate stepped backward as if to get a better view of his newfound treasure, but one more seductive smile from her gleaming lips and he suddenly became giddy. Her smile held, and his giddiness grew until his feet couldn't keep up with his fervor. He staggered to one side, dangerously close to the edge of the ship.

"Adieu, mon amour," she whispered as his own seemingly drunken stupor sent him overboard.

The pirate's mates roared with laughter and called him a drunken buffoon. Lise ran to her sister.

"How do you do it?" she asked. "How do you control their minds?"

"You don't control their minds, *ma fifille*; you control their hearts," Cosette replied quietly as Minette hurried to restore her modesty.

The reunion was cut short when the scuffed boots of the enemy captain hit our deck with a thud, sending everyone into silence. The hideous man had a wandering eye and a face like burned leather. On his shoulder rested a large red bird with a black beak and a long, exotic tail, the beautiful creature a stark contrast to the villainous group. It broke the tense silence by chirping a song, which on any other day would have sounded lovely, but today was eerie and mocking. As he rounded the ship, examining his new loot, the wind blew open his ragged overcoat, and the bird fluttered up and down.

His crew fidgeted with delight, eagerly awaiting instructions.

When the pirate captain finally stopped pacing, a smile spread under his untamed beard.

"Thanks be ta the king o' France!" he yelled in English, causing a roar from his constituency.

The crowd hushed as his eyes came to rest on me—I was the only lady on deck still in a dress. He turned on his heel and slowly approached me with a walk of grandeur, almost a dance. A dance that I wanted no part of. Nevertheless, he stopped right in front of me and asked, "Mademoiselle, why don't ya cry like all the otha birds?"

"Should you prefer me to cry?" I asked, struggling to form the words in English.

"I don't care what ya do, li'l lady, as long as ya do it lookin' like that." He gave me a wink, and that was when I realized his other eye wandered because it was not real. It was a stone: milky and iridescent like an opal.

His rank breath attacked me as he continued to say ungentlemanly things. Rage burned through my shoulders, and I became extremely frightened. Not of the hideous captain, but at what I might do, Papa. My fist balled to hide the sparks trying to escape.

"Then you shan't care that I do this," I muttered and spat in his false eye.

His monstrous hand collided with the side of my face, spinning me to the floor. He roared, like a true madman, and fell on top of me. "Ye'r' a feisty one, aren't ya?"

My head throbbed, and there was a buzzing in my ears. I dug my fingernails into the floorboards beneath me, struggling not to defend myself in ways that would cause alarm. I saw ten different things I could kill him with, but, remembering our audience, I let my head fall to the side in defeat as he spewed indecent things.

When no more words came from the captain's blistered lips, I looked back at him—his attention had moved from my face to my medallion, which had slipped out from beneath the fabric of my dress. Your gift, Papa.

He ripped the chain from my neck and became excited by what other riches might be aboard.

"Lock 'em below deck!"

His men chained us all together, along with the DuFrenses, and then packed us into the dining hall and bolted the door so they could raid the ship without distraction.

Whilst trapped, my thoughts spun. If I revealed my true nature, there was no guaranteeing I wouldn't be burned at the stake afterward, even if everyone on the ship was saved as a result.

It was the most dreadful night, Papa. For hours, we wondered which would be crueler: killing us immediately or leaving us on the open ocean to starve and bake to death under the unyielding sun. The orphans prayed with the nuns, as did some of the crew. My thoughts were with poor Captain Vauberci, whom the pirate captain had kept on deck.

The crew began to sing songs and sip flasks of spirits. The more time passed, the drunker they became, and the sadder the songs. By the time the sun rose again, most had made peace with God and were ready to walk the plank, but I was *not* content to rest eternally on the floor of the Atlantic.

And then the strangest thing happened, Papa.

Absolutely nothing.

No one came to get us. Eventually even the noises above deck went silent. Another hour went by, and still nothing happened. The others became restless, as the peace they had made with death faded.

From across the room, my eyes met Cosette's to tell her I was going to leave, and then I focused on the shackles that bound my wrists until the metal expanded enough to slip my hands out. Everyone was so excited when they saw I was free they did not even question how it had happened.

Opening the door, however, would have been an impossible task without being noticed, but then Cosette began to sing a lullaby. Minette joined a phrase later, and then Lise, until everyone was under the spell of the harmony—the diversion made it easy for me to focus on the inner workings of the padlock until it popped open. I slipped out before they began the second verse.

With haste, I ran down the deserted hallway and climbed the stairs that led to the deck, but when I tried to push the hatch open, it barely budged. Something was lying on top of it, trapping us below.

A little focus on the hinges, and they slowly pushed the heavy wood up. Sunlight infiltrated the crack, along with a dark drip. When I wiped it away, my hand came back smeared red. My heart pounded as the hatch opened, and the corpse weighing it down slid onto the deck.

When the scene came into full view, nothing could have prepared me for the sight. I ran to the edge of the ship as bile leaped up my throat.

The ocean breeze whipped my hair around, and the splashing waves glittered beautifully, as if the bloodbath behind me had not happened.

Despite knowing the answer, I wandered the deck to see if anyone was still alive. Bodies were strewn about as if it were the aftermath of a great battle, but there had been no battle. There had been a slaughter. Corpses draped from the blood-sprayed sails and hung from the railings like party decorations. Every throat had been ripped out, and every pirate had died with a look of terror on his face. My fingers tingled. I knew exactly what had happened. Who . . . *what* had answered our prayers.

Do not mistake me. I had no sympathy for the pirates, who had seemed so prepared to leave us locked up. Au contraire, a rush of excitement overwhelmed me, knowing we had not been defeated.

At the front of the ship, the pirate captain had been impaled with a large harpoon. The exotic red bird bounced up and down on the boom, screeching, as if confused about what had happened to its master. The pirate's remaining eye stared back at me, dead, the other socket now emptied. I pulled the sticky ring of keys from his drenched body, choking on the scent of blood, and then ran away, fearing the bird might attack me.

After releasing the others, I led the way back to the deck, hearing the gasps behind me as, one by one, they took in the carnage, each more stunned than the last. Screams fled the orphans, and the crew shed tears when they found the bodies of three of their brethren who had been left on deck, caught between the two deadly factions. The nuns, most confounded of all, fell to their knees in prayer, not knowing whether to thank God for our survival at such a cost of life.

"*Sacrebleu!*" whispered Minette as she held Lise.

"I do not understand," her sister said. "Are they protecting us?"

"They are not protecting us, *per se*—" I said.

"They are protecting their food source," Cosette finished as the pirate captain's bird squawked and swooped down, landing directly on her shoulder, singing a few notes as if in agreement.

As the crew raced around the ship, fearing irreparable damage, we found Captain Vauberci gagged, bound, and stuffed into a closet. He had only a few broken ribs and very little recollection of the previous night, although he twitched when asked about it. After many swigs from his flask, he became his steadfast self. "Prepare for a seaman's funeral!" he yelled. "With haste!"

Songs were sung as the sailmaker stitched the crewmen's corpses into their hammocks and weighted them down with lead shots.

"We owe these fine men our lives. They leave this life and enter the next heroes," the captain said as they were tipped overboard feetfirst. Of course, it was absolutely preposterous to think that the three men had taken out the entire pirate crew, but no one wanted to consider an unnatural alternative.

Following the funeral, the captain made the announcement we all feared: "The SS *Gironde* is beyond repair. We have no choice but to abandon ship. There is no time to lose; the sun will soon set."

Eager to flee the gory scene, every passenger, even Martine DuFrense, assisted in transporting our cargo onto the pirate ship. Once the orphans ensured their precious dowry cassettes were safely aboard, they scrubbed the cabins, but no amount of cleaning was going to remove the years of grime accumulated by the pirates.

While the crew scurried around, investigating the rigging, the triplets and I tackled the giant black rag on the flagpole and tossed it into the ocean. In its place, we hoisted the flag from the SS *Gironde*, and then Captain Vauberci claimed the ship for the king.

The night crew took their posts, and all the passengers retreated to their new cabins, while the Monvoisin sisters and I stole a few more minutes on deck. Drifting away, we watched the dark silhouette of the SS *Gironde* slowly sinking under the full moon.

"Is it possible we will be done with the monsters after tonight?" Cosette asked.

The three of us knew it was not the pirates to whom she was referring.

"We can hope," said Lise as the distance between the ships became greater.

I nodded slowly, but hope wasn't enough for me. I grasped their hands and concentrated on our old ship one last time.

We were stronger together.

Once again, we began to sing an ode to the moon. And soon enough, a fifth voice joined the lullaby—the pirate captain's bird, who perched once again on Cosette's shoulder, looking perfectly in place in the wash of blond waves.

"We shall call you Scarlett," she said to the bird. We all smiled and sang another verse with our new companion adding an extra harmony.

Soon, a flame grew on the black water, bright against the black sky. Our smiles deepened along with our song as the flames engulfed the ship, the pirate corpses, and anything else aboard the SS *Gironde*. When the last notes were sung, we retired for the night.

Both exhausted and enthralled, I entered the squalor of my new cabin. By what miracle of God could we have simultaneously survived a pirate attack *and* rid ourselves of our original predators?

I fell onto the rough mattress of a now-dead pirate and flinched. I expected to find a rock under my back but instead found a smooth, round stone: milky and iridescent, like a very large opal.

I sat up quickly, recognizing the glint from the pirate captain's eye socket. A trophy. Like a cat leaving a dead mouse as a gift for its owner. I didn't know whether to feel grateful or threatened. My intuition led me to the former, but the fiery itch in my palms begged to differ.

Upon second look, my medallion was there too—the chain broken but otherwise beautifully intact. I mended the metal and slipped it back around my neck. The familiarity brought an immediate sense of relief. This, of course, didn't last for long.

I didn't know *who*—but I knew *what*—had placed the treasures on my bed. We may have escaped the pirates, but we had not escaped the monsters.

CHAPTER 25
Willkommen, bienvenue, welcome

October 27th

Isaac	**7:22 p.m.**	Hey. Wanna hang out tonight? I know it's weird with the curfew, but maybe ur dad would let me come over?

I'd been staring at the text message for twelve minutes. In that time, I'd written at least six different responses and been unable to send one of them.

Determined, I typed in a dumb joke, but then quickly hit the back button until it vanished. My eyes flicked back to his message. *Like it's my dad's permission I'm worried about. He's never home anyway.* The thought of being here alone with Isaac made the knot in my stomach tighten. A knot that had intensified for the last three days, sitting six inches away from him in our mentoring sessions. All week we'd both pretended like nothing had happened. Like he'd never demonstrated some kind of magical ability in front of me. Like we'd never kissed. But ever since that night in the Tremé, it had been hard for me to focus on much else.

How am I supposed to think about Kafka, when every bird I see reminds me of Isaac . . . and then that kiss?

My fingertip traced the thick purple line on my cheek where the crow had attacked me.

"It's not possible, Adele," I told myself, smearing some more of the Voodoo ointment across the wound and then on my hand.

Brooke's words echoed in the back of my mind: *"Can't you ever just let something good happen to you without sabotaging it?"*

Was Isaac a good thing, and here I was convincing myself that he slashed my face open? *What kind of twisted freak am I?* Images of sketched feathers flashed in my mind.

"You're being ridiculous!" I yelled. "Isaac is *not* the crow."

My gut told me otherwise.

I grabbed my phone, but before my thumbs could get a word out, it buzzed with a lengthy text message from an unsaved number.

Unknown	**7:38 p.m.**	Hi, Adele. Little Sis initiation starts this week, and we thought it would be nice to include you since you weren't here freshman year. Slumber party at my house tonight. Wear ur favorite pjs! xo Annabelle

XO Annabelle? My phone buzzed again.

Désirée	**7:39 p.m.**	Did you get an invite from Annabelle? I told her I'd

> pick you up. Be ready at
> 8:30.

I love that Désirée just assumed I'd participate in these shenanigans.

Before I could overanalyze anything else, my thumbs flew over the screen, typed one little word, and hit send.

Adele   **7:40 p.m.**   Okay.

"Okay?" *Am I so determined to avoid Isaac that I'd rather hang out with Annabelle's clique?* "Seriously pathetic, Adele. You deserve whatever you get from Annabelle."

At least I was already dressed for the occasion.

From what I'd gathered over the week, Sacred Heart had a tradition of pairing freshmen up with juniors. The Big Sisters were supposed to guide the freshmen over the next two years and then pass on the Big-Sister title when they graduated. I had the feeling inclusion wasn't really what Annabelle had in mind for me tonight, but whatever stupid scheme she was cooking up seemed like marshmallows after reading about Adeline's and the triplets' problems.

Pirate problems.

Vampire problems.

Did I really just think that?

Dead blue eyes—*Do I have vampire problems?*

As I texted my plans to my father, images of pedicures, underage drinking, and rounds of Truth or Dare flipped through my mind: all things I could handle. *What's the worst that could happen at a slumber party?*

At least now I wasn't lying to Isaac when I texted him that I already had plans.

For some reason, guilt still plagued me. I don't know if it was him, the anticipation of prep school hazing, reading about the pirate massacre, or the fact that the overhead light was now flickering on and off, but I was soon in a tizzy. I closed my eyes and sucked air in through my nose until the lightbulb finally behaved.

I turned on the radio just in time to catch the DJ saying, "Two more bodies have been reported today."

A sound bite from the police chief followed: "We're not answering any questions. At the moment, all we can say is the victims showed no obvious signs of fatal trauma, yet suffered significant blood loss."

I sat at the vanity, aggressively separating my hair into two messy braids.

"As everyone knows, the city is operating with only one partially functioning hospital, and the morgue is completely overwhelmed, which means there's a queue for autopsies . . ." He sounded flustered. "Any further details are pending investigation."

The radio host cut back in. "And we have Jack on the line, a pastry chef from the Warehouse District."

"Yes, hello, Jack Whitaker here. Rumor has it the National Guard has set up shop in the old Brown's Milk Factory. Supposedly, they've hooked up generators to the old refrigeration system, and they're using it to store corpses waiting to be processed."

"There you have it, folks. The city is so broken we're stacking up murder victims like pints of Blue Bell. But this won't come as a shock to locals, who are still struggling to find food, gasoline, medical supplies, and, of course, their relatives. If these bodies weren't Storm related, then this message is going out to the killer: Just because the NOPD is backed up, it doesn't mean the rest of us don't have our eyes on you. Citizens, be alert. This is the Wolfman, signing off."

Chills crawled up my arms.

Without moving, I twisted the dial and welcomed the familiar trills of Mr. Jones's trumpet. The nostalgia lasted for only a few bars before being interrupted by obnoxious honking from the street.

An unfamiliar Porsche SUV, painted a shade of gold that could only be custom—not Désirée's white monstrosity—was parked in front of my house, engine running. I strained to see the driver. *Ugh, Annabelle.*

I grabbed my bag and ran down the stairs, but as soon as I opened the front door, Désirée pushed her way inside, backing me into the hallway.

"Hey—"

"Where's your room?"

"Upstairs, why?"

Without waiting for an invitation, she ran up, dragging me behind.

"Take off your clothes."

"What?" I snickered.

She began digging through my drawers, slamming each one shut until she got to my lingerie.

"What do you think you're doing?"

She spun around and stared me up and down with that look of disapproval I was getting used to. This time I was unsure why my ankle-rolled sweatpants and thrifted Mickey Mouse T-shirt were unacceptable for a sleepover. *Sheesh.* She tossed me a cream-colored, satin camisole from the drawer and then started pulling my shirt off. I swatted her hands away.

"You are going to have to trust me on this one," she said.

Coming from Désirée Borges, these were not comforting words, but the urgency in her voice made me obey. I ripped off my tee and slipped on the slinky cami I'd appropriated from a box of my mother's abandoned things. It barely covered my stomach. I was tugging on it when a pair of tiny black spandex shorts hit my face.

"Shorts, now. Do *not* say anything to Annabelle about changing your clothes, and especially don't say I made you do it."

Her comment activated my defenses for the night. *Is Désirée actually doing me a solid?* I slipped on the shorts, which had become far too short after I'd hit my final growth spurt.

"Where did you get that necklace?" she asked, watching me untangle the gris-gris from my chain and tuck it into the slip.

"Umm, your grandmother gave it to me."

"No, not the gris-gris. The other one."

"Oh, family heirloom."

"Hmm . . ." she said as if contemplating and then turned to dig through my closet. "Put these on." She tossed me a pair of plastic jellies. I let them fall to the floor.

"I'm not wearing those. There's still glass everywhere—"

"Flip-flops?"

"Ugh, no! How does that help?" I stepped into my boots to show her I meant it.

"Don't say I didn't warn you." She grabbed my arm and pulled me back down the stairs. Her behavior made no sense, especially since she was slumber party–ready in an oversized cotton T-shirt and leggings.

I caught a glimpse of myself in the hallway mirror as we went out the door. I looked completely ridiculous in the shiny shorts, burgundy Docs, two messily braided pigtails, and nothing but cream-colored lace covering my cleavage. I looked like a bumpkin teen prostitute.

Who cares? I thought with a sigh. *It's just a sleepover with a bunch of snobby girls.*

Annabelle honked the horn again as I pulled the gate closed, but I was mentally focusing on the gate's lock as I leaped down the stoop. When I reached the curb, I *felt* the mechanical pieces snap into place. *Success.*

"Hey, sorry to keep you waiting," I said, squeezing myself into the middle seat, next to Dixie and Annabelle's two minions, Jaime and Bri. "I couldn't find my phone."

From the front passenger seat, Désirée shot me a look of approval. *First time for everything.*

Four freshmen minions-in-training were crammed into the backseat, three wearing a mix of boxer shorts and kitty-cat scrubs, and one timid-looking girl, with black corkscrew curls, had on some kind of unfortunate muumuu.

For some reason being in a car with nine other girls made me immediately nervous. I could count my good friends at NOSA on one hand.

Jaime and Bri were in a Tweety Bird nightie and an XL Saints' jersey, seemingly with nothing on underneath. Dixie had obviously given careful consideration to her outfit: a purple satin nightgown and a matching robe. As if that weren't enough, she wore giant, purple, furry slippers that looked like tie-dyed sheepdogs. Jaime caught me looking at her leather ankle boots and had to tighten her lips to contain giggles. *Something's up.*

Just as my suspicions were aroused, I saw Annabelle Lee looking over my attire from her rearview mirror. A slow smile spread across her face. Something was *definitely* up.

"All right, ladies, per Sacred Heart tradition, you each have to wear one of these blindfolds until we reach the secret location."

"Secret location?" peeped a small blonde from the back.

"Don't ask questions," Jaime ordered.

"Where are we going, Annabelle?" I asked. Being blindfolded by a bunch of girls who hated me didn't seem like the smartest idea.

"It's not about where we're going. It's about how much fun we're going to have when we get there." She beamed a giant smile into the rearview mirror for only me to see.

I could sense panic from the backseat, but I refused to ask another question or seem alarmed in any way. I smiled back.

"Dixie," Jaime said, "you tie Adele, and I'll tie you."

"With pleasure," Dixie said, securing the black cloth into a bow at the back of my head—just a little too tight, letting me know who was in control.

The ride only took a few minutes, so I guessed we were still in the Quarter, or the Marigny, depending on how many stop signs she had blown through, although I couldn't really imagine the Queen of Uptown going past Esplanade Avenue.

Annabelle cut the engine. My door opened, and she helped me step out of the car. "Be careful. We wouldn't want any mishaps before the party even starts."

Suddenly the phrase "kill them with kindness" had a whole new meaning. I tried not to grow nervous as she linked her arm through mine and pulled me up the curb onto the sidewalk. Behind us, Dixie wasted her breath sucking up to Désirée, and, as per usual, Désirée ignored her.

We stepped on and off the curb three times. Three blocks? A loud creak gave away an iron gate. The echoes from one of the girls' clacking high heels made it sound like we were being shuffled down a narrow passage. *High heels?* I dragged my hand along the wall. Brick. *A courtyard?*

A damp breeze kicked up a familiar smell. It was dull, but I would've recognized it anywhere: the mix of booze and bleach that only a barroom could produce. I used to wake up to that scent as a child. Right after my mother left, my father had kept me with him at work until the wee hours, too scared to let me leave his sight.

Annabelle led me up a flight of wooden stairs and into a space that must have been incredibly dark; not even the faintest bit of light came through the blindfold. I grew very aware that it must be close to nine and we'd soon be breaking curfew.

"All right, this is good. You can take off the blindfolds."

It took only a second for my eyes to adjust to the minuscule amount of light shed by the single gas lantern in the dank room and only another second to realize the juniors were no longer sporting pajamas. Each was club-ready. Jaime must have been wearing the tight, turquoise halter dress underneath her Tweety Bird nightie. I yanked on my camisole, feeling seriously inadequate next to her. The girl could've easily been a swimsuit model.

Terror cracked through Dixie's pageant façade. She quickly shed her robe. "Flip-flops. Now!" she demanded from one of the freshmen, trading her ridiculous slippers.

My jaw clenched as I watched the rest of the juniors pull accessories from their bags, but I was more terrified of what would happen at school on Monday if I bailed. I peered down at myself. *Utterly ridiculous.* Annabelle Lee was looking at me too, laughing and saying something to Désirée, who gave me a look that wasn't exactly sympathy but implied, *I tried.*

I guess my outfit was a serious improvement compared to the others being hazed. In a more risqué closet, my camisole could've been a top. The group of freshmen looked completely childlike in their pajamas. One girl was irate, and I could sense a revenge plot turning in her head, while the other three were on the verge of tears, anticipating the public humiliation that loomed ahead.

"Everyone ready?" Annabelle asked. "Follow my lead."

An increasing sense of familiarity crept up as we walked a series of quick twists and turns. *Where the hell are we?* I searched for clues, but it was practically blindfold dark.

"Who do we have here?" a deep male voice echoed as we turned into a long hallway.

Annabelle signaled for the freshmen to walk past him.

"Let's see some ID."

Annabelle looked directly at the guy and said, "Are you sure about that? I think you want to let my friends in."

Man, that girl has guts.

There was a silent moment, and for a second I thought he might give in to her, but then he quickly shook his head. "I don't think so, sister."

His voice sounded familiar, but the flashlight he was shining directly on us was so bright I couldn't see his face.

Annabelle let out a toddler-like sigh in frustration, but then, to my surprise, she whipped out a plastic rectangle and showed it to the bouncer. He sighed but let her pass. Désirée, Bri, and Jaime each did the same and continued down the hallway.

Dixie stammered in her sweetest Texas beauty queen drawl, "Sir, it looks like I forgot my license. I can really be such a ditz sometimes."

Sometimes?

"No ID, no entry."

As Dixie continued to try to flirt her way inside, the freshmen scattered like mice. I didn't have a fake ID either. I relaxed a little and began to follow them out. But I didn't get very far . . .

"Little Addie—Adele, is that you?" The bouncer turned the flashlight on himself.

"Hey, Troy," I said, walking back over. An awkward smile spread across my face as I tried to act casual.

The gruff biker was a longtime employee of my father's. At least, he'd been before the Storm. My smile turned genuine as I realized there probably wasn't a bar in the entire French Quarter I couldn't get into, for better or for worse. He gave me a hug and then pulled up my arm to better examine my outfit.

"That's quite a different look you got going on, girl."

Dixie watched us with her mouth gaping.

"Don't ask," I begged, making him laugh. "It's a costume I'm testing out for a school play." I was appalled at how easily the lie flew out of my mouth. Maybe I was more like the Sacred Heart girls than I thought.

"Lookin' more and more like your ma . . ."

"So I hear . . ." I forced a smile.

He gestured at the door, allowing me passage.

"Do me a favor and tell your pa 'bout all these kids trying to get into this bar."

"Uh, okay," I answered, walking in. I had zero plans to engage my father in any conversation placing me somewhere that one of his old bouncers was guarding.

I took one last look back and saw Dixie glaring at me with her arms crossed. I wasn't enthusiastic about walking into this weird place, but I couldn't pass up the opportunity to have something Dixie wanted and couldn't get—this would probably be my only chance. I gave her a little wave before I pivoted on my heel and flipped my hair, like I'd seen Désirée do so many times before. Only my version involved braided pigtails.

The scent of cigarettes grew stronger as I approached a wooden door at the end of the corridor. A single gas lantern on the wall shed just enough light to see the handle.

Here goes nothing.

Muffled music and merriment flooded out as I slipped in. Two men in suits sipped cocktails near a candle-lined fireplace in the old parlor room. It felt as if I'd accidentally walked into a private residence. Others were huddled on couches, engaged in deep conversation. In a dark corner, a couple was kissing. The billowing cigarette smoke made my eyes water. An odd sense of familiarity washed over me again. I hurried along.

As I walked past a series of windows, I pushed aside one of the heavy drapes. Storm boards still covered the tall panes, but now, instead of keeping the weather out, they were keeping the flickers of candlelight and the noise inside, presumably to hide from the curfew. Slipping from room to room in the darkness, I felt like I'd unwittingly traveled to a night gone by.

The deeper I walked into the secret house, the more packed it became with folks from all walks of life. Young and old. Glitz and glam. Tattered and torn. I stopped in a ballroom, instantly taken aback by the scene, especially after the dullness of the last month. On a small, wooden, candle-lined stage, an androgynous female—wearing a flapper shift, oodles of metallic gold eye makeup, and a blunt bob—belted out "La Vie En Rose," while a pianist with a waxed mustache, bow tie, and bowler hat accompanied. People were draped over cabaret-style tables, soaking in the performance.

I felt leagues less cool than everyone else here. Paranoid about fitting in, I approached a makeshift corner bar to take my chances getting a drink. The bartender recognized me right away. By day, Mia was an architectural grad student at Tulane who used to work weekends for my dad, but now she better resembled Cleopatra. I glanced at Annabelle's group, which was scoping the room like a vulture ready to swoop. Mia's gaze followed mine, and without breaking the look of sympathy that followed, she simultaneously poured gin with one hand and tonic with the other into an iceless tumbler.

"You're gonna need it," she said with a wink of her ostentatious false eyelashes and slid me the drink. "Oh, wait"—she signaled for the drink back—"something from my secret stash." She reached under the bar and then plopped something into my glass, making it fizz over. "Just for you."

I licked the spillage from my hand and saw a limp, yellowish slice of lime floating in the bubbles. *Whoa, fruit.* I raised the glass to her.

"*Merci beaucoup.*"

I took a small sip, trying not to make a face at the wretched taste of alcohol, and then she gave me a strange look when I tried to pay for the drink.

"Our little secret." She winked again.

I thanked her a second time and turned to find where Annabelle's throng had landed.

Even by candlelight, I could see that the old house was falling apart—the paint was cracking, the wallpaper was peeling, and the furniture was a hodgepodge of hurricane-surviving pieces someone had likely collected in a hurry for the secret club. Despite the physical conditions, it was energetic and alive, as if the scene itself had a pulse. The kind of pulse only illegal activity could elicit.

The sultry singer held the final note, and the crowd roared—but only for a moment—then they began to shush each other, whispering, "The curfew! The curfew!" The shushing only contributed to the excitement. I felt like I'd time-warped into the Prohibition—people were ecstatic just to be out.

This place is so cool.

If it had been open pre-Storm, I'd have known about it, surely. *I wonder if Dad has heard anything?*

Dad.

I slowly turned a full circle. My pulse crept faster. It was certainly unrecognizable, but I *had* been here before. The alleyway, the bouncer, the bartender. I was in the *garçonnière* of Le Chat Noir . . . *my father's bar.*

These guesthouses at the back of properties were originally built for French boys when they turned fifteen. Bachelor pads for them to . . . er, become men? Le Chat Noir's *garçonnière* had been rented out to the same old man for as long as I could remember. When he died a couple years ago, my father discovered termites in parts of the building; he'd had the house treated, but we didn't have enough money to renovate it, so it had sat vacant since.

"Shit."

"Excusez-moi," I repeated continuously as I pushed past people, wanting to get away from the bartender who could bust me. As the evidence

became more obvious—the door to the bathroom, the chandelier, a rug that used to be in our living room—I tried not to show any outward signs that I was frantically composing myself on the inside.

You're a freaking idiot, Adele.

Not only was the room looking familiar, I began recognizing faces among the mélange of college students and gutter punks: our neighbors, a group of brass musicians who played with Alphonse Jones, and ol' Madame Villere, wearing pearls and white gloves and sipping a warm martini. Despite the volume level in the room, Ren still managed to make himself noticeable. He and Theis were sitting around a center table with a few other goths. Whatever story he was narrating had the full attention of his group.

Totally paranoid, I waited until I was safely hidden by a gang of people near the left corner of the stage before I continued scanning the crowd.

The room was filling up. *Is everyone back in town here?* I wondered, sucking limey gin-and-tonic through the tiny black straw. The main bar in the rear of the room was two deep with guys who looked like FEMA workers. *How am I the ONLY person who didn't know about this place?* I did a double take—Isaac's tiny ponytail. Sadly, I could also recognize the contour of his broad shoulders in his white T-shirt. He was sitting at the bar by himself. No. He was talking to my *dad*.

Ugh!

When the wall repairs had to be put on hold because of supply scarcity, Isaac had started fixing anything around the house that needed fixing in exchange for his art lessons. Not that my father cared; he'd gladly give Isaac free art lessons for life just to have another male around the house. But Isaac wouldn't have it any other way—which, of course, made my father like him even more. Apparently so much so that he was letting him stay in the bar, underage.

Knowing my father had told Isaac his big secret and not me compounded my irritation. My father and I did *not* have secrets. And to top it all off, Isaac hadn't told me either! *Ugh!* Talk about secrets causing scandal and distrust.

So much for Isaac trying to get closer to *me*. I imagined myself storming over to him and throwing the remainder of my drink in his face.

"Mademoiselle?" A tap on my shoulder interrupted my silent rage.

I turned and flinched—a man with a clown-painted face was extending a tray of small tumblers with clear drinks. *So. Random.*

"No, thank you." I shook my head, and the Marcel Marceau look-alike retreated with a bow.

I scanned the crowd again—Désirée was easy to spot because of her height as she walked across the room, the other Big Sisters in tow. Her trajectory led me to Gabe. *Shocker.* He was standing, sipping wine at a corner table directly across the room from me, with three other equally runway-worthy people. The two gorgeous blondes he was with seemed enamored by the words coming from his lips . . . but not in the way that Désirée seemed enamored. They radiated the kind of crushing confidence high school girls could only dream about—the kind where one look could have you questioning every decision you've made your entire life. They were enamored but his equals. *Are they the missing relatives?* The one I could see best had cascading, honey-colored curls that swept her vixen face and hung perfectly over her black-lace dress, which hugged her every curve. The other had long white waves, and her pale-pink, empire-waisted dress and perfect red pout made her seem more like a doll. A very sexy doll.

Now hyperaware of my working-girl outfit, I tugged on the thin satin and slouched a bit, hoping to cover my exposed stomach. I slowly sipped my drink, eyeing the table of Adonises. Sitting at the table by himself, watching the blond trio, was a dark-haired guy I assumed was Niccolò, although his back was to me.

The Big Sisters landed at their table and, to Désirée's liking, received a warm welcome by Gabe. Both of the blondes smirked, the vixen with intrigue and the baby doll with boredom.

Annabelle laughed loudly at something Gabe said. Anger boiled inside me.

What the hell is going on? Gabe and Niccolò are MY friends. How did I end up on the outside? We're downtown for God's sake!

The baby-doll blonde shifted away from Gabe after a barrage of high school giggles. Now it was me who smirked—until she draped herself on Niccolò's lap. I bit down on the lime slice, sending a sour squirt down my throat. She was *the* blonde. From Ren's tour. Face squirming, I finished the drink.

Why do I care who sits on his lap?

She whispered into his ear. I set my empty glass down on a table out of fear I might crush it. I couldn't see his reaction, but he certainly wasn't pushing her off. Without anything to occupy my hands, all I could do was stare like a jealous loser.

The woman brushed her glowing locks from her face and laughed.

The singer bellowed out another jazzy number.

Another tap on my shoulder distracted me: the clown was back. This time I gladly accepted a drink, just to have a prop. I slipped a few dollars into his flower-filled jacket pocket without ever really looking at him. The woman had put her jacket on as she spoke to Niccolò and now her arm was sliding around his shoulder. He pulled the hood of her jacket over her head, further concealing her whispers. I froze as her hooded silhouette in the candlelight stirred my memory again.

Was she the woman following me?

An uncomfortable silence crept over me, and I realized everyone nearby was looking my way and smiling, as if waiting for me to do something. I turned my head. The mime was dramatically bowing—a thank-you for the tip. I made a little curtsy, but it wasn't enough. He egged me on, the black paint on his stark white face amplifying his silent emoting. I tried to shoo him away, but he wasn't having it. I gulped down the drink, nearly choking on what I'd thought would be gin but definitely wasn't. I put the empty glass back on his tray, coughing, but he just spun it, offering me another.

I shook my head, fire coursing down my throat, and sucked in the coughs, trying not to draw more attention to myself. *What the hell is that stuff?* It tasted like rubbing alcohol.

He set down the tray and extended a gloved hand. More and more heads turned our way, until even the pianist stopped playing. The entire room hushed in delight, giving the mime permission to pull me into his silent world.

As the clown began a slow-motion spin, there was the loud clunk of a bottle landing heavily on the bar. I was afraid to look, but something told me it was the sound of my father's shock.

Midtwirl, my suspicion was confirmed—I caught a glimpse of him behind the bar, clutching a bottle of booze. It wasn't clear who was more busted: me for being dressed like a prostitute in an illegally operating bar after curfew or him for operating said bar and lying to me about it.

Isaac jumped from his bar stool in surprise.

The crowd began to slowly clap their hands as the mime twirled me again.

Clap. Clap.

Clap. Clap.

The slapping, clapping synched with the beats of my heart, tugging my chest.

As they sped up, so did the twirls. The clown brought my arm over his head, forcing me to turn him. The crowd cheered wildly, and the piano started up again. He spun us faster and faster.

"*Bravissima, bella!*" Gabe yelled, standing with his glass raised. Niccolò turned to see the source of the commotion, which made my feet freeze, jerking my partner to a stop.

All the sounds in the room seemed to fade away: Gabriel's shouts, the music, the whistling. I was only vaguely aware that the mime was now raising my hand for applause or that Isaac was walking toward me. The only thing I could focus on was the boy holding the blond girl—he wasn't Niccolò.

He was Émile.

Am I drunk? I blinked.

Am I losing my mind? I blinked again.

But there he was, staring straight at me. Smiling. *Did he come to New Orleans to see me?*

Behind him, Annabelle glared, as if I'd purposefully stolen the spotlight from her. I hated her for bringing me here.

My father moved from behind the bar. This was all his fault. *How could he not tell me about this place?*

The mime took a bow, while the crowd clapped with drunken glee. On his second dip, he bent my torso downward to join him. They whistled louder. As we came up, I let out an uncontrollable gasp—and every flame in the room extinguished.

The sudden blackout caused instant pandemonium. Squeals came from every direction. *This is my chance to get the hell out.*

"Adele!" my father shouted over the crowd.

Focus, Adele. You know this place. I pushed my way to the door. Tiny flickers of light appeared as people struck matches and held up their phones. *Faster.* With my eye on the handle, the door swung open, and I pushed past two FEMA workers with government issued flashlights. The door slammed behind me as soon as I crossed the threshold.

"Bye, Troy!" I yelled, dashing past him down the stairs. Into the courtyard. Down the alley, all the way to the curb. A cool breeze helped ease the sense of claustrophobia, but I kept running through the postcurfew streets. I could feel the alcohol coursing through my system as I sucked in the fresh air—my fingers tingled like they were on fire.

Maybe it's the alcohol . . . or maybe it's just . . . me. I took the corner too sharply—

"Dammit!" I yelled, slamming into someone coming from the other direction. My arm jerked in my shoulder socket as, once again, a guy kept me from hitting the ground.

"We really should stop meeting like this, *bella*," Niccolò said, holding me steady, smiling with one eyebrow cocked. "Not that I mind it."

I was still too shocked by the evening's events to engage in any kind of witty repartee.

"That's an interesting outfit," he joked as his eyes wandered, lingering in confusion.

I didn't laugh. I didn't budge.

"What's wrong, Adele?"

I felt like I was going to implode. This was *not* how I'd imagined our next encounter.

"Are you hurt?" His usual serious expression was back. "Why were you running?" He rubbed my shaking shoulders—his hands were barely warmer than my arms, but the friction helped. I could smell alcohol on his breath, but that wasn't the reason he was trouble, and I knew it.

"Adele!" Isaac shouted in the near distance, making me suddenly alert.

I flinched for only a millisecond, but that was all Niccolò needed. He grabbed my hand, and we started running. I didn't know where to, and I didn't care. I knew exactly what I was doing. I knew exactly who he was, or rather *what* he was. And it was precisely at that moment I decided I was okay with it.

For better or worse, I dove down the rabbit hole.

CHAPTER 26

Monster vs. Myth

Isaac's shouts faded as we sped through the narrow streets. I had no idea where we were going, but I was overwhelmingly eager to be there with Niccolò.

To help conceal our escape route, I flicked out the gas lanterns' flames as we ran, hoping Niccolò wouldn't notice. His fingers locked tighter around mine. The gesture was tiny, but I could feel his excitement. And his strength.

I struggled to keep pace in the heavy boots; he wasn't even breathing heavily.

Blue eyes flashed in my head. But I didn't stop Niccolò from pulling me along. I pushed myself to run faster. I wanted to get far away from everyone. Everyone who was hiding things from me. Tricking me. Lying to me.

We ran into St. Anthony's Garden, through Jesus's giant shadow. Yellow caution tape blocked the entrance to the alley behind the St. Louis Cathedral, but Niccolò didn't slow. The plastic popped against my bare skin as we ran straight through it to the back door. My brain fired off warnings about breaking into the church, but my heart unlocked the door just before Niccolò touched the handle.

As soon as we stepped inside, that unmistakable church feeling crept over me—a mixture of guilt, as if I'd been busted doing something bad, and total serenity, both wrapped into one.

The church was completely dark other than the muted moonlight shining through the stained glass windows and a bright, red emergency exit sign, yet Niccolò still managed to quickly navigate the towers of melted candles and the basins of long-dried-up holy water. He never let go of my hand.

We raced up the stairs, past the choir loft, and through the mezzanine that ran the length of the vast church. The cathedral was a historical landmark; I'd been inside countless times, but now all sense of familiarity was absorbed by the darkness, the emptiness. Now it was just us and our footsteps echoing back down from the domed ceilings.

I squeezed his hand as we entered a pitch-black hallway. A trail of glow tape spiraled up into the darkness. He pulled me in front of him, and I slowly made my way up the neon-taped steps, dragging my hand along the stone wall.

Each board creaked in pain under my weight.

His hands brushed my waist. I began to take the steps faster, confident he wouldn't let me fall. My quads burned with exhaustion, but I refused to slow down in front of him.

I made the final turn and halted abruptly at a dead end. An arched window allowed just enough moonlight to make the small wooden door visible. It was sealed with an antique iron padlock.

My heart thumped as the metal tempted my fingers. *Don't do anything stupid, Adele. He'll surely notice.*

Before I could think any more about it, he stepped ahead, onto the tiny top stair, and turned to me, blocking my view of the door. Strain pinched his face, and then there was a clank as the metal arch of the lock landed at his feet. I knew that the base was in his hand. *Is he trying to hide his strength so he still has the element of surprise, or is he, like me, simply not ready to reveal himself?*

I stepped past him through the little door into the bell tower and collapsed against the stone windowsill, discreetly trying to catch my breath. The slats in the eight long windows had been blown out, and the moonlight that flooded in seemed almost bright after the pitch-black church.

I looked out over the rooftops—this was certainly the highest point in the French Quarter.

When I turned back to Niccolò, his eyes were lit with rapt attention, watching me.

Other than the drop, there was only one way down, and Niccolò Medici was still standing in front of that exit, biting his lower lip.

"What are we doing here?" The cross breeze gave my voice a slight shake.

"You're upset about something," he said, moving closer. He pulled me away from the window, just enough to circle behind me. "I have an idea to make you feel better." Nervousness engulfed me as his hands slid up my arms.

I tried to steady my voice. "Unlikely."

He gently nudged me to the center of the tower, underneath the enormous church bell. The giant brass dome dwarfed all the other bells it was intricately rigged to—the clapper itself was bigger than my head.

Niccolò's chest knocked my shoulders, and I suddenly felt small next to him. Not something I'd ever paid much attention to until just then—the difference in our sizes. Our speed. Our strength.

Dead blue eyes.

My fingers tingled.

He swept both of my braids to the right side of my neck. *What are you doing, Adele?*

"On the count of three," he said, "I want you to scream as loud as you can."

"What?"

"One," he whispered into my ear.

Chills swept down my neck.

"Two."

I told you so, my subconscious scoffed.

"Three!"

He jumped up and jerked the thick rope down, and then his hands swooped back around to cup my ears. The clapper hit the brass rim right before the shriek left my lips.

The gong easily masked my scream, but under the protection of his hands, all I heard was a distant ping, which didn't at all match the resonant vibrations beneath our feet. It was exhilarating—screaming at the top of my lungs, high above the silent city. My throat became raw, and my knees started to buckle. His hands never left my ears as he followed my slow slump to the ground.

For a few moments, he just stayed cocooned over me, letting me be. Then he hooked my waist and drew me to my feet.

"Do you feel better?" he asked, still pressed against my back.

"Yeah, actually," I whispered, turning around.

"Bene." He brushed a tear that I hadn't realized fell from my cheek.

The wind tingled against the light sweat brought on by the unexpected run, making my teeth chatter. He removed his jacket but dropped it to the floor instead of handing it to me and began unbuttoning his green-and-black flannel shirt.

"What . . . what are you doing?"

A smirk slipped out. "Don't worry, your virtue is safe with me."

Blood flushed my cheeks as his black V-neck was revealed underneath.

"The wind is crazy up here. I can't take both—"

"Don't worry about me either." He draped the flannel over my shoulders.

"Fine. I don't think hipster-lumberjack is really your thing, anyway."

"Oh really? *Scusami, bella,* but you are in no position to be doling out fashion advice." A slight laugh slipped through his lips. "But you're right. It looks better on you."

I glanced down at my ensemble and became mortified all over again.

He gently lifted my chin so my gaze was back on him. "Stop worrying. It's very Seattle circa 1992."

The statement was very matter-of-fact, as if he'd been there, onstage with Kurt Cobain. Unconvinced my outfit had achieved Courtney Love status, I buttoned up the shirt for maximum coverage and turned to the nearest window, making room so we could both fit into the tight frame. Even in the darkness, the view was magnificent, high above the history of three centuries. Three hundred years of mysteries, of ghost stories, of love affairs.

The lingering silence suddenly caused anxiety to rush through me—despite not knowing his real intentions, despite not really knowing him—I didn't want to leave.

I also wasn't sure what I wanted from him: Answers? Proof? Or . . . something else.

Dead blue eyes, Adele.

I slunk down under the window's stone ledge and wrapped his jacket around my bare legs. He slid down next to me, and we both just sat in silence in the cone-roofed tower.

Soon I began to feel like a player in a game of Who's Going to Talk First. I wanted to play it cool, but I also wanted to know how many years of history he'd seen unfold in this city.

"Niccolò—"

"You can call me Nicco. It sounds funny when you try to say my name."

"Oh." I blushed, repeating his name in my head, trying to figure out what was funny about the way I pronounced it.

"Nicco . . ."

"*Sì, bella?*"

It felt like he was baiting me, pulling the words out. Not knowing how many questions I would get, I chose carefully.

"How's the *hunt* going?"

"What?" he asked sharply.

"The hunt . . . for your *family*?"

His eyes lit up, searching my face as if seeking some kind of underlying hint that I was blowing his cover. When I gave him nothing more, he quickly restored his poker face.

"Everyone is accounted for, actually."

"Oh good."

"Well, all but one, but I'm quite certain we lost her. She jumped out . . . she didn't stay in the attic with the others."

"What happened to them? Are they okay?"

"You know how the story goes . . . the trauma after being trapped in an attic for so long. Abandoned. Malnourished."

The slight smirk that followed made me believe we were no longer talking about victims of the Storm, but we continued to speak obtusely, neither confirming nor denying my suspicions. The fleck of excitement in his demeanor remained.

"So, does this mean you'll all be going home to Italy?"

"They are not well enough to travel, yet."

"But then?" I pushed, daring him to answer.

His eyes slanted with slight suspicion.

"We'll see . . ." He relaxed back into the wall. His attention went out the window to the stars, giving me nothing more.

But I tumbled deeper down the rabbit hole. The question flew out of my mouth, and that was the moment everything changed:

"Did Adeline ever tell her father you called?"

And that was the moment everything changed. His jaw jolted, and a hushed snort forced its way out of his nose. I had no idea what to do next, but the hairs standing on my arms told me to proceed with caution.

"*What* did you say?" he asked, one hand strategically placed over his mouth.

I stood. He stayed down, like an animal ready to pounce.

My words were sweet; I was careful not to come across as mocking. "Paris. 1728. Did Adeline ever tell her father that you called . . . , *Monsieur Cartier?*"

Pain rippled through my shoulders as they made sudden contact with the stone floor. His head hung directly over mine, his cool green eyes assaulting me. I froze underneath him, terrified I'd pushed him too far. His breathing became heavier with each inhale and exhale through his nose.

Despite beginning to tremble, I held out, waiting for an answer. He kept his mouth clamped shut.

After another breath, he pushed himself up into a crouched position over my lap, allowing me to sit up, so we were eye to eye. He rested his hand nonchalantly on his jaw, covering his mouth.

"Do you trust me, Adele?"

It was a perplexing question, but I knew he was serious because he'd used my real name rather than the endearing Italian nickname. A fiery sensation spread to every shred of my physical being, urging me to scream *no*, but instead I whispered, "Yes."

"Never trust a vampire, Adele!" he yelled, slamming my shoulders back to the ground.

A second surge of pain ripped down my back, but my attention clung to his words. The one word I had been waiting to hear from something more than a book or a tour guide.

Vampire.

———

His mouth hung open somewhere in between a hiss and a growl, revealing the evidence that, up until this point, he'd gone to such great lengths to hide: two incredibly enlarged fangs. Perfectly pointy. Perfectly lethal.

His breath was cool on my burning face, and his eyes pulsed with need, letting me know that if I made one wrong move, everything would be over. And then, just like that morning on the street, his eyes stopped pulsing and glazed over, as if he were no longer with me.

"Nicco . . ."

His nostrils flared as his face came even closer.

Suddenly everything became very real. Too real.

Trying to control the tremors rippling through my body only shook me harder. *What would Adeline or Cosette have done?* Through the window behind Nicco, I could see an iron cross affixed to the neighboring steeple. Adrenaline raced through my veins like electricity, shocking me into action.

I gave the cross one desperate tug with my mind, and it broke off with a crack, whipped through the window, bent around his pale neck, and boomeranged back, slamming him against the wall. The tiny bell tower shuddered as the iron cross plunged into the rock, pinning him in place.

I jumped up, closing the gap between us.

"I am *not* having a good night," I spat, heart pounding.

His fangs protruded even farther as he reeled from the power reversal. "That's it, Adele!" he hissed. "Trust your instincts, *not* your intuition. Instincts exist for your survival. They will keep you alive. Intuition is muddled with emotion." He attempted to compose himself beneath the makeshift shackle. "Emotions will get you killed."

My instincts told me to run as he pulled at the cross, but I easily held it in place. The tug-of-war only further charged him. He slammed his neck into the iron with excited rage. The burst of emotion made me back away, but I kept my mind locked on the restraint. The more I focused, the warmer it became, until the iron nearly glowed and he had to stop pulling or risk searing his neck.

And then we were back to silently staring at each other.

I had no idea how much time had passed. Ten minutes? Twenty? Thirty? The only thing I knew for certain was that I'd never beat him at the silent stare-off. Niccolò Medici had the patience of a marble statue.

I loosened my grip.

In a flash, he ripped the metal from the wall and whipped behind me. One crushing arm wrapped around my chest and the other around my head, forcing my neck to bend. With his lips against my nape, his sharp teeth grazing my skin, he quietly asked, "Did you hear anything I said, *bella*?"

My upper arms were pinned to my sides, but my hands were free. Burning. The dead man's blue eyes blazed in my mind.

He shook me in a violent rage. "Did you?"

"*Sì!*"

My fingers spidered outward, and with every ounce of momentum I could muster, I grabbed the tops of his legs. He howled in pain and fell back.

I scurried to the wall, not totally sure how I'd gotten the upper hand.

"So, it's true," he mumbled under his breath. "You *are* the one."

A killer's instinct shone through his eyes, but his smile said otherwise. I followed his gaze to my own palms and jumped back, only then feeling the heat. A small sphere of fire sat in each palm, miraculously not burning my skin.

What the hell? My heart raced as we both slumped against the walls on our respective sides of the tower, me trying to hide the shock.

Wincing, he carefully pulled the burned denim away from his thighs, and I watched in astonishment as his charred skin began to regenerate—my eyes flicking back and forth to the flames still hovering in my palms.

Minutes later, there were two singed holes the size of my hands in his dark jeans, but they revealed nothing but his pale china-doll skin.

I sucked in air, still struggling not to panic.

Eventually my heartbeat calmed and my palms extinguished, bringing back the darkness. The burning sensation in my arms and the tingling in my fingers, however, didn't go away so easily.

We waited. Watching, wondering if the other would make an aggressive move, but neither of us stirred.

Finally, he spoke. "You fiddle with your necklace just as she did."

I looked down. My fingers were around the charms on my chain. I hadn't even realized I was doing it.

I looked back up at him. "So, I guess the whole 'church is a sanctuary from vampires' thing is not so much?"

He laughed. My shoulders relaxed a little.

"No, not so much. Antiquated Christian propaganda. Recruitment strategy."

"Coffins?"

"Hmm . . . derived from a multitude of Eastern European superstitions, but you can mostly blame the novel *Dracula*."

I tried not to stare at the two fangs he no longer attempted to hide from me.

"Oh, and that atrocious German expressionist film *Nosferatu*, in the twenties."

"House entrances?"

"Philosophically, most vampires believe any creature should be able to find asylum in its own home, but, no, there is no physical reaction to crossing a threshold without invitation."

"Holy water?"

"See 'church.' As with crucifixes, rosaries, and exorcisms."

"Silver?"

"Most have a severe sensitivity to silver, but only in extreme cases would it have a grave effect like anaphylactic shock."

"Garlic? No, wait . . ." Ren's accent crept into my voice. "Crypt keepers in New Orleans used to wear strands of garlic around their necks to help cover the stench of the corpses, not because they actually thought vampires would rise from the ground."

"*Molto brava.* And, centuries ago, people used to stuff cloves of garlic into the mouths of their beloved dead so the deceased wouldn't return as vampires and hunt them . . . because the first thing on every newborn vampire's mind is to terrorize their previous family."

"Is that true?"

"The garlic? No. Terrorizing one's previous family? Not . . . *usually.*"

"Blood?"

"Sustenance."

"Mind reading?"

"No. Mind . . . altering, yes."

"Mirrors?"

"Myth."

"Murder?"

"Inconsequential."

I looked away, trying to digest his blasé answer to my last question, but then forced myself to look back at him. I couldn't afford to be terrified if I wanted the truth.

"Two more questions."

"Just two, *bella*? I have a sneaking suspicion there will be more, but please, go on."

"Sunlight?"

"Vampires don't need vitamin D to survive. Our senses are heightened by the darkness and dulled by the daylight, so that's why most of us are nocturnal." He paused, smiling to himself.

"What?"

"We are very susceptible to sunburn, but you won't find any vampires who will spontaneously combust day-walking, if that's what you were wondering." He became serious again. "Humans think many things about vampires, almost none of which are true. Some think we are creatures spawned from Satan."

"Are you?" I felt foolish as the words slipped off my tongue.

"Do you believe you descended from God?"

I stumbled over the question, picturing Jeanne and Sébastien sighing at me in the name of science. "Um, I don't know."

He smiled. Luckily, my answer was exactly the point he was trying to make.

"Well, then, where *did* vampires come from?"

"Whoa, so existential . . . It's going to be one of those kinds of nights, then?" His long index finger stroked his well-defined chin. "The mythology is vast. Some vampires believe we descended from Cain and Lilith, some believe we are fallen angels, others believe we are alien life-forms, et cetera. Most just believe the obvious—that we evolved from humans. Just the way humans evolved ages ago."

"It's not the same. Human beings evolved over an insanely long period of time, as a species, but you *used* to be a human, right?"

"Of course I did. And, of course, we have a far superior evolution-ary process. I was just trying to make things as linear as possible to explain—"

"The point is, no one knows."

"Exactly. There are many theories for the genesis of man, vampires, and all other life on the planet."

We both gripped onto another moment of silence, contemplating the origin of the universe. I wanted to ask him how *he* became a vampire . . . but for whatever reason it seemed too personal to ask.

"What is your second question, *bella*?"

I didn't want to ruin the mood by asking if *my* family had locked *his* in an attic for three hundred years, so I opted for triviality with a pressed-lips smile. "Did you . . . ever meet Leonardo da Vinci?"

He let out a hearty laugh. "I'm not *that* old, *bella*," and then joked in a faux American accent, "Leo died, like, waaaaaay before I was born."

The jest sounded strange coming from his lips. I smiled. His fangs retracted.

He may not have met da Vinci, but he had a million and one family stories to share about the Italian Renaissance. My knowledge of Italian history was slim, so I asked a lot of questions, listened intently, and tried not to become too mesmerized when his eyes lit up over and over as he zealously bopped from eighteenth-century Florence to Mussolini's Rome.

Hours escaped, and the city became even quieter—it felt like we were the only two people in it. Like we were the only two beings in existence. Somewhere in the middle of the rise of Italian cinema, he had moved beside me, causing my heart to pitter-patter and my brain to forget about the first half of the night.

"How is it possible you've never seen *La Dolce Vita*? It's Fellini's best!" His accent became thicker the more passionate he became. "A cinematic masterpiece . . . You have a lot of homework, *bella*," he said without a trace of judgment.

I mentally filed away the name Federico Fellini, trying not to swoon. I wanted to hide here forever. With him.

But before I could fall too deeply, a bloodcurdling scream shattered our night. We both bolted up and leaned out the back window of the tower just in time to see a dark figure dart through Jesus's shadow in the garden below. The screams didn't stop after the first one, and they sounded close. Very close.

"Emi . . ." he muttered.

"Huh?" I turned to ask. But he was already gone—the rickety door bounced against its frame.

I ran down the dizzying stairs after him, but catching up was a lost cause.

Black lines of makeup streaked the face of a hysterical woman, who was on her knees at the base of the statue. She murmured words in Spanish, which must have been prayers, because I kept hearing the word "Jesús" over and over.

"What happened?" I squeezed my arms around her shoulders while searching in either direction, but I saw no one else. "Are you hurt?"

"Not me." She seemed reluctant to look up but pointed a shaking finger at the shadow on the cathedral wall. "Jesús."

Upon closer look, the shadow seemed distorted, as if Jesus had a humpback. I turned slowly to look at the statue. Trickles of blood dripped down the slick marble to Jesus's knees.

"Oh my God," I yelled, pulling us farther away. Two arms hung around his neck. Two human arms. I gagged, forcing vomit back down my throat. A bloodied man was hanging on Jesus's back.

I whipped around, catching the ruffling of a large, black bird before it took off. I wanted to follow it, but the woman clutched my arm. I had no idea what to do.

Breathe.

Then, through the fog, the muffled sounds of footsteps approached down Orleans Avenue. My grip on the poor woman tightened until I saw it was Ren leading the way, flanked by Theis. It must have been the crowd from Le Chat Noir. Or, part of the crowd. No sign of my father, thank God. Or Isaac. Or . . . Gabe's crew.

"*Bébé!*" Ren ran and scooped me into a bear hug.

"*Ça va bien,* Ren."

He set me down, casually pushing back both of my braids while Theis looked at me with suspicion.

I suddenly remembered all the freshmen girls scattering away from the bouncer. *It was after curfew by then. I should have made sure they got home! What was I thinking?*

I scanned the crowd for them.

Jaime and Bri were taking photos with their phones. Annabelle was crying but was obviously enlivened by the drama. She buried her face into the pecs of some frat boy. *Wait. We're one Big Sister shy.*

There was no sign of her.

I frantically hurried over to the girls. "Where's Désirée?"

"She went off with Gabriel," Annabelle said with an exaggerated tongue roll on the *r*.

"*What?* No. Do you know where they went?"

She shook her head, utterly unconcerned. My cheeks flushed as she scanned the two additions to my grungy ensemble.

"Where did you get off to, by the way?" she asked. "That hot ponytail ever catch up with you?"

I ignored her and checked my watch. Two a.m. *Is Gabe a vampire too? Are Gabe and Nicco really even brothers?*

Nicco's words echoed in my mind: *Never trust a vampire.*

Tires screeched to a halt. Lights flashed. Doors slammed. A voice on a megaphone told everyone to vacate the garden. *Dammit*—Detective Matthews. *This is way worse than being busted out past curfew.*

You didn't do anything else wrong, I reminded myself.

A plainclothes cop started shooing people away, and I eagerly took the opportunity to exit with the crowd.

"Adele!" Detective Matthews said, accidentally speaking through the megaphone.

Everyone looked at me as I stopped in my tracks. He hustled over.

"Were *you* the first one to arrive at the scene?"

"Um . . . not exactly."

"Oh my God!" Annabelle shrieked as a cop on a ladder lifted the corpse's head. The crowd gasped.

Blood dripped from the empty sockets where his eyes had been plucked out. A lump formed in my throat. It was Wilson "the Wolfman" Washington, the DJ who, on that very evening, had warned the city to keep their eyes peeled.

Over the next hour, the crime scene tape was rolled out. Cameras flashed as evidence was documented. My back stiffened as Detective Matthews continued to interrogate me, going back and forth with another cop. I wanted to leave to go look for Désirée. *Is she in danger? Should I tell Detective Matthews?* Warmth spread through my body, making me shake as he asked what felt like the hundredth question. Just as I was about to explode, an arm pulled me backward.

"What the hell is going on here, Terry?" my father asked, pushing through a couple of forensic techs.

"I'm sorry, Mac," said the bleary-eyed detective. "Protocol."

"Well, my daughter is a minor, so all your protocol can go through me from now on. Got it?" There was more aggression in his voice than I'd ever heard before.

"Of course, Mac. I think we've gotten everything we need. Why don't you take little Addie home?" My fingers twitched. One minute I was being grilled like a murder suspect and the next being treated like a toddler. He patted my shoulder and began to walk over to his partner.

"Wait, Detective—" I said. He turned back around. I hesitated. What if Désirée wasn't missing? What if she was just somewhere hooking up with Gabe? She'd *kill me* if I started a search for her. *Shit.* "I hope you find whoever did this."

"We will, kiddo," he said and turned back to his team, leaving me with my father.

"Adele, where the hell have you been? I've been calling and texting you for the last—"

"I'm sorry, Mac. She was with me." And suddenly there Isaac was, staring straight at me, offering me an out. *How long has he been standing there?*

"Dammit, Isaac—"

"I know, sir. I'm sorry. We were just sitting by the river talking, and we lost track of time." Isaac looked at the leather jacket I was huddled in and the shirt hanging out below it. He knew exactly whom they belonged to. He turned back to my dad, blinking away the sting.

"I expect more from you . . . !" my father proceeded to yell.

Isaac quietly accepted the lashing.

When my father finished, Isaac wouldn't even look my way. Guilt pummeled me.

A policewoman closed up the body bag with a loud zip. My gut told me I was responsible for this insanity.

And the vampires.

My lungs pinched.

Where the hell is Désirée?

CHAPTER 27

It's a Bird

October 28th

"Your hair is uh-mazing, Adele," said a girl with a faux tan and diamond hoop earrings, sitting in front of me in physics lab.

"Uh, thanks?" I replied, hoping she'd turn back around. There was definitely nothing amazing about my hair, other than it being genuinely dirty and disheveled rather than purposefully styled that way. The girl asked me a question about my hair products.

Why didn't I skip today?

I certainly could have, considering the circumstances, but after the huge fight I'd had with my father when we got home last night, escaping the house seemed like a good plan. Now I needed pencils to hold open my eyelids, but I couldn't just blame my father—besides the crime scene, a multitude of other things had stolen my few remaining hours of sleep: for starters, the beady-eyed crow had perched on our neighbor's balcony all night long, and I spent a good hour convincing myself it wasn't Isaac. Then there was the fact that Désirée was still MIA. She hadn't returned any of my texts, nor had she picked me up for school. Lastly—and this was horrible, given the circumstances—I couldn't stop thinking about Nicco. *He knows my secret. And I know his.* Yet he'd told me not to trust him. *What the hell?*

"We should hang out sometime—"

"Face forward," Mr. Anderson told the girl.

Thank God.

Maybe I was just delirious, but out of all the bizarre things that had occurred over the last few weeks, today was the most confounding. A jock had helped pick up my spilled books, and a cheerleader had complimented my necklace, which was hardly fashionable. At least half a dozen other upperclassmen had smiled, waved, or said hello in the hallway. All before first period.

I waited for Mr. Anderson to turn his back and then leaned close to Tyrelle. Being my lab partner, he was forced to talk to me.

"What is going on today?" I whispered as he carefully connected tiny wires to a circuit board. "Why is everyone being *nice* to me?"

"Because you have something they want," he said without looking up. "Something that not even their parents' money can buy them."

"Huh? What?"

"Permanent entrance to the coolest underground club in town."

"Ugh . . ."

My mind instantly went back to last night. *I should have told the detective about Désirée.* "What was I thinking?" I accidently yelped out loud, and a long spark zapped from the circuit board.

Tyrelle jumped back. "What the—"

I didn't know what was worse: that everyone in school knew about Le Chat Noir's illegal operation or that they were being nice to me because of it. Tyrelle looked at the circuit board plug, which was resting on the table, and then back to me with confusion. All I could do to cover up the blatant magic was shoot back the exact same *what just happened* face.

He stared at the blur of my pencil as I frantically tapped it. "You need to chill."

I wiped my clammy forehead with the back of my hand. The bell rang, and I jumped up.

"Welcome to my world," he said, packing up. "Everyone always after something your pop's got."

"That sucks," I said, and for the first time we walked out of class together.

When we got to our lockers, the queen herself was waiting. "Good morning, sunshine," Annabelle said as I swapped out my books.

"Pfft," Tyrelle sighed traitorously, looking at me.

Lacking the energy for hallway politics, I shot him a snarky look back. My locker slammed shut on its own, and I reflexively slapped it as a cover-up. Pain shot up my arm.

"Dammit!"

Tyrelle shook his head as if I were the biggest spaz on the planet.

I checked my phone for the umpteenth time as I rubbed my hand. "Have you seen Désirée?" I asked Annabelle, too concerned to realize we'd started walking to class together.

"No, but she can't ditch French because of our midterm."

"Bonjour, mesdemoiselles," said Madame Cecilia as we entered the room.

"Bonjour, Madame Cecilia," we chimed in unison.

And, sure enough, Désirée was at her desk, giving her best deviant smile to the other minions.

I exhaled loudly as Bri shrieked, "You *have* to give us more details than that!" I dropped my stuff on my desk with a thud. They all looked over. Now that I knew Désirée had a pulse, I was pissed.

"What the hell? I've called you like fifty times. I thought you were dead!"

Bri's mouth hung open at my total disregard for social hierarchy.

"Yeah, Dee," Annabelle demanded. "Time to spill it."

I glared at Désirée. What she did or didn't do with Gabriel Medici was *not* my concern, and I was pretty sure she knew that.

"Calm down, Adele. Obviously, my father was alerted when the Wolfman's body was found, so he was waiting up for me when I got home at four a.m. He freaked and took away my car and my cell. One of his jocular security guards dropped me off at school."

The bell rang, shrieking through my head. "You could've at least found me this morning. Are you sure you're okay?"

My eyes frantically scoured her neck. She seemed perfectly normal. In fact, she seemed better than normal. She seemed . . . happy. Must have been the Gabe effect.

"I'm sorry. I just really thought you were in trouble . . . or something."

She leaned over. "I do *not* have trouble with boys." Her eyes locked with mine.

Wait . . . Do we actually understand each other? Does Désirée know vampires are roaming the streets? Her gaze went to my necklace. My fingers automatically touched it. *Does she know about me?*

"Take your seats and put everything away," Madame Cecilia instructed in French.

Everyone scrambled with varying groans. Luckily for me, my current level of French was far more advanced than anything we'd learned in class. No studying required. I threw my books underneath my chair, and when I looked back up, there was a note on my desk.

We need to talk. VP 6 p.m.

Désirée looked back at me for a moment, and I nodded.

The message momentarily calmed me. Suddenly, I didn't feel so alone. *She knows something,* I thought as I slipped the note in my pocket and resumed my pencil tapping.

Dixie walked in late. "*Désolée, Madame Cecilia*. I wasn't feeling very well this morning."

"*Ça va bien*, Mademoiselle Hunter. You look rather pale?"

"I'm fine. I mean, *très bien*." The French words sounded completely ridiculous with Dixie's thick drawl.

She walked to the empty desk in front of mine—she looked like she hadn't gotten much sleep. Her skin tone was more emo than her usual Malibu Barbie shade, and she clutched the chair as she lowered her body into the seat. But my pencil tapping came to a halt when I noticed the Gucci neatly tied around her neck.

"Nice scarf," I whispered, leaning forward.

"Thanks. It was a gift." She smiled smugly.

Désirée's gaze moved from her test, to the scarf, and then to me.

"So, Dixie," I whispered, trying to sound casual, "where'd you get off to last night?"

"Wouldn't you like to know!"

"*Je demande le silence!*" Madame Cecilia threatened.

Was Dixie's hostility warranted? I had kind of left her hanging at the bar. I *could* have helped her get past the bouncer. *What about the freshmen?*

I tried to concentrate on the test questions, but fear for the other girls distracted me. *Why do I even have to take this class?*

Focus, Adele.

I shut my eyes, took a deep breath, and attempted to push away all the images of the Little Sisters getting their throats ripped out.

It was strange, walking down the silent halls on my way off campus. Even though I was only scheduled for half a day, my step quickened walking past all the closed doors, as if I were going to get caught skipping.

When I opened the grand front door, it nearly smacked a girl.

"Sorry!"

"Adele!" she returned with glee, although smiling appeared to be a struggle for her—she was the freshman from last night, with the black corkscrews (currently sticking out in every direction), in the God-awful muumuu. I felt bad I didn't even know her name.

"Hey, are you just getting to school?"

"Yeah, I wasn't feeling so well when I woke up, but I'm okay now." Her skin gleamed as if a fever had just broken, and her arms were wrapped tightly around her torso, but then her face brightened up. "Are you my Big Sister?"

"Um . . . I don't think any decisions have been made yet, with all the commotion last night."

"I hope you are!" she said, her gaze dropping to the floor. "I have to get to class now."

"Me too," I said as she quickly walked past me. There was something off about the entire exchange. *Wait.* I spun around, just in time to catch a final glimpse as she walked into a classroom—there was a pink Dior scarf fashionably knotted around her neck.

What the . . . ? Not exactly the same as Dixie's Gucci. *It couldn't be a coincidence.*

Great job I'd done guiding the freshmen.

I buttoned my school-issued blazer as I walked into the perfectly manicured garden. The sun shone, but the air was damp. A part of me wanted to turn around and see how many of the other girls were wearing silk scarves. Another part of me wanted to run home as fast as I could and never come back. But when I thought about going home to my apprenticeship with my father and Isaac, a whole new wave of anxieties set in. *I can't believe Isaac covered for me last night.*

They had both completely invaded my routine. I missed my old life, back when I liked my nerdy art school. I missed Brooke. I missed working with Jeanne and Sébastien. Central air and heat. Fresh produce. Sweet potato Hubig's Pies. Thanks to the Storm, nothing was sacred anymore. I ripped the bun from my head and let my unwashed waves ripple down my back, feeling an immediate release of tension.

At least I knew Désirée was alive.

I forced my shoulders to relax and hopped down the remaining stairs, but when I lifted my head to open the front gate, I saw *him*. Directly ahead of me, leaning against an oak tree, was Émile. He was waiting for me. With all the chaos, I had somehow managed to forget about him.

I had no choice but to walk straight over.

"Bonjour, Adele, est-ce que je t'ai manqué?"

Despite his soft lips brushing each of my cheeks as I greeted him, I was still stunned to see him here. In New Orleans. I had practically convinced myself that he was a figment of my imagination, brought on by trauma.

"Did you miss me?" He repeated the question in English, as if my language skills were the problem in this scenario.

"What are you doing here?" I asked, the last word not much more than a gasp.

"I'm sorry for just showing up. I whuz so excited to see you last night, but zhen you disappeared before I could get to you. How are you? Missing our adventures?"

Everything felt different now. He was no longer exotic and mature. He was my babysitter. He always had been. I felt stupid and childish for ever fantasizing about him chasing after me. There had never been anything between us. I wasn't sure we were even friends. He was just an employee of my mother's.

"Adele, what's wrong?" He took my hand, and an electric shock zapped us.

"Static," I said, trying to pull my hand back, but he held on. "You didn't answer my question, Émile. Why are you *here*? In the States?"

He paused, and his usual confident expression turned puzzled. "Didn't she tell you? Your mother invited me to accompany her to New Orleans to assist on her new assignment."

I yanked my hand back. "What?"

"Adele, I am here with your mother—her grant from zha government of France to restore some historic French exhibits damaged by zha hurricane. Didn't you know?"

"Of course I knew!" I crossed my arms. "I just didn't know you were coming with her."

I wondered if he could tell I was lying. During our many bouts of espresso drinking, I'd complained a lot about my mother. He'd always listened attentively, but he'd also *always* found a way to defend her. "She has a very stressful career at zha museum. It's just her artistic temperament. She's just French." Blah, blah, blah. Sometimes I'd wanted to slap him for knowing more about my mother than I did.

"Is zhere somewhere we can go and talk? We have so much to catch up on. A coffee, maybe?"

I shook my head, feeling like I might cry if I opened my mouth. My mother was in town, and she hadn't even bothered to tell me.

"Can I give you a ride?" He nodded to a museum-worthy motorbike.

I shook my head again.

"Can I at least walk you home?"

I couldn't manage to get a "no" out, so when I started walking, he stepped beside me by default. I choked out a question about his flight. Luckily, he liked the sound of his own voice.

It felt like a year since I'd been in Paris, since Émile was the only person able to comfort me, since my stupid schoolgirl crush. It was typical Émile to just rock into town and slip in with the cool kids. The bad memories from the bar flooded back, and the cracks in the cement became blurry as I blinked away tears. *Glad to know art can get my mother back to town.*

When we approached the last couple of blocks, I stopped. My father crossing paths with my mother's hot, young assistant didn't seem like a good idea.

Fortunately, Émile took the hint. He kissed my cheeks and smiled his stupid smile. "*Demain.* Same time, same place. See, it's just like Paris. *À bientôt.*"

Nothing was like it was in Paris.

The Storm. Sacred Heart. Telekinesis. Vampires.

They were all things I'd never thought would happen. But for some reason, knowing that my mother was in New Orleans was the thing that made the whole world seem off-kilter.

My pace quickened as I approached the house, continuing to stare at the sidewalk, continuing to blink back tears. I didn't think I could feel any worse, but then suddenly I did.

"Are you going to avoid me forever?" Isaac asked. He was sitting on my stoop, examining a thin silver object in his hands. He looked exhausted.

"That doesn't really seem possible, given you are at my house every afternoon," I snapped, immediately regretting it.

He stood to leave.

"No, I'm sorry. I'm just confu—It's just that . . ." I stopped and took a breath. "Do you ever just feel crazy?" I didn't even know what I meant by the question, but I found myself standing directly in front of him, with my hand on his chest.

"These days? You have no idea." He looked at my hand, which I promptly removed.

The hurt in his eyes was evident. I asked myself how it would have felt if Nicco had turned his back on me after seeing flames rise from my hands, the way I'd done to Isaac after he'd revealed so much of himself to me.

I would have been horrified. Humiliated.

Of course, Isaac hadn't revealed *everything*. My legs became wobbly.

I sat next to his feet, and he sat back down. The knot in my stomach pulled so tight I couldn't even sit up straight, so I rested my head on my knees, looking at him. I knew we were bordering a moment of truth. A wave of hair fell over my face. I closed my eyes, trying to ignore the thoughts I'd been having about him—about the crow—but his sketchbook pages flipped through my mind.

Feathers.

Feathers.

Feathers.

He gently moved the hair from my face and tucked it behind my ear, causing butterflies to rush my stomach. "The cut's getting better," he said, tracing the mark. Heat rushed to my cheeks as his fingers lingered. "It's hardly noticeable."

Liar, I thought. But then my lashes fluttered open, and the concern in his golden-brown eyes gave me the answer. I asked the question anyway.

"Did you do this to me?"

His gaze fell to the ground and then came back to me. "Yes."

I jumped up, defenses skyrocketing. He did too.

"I'm so sorry, Adele. I didn't know what I was doing . . . I still don't know what I'm doing. I didn't mean to . . ."

And with that, the whole world seemed to tilt another degree: Isaac had admitted he could turn himself into a bird.

"What else have you lied to me about?" *I knew it wasn't a coincidence when he showed up at our house to fix the wall.* "And what were you doing in my house that night you attacked me?"

"I didn't attack . . . I can explain—"

"I think you should go now," I said, despite hearing the desperation in his voice.

His head bobbed in agreement. If I wasn't mistaken, there were tears in his eyes, but I couldn't be sure, because I was fighting my own. *Had anything between us ever been real?* My chest tightened, thinking about our kiss.

"I'm really sorry . . ."

My breathing became erratic. I looked at him one last time and slipped through the door, barely getting it shut before I collapsed on the other side in tears. Not just a few tears, chest-heaving, would-be-screaming-if-I-could-breathe tears.

"Isaac?" my father yelled from the back of the house. "Adele?"

The sound of my name sent me into a panic. I didn't want to talk to my father, or see him.

He entered the hallway, and I nearly knocked him over as I sprang to the staircase.

"Adele, what's wrong?"

"Leave me alone!"

He ran up the stairs behind me, but I slammed my bedroom door, not caring whether he'd seen the door fly closed by itself. I felt the bolt in the lock click as I flopped onto my bed.

"Adele, what happened? Come on, sweetheart, open the door," he pleaded, jiggling the handle.

My chest burned like something had clawed it raw. Like some-*one* had.

"Please let me in. Did something happen at school? Is this about last night?"

My chest grew tighter and I began to wheeze.

"Adele, *use* your inhaler."

"Go away!" I yelled, gasping.

I threw my arms over my head. As soon as I got my breath back, my tears stopped.

My dry eyes confused me. With the amount of emotion pummeling through my body, I'd expected them to continue like an endless river. *Even my emotions are betraying me now.*

The thought made me feel like a melodramatic child. I jerked myself from the bed and approached the door. I knew I was causing my father pain, but I didn't care.

Everyone I knew was lying to me.

And to top it off, it felt like electricity was running through my bloodstream, and I had to focus on not spontaneously combusting.

My forehead pressed against the wooden door as I mumbled, "Did you know she was in town?"

"What, sweetheart? I can't hear you. Can you open the door, *s'il vous plaît*?" Resorting to French meant he was desperate.

"Did. You. Know. That *she* was in town?"

"Honey, you're not making any sense. Did I know who was in town?"

My jaw was clenched so tightly I barely got out the words. *"Madame Brigitte Dupré."*

Silence.

Even through the thick wooden door, I knew my father was trying to compose himself. I felt as if I'd put a knife through his heart. Learning that my mother had arrived back in town for the first time in twelve years without a peep was possibly even more painful for him to swallow than for me. And the sick thing was, in that moment, it made me feel a little better, having someone to share a little bit of my pain. My confusion.

"Your mother is in town? In *New Orleans*?" His voice cracked on the *O*.

"That's the word on the street."

"According to who?"

I opened the door a couple of inches and saw him quickly wipe his eyes. "I ran into her assistant on the way home from school."

"What's she doing here?"

"Apparently something for work," I answered coldly.

The words stole the glimmer of hope from his eyes.

"I'm going to take a nap, okay?" I said.

He nodded. "I think I'll close the bar tonight and stay here with you."

"Don't bother . . ." I managed to refrain from commenting on *that* still-sore subject. "I have to meet up with Désirée to study for midterms. Probably till late."

"I don't want you on the streets at night, Adele."

"I know, Dad. We're meeting at Vodou Pourvoyeur, so it's just a couple blocks. She'll drive me home afterward."

"All right," he said, defeated. "I love you, Adele."

"I love you too, Dad."

Guilt set in before I had shut the door again. I'd never seen my father cry before. I didn't know what to make of it.

Counting on the distraction, I pulled out my copy of *The Metamorphosis* and tried to convince myself to start writing my English term paper, an essay on symbolism. I took one look at the cover and, for the first time, started to fathom how Gregor Samsa could have woken up one morning and not seen his own giant bug head in the mirror. I hardly recognized myself anymore.

CHAPTER 28

Voodoo Queen Dee

Incessant beeping from the alarm on my phone pulled my mind from the deep bowels of a REM cycle, but even as I became semiconscious, my eyelids remained swollen shut. Desperate for more sleep, they'd encrusted themselves with a layer of gunk during my nap. I hobbled straight into the shower—while sleeping for eternity seemed like a great option, I was eager to meet up with Désirée.

The steamy shower didn't do much for the giant circles under my eyes, but at least it pulled me out of the zombielike state.

Black jeans. White cotton T-shirt. Docs. *Good enough for me.* Beneath my shirt, the gris-gris was damp against my chest. I hadn't taken it or the medallion off in days.

I tossed a couple of books into my bag, in case we needed evidence that we were studying, and, of course, Adeline's diary, which I carried around as if it needed protection.

With five minutes to spare, I was down the stairs and out the front door. I'd be right on time.

My boot sent something skidding across the pavement as I hopped down the stoop. When I slowly lifted my hand, the small metal object leaped into my palm—the feather Isaac had made during our casting lesson. The silver version was stunning beneath the autumn sunset. He must have dropped it during our fight. Guilt sank my heart as I slipped it into my pocket and hurried down the street.

Adele, you cannot feel bad for a boy who broke into your house, attacked you, and cut your face open.

I didn't see so much as a shadow or hear a second set of footsteps until it was too late. A hand slipped over my mouth, muffling my screams, and a strong arm hooked my waist, forcing me into an alleyway. Before I could react, my hands were crushed together by inhuman strength.

"Shh . . ." A voice hushed into my ear.

I arched my back and bucked all my weight against the faceless person. My captor didn't so much as wobble but simply straightened to full height. My legs kicked as my feet left the ground, but then I froze when a woman's voice whispered sweetly in my ear, "Don't bother, *ma fifille.* I can drain you dry in less than a minute if I like."

A woman? A woman with a very thick French accent . . .

The more I struggled, the more riled up she became. Her fingers tightened around my hands, and I winced as my palms burned against each other. She pressed her nose into my neck, her nostrils flaring against my skin as she sucked in my scent as if in ecstasy. Then her cold, wet tongue slid from my collarbone to my ear.

With a shudder, my body went limp, like a rag doll.

A second shudder rippled, this time from her—a shudder of restraint.

"But I am not going to do that, Adele. Not yet. I am just 'ere to warn you: if you don't finish breaking the curse, bad things are going to happen *dans le Vieux Carré.*" Her hand slipped from my mouth to my forehead, holding my head tightly in place, so I couldn't see her. "Very bad things."

"I can take care of myself, *merci beaucoup*," I grunted.

I could sense her lips spreading into a smile, but she didn't mock me. "It's not you they will hurt, *ma fifille*, but every person you love. They will show no mercy, for this is a very old grudge, and they play by very old rules. They will destroy your *famille*, just as they destroyed mine."

"What grudge?"

"Whatever it is they want from your *famille*, you'd better give it to them, or you will regret it. *Je vous le promets*."

Then I was in a heap on the ground. Alone.

"Give *what* back to *WHO*?" I yelled down the alley.

My own voiced echoed in return, taunting me.

I dusted off my burning palms, cursing under my breath. *Finish breaking the curse, or bad things will happen in the French Quarter?*

"*Finish* breaking the curse? What the heck?"

I picked up my bag and power walked the rest of the way.

As I approached the shop door, another figure stepped from behind the shutter, nearly sending me into cardiac arrest.

"Jesus, Ren! I almost decked you!"

"Aw, *bébé, pardon moi*."

He was carrying too many packages to sweep me up into his signature hug, so he shuffled his bags until he could remove his top hat with a couple of free fingers.

"No tour tonight?" I asked.

"Er, it's supposed to rain later."

I looked up at the clear sky, not that a lack of clouds really meant anything. It was New Orleans, after all; the weather was anything but predictable. "What are you doing here?"

"Oh, ya know, just makin' groceries."

"At Vodou Pourvoyeur?" I got the feeling he was being purpose-fully vague.

"And what are you doing here on this fine evening?" he deflected with a wink. "Love potion, perhaps?"

I tried not to scowl as I patted my bag—two could play at this game. "Studying for midterms with Désirée."

As he shifted the weight of the bags around, a strong, botanical whiff blew my way. I peeked into one of his sacks: an assortment of herbs. I sneezed.

"Did you leave anything in the shop? Whatcha got in there?"

"Oh, a little bit of this, a little bit of that. Juniper berries, green cardamom, coriander, lavender, and a pinch of black peppercorn for a little zing! Tryin' to class up the ol' bathtub gin while tours are slow. People in New Orleans will drink just about anything, but, to quote your pa, 'Why put hair on people's chests if we don't have to?'"

I nodded as if I knew what he was talking about. *So, Ren is making that God-awful liquor the clown was offering at the bar?*

"Plus, if we can get the 'shine to taste more like the store-bought stuff, there's less chance of the law finding out, right?"

"Speaking of the law, has there been any news . . . about the Wolfman?"

"The wind in the willows says more than eighty percent of his blood was drained."

"What? There wasn't *that* much blood at the crime scene."

"No, there wasn't, *bébé*." He paused, as if trying to silently lead me on. "I hate to say it, but it kind of reminds me of the story from my tour. The one where the two documentarians were found in front of the chapel at the Ursuline Convent, blood drained."

"When did you say that happened?"

"About twelve years ago."

"All your other stories are so much older."

"*Oui*, centuries of unsolved crimes in this city."

"So they never found the murderer?"

"No."

My pulse skipped. The first time we met, Nicco said they'd been to New Orleans before. *I wonder when . . . ?*

That's a horrible accusation, Adele. But the questions lingered. *Would Nicco do something so barbaric? Even if he needed blood to survive?* I wanted to think, "no," but his statement about murder being inconsequential rang loud in my mind.

"All right, darlin', I need to get moving. Theis and I are cooking up a batch of hurricane gruel tonight."

"What's that?" I asked, scared to know the answer.

"It's when you break out the biggest gumbo pot ya got, close your eyes, and dump in about a dozen random canned goods."

"Ew!" I choked out a giggle.

"Laissez les bons temps rouler!"

As gross as it sounded, the very mention of food made me purr. The only thing that had entered my stomach today was anxiety.

"Eh, it all tastes the same after you add enough cayenne." He took a swig from his pocket flask and bent forward to kiss the top of my head. "Get some sleep, *bébé*, and go easy on your papa about the distillery. He was really torn up about hiding the hurricane hoochin' from ya."

"Distillery?" The question flew out so quickly I was unable to hide my surprise.

"Oh, er? I thought you . . . Oh, don't listen to anything I say. You know it's all baloney. *Bonne nuit, ma chérie!*"

He walked away, cursing himself under his breath. "Geezum, Ren, *tuat t'en grosse bueche.*"

"*Non, Ren, merci beaucoup* for your big mouth." My voice faded into the night, and again I was alone.

Inside, the smell of wood, lilacs, and cinnamon permeated the air. *I can't believe I'm here, looking for answers,* I thought as I walked past the Voodoo dolls, tourist thrills, and alligator skulls. Désirée was at the counter, doing what I assumed was homework. It turned out I was wrong; at least, it wasn't homework in the traditional sense.

She nodded to acknowledge my presence and shut the encyclopedia-thick book. I stared into the dust that clouded out. The atmosphere became awkward. We weren't even friends, but something about the meeting felt natural, and that's what *really* felt weird.

"So . . ." I said.

"I want to show you something. Wait right here." She disappeared behind a thick fuchsia curtain on the far wall.

Voices murmured, and then she returned with an oil painting in a hand-carved wooden frame. She set it on the counter, crossed her arms, and asked, "Who is she?"

"Huh?" The painting looked old. Like colonial old—teenage girls, posing for a group portrait. I laughed. "How would I know any of these people?"

"Focus." Désirée snapped her fingers in my face.

"Okaaaaay . . ." I looked back down. There were seven girls posing in a garden. "Wait, is that the Ursuline Convent?"

The garden was sparse, as if it had recently been planted, but the building was the same.

"Mmm hmmm." She eagerly leaned over the painting.

It was hard to pinpoint the time period. Each of the girls' style of dress was so different—from peasant blouses, with externally laced bodices, to silk that reflected the sun—it was almost like they were in costume. The fanciness of their clothes might have varied, as did the color of their skin, but it was obvious they were kindred spirits. Even through the stoic expressions, you could tell they were all close. Like they all shared a secret.

I instantly fell in love with them.

My gaze stopped on a brunette holding a parasol; everything else blacked out. Her dress was fancier than the rest, with layers of delicate lace ruffles at the collar and sleeves. The structured boning made her posture stiff. Aristocratic.

"She's . . . she's wearing—"

"Your necklace?" Désirée finished.

I looked at the painting again. Her necklace was small, but there was no denying that she was wearing the same medallion. The opal was hard to mistake.

"*Adeline*," I whispered. And even stranger, despite having never seen the painting before, this wasn't the first time I'd seen her face—Isaac had captured her perfectly in his drawings. *He hadn't been sketching me . . . He'd been sketching* her. *But how could he—?*

"Do you ever hang out with Isaac Thompson?" I asked.

"Ugh, *no*," she answered with a quick lift of her eyebrow.

"*Where* did you get this painting?"

She ignored my question as a little excitement slipped through her placid demeanor. "I have a theory . . . But first, who is she?"

I looked back at the girl, and it was as if she looked back at me. Her expression was exactly how I had imagined her: both dreamy and defiant at the same time.

"Adeline Saint-Germain." I took off the heirloom and dropped it into her hand, showing her the initials.

"This stone is so weird."

"I know . . . I'm pretty sure it was stolen from a dead pirate captain. Which is kind of gross, now that I think about it."

"And how would you know *that*?"

"How do you have a painting of my great-great-great-whatever-grand-something?"

"Because it's also a painting of my great-great-great-whatever-grandmother Marassa Makandal." She pointed to the girl next to

Adeline, who wore a knotted head scarf similar to the tignon that Désirée's grandmother often wore.

"What?" I lowered my voice. "This is so nuts!" I wasn't sure why I was whispering, but it definitely felt like we were on the verge of discovering something that had been hidden for a very long time.

Ritha Borges emerged from behind the curtain. "Our ancestor Marassa Makandal was a remarkable woman. A very powerful woman." She walked behind the counter and stood beside Désirée, with a large leather-bound book in her arms.

"She was beautiful," I said.

They both nodded in agreement.

Ritha slid the painting down the counter to make room for the ancient-looking book. "And this . . . was her grimoire."

"Come again?" I asked. "Grimoire?"

"It's where Marassa kept all of her most secret thoughts, and experiments," Ritha explained, pride resonating in her voice. "You can think of it as a Voodoo spell book that's been passed down for many generations. Most of the magic sold in this shop is still based off of things from this book."

"This is *Marassa Makandal's* grimoire?" Désirée asked with a surprising bout of emotion in her voice.

"It was. And now it's yours, my dear."

"I . . . I'm still not joining your . . . you know." Désirée seemed uneasy with me being there for all the talk of Voodoo and magic, but not more than I was.

"You will." Ritha said. "In time."

Désirée turned the book sideways, so we could both see, opened the leather cover, and carefully turned a few of the thick, browned pages. Intricate sketches and diagrams were drawn between lengthy passages and lists that resembled recipes. I could only understand about half of it, and those parts were in French—and that was just the linguistics—it's not like I knew what any of it meant.

"It's a Haitian *Kreyòl* dialect," Ritha said. "Very old."

"Looks old. What are all these notes on the sides?" I asked.

"The entire volume has been translated over the years by different witches from different generations of our family."

Witches?

"The marginalia discuss discrepancies in translations. New interpretations."

"I know all about translating old French text . . . I've been translating Adeline Saint-Germain's diary—"

"Wait, Adeline Saint-Germain had a diary?" Désirée asked.

I patted my bag.

"And you *have* it?"

"Is that really so weird? You just pulled out a three-hundred-year-old spell book."

"Touché."

I procured Adeline's diary and gently rested it on the counter. I was suddenly nervous, unsure whether I should confide in the Borges, but it felt so good to uncork the bottle I could barely control what came out of my mouth. *Bad things will happen in the Vieux Carré.* I was out of time. I was going to have to start taking some risks.

"Adeline came from France to New Orleans in 1728, with *les filles aux cassettes—*"

"Adeline was a casquette girl?" asked Désirée.

"Not exactly, but she came over with a couple of other aristocrats on the same ship. Her father gave her this diary and asked her to record her journey . . . every single detail. He was pretty adamant about it." I pushed the diary across the counter so she could see it.

"Weird . . ."

"The things parents ask of their children," said Ritha, "often seem silly at the time, but rarely are."

"How did you find it?" Désirée asked.

"Uh . . . ," I stumbled, unsure if I was ready to reveal so much about *me*.

"Sometimes when things need to be found, they find you," Ritha answered. I nearly chuckled at the truth in her strange statement.

"Ugh, is this whole diary in French?" asked Désirée, turning the pages. *"Ma français est pathétique."*

"Don't beat yourself up too much. My French is okay, and it's still taking me forever to translate it. I'm just up to the part where some, er, stowaways helped them survive a pirate attack."

"How adventurous."

You have no idea.

We all got lost in the old texts for a moment, but soon, the silence pecked at me until the question escaped my mouth: "Mrs. Ritha, can I ask you something . . . about magic?"

"Sure, suga', what's on your mind?"

"What happens to a spell after the caster dies?"

"Unfortunately, there's no simple answer, since all spells and all witches are so different. In most cases, the spell is passed down to a descendant. If the witch dies without any progeny, then the spell should break instantly."

I struggled to keep my face composed at her casual use of the *W* word. "And if the spell was passed on, would said progeny be able to break it?

"Oh yes. Break it. Bend it. Enhance it. Once the spell is passed on, the new witch has complete control of the cast."

Am I a descendant? Did I inherit one of Adeline's spells? Just because she could do magic, did that make her a witch? The medallion started to vibrate on the wooden counter. I quickly slipped it back on and hid it under my shirt.

No.

No.

No.

Did I . . . ? Shit. No. The shutter. The whoosh of energy. The metal stake rolling to my nose. *Did I break a spell?* I remembered the woman from the alley's demand for the rest of the curse to be broken.

"Is there a way to *partially* break a spell?" Désirée asked. I paused my internal freak-out to listen.

A smile crossed Ritha's face. I got the feeling Désirée wasn't usually so interested in the family business.

"Hmm . . . No, a spell is created with a very specific effect in mind, and it requires an exact recipe: certain words, ingredients, sacrifices. Even an individual's specific bloodline can matter. Each spell is its own little perfect storm. A bond between the caster and the castee. A witch can enhance or mutate a spell if she desires a new outcome, but she can't partially break a spell that was cast for a certain effect . . . not without destroying the integrity of the spell."

I was confused, but still, a wave of relief washed over me.

"Of course," she said, "that all goes out the window if the spell was cast by a coven."

My brow furled.

Coven?

"If the spell was cast by a coven instead of just one witch, each descendent can break the part of the spell her ancestor was directly responsible for: the part she inherited."

I looked back at the painting of the girls. "And if the spell was cast by a coven, how would you break it completely?"

"To completely break an old coven's spell, you'd have to re-form the original coven with the new generation of witches who inherited their ancestors' powers," Ritha said. "Of course, there is one other way to break a coven's curse."

"How?" Désirée and I said at the same time.

"The same way you can break a spell by a single witch. Break the spell line. The original coven's spell will break, piece by piece, until the last inheritor is gone."

A breath escaped my tight-pressed lips.

"Death?"

Giant flames exploded in the fireplace, causing me to jump back. Désirée gave me a slanted look, but Ritha didn't blink an eye.

"Mother Nature has a way of bringing people together in times of woe."

"That's very esoteric," I said.

"Welcome to my life." Désirée cracked a smile. She placed her hand on the painting and hesitated before asking her grandmother: "Were they a coven?"

"Don't be silly, Désirée Borges," Ritha said with absolute authority. "You know Marassa Makandal was the high priestess of an *all*-Haitian *Kreyòl* coven—the first recorded coven in all of New Orleans, dating back to 1730."

It was weird seeing someone shut down Désirée. I found myself asking on her behalf: "So there's *no way* these girls were a coven?"

Désirée's attention perked up, waiting to see how her grandmother would respond to me.

"Covens are formed by witches of the *same* house of magic. It's the only way for a witch to reach her *true* potential."

I didn't know what that meant, but I felt Désirée silently egging me on, so I probed: "Always?"

Ritha hesitated for a moment, as if reluctant to speak the truth. "Good night, girls," she said and disappeared behind the curtain.

"*Bonne nuit,*" I said, and waited until the curtain was motionless before I continued. "What was that all about?"

"*Nothing.*" Désirée diverted her attention to Marassa's grimoire, and things went back to being awkward. I tried not to sigh in frustration.

"Can I take a few snaps of the painting?"

"Go for it."

It only took me a minute to photograph every possible angle, but by the time I was done, Désirée's attention was consumed by the grimoire. I knew the feeling.

"I should go," I said, gathering up my things. "Curfew and all."

She didn't look up as I headed for the entrance.

"Oh," I said, turning back. "You said you had a theory . . . What is it?"

"Oh . . . nothing. It's *silly* . . . See you in the morning for carpool."

"What about your car?"

"I'm sure I'll figure out some way to coerce my father into giving it back. He can never really stay mad at me for more than a day."

I guessed we had that in common.

On my way out, I saw Désirée's mother in the front of the shop, talking to a woman whose back was to me.

"Calm down, Ana Marie," the woman said, "you have much bigger problems on your hands than me being back in town."

I turned my head as I passed them, and the woman looked me directly in the eyes. Horror struck. I rushed through the door without saying a word.

The woman was my mother.

CHAPTER 29

Blood sucré

The surest way to push me back into my father's arms was certainly the sight of my mother. I ran (literally) straight to Le Chat Noir.

Without the pounding from the piano and the urgent whispers of the crowd, the ballroom in the *garçonnière* felt like less of a scene, but it wasn't even nine o'clock yet, and in pre-Storm New Orleans that would've meant the night hadn't even begun. I headed directly for the bar but stopped short when I saw Detective Matthews sitting over a glass of clear-colored spirits, talking to my father, who was drying tumblers with a rag.

". . . I'm just saying, it's a little strange that she reported one of the victim's bodies and then was first on-site to another crime scene."

I slipped beside an armoire and strained my ears to listen. *Are they talking about me?*

"You'd better not be insinuating what I think you are, Terry."

If I wasn't mistaken, there was more than a bit of threat in my father's tone.

"I'm not trying to cause trouble here, Mac. It's my job to look at all the facts. Don't you think it's a little peculiar that most of this picked up right after she arrived back from France?"

Does the detective actually consider me a suspect? Of murder?

Detective Matthews continued. "The way the Wolfman was drained and hung over the statue reminds me an awful lot of those two dead filmmaker kids."

This time my father wasn't so quick to defend. He dried two more glasses before looking up. "I can't believe I'm about to say this . . ."

"What is it, Mac?" The disheveled detective leaned closer to my father.

"Dammit . . ."

"Mac?"

"Well, I've gotten wind Brigitte is back in town."

"Your ex-wife?"

"Wife."

"What?"

"Technically we never got a divorce. After she skipped town, there was never a real need to." He paused. "And I guess I always hoped she'd come back."

"I'm sorry, Mac, but this is just too much of a coincidence. Do you know when she got back? Where she's staying?"

"Nope. Haven't heard from her, so I'm guessing she's not here to see me," he joked, but disappointment clogged his throat.

Whatever animosity I'd been harboring toward my father totally dissipated. He was the only person who'd always been there for me. I sheepishly stepped out of the shadows.

"Hey, Dad."

"Sweetheart!"

"Addie," the detective chimed in, "what a pleasant surprise."

"Hi, Detective," I greeted him through gritted teeth. "How's the case coming?"

"Slowly but surely. Just got a new lead, actually. I need to run. Take my seat."

My mother is a new lead? What the hell is going on here?

The detective coughed as he drained the booze. He shook my dad's hand. "Mac." And then he turned to me. "Adele, I hear your mom's back in town. You seen her?"

My father set down his glass, waiting for my reaction.

"No," I lied. It wasn't like I knew anything about her whereabouts.

"Do you know where she's stay—"

"Terry, minor. Out!"

The detective gave my dad an apologetic look and headed for the exit. Once the door closed behind him, my father treaded with caution. "Did you get some studying done with Désirée?"

"Yeah, it was far more educational than I ever expected."

"That's good."

"I'm sorry, Dad. About last night. About everything. It's just that everything is so different now."

"Sweetheart, I'm not sure the city is ever going to be the same, but I do know that we'll recover, no matter what the rain, wind, or crooked politicians throw at us."

But what about vampires, curses, and covens?

"Everything's so surreal now," I told him. "Sometimes it's like I can't even tell what's reality anymore. I hate it."

"I know it feels like we're living inside a Dali painting—"

"*Pfft*. Dali? Try Jackson Pollock."

He paused, smiling at me. "How did you turn out so amazing?"

I groaned.

"I'm serious!"

"Clearly not from my maternal side . . ."

He didn't laugh—the comment would have been funnier on another day.

His voice softened. "She'll turn up eventually, Adele."

"That's not very comforting, Dad. Why do you think she's really here? For work?"

"I don't know, but I'm sure it's got something to do with you. She probably couldn't stay away after having you for two months."

I gave him my best get-real look. *Does he not remember her shipping me off to boarding school the second she had the chance to be with me?*

"Your mother loves you, Adele."

I took a deep breath and, just for him, managed not to roll my eyes. "Is it okay if I just sit here and study for a while?"

"Sure, but don't tell Terry I let you stay out after curfew." He winked.

"Me being out after curfew is the least of Detective Matthews's problems."

"Ain't that the truth?" He popped the cork from a bottle of cabernet and poured a heavy glass for a bar patron. "Only two more bottles left."

I looked at the empty bottles lining the floor behind the bar: various wines, rums, bourbons, and vodkas. Sazerac. Pimm's. But on the shelf sat a dozen bottles of gin, all full.

"Hmm." I shook my head and kept my mouth shut as I took out Adeline's diary and my journal and began translating.

5th May 1728

That first night aboard the pirate ship, I had gone to sleep with an odd feeling of gratitude toward them, our monsters. Despite their brutality, I could not deny the fact that they had saved us, even if their real motive was self-serving. Of course, this feeling of thanks disturbed me greatly. I wasn't so naïve as to have forgotten that they were our original predators, leeching on us before the pirate attack.

Now, nearly two weeks later, my gratitude has drained, along with the happiness that arose from our victory over the pirates. It is with a heavy heart that I report the death of Monsieur Claude DuFrense. He never recovered from his "seasickness." Needless to say, poor Martine is completely distraught, for she had never wanted to be on the voyage to begin with. At times, she becomes completely hysterical and demands the captain return her to Paris. Cosette is the only one who can calm her down—with her smiles and her lullabies and her herbs.

Tonight, just in case my feelings of sympathy ever resurfaced, I warmed my medallion in my hand, and when it was glowing hot and pliant, I pressed the pirate captain's opalescent eyeball into the metal. From now on, the medallion will not only remind me of you, Papa, but of the slaughter aboard the SS *Gironde* and what happens to those who get in the way of the violent nature of monsters.

10th May 1728

After more than two months of endless ocean, I did not think water could impress me, but as we entered a waterway called the Caribbean Sea, the wild spectrum of greens and blues sparkled like a million jewels leading the way to adventures, romances, and happily-ever-afters. I hoped all of these would be our fate.

The last two weeks aboard the ship went by without incident, but you won't hear me complain of boredom. The orphans finally began to relax, and the crew was elated, as much by the strong gales as by the endless barrels of sugary rum the pirates had hoarded. The best news was no one came down with the "seasickness." After all, our children of the night had just feasted like vampire royalty. Regardless, each dusk, I couldn't help but wonder if tonight would be the night their thirst was unquenched. How long would the pirates' blood hold them over?

Luckily, we made very quick progress. The captain was eager to be rid of the pirates' vessel, so he slept very little, pushing the crew to our first port of call.

We were in high spirits when we entered Port-au-Prince in the French colony of Saint-Domingue. This small isle was like a page from Daniel Defoe's novel *Robinson Crusoe*, with trees that stretched toward the sun and bore fruits with hard shells and hair.

We were greeted with a grand welcome, and I, along with Martine, Captain Vauberci, and the top members of the Holy Order, was invited to dine at the governor's mansion, or plantation, as the châteaux are called here. At dinner, the governor told us his plantation yields enormous crops of sugar, coffee, sisal, and indigo.

"Very lucrative," he said.

"Lucrative but labor intensive," said the captain, gritting his teeth before excusing himself from the table.

When the dessert came, even though it was my favorite, crème brûlée, I politely excused myself and slipped out to find him.

Outside on the second-story balcony, overlooking the expansive back of the property, I found him in a chair, smoking his pipe and taking swigs from his flask. I took the chair next to him.

"Lovely night," I said, breathing in the warm, wet air.

He stayed silent.

"Everything seems so much more vibrant on this island, or maybe I am just used to the monochromatic palette of the ocean?"

"I prefer the sea," he said, and aggressively spat over the rail.

A moment later, he looked at me with the concerned expression of a father. "Adeline, now that you are out of the aristocratic monolith of Paris, there are many things you are going to learn about the French. About men."

Oh, the irony in that statement, monsieur, I thought, but held my tongue and looked at him with innocent eyes.

"This isle has become nothing more than a miserable hive of filth and depravity. It's a haven for pirates, bootleggers, and smuggled slaves. And it flourishes, partly thanks to the French."

I asked him to elaborate. He nodded, but first unscrewed the top of his flask with a single flick, took a swig, and then offered it to me, a gesture he had never made before. It seemed impolite to refuse. I took too large a sip and immediately coughed as the fiery pirate rum trickled down my throat.

"Easy, now," he said as I passed it back. He took another swallow and began again. "The despicable triangular trade: French ships travel to Africa, exporting European goods in exchange for slaves; then they sail to Saint-Domingue, sell the slaves en masse, and return to France with 'white gold' from the New World."

I gasped, thinking of the countless spoons of sugar that had passed between my lips in Paris, wondering if any of the delightful confections had come from this tropical isle. I hoped not.

"And that, *chérie*, is how this island's become the richest colony in the West Indies." He guzzled the remainder of the flask and leaned back in his chair.

"That is preposterous! How could the king allow this to carry on?"

"Gold, Adeline. Gold and power. Power and gold. The more a man has, the more he wants," he answered, but his mind seemed to be drifting far away. Without the familiarity of the waves, we rocked in our wooden chairs and lost our attention to the waxing moon.

Later tonight, just as I was dressing myself for bed, there was a light knock at the door. I thought it would be one of the triplets, looking to gossip, so I was surprised to find a pretty *Kreyòl* girl carrying a tray. *"Bonsoir,"* I said and opened the door to let her pass.

"You left before dessert, and I saw how you was eyein' dem sweets. My mama makes the best *vani krèm* on dis island," she bragged with a smile as sweet as the crème.

And she was right, Papa. It was an amazing crème brûlée, although I was only able to take one bite out of politeness as she lingered. Once the girl left, I had a hard time even looking at the dessert, remembering what the captain had said about the sugar.

22nd May 1728

We stayed on the island of Saint-Domingue for seven more nights while a new ship was prepared. Tonight, on the eve of our departure, the governor's wife threw a soirée in our honor, to which all of the orphans were invited. Even Scarlett, the pirate captain's red bird, attended the party with Cosette. We were having so much fun, dancing and singing around the piano, we almost forgot we were not in Paris, for everything was prepared in such exquisite French style.

After hours of socializing with the crème de la crème of island *société*, Cosette and I escaped to the balcony for some fresh air.

We leaned over the railing and let our minds disconnect from the fête inside, but after a moment of silence, we heard drumming in the near distance.

"What is that music?" Cosette asked and then pointed out into the darkness. "Is that a fire?"

The light was so faint and flickered so quickly it was hard to be sure. With a mischievous grin, I answered, "There is only one way to find out."

We snuck down the stairs and out through the gardens, letting the drum guide us. The beats were so round and full they seemed to reverberate through the earth and pull us through the lavish flower beds and intricate patchworks of vegetables. We passed fields of crops and finally came to a path dotted with small wooden houses, one of which was not only the source of the drumming but of several strange, rhythmic sounds, foreign to my ears.

I never felt fear, only pangs of guilt for trespassing, but we were too far under the spell of curiosity to stop ourselves from taking a peek. Entranced, we approached the house and then, like children, perched our heads on the sill of the glassless window.

The house was nothing but a simple square room, crudely made of wood and leaves. An old man, with the darkest skin I had ever seen, sat in the corner with closed eyes, smacking his large hands against a drum made of animal hide. A woman, whose mind seemed to be in another world, danced in a way my body has never moved, as if her spine were possessed by a serpent. She carried a gourd attached to a stick, all decorated with strings and feathers that made a hissing noise when she shook the stick. Another man, holding a glass bottle, danced with no regard to the liquid he spilled onto the packed-earth floor.

There was a table in the middle of the room with a centerpiece of unrecognizable wooden statues and bowls, which must have contained liquid of some sort, because flames floated in them, like magic. "Enraptured" hardly describes what I felt as I watched the little flames bob in the bowl.

Three others were gathered around a *Kreyòl* girl at the head of the table. Her face was covered with a scarf, and her lips moved hurriedly under the fabric, as if in song. Two women gently held her down while a man drew a knife and carefully cut her left upper arm, chanting as he worked. I would have been screaming in horror, but the girl seemed to be in no pain—it was one of the strangest events I have ever witnessed, Papa.

Before she lost much blood, the man packed the wound with a concoction of herbs and then dressed it with a tightly tied red scarf.

I was enthralled by the whole ceremony.

I knew not whether it was barbaric or divine, but the power in the room was undeniable. Lost in my own thoughts, I only noticed the fiery itch flare in my palms after rough hands were already over our mouths, dragging us away from the house.

"You are brave li'l girls to be out in da night spyin'!" a man said in a strange French dialect. He pulled us down a path between giant rows of sugarcane stalks.

When we were hidden in the patch, he let us go. Reflexively, two flames bolted from my hands, aimed straight at his chest. The balls of fire disintegrated into thin air just before they singed his bare skin. He did not even flinch—only stood smiling as if we were playing a game. Cosette smiled back at him without a flicker of fear in her eyes.

"Your witchy juju isn't gonna work on me either, *ma chérie*," he said with a deep-throated chuckle.

The *Kreyòl*, who could not have been but a few years older than us, also had a red scarf tied around his left upper arm, which was now dripping with blood. I wondered if he had participated in the ceremony like the girl.

The fiery feeling in my palms subsided, and my shoulders relaxed. I apologized and told him we hadn't meant to intrude.

"And I apologize if I scared you," he said. "Do not worry, mesdemoiselles. I bring you no harm. It is quite da opposite. My name is Makandal, and I have a favor to ask of you."

Cosette and I exchanged glances, and I motioned for him to continue.

"I realize dat what I ask of you is as enormous as the moon herself, but it is a matter of life or death. I've been watching da two of you since your pirate ship arrived in our docks. A strange sight, indeed." He looked at Cosette. "Yesterday, I would have never dreamed of speaking to you about my affairs, but now I feel fate has intervened and brought you to me. You have been blessed by Mother Earth, and der is no one else whom I can trust with this favor."

"I am sure the governor can sort out whatever it is you need—"

"No," both he and Cosette said at the same time.

"The governor can never know," he said. "No one can ever know."

"What do you need?" Cosette asked. She more immediately under-stood him than I did. She was instantly ready to fight his battle.

Before he answered her, I swear, Papa, the wind blew around us in swirls of warmth, slightly bending the wispy crops, as if to protect his words from unwanted ears.

"Der is no hope for us here. My people've become restless. They look to me to lead, but it is an impossible task, when I know they will show her no mercy for my actions."

"Who?" I asked.

"My only family. My sister." He came closer and bent one knee to the ground. "I will be forever in your debt if you oblige. I beg you. Your ship sets sail tomorrow for *La Nouvelle-Orléans* . . . You must take her with you, or they will kill her in a most brutal fashion as to set an example."

The stories Captain Vauberci had told me about the slave trade rippled through me in feverish waves as Makandal pleaded his case. One look from Cosette, and I cut him off.

"No more explanation is required. Of course we will take your sister," I pledged in a way that committed our absolute loyalty.

I believe it is what you would have done in a similar circumstance, Papa. And so, Cosette and I agreed to meet Makandal just before dawn.

And now, tonight I refuse to rest out of fear of oversleeping.

23rd May 1728

As I write, my heart still races, thinking about this morning, Papa!

Just before dawn, Cosette and I arrived at the rendezvous point in the sugarcane field. Makandal was already waiting there in the dark, hugging the girl we had promised to sneak onto the ship before every-one else boarded.

I was shocked to see his sister was the same beautiful girl who had brought me the crème brûlée. She too wore a red scarf around her left upper arm.

"I present to you my sister, Marassa Makandal," he said to us, a slight shake in his voice.

"Enchanté," we both whispered.

She stared back at us with wide eyes and then turned back to her brother, speaking rapidly in a language we did not understand. I suspect they were not in complete agreement about parting ways.

Cosette and I retreated into the sugarcane to give them a moment of privacy. We all knew it would be their final exchange, although none of us dared say so aloud.

"I promise I will be right behind you to live our new lives together," Makandal told the teary-eyed girl as he embraced her.

The girl cried, making giant tears roll from his determined eyes. In that moment, it was obvious the boy loved his sister but was willing to let her go to serve a greater cause. And it was an honor to help in our small way.

But our plans were about to become a lot more . . . shall we say, complicated?

Suddenly a voice bellowed, "What have we here?" A large white man was standing right behind the siblings, outrage visible in his eyes.

Fear flooded Marassa's face—he was the foreman of the plantation.

"Surely the makin's of Maroons," he yelled. "Just wait until the governor hears about this!"

With one solid shove, Makandal pushed his sister into the stalks, toward us, and yelled to the foreman, "This is no concern of yours."

The white man's lumbering fist pounded onto Makandal's face.

Cosette covered Marassa's mouth to muffle her screams as blood gushed from her brother's split nose.

"Take her now!" I whispered. "I will be right behind you. Be safe!"

The foreman continued to assault Makandal, who did nothing to retaliate.

My senses were drawn to a rusty machete blade left lying on the ground in the stalks—a tool used by the slaves to hack down sugarcane. Blood sugar. Anger rose inside me like a growing fire. I could not let Makandal die in a sugar field after he'd helped his sister. *But could I really kill a man?*

There was no more time for thinking, only for action.

I focused on the machete, and it slowly rose from the ground. Up and up it floated, until it was high above the crops. Then, with a flick of my wrist, I sent it plunging toward the foreman's back.

I watched in astonishment as the blade pierced the earth, missing him—and yet he still fell to the ground with a bone-crushing thud. A blond man had appeared out of nowhere and was now crouched over the foreman's chest, pinning him down. His teeth flashed before they sank into the foreman's neck, spraying crimson across the tall stalks.

Goose bumps tore through my flesh as the foreman's cry for help faded with his life. I told myself to run, but my legs seemed paralyzed.

The sun began to rise, throwing a million shades of pink across the sky as the blond head bobbed up and down, feeding, feasting, finishing off the foreman. I hardly want to admit it, but I was oddly exhilarated by the display of sheer power.

Makandal managed to push himself a few feet away, but then fell back down, barely conscious. "What have I done?" he whispered, gazing at the creature with horror.

I rushed to his side. "Please don't be frightened," I begged, but my fingers trembled as I squeezed his hand. "Your sister will be safe with me, I promise."

The blond looked at us with rabid eyes as crystalline as the Caribbean Sea. He remained in a crouched position and edged our way, squinting in the dawn's light.

Protectively, I hovered over Makandal, but the monster pushed me aside with one sudden movement. My protests tapered when I saw he wasn't looking for a second course. Instead, the vampire rolled Makandal onto his back, looked into his dark brown eyes, and said in a soothing hum, "Everything went as planned. You succeeded in finding a way to get your sister off the island. She is going to be fine. You are free to do great things."

An aura of triumph washed over Makandal's face, and his breathing slowed.

The monster drew his own wrist to his mouth, bit down deeply, and then held the bleeding punctures over the boy's mouth. He waited patiently as the blood dripped over Makandal's lips and seeped down his throat.

I found myself inching closer, watching in amazement as the split across Makandal's nose began to fade. I heard a crack, and then Makandal winced in pain. The vampire had to stop feeding Makandal his blood and hold him to the ground. I heard another crack, and my gaze moved to Makandal's chest, where his shirt had ripped open. There was movement beneath his skin. If I wasn't mistaken, his bones were sliding back into place. The vampire blood was healing his wounds! What is this miracle, Papa?

Makandal's eyes slipped shut as his wounds continued to heal—his smile serene like he was no longer in pain.

My senses were wildly confused as the vampire rose. He looked so much like a man, and not at all like the hideous creature I had dreamed about all of those nights at sea. The burning in my hands pulsed, as if unsure whether I was in danger or not.

He looked at the foreman's corpse and then back to me and said in perfect French, "Every species has its monsters."

I nodded and stood. "Are you the man who—Do I even call you a man?"

"Well, I am certainly not a woman," he answered and taunted me with a devilish smile.

"Of course not. Are you the man who met the triplets on our last night in Paris?"

"*Sì, signorina.* Stubborn, those three." He smirked and licked the foreman's spilled blood from his own hand. "Mmm . . . sweet . . . tropical."

He focused on the task for another moment before raising his head back to me. "Luckily for me, I found someone else willing to oblige. Unfortunately, my baby brother wasn't so lucky." He searched my eyes for acknowledgment, of which I gave him none. "But don't fret; I am sure he found a willing passenger on the next boat out from Paris. My brother can be very . . . persuasive." He walked closer and reached for my hand. "But apparently, so can you. Gabriel Medici. *Enchanté.*"

"Adeline Saint-Germain," I whispered. The brush of his cool lips on my hand sent a shiver up my arm, clashing with the fiery defenses wanting to leap from my fingers.

"Of course," he said. "We all know who you are, *bella.*"

"Medici?" I stuttered, not understanding why a vampire would know who I was. "That's quite a famous name."

"*Sì.* But not nearly as infamous as yours." He took another step closer, his leg brushing my skirts.

"You know, I had everything under control here." I tried to assert myself, but my voice cracked at an unfortunate moment.

"*Sì, sì.* I didn't kill that man because you were in over your head, Signorina Saint-Germain. I killed that man so you wouldn't have to."

He licked the rest of the blood from his teeth, and my heart pounded so deeply I felt like I was standing on top of a Kongo drum. His fangs slowly retracted, making him appear alarmingly like a normal man. He then came one step closer, causing me to step back. My shoulders knocked against the tall sugarcane stalks, but closer still he leaned, until it was more than my skirts that he touched.

"I am sure one day you will have to kill a man, but there is no need for that day to be today."

"Merci beaucoup," I whispered, trying not to choke on my own breath.

Then a loud whistle from beyond the fields grabbed my attention, and I whirled toward it. "The boat is boarding!" I yelled in panic. But when I looked back to Gabriel, all I saw were the sticky stalks of sugarcane bending in the breeze.

One final time, I lowered myself to Makandal's side.

"I will be fine," he whispered beneath the tremors of a breaking fever. *"Vive la révolution."*

I wiped the sweat from his brow and kissed the top of his head. "Marassa and I will be like sisters," I promised. "We will be waiting for you in *La Nouvelle-Orléans*."

He brushed my cheek, and his eyes rolled back as he began chanting.

I gave his hand one final squeeze before I took off running. I told myself Captain Vauberci would never set sail without me, but still I was frantic.

When I arrived at the dock, everyone was waiting for me. Both the governor and the captain looked relieved when I approached, but neither of them more so than Cosette, who stood by herself in the background.

With Scarlett on her shoulder, she took off below deck as I apologized to the men for being late. I told them I took one last stroll in the beautiful garden and lost track of time. The captain glanced at the state of my dress and raised an eyebrow, but said nothing. The governor accepted my excuse with good cheer and presented a gift he had loaded onto the boat for you, Father, as a gesture of goodwill: six mammoth barrels of sugar, along with the message that you are welcome in the Caribbean anytime. Papa, the vastitude of your reputation never ceases to amaze me.

When the crew weighed anchor, I hoped that, by some miracle, our original stowaways had seen this tropical oasis and decided to stay on the island, but the chills rippling up my arms as the boat set sail told me otherwise.

That night when I dreamed, our monster's face was no longer horrid. He had the face of Gabriel Medici.

CHAPTER 30
Plastic Cheese

"Gabriel Medici," I whispered, the name on the page staring back at me. *Gabe was on the SS* Gironde.

My fingers circled the stone on Adeline's necklace. A stone that, apparently, *Gabe* had pulled from a dead pirate captain's eye socket. *Maybe I was hitting up the wrong Medici brother for answers on Adeline . . . ?*

"Sweetheart, you should really get home," my father said. "It's a school night, and you have midterms. I'll ask Troy to walk you."

"I can escort her home," came a voice from behind me. "If that's okay with you, Adele."

I turned around, but I already knew from his accent that it was Nicco.

"And who are you?" my father asked. *My key to figuring this all out. And possibly the most attractive guy ever to know my name.* "I've seen you around here with that blond guy. Quite the ladies' man, that one."

"Niccolò Medici, sir. And I can assure you, my brother Gabriel is harmless. He's just been cooped up for a long time."

My father raised an eyebrow.

"In the library," Nicco quickly added. "He just finished writing his dissertation."

You'd think someone who'd been around for so long would be a better liar. The idea of Gabriel Medici sitting in the library, writing a dissertation, was absurd.

"Dad, Nicco and Gabe came to town looking for missing relatives. They were staying with the Palermos for a while, helping Mr. Felix clean out the shop." I think that was all actually true.

"Well, welcome to New Orleans, son. I hope everything is all right with your family." He poured a stiff drink and slid it across the bar to Nicco.

Nicco brought the drink to his mouth, and I could tell he was trying not to make a face as the scent hit. He glanced at my father and then at me, set the glass down, and slid it back. "I'd better not."

"Correct answer."

"So this city can't get a real food or petrol supply, but you can get liquor?"

"No, no, no. That which you just turned down is the finest Hurricane Hooch your lips will ever taste. And by the finest, I mean the only."

"And who distills this magical moonshine?" asked Nicco.

"Yeah, Dad, who distills this magical moonshine?"

He looked at me, knowing full well he was busted. "Er, an old family friend."

I shot him a *no-more-secrets* look. He returned a look of concession that also begged to drop the subject. I smiled, satisfied with our exchange, and he stepped away to help a customer.

Nicco turned to me. "You know, at one point in time it would have been insulting *not* to accept that drink. It's strange the way humans have evolved."

"You know, at one point in time, the general populace believed in vampires."

"Like I said, it's strange the way humans have evolved."

"Touché." I tried not to sound smitten. "Where did you come from, by the way? I didn't even realize you were here."

"I've been sitting in the corner, waiting for an opportune time to approach you."

"What do you mean?"

"Well"—a small smile flashed across his face—"it's a little intimidating."

I laughed. "What could possibly be intimidating?"

"I mean, with your father and all . . ."

I looked at my dad, who was slinging moonshine but still watching us, and then back at Nicco. I didn't know what to make of a vampire being intimidated by my father.

"Three hundred plus years old, and you're still intimidated by the fathers of girls?"

"Not the father of *any* girl."

The task of inhaling suddenly felt very difficult. "Then let's get out of here," I barely squeaked, gathering my things. When we were nearly at the door, I yelled good-bye to my father, not giving him a chance to stop me.

"Be careful, and go straight home!" he yelled back.

When we were out of Troy's view, Nicco asked, "Where to, *bella*?"

"*Anywhere* but home," I answered, joking, but not, as we stepped onto the postcurfew street.

"How rebellious," he said with his not-so-innocent smile and then extended his elbow. I curled my palm around his arm, internally smiling at his completely nonrebellious, old-fashioned gesture. The same arm that Adeline had curled her palm around at the salon in Paris. *Had Adeline been the one to curse the attic?* My *ancestor?*

My pulse sped up. Nicco's arm squeezed my hand.

Never trust a vampire.

Nothing about my hand tucked in Nicco's arm felt untrustworthy.

I pushed his warning away and racked my brain for a place to go. It was too cold and too illegal to just wander about. But then Nicco stopped midstride, pulling me back, right in front of the Clover Grill.

"What?" I asked. "It's not like they're open."

"I beg to differ . . . I can smell the gas from the grill." He pushed the door, and to my surprise, it opened. A smile crept over my face.

Inside the old diner, the temperature was barely warmer than outside, but the counter was lit by a row of tea lights, music was playing, and the smell of recently heated grease hung in the air.

We were greeted with a menacing growl as a pit bull appeared from behind the counter. Nicco stepped ahead of me, but I knelt down to greet the chocolate-colored canine, who, in turn, ran her drool-covered tongue over the line on my cheek.

"Stella, gross!" I wiped my face with my sleeve.

"Addie! Little Addie, is that you?" shrieked a voice from behind the grill. "You come over here right now and give Blanche some love!"

The Clover Grill was an institution known equally for its flamboyant staff and its hangover-curing patty melts. There was usually a line outside—I'd never seen the place empty—but tonight it was just us and the feeling that we were getting away with something.

I scurried to the other side of the counter to embrace Blanche, a downtown celebrity, famous for both his mammoth omelets at the Clover Grill and his drag performances a few blocks over at Lucky Cheng's. Tonight he sported a pink-ribbed tank, baggy camos, and false eyelashes accentuated by glitter-swept eyelids.

"Well, you look fabulous," I said.

"Of course I look fabulous. You think Imma let some little thang like a hurricane keep me from lookin' fabulous? I don't think so, honey!" He snapped his finger and did a full twirl. Blanche talked faster than anyone I knew and rivaled Ren in Oscar-worthy performances.

"Wait. Stella and Blanche?" Nicco asked. "As in Blanche DuBois?"

"As in Blanche Du-whoever-I-felt-like-when-I-woke-up-this-morning, thank you very much." He rolled his head to me. "He's quick."

I had to hold back giggles. "Nicco, this is Blanche. Blanche, Nicco."

"En-shan-tay, baby." Blanche grabbed Nicco's hand and raised it to his lips. "You a quick one, and you pretty too."

Blood ambushed Nicco's pale cheeks, making him look more human. My imprisoned giggles burst from their holding tank.

"Take any seat ya like. As you can see, folks ain't exactly beatin' down da do'."

I slipped into one of the red leather booths, and Nicco grabbed a candle from the counter before sliding across from me. It was almost, dare I say, romantic. Not a word I ever dreamed I'd use in reference to the Clover Grill.

"What are you doing open?" I asked as Blanche came to take our order. "What about the curfew?"

"Honey, if they want me to close, they gonna haf to come down here and drag me to the Orleans Parish Prison in cuffs. And I know that's not gonna happen 'cause there ain't a single pair of cuffs ta spare. They ain't got no room in that OPP to arrest a gurl for makin' omelets." He waved a spatula in a tizzy. "But you know after that curfew hits, ain't no one gonna come in here for the rest of the night. You know who the only ones comin' up in here are?"

"Hmm?"

"The po-pos! So I end up jus' fryin' eggs for half the parish precinct. But that's okay, honey." His voice dropped an octave. "'Cause I love a man in uniform."

Nicco seemed a little taken aback, which made me smile, considering how much he must have seen over the last three centuries.

"Whatchou want, baby? I got omelets, and I got omelets. My egg guy seems ta be my only guy back in bidness. Well, not my *only* guy, if ya catch ma drift." He hooted and slapped his knees. "Wahoo! It's good ta see ya home, Addie Le Moyne. And how is your mighty-hot daddy?"

"He's fine," I responded, cringing when I realized the word I'd chosen. This time it was Nicco who couldn't refrain from laughing. "Welcome back to New Orleans," I said through blushing cheeks.

"How 'bout I jus' bring y'all the Hurricane Special?"

"The Hurricane Special sounds perfect," I said.

Blanche's hip cocked as he turned to Nicco.

"When in Rome . . ."

"Alrighty, baby." Blanche went back behind the counter, fired up the grill, and cranked an old boom box, blasting a classic Mariah Carey album. Stella rested on the floor at our booth, never taking her eyes off Nicco. And Nicco never took his eyes off me.

"Tennessee Williams," he said, "such a tragic fellow. You know he used to live not too far from here?"

"Everyone knows that, son!" Blanche yelled from the grill without turning around.

I raised my head to peek at the boom box and turned the volume up just enough to mask our conversation.

My attention came back to the table just in time to see Nicco finishing a silent exchange with someone on the other side of the window. She rushed off, her bright blond mane swinging behind her, luminous in the night. I could swear she'd given him a threatening look, which he'd returned with an equally hostile expression. His demeanor changed as his gaze dropped from the window.

"What was that all about?"

"It's nothing."

"Who is she? The blonde?" I tried my best not to sound like a jealous lunatic. "She keeps showing up—the night of the tour, last night at the bar, and she's the one who was following me that morning, right? When I ran into you?" I paused, but then continued before he had the chance to answer. "Is she the one biting my classmates?" Anger edged my voice. "The one killing people?"

Our eyes locked. I focused on keeping my mouth shut, so he could speak.

"*Sì*, she was the one following you. I'm not sure if she is the one killing people, but it's likely. She's volatile on a good day, but, in her defense, self-control would be difficult for any vampire who'd just spent three hundred years *banished* to an attic."

I froze. Last night, he'd alluded to his family being trapped in an attic, like Storm victims, but this was different. This was the first time someone had actually said it out loud. The legend was *real*. My heart thumped against my chest in an alarming way.

"Being a newborn, it's a *wonder* she even made it out alive." Now his voice also had a bit of an edge. "Surely some sort of *magic* aided her survival . . ."

The mention of magic made my nerves curl.

"As for whether she's the one biting your friends, who knows? All vampires bite people, Adele."

"All . . . ? Even you?"

"What would happen to you if you stopped eating?"

"Sorry, stupid question. It's just so hard to fathom humans not at the top of the food chain."

"That's because humans are arrogant."

"And vampires aren't?"

"Touché." He smiled.

"Was she the one who attacked *me*—?"

"What?" His eyes flickered. "When? Were you hurt?"

"No, I'm fine." I paused. "She just threatened me . . . or warned me. Or something. I don't know."

"Tell me *exactly* what happened."

As I relayed the story, he gently strummed the table. With each tap, his energy rippled from the tips of his fingers, through the tabletop, to my resting arms. I could feel his strength, his anger and power. *How many people have those fingers hurt?* I became quiet, but then he touched my hand, and I couldn't imagine him ever hurting anyone—and that scared me even more.

I continued. "She said 'they' would hurt every person I love . . . destroy my family." My heart raced as he looked at me. He was not happy. I had every intention of stopping there, but then I said, "Meaning *your* family would destroy *my* family, right?"

His silence answered for him, which had a dizzying effect on me. I desperately wanted to know why, but the implosive look on his face warned me not to push it any further.

"That's all she said?"

"Yes. Do you think she was your blond friend?" He remained completely calm, but I could feel the wheels whirring through his mind. "Who is she? Is she dangerous?"

Silence.

It was as if he were trying to decide how much information to reveal, which only further frustrated me. Blanche belted another Mariah verse in the background, but I refused to allow my gaze to wander. Then I saw it—a quick fleck in his eyes—the exact moment he gave in.

"Her name is Liz. She's a . . . friend of Gabriel's. And all vampires are dangerous, Adele. *All.*"

My heart ricocheted against my chest. "Even you?"

"Especially me."

"Why especially?" I intertwined my fingers with his. The small gesture was bold for me.

"That's why." He yanked his hands away and dragged them through his hair, causing my self-esteem to plummet.

"I'm sorry—" we both said at the same time.

The awkwardness that followed made my stomach's knot come back tenfold. I desperately wanted to get back to the place we'd been last night, in the bell tower. Telling each other secrets. I wanted to jump into his side of the booth and wrap myself underneath his arm. Instead, I twisted a napkin until it morphed into a ropelike shape. I wanted answers more.

I laid a card out on the table:

"Did Adeline curse the convent attic? Your *family*?" I barely managed to whisper the next part. "Did I break Adeline Saint-Germain's spell when I opened the shutter?" His eyes flickered again, and I realized that was the first time I'd ever admitted to opening the attic window. "Is that how they escap—?"

"What do you know about Adeline Saint-*Germain*?" He nearly spat out her surname, sending a wave of energy rushing through my limbs, collecting at the tips of my fingers. The chain around my neck gently rippled against my skin.

"Nothing really," I lied. "When I found Adeline's necklace, there was also a letter she wrote to her father, describing her last night in Paris. The night she met you."

Lying to him hurt me more than I could have imagined, but something deep inside pushed the words out, and to make it worse, I knew that *he knew* that I was lying—a pinch of hurt slipped through his unflappable expression while he looked at me.

His voice became soft again. "You have to break the rest of the curse, Adele."

"What?"

My chest tightened while he started rattling on about the curse, and I had to focus on breathing—if I *was* the one who broke Adeline's spell, then that meant *I* was responsible for all of the recent deaths in town. I glanced at Blanche, who was using the spatula as a mic and riffing trills. "I don't know anything about Adeline's curse!"

"Adeline is *dead*. It's your curse now—"

"No. No," I whispered loudly, leaning across the table, the Wolfman's bleeding eye sockets hammering in my head. "I don't want any of this!"

"Do you think I did?" He jerked forward in his seat, his nose suddenly brushing mine.

Despite keeping my gaze fully locked on the green eyes, only inches from mine, I knew his fangs were extended, because my fingers ached. The song ended, leaving a moment of silence. The soft sounds of air pushing in and out of his nostrils sent a shiver down my spine. *There's one other way to break an inherited spell . . .* "Break the spell line."

Death.

Would Nicco kill me?

His breathing slowed, and his fangs retracted. We both sank back to our leather cushions. I sat on top of my hands for a minute.

"There's *no* more time, Adele. I cannot control what will happen— not that I haven't been trying. People *will* die in retaliation if you don't break the curse."

I shook my head. "Opening the attic window was an accident . . . and Ritha Borges said you can't partially break a curse, unless—" I stopped, suddenly unsure if the coven speak at Vodou Pourvoyeur should stay there.

"Unless Adeline had help creating the spell," he finished.

"How did you know that?"

"It's the only thing that makes sense. I may not have known Adeline as well as, say, Gabriel did," he smirked, "but in 1728, there was no way Adeline could have cast a spell *so powerful* it held three vampires for nearly three centuries. She must have had the help of—"

"Of her co—"

"Of her father," he said before I could complete the thought.

"The Count?"

"*Sì.*" His jaw tightened. "But that doesn't change anything, Adele. The spell would still be passed to you. You have to break—"

"I don't know anything about binding or breaking curses!"

"They're going to kill you!"

"Well, that also doesn't change the fact that everything I know about magic involves metal or fire!"

The words came out slightly desperate sounding. I wanted him to trust me. I wanted him to be on my side.

His foot knocked into mine. I was surprised when he didn't immediately pull it back.

"I won't let anything happen to you, Adele. *Prometto.*"

Over the next few moments, our legs slowly crept around each other's and locked together. The bend was awkward but somehow still felt perfect. I knew he could feel my pulse speed up—a small smile hid under his serious disposition.

"What's it to you?" I asked. "You're not cursed . . ."

He paused before answering, and for a moment I wondered whether I might have something to do with his caring. "I usually let my brethren clean up their own messes, but I'm not fond of my family members being cursed."

"Gabe," I whispered. *Had he been one of the vampires trapped in the attic?* Of course. He'd been on the ship with the casquette girls. *Shit.* "Nicco, if Gabe was there . . . wouldn't he know who helped Adeline curse him?"

"Gabriel doesn't have any recollection of that day or night . . . None of them do. More evidence of witch magic in the attic: some kind of memory-altering spell."

"I thought you said mind altering was a vampire thing?"

"It is . . . but not on each other. Vampiric thrall is a predatory mechanism to aid in hunting, and to help camouflage our species after feeding. This is different—it's like a twenty-four-hour period has been plucked from his consciousness—"

"One Hurricane Es-pec-i-al," Blanche said, dropping a single plate with a mound of eggs, dripping in gooey cheese, and a mysterious, powdered sugar–dusted log. "Bon appétit." He placed a fork next to each of us, not knowing we only needed one.

"Wow, Blanche, you really outdid yourself."

"This really is . . . special," said Nicco.

"Always, baby."

"What is this?" I poked the long lump of fried dough. "A Twinkie?"

Blanche opened his mouth.

"No Twinkie jokes!" I yelled.

He mimed zipping his lips. "Yeah, baby, that's a fried Twinkie. You know that shit'll survive the apocalypse."

Gross. I waited for Blanche to return to the grill before I pushed the sponge of fried preservatives to the side and tried to separate some of the eggs from the cheese.

"This is something you have to explain to me," Nicco said, suddenly serious.

"What?" I was fully intrigued by something *I* could explain to *him*.

"This stuff you Americans eat. This American cheese. Is it good? It looks like—"

"Plastic," we both said simultaneously.

As the last syllable came out of my mouth, a series of latent memories, buried deep in my subconscious between jet lag and underage drinking, flashed through my mind like a camera bulb:

Plastic cheese.

Part James Dean, part Italian Vogue.

Leather jacket.

Innocent smile . . . deceptively innocent.

Fork clank. "Don't worry, honey, I'll bring ya a new one," the waitress yelled.

The room began to spin.

"Adele . . . ?

"Adele . . . ?

"Addie? Hel-lo! Girlfriend, you in outer space right now." Blanche handed me a fork. "Here ya go."

When I looked down, I realized mine was missing.

"Try not to take my eye out with this one, m'kay?"

Clutching the fork, I nodded, and Blanche walked back to the grill.

Breathe.

I looked back at Nicco.

"I've said something to offend you?" He sounded genuinely concerned. "Are you okay?"

Was Nicco at the Waffle House? In Alabama? I stared at him for another moment. My body tensed. *Dammit! I knew he looked familiar. What the hell?*

"Adele, what's wrong?" He covered my hand with his own, until his fingers rested beneath my wrist, gently stroking the delicate skin.

I tried my best not to recoil, so he wouldn't think I was on to something. *If I am on to something.*

"Are you okay?" he repeated.

"Oui."

"You're lying. I can hear your heart racing."

I tried to mimic one of Désirée's sultry smiles. "My heart's racing for a lot of different reasons right now."

"Oh really?" He leaned closer over the table, as if daring me.

Never trust a vampire.

And that's the first time I thought: *What if the rest of the curse shouldn't be broken?*

I leaned back into the booth. "American cheese, it's kind of an acquired taste."

His brow crinkled. He knew I was still lying. And for whatever reason, he seemed upset by it.

"Are you sure you're okay? Or is there something else on your mind?"

I poked the eggs, trying to think of something to cover for my sudden nervousness. "I do have another question."

"Go on," he said with confidence and leaned even farther across the table.

"The Carter brothers, John and Wayne . . . the story Ren told on the tour." I looked up at Blanche to make sure he was still preoccupied. "John Carter? *Monsieur Jean-Antoine Cartier*?"

As the words left my mouth, a gigantic flame shot up from the grill, causing a high-pitched yelp from Blanche.

My gaze fluttered to the grill, but Nicco's eyes never left me.

"*Sì*. My brother and I," he said quietly. "It was the Depression. Everyone rationed."

I had to consciously keep my mouth from gaping at his flippant response.

"Times were . . . complicated," he added.

Is he really comparing saving half a potato to stringing people up and slowly bleeding them to death?

I barely heard the words come out of my mouth as I asked him something trivial about life in the French Quarter during Prohibition. I swallowed a few bites of egg and slowly drank my coffee, trying not to rouse suspicion.

"People always want what they can't have," he said, a bit lost in his own thoughts.

"Nicco?"

"*Sì, bella?*"

"If Gabe spent the last three hundred years locked in the Ursuline Convent, how was he rationing people with you during the Depression?"

"It wasn't Gabriel roaring through the nineteen twenties with me." He sighed. "It was my other brother, Emilio."

I wheezed as I gulped my last sip of coffee. "You have another brother?"

"*Sì*, although we're a bit estranged now. That's also why I've been eager to get Gabriel back."

I felt as if I'd been bitten by a snake and the venom was slowly coursing through my veins, taking over the function of each organ. At the bar last night, Émile had been sitting at the table with Gabe's crew. *Is he Emilio Medici? My mother's Émile?* I felt very tiny, like a pawn in a life-size game of chess where the stakes were real. *How many wrong moves have I made, unaware that I was even a player?*

Player.

I had been played.

How could I have been so stupid? Energy streamed through my system like fire, burning out all the venom. All the fear.

Worry that he'd lost me now shone in Nicco's eyes. He didn't know how or why, but he knew everything had changed. Why did he care? *Did* he care?

Maybe he just needs something from me? What did he need Adeline for all those years ago? Was it really only passage and a meal ticket aboard a ship?

There'd been nothing coincidental about their meeting. It had all been so perfectly romantic. So calculated.

"Mademoiselle Saint-Germain, do tell your father I called, s'il vous plaît . . ."

When had Adeline realized she was just a pawn?

Suddenly the idea of trapping the players in the attic made the corner of my lips gently twitch. My palms burned.

Then I looked back up at Nicco and just wanted it all to go away. It was so easy to get lost in his stories, in his smiles, in his leather . . .

"I should go," I said.

The look of disappointment on his face seemed genuine, but he conceded and walked me home.

For weeks I'd felt like I was being watched—now I knew I had been. By Émile. By the blond woman. By Niccolò. And by the crow, who had followed us from the bar, to the diner, and then to my home, patiently waiting in the shadows while I flirted with a monster.

CHAPTER 31

Mad World

Why did I tell Nicco anything? What was I thinking?!

Engulfed in paranoia, I ran from room to room, locking the windows and doors. Not that they really offered much protection, considering the back wall was still half blue tarp, but it made me feel better.

"Philosophically, most vampires believe any creature should be able to find asylum in its own home . . ."

Asylum? Maybe. Solace? No.

When I peeked through the kitchen door's curtain, I saw the crow perched on the fence, just as he had been last night. Isaac had looked so tired before our fight, like he was getting even less sleep than I was, and now I knew why. Part of me wanted to invite him in. Instead, I closed the curtain—on the door that *he* had fixed—and made coffee, thankful for the solitude. But then the necklace rippled against my skin once again, and I didn't feel alone.

This is not my problem. This cannot be my problem.

The front burner on the stove exploded with flames.

"Then help me, Adeline!"

I blew out the fire, but the flames just popped right back up. So I opened the stove, blew out the pilot light, and turned back to my chair.

Instantly I felt the glow beckoning from behind. My fingers also burned. When I turned my attention back to the stove, rings of fire lit around the other burners, until all four were ablaze.

Focusing on the flames, I took deep breaths, trying to calm myself. The fire slowly simmered into nothing, and the burning in my palms dissipated to a tingle.

"Okay, Adeline, it's my curse now."

I sat back down, gulped the coffee, and began to translate.

20th June 1728

For four weeks we hid Marassa in my private cabin with little effort. That was until this morning, when the vessel jerked to a halt and flung us both from my bed. I ran out of the room with such haste I forgot to lock the door behind me.

Half the crew, including the captain, was leaning over one side of the ship, while others flooded up from below deck.

"Captain, looks like we hit a sandbar," said one of the men. "Good thing the winds were calm."

Our vessel might not have incurred any damage, but we were, indeed, stuck.

Hours went by as the crew attempted to maneuver the ship without getting it to so much as budge. Finally, the captain ordered the men to start tossing things overboard to lighten the ship's load and float us off the sand.

First, he ordered the thirty-seven barrels of pirate rum to be thrown over. Watching the crew lament the spirits, you would have thought they were throwing over their own mothers. Sadly, it was done in vain.

Next went forty-two barrels of wine. When this didn't change our fate, the captain ordered the cannons overboard. I stayed on the deck and focused on each of the iron weapons, lifting them up just enough to take some of the burden off the tired crew. Two more stagnant hours went by. People grew restless, knowing we had abandoned our weapons in vain.

"Mesdames et messieurs," said the captain. "I was hoping we could avoid it, but it appears the time has come when we have no choice but to throw the passenger luggage overboard if we are to stand a chance at survival."

"Isn't there something we can do?" I whispered to the triplets.

"Unfortunately, I can only persuade the hearts of men, not sand," Cosette responded, looking at me with hopeful eyes. "Can you not do something?"

"If only our ship was made of steel . . ."

Being ladies of God and without attachment to their material possessions, the nuns volunteered their luggage first. The orphans wept, realizing their cassettes would be next. The long boxes containing their gifts from the king were the only security they had going into the New World.

After the nuns' luggage was tossed and the ship still didn't move, the captain ordered the cassettes to the deck. The girls tried to hold back their emotions, as they knew our survival was more important than their dowries.

"But what kind of life are we surviving for?" one of them cried and burst into tears.

The men emerged from below, carrying the first wooden box like casket bearers. The mood was somber as they passed the mourners on deck.

That is when everything suddenly made absolute sense, Papa.

How did I not see it before? On our last night in Paris, Monsieur Cartier, or Medici, or whatever his real name is, had asked if I would hide him in my luggage. The blond man, Gabriel Medici, had asked Cosette if he could stow away in her cassette. How many other vampires had visited how many other orphans and tricked them into giving passage—and meals?

I recalled the crew moving the cassettes from the SS *Gironde* to the pirate ship and then to our current vessel. These vampires had made it so far, and now they were about to inadvertently walk the plank. We would finally be rid of the monsters for good!

My head spun with images of Sophie and Claude dying, and the bloody massacre on the SS *Gironde*—but also with the compassion Gabriel had shown Makandal that night in the sugarcane field. Was it even possible for such a creature to have compassion?

"Wait!" I found myself yelling. "*Attendez!* Stop!"

All eyes on deck turned to me.

"*Oui,* Mademoiselle Saint-Germain?" asked the captain.

"*Le sucré! Le sucré!*" I gasped, running to help the men keep the first box from tipping overboard. "The sugar! Throw over the sugar! You have to try at least before we toss their dowries." My heart pounded, knowing Gabriel might be inside the cassette.

Relief spread through the orphans, and a smile crossed the captain's face. "You heard the lady: bring up the sugar!"

The men finished dumping the governor's golden gift overboard, and all the passengers ran to one side of the boat to redistribute the weight. We anxiously waited as the rudder fought, but it still wasn't enough. Another half hour went by, and we were no freer than before.

I could feel the heart of each passenger beginning to sink, when, all of a sudden, a wave rocked the boat, and then another. They grew in strength, and the boat lurched, knocking everyone to the deck.

I gripped a thick net and hoisted myself up against the wind. Even now, I can hardly believe what I saw: underneath the splashing sea, the sand was taking on the shape of the waves, rippling over and over again, until the earth released the ship.

"A miracle," one of the nuns rejoiced, crossing her chest.

Another jolt knocked me back onto the deck, and that's when I saw her. In the crow's nest, with her arms held out to the sandbar and her head rolled back, was Marassa, speaking into the wind, and Scarlett, flying in a tight circle around her, mimicking her song.

Confounded, my gaze brought everyone's attention to the *Kreyòl* girl.

"Who is that?" yelled one of the orphans.

"Stowaway!" shouted one of the crew.

"What is she doing?"

"Who smuggled the contraband!"

"Witch!"

The crowd gasped.

"Witch!"

"Come down here, girl!" yelled the captain. "We won't hurt you."

The nuns pulled out their beads and began to pray. Panic spread throughout my body as Marassa slowly came down the pole. Her feet hit the deck, and she took off running. The first mate raced behind her as she fled below. The captain yelled for order, but I flew past him, with the triplets in tow, chasing them straight into the DuFrenses' first-class cabin.

I burst into Martine's room, yelling, "Get off of her!" as the first mate grabbed the back of Marassa's neck.

The captain and mother superior entered the cabin as the sailor yelled back at me, "Did you steal her from the island?"

"I didn't *steal* her," I hissed. "You can't steal a person. She's not a possession!" My heart pounded, Papa. After all of the trouble—after weeks of hiding—we were finally exposed.

But then a voice of superiority rang loud and clear. "What do you think you are doing? Take your hands off my property at once!"

A small hiccup prevented Martine from any more speech, but she grabbed Marassa's arm and pulled the girl to her side. Everyone looked on in shock, including me and Cosette.

"Pardon, Madame DuFrense," said the first mate. "This girl belongs to you?"

"What do you think I spent all of those hours shopping for on the island? Sugar? Do you think I have ever baked a tart in my life?" She stood in front of the frightened girl in a protective stance.

"Our apologies, Madame DuFrense. You should have let us know, to ensure she was properly added to the passenger manifest." The captain halfheartedly scolded her, but his eyes never left me.

I made a face to declare my innocence, and I knew he had to concentrate, lest he betray a smile.

"Well, add her to your documents!" Martine said. "Now, don't you have a ship to navigate? Get out of my cabin, all of you!"

As soon as everyone but the triplets and me cleared the room, Martine fell onto the chaise and let out another hiccup. The four of us fell to our knees beside her, showering her with thanks.

Marassa stood frozen in bewilderment.

"Don't fret, *ma chérie*," Martine told her as she poured rum into a glass and quickly swallowed the drink. "I would no sooner own a child than I would birth one of my own accord."

"And then there were five," I said to myself. Five witches trapped on a boat with vampires, and one of those vampires was Gabriel Medici.

I grabbed my phone and opened a photo of the painting. This time, rather than focusing on Adeline and Marassa, I looked at the other girls. Almost instantly, my heart pounded. There were five unidentified girls, but three of them, beneath their different hairstyles and hats, bore more than an uncanny resemblance to each other.

"The triplets," I gasped.

They *had* to be the Monvoisin sisters. I blew the photo up as much as I could. Stunning blond beauties. Based on the description from Adeline's diary, I easily identified Cosette Monvoisin. Lisette had been right: the eldest sister radiated a sexuality that shone through the painting, even three hundred years later. At the bottom right corner of the painting was a tiny number in white paint: 1728. The same year they all met, the same year they came to *La Nouvelle-Orléans*. And I would bet . . . the same year as the curse.

It all couldn't be a coincidence—a group of girls, five out of seven of whom were definitely witches.

"Adeline, Cosette, Lisette, Minette, and Marassa *were* a coven." Fire exploded on the stove behind me, but my hand shot up and extinguished it with the same quickness.

Désirée was right.

I guess saving a town from a family of vampires was a grave enough circumstance to mix houses of magic.

Not caring that it was almost two in the morning, I grabbed my phone and texted Désirée:

Adele   1:59 a.m.   Your theory... it's right.

I frantically tapped my pen, waiting for her to text me back. *Who are the other two girls? Surely they were in on the magic too. The curse.* Fighting a yawn, I uncapped the pen and went back to translating through watering eyes.

2nd July 1728

I have spent the last two weeks in agony, Papa, wondering whether I made the right choice by saving the vampires from being tossed overboard, and today my greatest fear has played out: two orphans woke with symptoms. The guilt consumes me. I torment myself with regret.

Every morning I pray with the nuns for good weather and strong winds to expedite the journey.

5th July 1728

One of the girls has woken, thank God. I spend night and day with the remaining unconscious girl, Noëlle.

6th July 1728

Despite all of Marassa's herbs, today, Noëlle's chest stopped moving up and down. I became hysterical. Cosette did her best to calm me, and the captain assured me we would reach *La Nouvelle-Orléans* in two days' time.

8th July 1728

Thank heavens the captain was right. This morning I woke in *le port de La Nouvelle-Orléans*. It was the most peculiar sensation, at last arriving at our destination, finally knowing that we had survived each of the perils at sea. The strangeness of the land exacerbated the feeling—although it's not an island, there is water everywhere—a great river, a great lake, and many bayous. Even the land is wet, making the air always thick and damp. The heavy atmosphere holds the scent of creamy blossoms as large as my face, and vines of honeysuckle wrap themselves around anything that obstructs their path, marking their territory with a lingering perfume. The tree branches, which are covered in a hairy moss, droop to the ground as if Mother Nature herself is weeping.

This melodramatic atmosphere was the perfect place for my heavy mix of emotions upon arrival—elation that the passengers I had come to know so well were no longer trapped at sea with the deadliest of predators, but at the same time fear for the unsuspecting citizens of this new land.

I never told the triplets my theory regarding the cassettes. I hated carrying this secret, but knowing an innocent girl had died after I saved the monsters was too shameful. Despite my heavy mood, the girls made me celebrate our arrival by attending a parade commencing that very afternoon, honoring the completion of the new Ursuline Convent on Rue de Chartres.

It was impossible not to get caught up in the festivities: children led the way, twirling long ribbons tied to sticks. Women tossed flower petals onto the newly stoned streets, while the men beat drums and blew horns, and an elderly man rode a mule, waving the king's flag. The parade did raise my spirits, mostly because I couldn't help but marvel at the procession of people. There were rich and poor. Men of the holy cloth and women of the very unholy cloth. White. Black. Dark. Light. Young girls, with tanned skin and shiny black hair tied into intricate braids adorned with feathers and beads, held hands and walked side by side with the sisters. I overheard a local Frenchman call them "savages" as they passed.

Most of the colonists are French, but I occasionally hear words of Spanish, English, German, and other languages I do not recognize. The mixture makes *La Nouvelle-Orléans* seem so progressive, so scandalous! Of course, I immediately fell in love with this land. Maybe it really is true that a person can start over here . . .

"Adele, wake up," my father said, frantically shaking my shoulder.

"What?" I carefully peeled my face from my journal, realizing I'd fallen asleep sitting at the kitchen table.

"Sweetheart, there's no easy way to tell you this." He squatted down so he was eye level with me and took both of my hands.

"Dad, what's wrong?" The look on his face made my eyes well.

"Something horrible has happened at the café."

My heart leaped out of my chest.

"Jeanne and Sébastien?"

"No, honey, the kids are fine."

"Then . . ."

"It's Bertrand and Sabine."

"Has there been an accident?" I choked out. Tears began to pour down my face as Nicco's comment about retaliation echoed in my head.

"It wasn't an accident, darling." He squeezed my hand—the pressure instantly transferred to my lungs.

He didn't have to say anything else. I knew Mémé and Pépé were dead.

Blue. White. Red.

"Adele?"

Red. White. Blue.

I stared directly into the flashes of light, and the colors began to blur together. Everything faded into bright white, and then went black. A spectrum of spots began dancing in front of my eyes, until dizziness filled my head like a balloon. I wanted to float away.

"Adele, please answer the question."

I blinked a few times, and the detective came back into focus. My nose was cold, as were my ears, but my cheeks were warm from two steady streams of tears. He continued to say my name. I watched my breath vaporize in the chilly, dark air and wrapped my hands around Jeanne's freezing fingers. She'd buried her head in my lap, whimpering.

"Adele, where were you last night from the hours of nine o'clock to midnight?"

"Back off, Detective," someone said, almost as if he were pulling the words from my mind. "You heard what Mac said."

Sébastien. He was sitting next to me on the bench, one arm around me. I'd never heard him say my father's first name before. It sounded strange. His arm tightened around my shoulder.

"I know this is difficult, Sébastien—"

"Back off, she's in shock!" he yelled, standing up so they were eye level. "And you heard Mac, she's a minor."

Sébastien *never* raised his voice. It made Jeanne cry harder, but Detective Matthews got the message and walked away to consult with his team.

"Merci beaucoup," I whispered as he resumed his position next to me.

I had no clue how long the three of us had been sitting in front of Café Orléans, but the sun still wasn't showing signs of rising, and my back was numb from the cold bench. My father wouldn't let us inside, and we didn't dare look behind us through the window where the two bodies were being cataloged.

A man with a portable crime-scene lab walked past us, yawning, and entered the café. "Did you guys really have to wake me for this one? I've worked three shifts in a row. I don't even see any blood spatter."

"That's just it," answered one of the investigators. "There's no blood on site. No blood at all."

My stomach lurched, causing Jeanne to lift her head from my lap and sit up. I pinned my lips shut and bolted as vomit rose in my throat—I made it just far enough to turn the corner of the café before the contents of my stomach spewed into the gutter. It didn't take long before my system was totally void of plastic cheese, but I couldn't stop gagging, and soon I was staring into a puddle of neon-colored bile. The stomach acid burned my throat, but all I could think was that I deserved it.

This is all your fault.

In between my wheezing and coughing, someone scooped back my hair. I continued to dry heave as a strong but delicate hand rubbed my back.

"Respirer, mon cœur," a woman whispered. "Breathe."

I whipped around, and my mother steadied me as I barely avoided a tumble into my own vomit. I quickly regained my balance and jerked away from her. "What are you doing here?"

"I'm so sorry, Adele." Her voice was as solid as her touch. "I wish I could take away your pain."

"Ha!" my raw throat croaked. "All you've ever done is cause pain!"

"I know. This is all my fault. I never should have left you. You were so young. I don't expect you to forgive me, nor to understand."

"Understand?" I shouted. "Do *not* patronize me."

"That wasn't my intention. I simply meant things are complicated . . . more complicated than anyone should have to deal with. Especially a sixteen-year-old girl as sweet as you."

Her words induced another wave of nausea, but there was nothing left in my stomach but pain. Somewhere deep down inside was a little girl who wanted the comfort of her mother, who wanted to cry into her mother's sweater and confide everything, but I had no recollection of what a mother's comfort was. There was nothing my mother could do to help. The horror would continue unless I took care of it myself.

"I can't do this," I mumbled and walked down the foggy street, wiping tears and snot onto the back of my hand.

It was my turn to make a move, but I didn't know the play.

I managed three blocks alone before I saw Isaac coming toward me in his work boots and barely there ponytail. Yesterday I would've crossed the street to avoid him, but my issues with Isaac didn't matter anymore. All of my energy was used up hating myself.

He stopped when I got close.

"Not now, Isaac," I said, defeated.

"Your dad just texted me. I know I'm the last person you want to see, but I just want you to know that I'm here for you. Okay?" He pushed the loose hair from his face, revealing his concerned gaze.

I was already tired of getting that look from people. I didn't deserve sympathy. If they only knew what I'd done. "Okay."

"Oh, and check your phone. Mac's looking for you."

I nodded and hurried away, hoping the dense morning fog would quickly hide me from the worried gaze I could feel on my back.

The shrill of Désirée's car alarm being activated made me wince. It was now light out, but I hadn't even noticed the sun rise. My hand trembled as I squinted at my watch—I'd been sitting on the stoop at Vodou Pourvoyeur for twenty-three minutes, but I hardly remembered calling Désirée.

The entire morning felt like a dream—a very *bad* dream.

"Jesus Christ, Adele! You're shaking," Désirée said, crouching down in front of me. "Why didn't you ring the bell? Gran would have let you in."

I tried to think of an answer, but the question felt overly complex, and I just ended up staring at her blankly.

She helped me up from the step. And as she reached for her keys, I felt the internal mechanisms inside the door start to turn, but I didn't try to stop it or hide it. Before she could fit her key in the lock, the lock spun, the doorknob twisted, and the hinges pushed the door open.

"Or . . . why didn't you just let yourself in?" she asked, ushering me inside.

When she closed the door, the dead bolt snapped shut on its own—she raised an eyebrow to me but still didn't ask questions. Instead, she motioned for me to follow her to the back room, where I collapsed next to the fireplace and concentrated on taking shallow breaths. She bent to light the hearth.

The memory of begging my father to return us to town—the way I'd forced him—became very vivid. This could all have been avoided had I just stayed in Paris at boarding school. With my mother. With Émile.

Émile. Emilio?

My stomach twisted. *Had all of this really started in Paris, just like it had for Adeline?* My memories spun. Sneaking around Paris with Émile. His promise to see me soon when I left France. The Waffle House. The crow attack. The convent. The rain of metal as the nails dropped to the ground. The shutter flapping, drawing me closer and closer. Controlling me. Crashing. Only now was I starting to recognize that sensation of supernatural energy—the whoosh as the monsters had whipped past me.

Me.

So stupid.

So *naïve*.

Flames exploded in the fireplace, and Désirée jumped back, holding her chest.

"I'm sorry!"

"You need to *calm* down," she said as the bright-orange flames leaped higher.

I nodded and shut my eyes.

Beneath the darkness of my eyelids, I felt a wave in front of my face, and a sharp scent filled my nostrils, followed by sweet notes. Citrus.

"What is that?"

"It's just oil: sandalwood, blood orange, and sage. It should help you chill out." Her warm fingers rubbed the oil into my temples.

Breathe.

The fire crackled. The warmth from the fireplace made my face tingle, as if it were defrosting. She released my head, and for a moment there was just perfect silence. And I let everything else drown in the darkness.

Breathe.

"Adele . . . ?"

Breathe.

"Adele," she said louder.

I opened my eyes.

Little flames flickered all around the shop. From tea lights to gallon-sized candles, every wick was lit. Pink, black, blue—some candles twisted into different colors; others floated in vases of water. Every mirror in the room multiplied the number of flames.

Then I felt the big tears begin to slide down my cheeks. "She warned me." My voice cracked. "She warned me last night, on my way here, but I didn't know they would act so fast. I should've listened . . . done something, but I didn't know what to do—"

"Who warned you?"

Even Nicco told me they would retaliate.

"There was nothing you could've done to stop this, Adele." She held my shoulders. "This is *not* your fault."

Her words just made me cry harder, and then I couldn't stop. My chest began to tighten, and I felt the panic coming on.

A pop came from the hearth, and a flaming ember leaped onto the wooden floor.

"Shit." Désirée said, smacking out the flame with one hand while her other shot up and a jar flew from one of the shelves, slapping her palm. The cork popped out and fell onto the floor, and then she dumped out a handful of small yellow flowers, whispering unfamiliar words under her breath, almost like a chant. And then her big, almond-shaped eyes widened as she blew the fistful of flowers above my head.

My mind began to drift. The physical pain numbed, as if someone had given me a jumbo dose of morphine.

"What did you do? I feel really light." And I did—weightless and safe. Like there was some kind of protective filter between me and the rest of the world.

Désirée held my chin tightly and looked into my eyes. "Jesus, you have a low tolerance . . ."

"Huh?"

I straightened suddenly; my head slipped from her fingers and turned toward the window, and—I could have sworn something ran by outside. I didn't see anything, but I could *feel* something.

"Don't worry," she said, "there's a protection ward on the house. The vampires can't come inside."

My heart nearly stopped. *She knew.*

Something was preventing my pulse from speeding up, forcing me to remain calm. When I looked up, I saw all the little buds of chamomile floating around me. Every time I blinked, they twinkled like stars. I reached up to poke one, and it bobbed higher into the air.

"They're going to kill me," I said.

"We'll figure that out after you get some sleep."

"There's no time for slee . . ."

CHAPTER 32

The Brothers Three

October 30th

My nose nuzzled into a soft, warm fabric. I felt rested for the first time since we'd been home—since before the Storm, even—and for a few seconds I was awake without remembering the nightmare that had become my reality. Then, as I sat up from the cocoon of brightly colored blankets and pillows, it all rushed back like a boulder to the chest.

Where the hell am I?

My stirring caused a head to peek through a fuchsia velvet curtain. "Finally, you're awake," Désirée said, dropping to her knees next to me.

The altar room at the Voodoo shop. I focused on my watch. "Holy shit! It's six p.m.? How did I sleep that long? Did you drug me?"

"No. Yes. No. Well, kind of. I've been digging through Marassa's grimoire and found this herbal . . . remedy. I'd like to take credit, but I think in your case it was mostly extreme exhaustion—"

"Do *not* do magic on me without my permission."

"Then don't be so emotional," she said as she exited through the curtain. She returned a few minutes later with two cups of coffee.

"Thanks." I took a sip, wishing for milk. "Did you get my text message last night, before everything happened?"

"The one about my theory? My gran is right. We already know everything about Marassa and her Haitian coven." She threw me an unmarked bottle of clear liquid. "Pretty sure you were puking earlier."

"Thanks."

"Marassa was a master at hiding her secrets from the world, but she kept them well-documented for her children. We have everything preserved all the way back to 1730."

"Exactly. But what about pre-1730? These girls were together in 1728."

"Hmm . . ."

Giving her a minute to mull over her theory, I took the homemade mouthwash, forced my stiff body to stand, and reentered the land of the living.

I felt brave enough to look at myself in the bathroom mirror only after I had washed my face and gargled until my throat burned—my eyes were red and swollen, and my hair resembled that of a 1980s power-ballader. My stomach was back in its semipermanent knot, but the sleep had done wonders for my mind. As the lingering effects of the chamomile wore off, I felt alert, focused, ready for the battlefield, but as soon as my mind became more active, the misery also flooded back in.

How could Mémé and Pépé be dead?

My gut wrenched, recalling the warnings I'd received. I couldn't even think about Jeanne or Sébastien getting hurt too; or, God forbid, my father.

I pulled out my phone as I went back into the altar room—seventeen text messages and way more missed calls. *How had I slept through that?*

Sébastien	5:37 a.m.	Adele, you disappeared. Are you okay?
Sébastien	5:51 a.m.	Detective Matthews is gone. You can come back now.
Dad	6:00 a.m.	Adele, where are you?
Jeanne	6:12 a.m.	Où es-tu? You're scaring me.
Dad	6:15 a.m.	Come home now, sweetheart. The streets aren't safe.
Dad	6:25 a.m.	Adele, where are you? I can come and get you.
Dad	6:40 a.m.	Please call me.
Sébastien	6:53 a.m.	You don't have to return, just let me know you're okay. I'm about to call the detective back.
Isaac	7:00 a.m.	Your dad is freaking out.

I'm coming to look for u.
Don't be pissed if I find u.

Isaac	**7:01 a.m.**	This is Isaac, btw.

Unknown	**9:17 a.m.**	I had no idea this was going to happen last night. It doesn't change things, but I need you to know, bella. Sentite condoglianze. ~Niccolò

Émile	**11:26 a.m.**	Your mother sent me out to find you. Où es-tu, ma chérie? You can't hide forever.

Isaac	**3:42 p.m.**	You've been sleeping all day. Starting to think D put some kind of Voodoo spell on u.

Isaac	**3:43 p.m.**	That was a joke, btw.

Jeanne	**4:07 p.m.**	Isaac found you asleep at Vodou Pourvoyeur???? I feel like I'm in The Twilight Zone.

Dad	**4:21 p.m.**	Call me when you wake up if I'm not at the Borges'. I love you.
Brigitte	**4:49 p.m.**	Adele, I'd really like it if we could talk. Bisous.

I plopped back down on the pallet next to Désirée, who was reading Marassa's grimoire. "My dad is freaking."

"My mom talked to him," she said without breaking focus from the book. "She told him you could stay here tonight while he worked, if you want. Oh, and Niccolò came by at least three times. There's a good chance he's still perched outside like a hawk, which, I have to admit, is something I sooner expected from that Isaac guy."

A halfhearted chortle slipped out.

"What?"

"Nothing. I'll explain some other time."

"Whatever."

I touched the crow's mark on my face. *I was such a jerk to Isaac.* He'd clearly been trying to make amends, and I didn't even give him a chance to explain. "I'll be right back. Gonna see if phone reception is better outside." That's what I said, but I really wanted the privacy. My nerves fluttered, knowing I'd have to apologize.

Under the setting sun, I tapped the callback button. I immediately began pacing down the sidewalk, but before the second ring, a figure whipped down the street. My phone dropped into the gutter, and my feet glided on air as Nicco pinned me against the wall of a neighboring house. The rough stucco scraped my back through the thin T-shirt.

"Are you okay?" he asked, jerking my head to the side.

"I was unt—"

He pushed my head again, closely examining the other side of my neck.

"That hurts, Nicco!" I still had bruises from our night in the bell tower.

"I'm sorry." His grip loosened. "I didn't mean to hurt you. Sometimes I forget how delicate you are."

"That's bullshit! I can touch a rabbit without hurting it. Or a child—"

"You're right. I'll try to be more careful with you."

"I'm not asking you to try. I'm telling you to stop!" My fists slammed into his chest.

He grabbed both of my wrists and gently lowered my arms to my sides. My muscles shook, trying to fight him.

"Don't, *bella*, you'll just hurt yourself."

He was so close I could smell him. Leather and soap, just like . . . Emilio. I couldn't bring myself to look at him after what had happened last night.

Mémé and Pépé are dead. Dead, *Adele*.

"I don't understand," I choked out, battling tears. "Why don't you all just leave?"

"Do you want me to leave?"

His calmness was a stark contrast to my emotional wreckage.

A sharp pain tugged in my chest. I wanted this all to go away. I wanted Nicco to be normal. *I* wanted to be normal. A part of me wanted to destroy him for everything he'd done, whatever his role. For following me. For not telling me everything. For letting me fall for him. I hated myself for wanting to cause him harm. I wanted him to be stronger, to change, to want the same things as me. I wanted *him*.

"Yes, I want you to leave," I whispered, looking past him.

"I don't believe you, *bella*."

His stare burned into my face. My pulse raced as I forced myself to look directly into those perfect green eyes. My vision became blurry. Not being able to see him clearly gave me the courage to repeat myself. "I want you to leave."

I lost all ability to contain myself, to retain any sense of maturity. "Leave," I yelled, attempting to push him away, but only ended up shoving myself backward into the stucco wall. He didn't waver. "Leave!"

"As if it were that simple, Adele." His tone was much sharper. "You know we can't just leave."

"Of course you can! Surely you're all strong enough to travel by now. You've all certainly had enough *sustenance*." My voice lowered on the last word.

"Ironic request," he shouted, "coming from the keeper of the keys herself!"

I shrank back. The raised voice of the usually demure Italian was far more distressing than his physical strength.

He quickly quieted, but I could tell he was barely restraining himself.

"After three hundred years trapped in this town, don't you think they'd leave if they could?" He snorted. "You may have opened the window, Adele, but don't forget parts of the curse still remain. So here my family will remain, confined to the city limits of *La Nouvelle-Orléans*—and not even the entire city, just the part that existed in 1728, when the spell was bound." He bit down on his lip.

"What?"

"How do you not know this?" He sounded exasperated. "The spell has been passed to you. You should be able to feel it. Change it. Break it. Whatever you want."

"So you're telling me that not only did I let a group of vampires escape, but now they're confined to the French Quarter?"

He rested his left elbow against the wall next to my face and bowed his head just above mine. *"Sì, bella."*

"But you weren't cursed. You weren't trapped in the attic."

"*No. Grazie a Adeline*, I didn't make it on the ship, so I wasn't trapped in the attic with them. I can leave whenever I want." He leaned so close it felt like we were touching.

And then we were.

His fingers brushed my face. My head moved slightly so his cool hand cupped my cheek; my lashes batted shut as his face came closer to mine. Tingles erupted. Maybe out of excitement? Maybe as a warning to stop flirting with the enemy?

Maybe because someone else was there.

Nicco swung around.

Émile was standing in the middle of the street, watching us. He slowly clapped his hands. "So, this is why I'm getting the cold shoulder, *ma chérie*?"

In the silence that followed, I heard the faint sound of my name being shouted over and over again. "Adele! Are you okay?"

All eyes went to the sidewalk, to my phone.

Dammit. The call must have been connected this whole time.

Before I could reach it, Émile scooped the phone off the ground. "I'm sorry, but Miss Le Moyne is occupied at the moment. Can I take a message?" His French accent was totally gone, and he now sounded just like Nicco, but more bitter and slightly insane.

He moved the phone from his ear as Isaac yelled on the other end, "Go to hell, bloodsucker!"

Ugh. Isaac . . . Wait, bloodsucker?

"How sweet," Émile teased, hanging up the call and handing the phone back to me. "A love triangle." There was no anger in his voice; he was just taunting us. Smiling. "*Fratello*, please don't tell me you're really competing with a bird for the affection of a human? *Tragico*."

Embarrassment boiled over inside me, and then anger, but I focused on controlling myself. One of the only things I had going for me in this nightmare was the element of surprise—that is, if Nicco hadn't already told his brothers about my abilities.

"Go back inside, Adele," Nicco muttered, pushing me behind him so forcefully I nearly fell to the ground.

"I can take care of myself," I said, trying to keep my balance.

He ignored me and yelled something in Italian to his brother, which only made Emilio scoff. "Of course I would get to her first, Brother. Please . . ."

Get to me first?

"This really is adorable," he continued, wrapping a lanky but intimidating arm around each of us. An arm I used to love having wrapped around me when we rode his Vespa together.

"Je ne comprends pas, Émile," I said.

"Well, then, let me make it perfectly comprehensible for you, since my little bro is probably being vague—it's his specialty." He twisted me away from Nicco. "As you already know, I am very direct."

Nicco's fangs snapped out.

I stepped away from both of them, nauseated by my own naïveté.

"Do not listen to anything he says, Adele," Nicco told me.

"What? Why?" I yelled. "Don't tell me what to do unless you're going to tell me *why*—"

"That's my girl!" Emilio said. "Don't fall for his overromanticized, always-the-dark-knight bullshit, Adele."

"Shut up, Emilio." Nicco turned to me. "Because he is my brother, and you are just going to have to trust me on this one."

"Ha! Never trust a vampire," I snapped.

Emilio sneered in delight, practically dancing around me.

"Leave her alone." Nicco's voice neared a growl. "She doesn't know anything—"

"What the hell?" I yelled.

Nicco's face pleaded with me to stop, so I whipped around to Emilio. "What don't I know?" I just wanted answers. I didn't care who they came from.

"She doesn't know anything more about the curse," Nicco said. "Or the Saint-Germains."

"She's lying."

"She's *not*."

"And how do you know that, Brother?"

"I just *do*."

"You just *do*? How cute, Brother. Chiaroscuro worthy of a gilded frame, the two of you are, Niccolò. Haven't you learned anything in three and a half centuries, Brother? Wasn't it your *inexorable* gullibility that got us all into this predicament in the first place?"

Nicco moved in front of his face. "I am hardly the reason—"

"You and Gabriel are pathetic!" he said, shoving Nicco backward. "He's been free for weeks. Father is rolling over in his mausoleum at the two of you." When Nicco didn't push him back, Emilio walked over to me and touched my face, just as he had done so many times in Paris, but this time, I swatted it away. The aggression only made him smile.

"*Ma chérie*, this is quite simple. The curse will be broken one way or another. You have until *tomorrow night* to do it your way, or I'm going to rip her throat out," he said, pointing to Vodou Pourvoyeur. "Then your father's throat. The twins'. I'll pluck every feather from your little bird friend, and tear that hot redhe—"

A flash of flowing chiffon rushed past me and knocked Emilio into the street with a bone-cracking thud. "Over my dead body, Medici!" my blond stalker growled, her exposed fangs just inches from his face.

"It appears my brother already beat me to your dead body—"

She cut him off with a hiss.

"Aren't you plucky? Three hundred years old but still with the unpredictability of a newborn."

"Do not test me," she said in French, glaring at him.

"Gabriel," Emilio said, "can you please control your progeny?"

Gabe stepped out of the shadows. "Lizzie, please remove yourself from my brother."

Jesus. They're everywhere. How long has he been standing there?

She hissed one last time before she retracted her fangs and stepped off.

Laughing, Emilio popped his arm back into place and rolled over, propping his head on his hand. "Now where was I? Ah, yes, Adele, then I will drain you and break the curse myself, the old-fashioned way. No witch, no curse. We go home."

Nicco grabbed Emilio by the collar, forcing him to stand up. "This is about more than a curse, Emilio!"

"Come on, Niccolò! It will be just like the twenties all over again—"

"And what good will that do? Killing the only link we have to *him*?"

Gabriel intervened, pulling his brothers apart. "For starters, *we'll* have our freedom back."

With that, a woman in tight red jeans and black patent leather pumps jumped down from the roof like a cat—I recognized her from the night at the bar. As she crept closer, blocking the street, her fangs protruded. My head swept around—I was completely surrounded.

"Gabe!" I yelled.

"I'm sorry, Adele, but this feud has gone on for entirely too long. I've grown bored of it."

"I want to go back to Paris," the woman said, with a deadly pout half-hidden by her honey-colored curls.

"That's the spirit!" Emilio yelled.

As she edged toward me, I got the feeling she might be even more bat-shit crazy than Emilio. She lunged, and before I could back away, Nicco shoved me behind the Borges' property line.

"*Go* inside," he said with a clenched jaw.

I scurried to the entrance.

"That girl makes you weak, Niccolò," I heard Emilio say as the door slammed behind me.

I stormed back into the shop, trying to keep my fingers from frying themselves off. *What feud? How am I going to tell Désirée that her life is in danger because of me?*

I threw open the fuchsia curtain to find her, mug in hand, examining the painting of the casquette girls, which had been rehung on the wall.

I walked straight over and pointed to the blonde standing behind Adeline. "Cosette Monvoisin." Her eyes followed my finger as I pointed to the other two. "Lisette and Minette. Parisian triplets. Casquette girls."

"I know," she said without looking at me. "I started reading your journal while you were sleeping."

"Oh," I said, surprised by my lack of sensitivity toward Désirée Borges, of all people, invading my privacy. "Then you should also know they were witches too. They *had* to be a coven. And they . . . This might sound crazy"—I looked up for a moment at the altar adorned with human teeth and sequins—"Or maybe it won't . . . but I think the coven cursed the convent attic, trapping the Medici for the last three hundred years." My throat began to tighten, feeling the confession coming on. "And you should also know that I was the one who opened the attic . . ."

"I heard everything, so you can skip the part about the vampire witch hunt to break the rest of the curse."

"I'm sorry. I swear I didn't know what I was do—"

"Actually"—she moved to the floor, taking her time settling into the cushions—"I kind of have a confession too."

I joined her. "This should be good."

She let out an exasperated sigh. "A few weeks ago . . . I-kind-of-might-have-broken-Marassa's-part-of-the-spell."

"What! You've known about the curse this whole time?"

"Adele, where are you right now? Please. Nearly every spell cast in this city has come through these doors in some way: ingredients, advice, blessings, dolls, gris-gris."

I touched my necklace through my shirt, and she pulled out a similar one from underneath hers. "My grandmother forced this around my neck the morning you first came in the shop. The morning of the incident."

"What incident?"

"The incident at the convent."

"*Excusez-moi?*"

"I was in a bad mood that morning you came into the shop, 'cause Gran and I had been fighting. Ever since my sweet sixteen, she's been on my back about preparing for this ritual."

"Ritual?"

"Yeah, the ritual to join her coven—"

"You're part of a coven?"

"Ugh, *no*. I didn't want any part of all of this hocus-pocus, especially not some coven prearranged by my gran. I mean, what year is this, 1650?"

"Er?"

"She was refusing to eat until I joined, like she's Gandhi or something, so I was in a foul mood. I ditched first period and walked around the Quarter for a while. You know, checking out Storm damage. I felt guilty about our fight, so I began practicing this spell that she really wants me to master—and that's when it happened."

"That's when what happened?"

"First, I accidentally turned a bird into a cat. I tried to bail, but the cat was *freaking* out. It followed me for like four blocks. We were right in front of the Ursuline Convent when . . ."

"Uh-huh?"

"I felt bad for the cat, so I started casting every reversal spell I knew to try to turn it back into a bird."

"And?"

"And, I think I may have overshot it."

"What do you mean?"

"The cat turned back into a bird, but then my hair got really frizzy."

"Huh?"

"The straightening spell I'd performed last year vanished, duh, along with every other spell I had ever cast. It was like I accidentally hit the reset button. The entire side of the block where the convent is warbled like there was a glitch in the Matrix or something. Then there was this really loud noise, like a rooster waking up the sun."

"Then what happened?"

"Then I left."

"You left?"

"Yeah, my hair was crazy, and I needed to redo the spell.

"I went back later, and the shutter was busted open, and then after Gran gave me Marassa's grimoire, I found a slumbering spell from the 1700s. This whole time, I thought I was the one who released them."

"Riiight," I said in disbelief. "And here we are."

"And here we are." She smiled. "A new coven comprised of the new generation of witches."

"Two out of seven—we don't even know the *names* of two of the original coven members, much less their descendants."

"With less than thirty hours to break a curse we don't know anything about."

"Well, I might know one thing . . . Nicco told me that none of the cursed remember anything from that night."

"A memory spell?"

I shrugged. "And he said they're all stuck in the Quarter."

"Yeah, Gabe told me whenever he tries to leave, a giant gust of air pushes him back in. Must be some kind of trapping spell."

"So Gabe just told you about the curse?"

"He was after some kind of quick fix. I'm pretty sure he thinks he vamp-zapped my memory afterward. I guess he's a little rusty on how that works."

I opened up my journal and made three new lists, the first with the names of all the original witches, along with two question marks. The second was for their descendants, which were mostly question marks. The third was for the known parts of the curse, which I labeled: seal, slumber, trap, memory.

"So, *you* woke them from some kind of eternal slumber, and *I* broke the seal," I said, staring at all the question marks on the page. *We're screwed.*

"I'll work on the curse," Désirée said, opening Marassa's grimoire again. "You work on the coven."

My anxiety levels climbed as I opened Adeline's diary to my bookmark. I translated the next three sentences before I paused.

"Dee, one more question."

"What?"

"What kind of bird was it that you turned into a cat?"

"Um, a freakishly giant black crow," she said without looking up.

CHAPTER 33
Death of a Diva

(Translated from French.)

22nd July 1728

La Nouvelle-Orléans is unlike anything I have ever experienced, Papa! There are no words to describe the sticky heat. It is absolutely impossible to maintain Parisian fashion, and I find myself wearing less and less clothing each day, so I fear for what will be left when August comes!

To call this place a miniature version of Paris would be preposterous. In truth, it is quite the opposite. While Paris feels like the epicenter of the world, *La Nouvelle-Orléans* feels like the fringe. It's as if we could sink into the marshy glades and no one would ever know. I may still curse you every night for not taking me with you to the Orient, but coming to this foreign land on my own has given me an understanding of your sense of adventure and your longing for independence above everything. The people here seem to share this sensibility, making the city a very lively place to be. Even on the streets, there is always talk of what's to come rather than of past traditions, which dominate the conversations of the French aristocracy.

Martine, Marassa, and I stayed with the Ursulines for one week while the DuFrense estate was prepared. The convent is simple but large, with a labyrinth of shrubs, a vegetable garden on either side, and a special building to house the orphans, including the triplets, while the nuns mold them into ladies fit for society. I never thought I would be happy to stay in a nunnery, but after such a perilous journey, it was like heaven.

Unsurprisingly, the DuFrense estate is even more grand than the original in Paris, just as Claude promised Martine it would be. Naturally, Martine is still distraught, and being stuck in this new land without her husband is testing her health. The opera star's tongue has become sharp to anyone who crosses her path, mostly because she is drunk for more hours of the day than not.

Marassa continues to live under the guise of being Madame DuFrense's slave, residing in a private house across the back courtyard of the property. Marassa and I attend a religious class on Sundays, but I confess to only going to this catechism so as not to miss the chance to see my confidantes, and because Marassa is allowed to attend. It is a fascinating afternoon, for this is the day the nuns welcome all the girls from the community to attend class, including slaves and those from the indigenous tribes.

Much to Martine's dismay, I have taken a liking to a large, black-haired wolf-dog, who seems to be as independent as you, Father. Louis, as I have named him after my good friend the tailor, refuses to come into the house at night but is always waiting at the door in the morning to escort me on my daily errands. It has become a joke around town that Adeline Saint-Germain no longer requires a chaperone.

Others whisper behind my back, "The daughter of *le Comte de Saint-Germain* has turned her chaperone into a wolf!"

I ignore the whispers, but it does make me fear that I will be alone forever. What man would court a girl who might turn him into a wolf?

Cosette and I, along with Louis, often escape for late-night strolls along the river, which I have heard the local people call "*Mi-ssi-ssi-ppi*," a horrendous word to say the first dozen times, until the tongue is trained. Cosette mourns the absence of Scarlett, who seems to have taken flight when we docked, and then jokes about her own flight from French court. Sometimes I feel that perhaps I was fleeing Paris as well, unbeknownst to me at the time. But I suppose I won't know for sure until I receive a letter from you regarding our next rendezvous, Father.

As far as our dark-natured friends, I know they are still here.

The streets have been paved with new stones, and the buildings are freshly painted, and yet sometimes when I am out walking, I can sense things far older hiding in the shadows. I pray their plan is to move on to some land far away from this one. Although . . . I confess, sometimes when I am alone, late at night, I can't help but wonder about Gabriel Medici and why he was aboard the SS *Gironde*, and how he knew my name.

27th July 1728

I worry more about Martine every day. At night, she can sleep only if Cosette slips an herb solution into her brandy, which she consumes as if she is looking for death—and death, I'm afraid, is far too easy to come across in this town. Conditions are poor for most people. The streets are filthy, and disease runs rampant. People do not understand the real epidemic that unleashed when our ship docked in the port de *La Nouvelle-Orléans*—the true reason bodies are turning up, scattered across the city.

Each night more of the population disappears, but no alarm bells are rung when they go missing: a faceless prostitute, a nameless pirate deckhand, an orphan girl sent by the king.

But I notice, Papa. And I am overridden with guilt.

After so many months coexisting with these predators, developing this strange bond through the shadows, I have become complacent. I have to remind myself constantly that the relationship could turn lethal for me if there is any disruption to the current arrangement of shared bloody secrets: let live and let live.

31st July 1728

Protecting *les filles aux cassettes* from the monsters has become my obsession. I cannot sleep at night, knowing they are cooped up together, unprotected, like animals waiting in the slaughterhouse. I have no idea how to rid the town of the monsters, so I am desperate for the girls to be married and separated off. That is why, today, I was having luncheon with the mother superior at the convent. My goal was to persuade her to host a ball to give the orphans an opportunity to mingle with the town's bachelors. I thought nothing could distract me from this mission, but then fate intervened, dropping a new goal directly into my lap.

We took tea in the drawing room, and from the moment I sat down, I felt the servant's icy blue eyes noting my every move. Her red curls were fiery against the simple uniform dress, spilling from her bonnet, hiding her face but not her stare as she asked, in English, if I wanted a cup. I returned her gaze with equal suspicion as she poured the bergamot-flavored tea. Our fingers brushed as I refused the sugar, and a jolt of energy swept through me so quickly I couldn't keep the silver spoon from stirring itself.

My intuition told me I may have found a new *friend*—and my intuition rarely leads me astray.

I tried my best to remain calm as I finished mixing in the crème myself, but I became overwhelmed by the sudden surge of possibilities a sixth member would bring to our circle. My growing excitement made the flame in the glass wall lamp pulse bigger—and that's when the idea came.

While chatting with the mother superior about the ball, I slowly unscrewed one of the little bolts that held the brass lamp to the wall. I could sense the maid's nervousness when the second bolt dropped to the floor with a tiny *tink*. She continuously looked to the fixture and then to me, my eyes daring her to do something about it. Beneath her simple uniform and position of silence, I knew she was floored.

"A ball would absolutely be the quickest way to find suitable husbands for the orphans," I said, "and a fully chaperoned environment."

The mother superior paused at the window to contemplate my suggestion, and I pulled the last bolt from the wall, letting the heavy lamp drop. In retrospect, my behavior was brash and risky, but, as I suspected, the servant's natural reflex wasn't to move or reach out for it. Instead, she sent a burst of wind upward, and the brass fixture bobbled in the air like a marionette—the flame staying intact the entire time. Her eyes darted to me, and a taut smile spread across her face as the lamp gently floated into her freckle-dusted hands in one piece.

"Heavens!" yelled the mother superior when she turned around. "Give that here! We will not be responsible for burning down the town!"

Mark my words, Papa. We *will* have a ball for the orphans, and it *will* only be a matter of time before the English-speaking servant joins our circle.

8th August 1728

For the last few Sundays, after the Catholic service, I have invited the girls back to the DuFrense home, where we sing around the piano, paint, or share French lessons with Marassa and the new girl, Susannah Bowen. Yes, that's right: the convent's servant girl. I've yet to extract her entire story, because her French is poor, as is my English, but I have gathered she is of British descent by way of the isle of Bermuda. Speaking a common language would make it so much easier to communicate, but I believe this barrier has brought us together in a strange, intimate way. In lieu of mindless gossip, we share our secrets by teaching each other things passed down by those before us: Susannah and Marassa spend hours exchanging notes and diagrams on the healing properties of herbs and flowers; Cosette teaches Lisette the ways to a person's heart by showing her first how to speak to animals; and I have found an unsuspecting partner in Minette, who has quite an aptitude for the sciences. Her curiosity about the origins of material sometimes reminds me of you, Father.

It's such a strange relationship, Papa, having grown up without siblings and with no close friends amongst France's crème de la crème. I never learned to trust anyone until now. Other than you, I'd never met anyone like myself. You've always told me that people are brought together for a reason, and I keep that wisdom close to my heart. I wonder if there was a time in your life when you weren't alone with your magic?

13th August 1728

At night, I can feel them following me. Watching, waiting for me to waver. I am beginning to suspect they, the monsters, want more from me than just silence, and yet my intuition tells me it's not my blood they are after. What they expect from me, I have no idea, but the simple fact that they have never tried to harm me leads me to believe that whatever they want is *very* important to them. The way they said my name—both Jean-Antoine, just before his carriage took off in Paris, and Gabriel that night in the fields—makes me wonder if it has something to do with you, Father. I lie in bed at night, wondering what they are after. Unless it is simply *you* they want?

23rd August 1728

I feel like I am going mad, Papa, feeling *their* presence but never seeing them, not knowing why they are here, and knowing that the question is *who* they will kill next rather than *whether* they will kill. It creates a constant, looming fog around me, rendering me unable to see or think clearly.

Marassa made me a necklace she calls a gris-gris. She fears I need protection and says this little satchel, strung on a ribbon, will help repel evil. Perhaps her concern for me is because of the sad news that Louis has gone missing. I haven't seen my furry companion in days. I always felt safer with him near—he seemed to have a sixth sense for knowing when danger was lurking.

Darker days are coming. I know the other girls can feel it as well.

Even more disturbing, a boy from one of the local tribes—the only son of the chief—has gone missing. His family suspects foul play, and they are causing quite a stir here in town, trying to find the culprit. His sister, a stunning girl named Morning Star, who attends the religious class on Sundays, has taken to questioning me on the street. I do not know why she thinks I know something about her brother's disappearance, but her interrogations bring me to tears. I can only guess what, or rather, *who*, has caused her brother's sudden disappearance, and I can't help but feel responsible. If it weren't for me, the monsters would be at the bottom of the ocean instead of terrorizing the population of *La Nouvelle-Orléans*.

I know something needs to be done, but I am not strong enough on my own, and I don't know if I can jeopardize the lives of the five girls I hold so dear. I don't know what to do, Papa.

Your silence is making me fear the worst. You should have arrived by now. I tell myself I should be used to your unpredictability . . . I never gave a second thought to your erratic behavior in Paris, but here, where everything is unknown to me, it's unsettling.

I pray you are well. You always are.

2nd September 1728

I suppose I always knew this day—or night, rather—was bound to arrive. I just wish the catalyst hadn't been what should have been such a joyous occasion . . .

This evening, Lisette ran to the house, announcing that she had received a marriage proposal from one of the local townsmen! It is no surprise that she was the first: so beautiful and alluring, with her child-like innocence.

"I can't wait for you to meet him, Adeline!" she shrieked, the sparkle in her eyes brighter than the stars at night. As I hugged her, fear suddenly struck me: what if hers was one of the cassettes that had been used as a sleeping compartment on our journey? The thought of her dowry missing made my heart ache.

I went immediately to the convent and followed the nuns to the attic to retrieve Lisette's cassette, saying that I wanted to add something to it as a surprise. It wasn't until we were halfway up the stairs that I began to worry about something far more grave than a missing dowry: What, or whom, might we find in its place?

My heart pounded like death knocking as the mother superior opened Lisette's chest from the king—all at once, the holy sisters gasped—I braced myself in a defensive position. But nothing happened.

Nothing was awoken. Nothing sprang forth.

I breathed a sigh of relief, realizing they must be out feeding. How horrible is that, Father? I was thankful they were out feeding on other humans! What kind of monster have I become?

The sisters scattered through the attic like a flock of geese pecking at each box to examine the contents. After thorough examination, only three came back empty. All three were marked: "SS *Gironde.*"

"We've been robbed," said one of the novices.

The local nuns panicked, but the postulants who had traveled on the SS *Gironde* did not. Though none of them dared say the words aloud, I could see suspicion in their eyes about why the boxes might be empty. No matter how strong their faith, they could not deny the supernatural events that had occurred on our voyage from Paris. The mother superior said something in Latin, and they all fell to their knees, hands pressed together.

When we finally got a hysterical Lisette to sleep—I assured her that we would not let her engagement be jeopardized—the mother superior called me into her private quarters and told me the most peculiar thing, Papa. She said, "We have more troublesome things to worry about than missing dowries, Mademoiselle Saint-Germain."

My fingers pulsed. I knew not what to say, but I knew what she was hinting at. My concern was whether she was referring only to the vampires, or including other magical . . . occurrences.

"But don't fret," she said. "I took action the very day we set foot in Saint-Domingue, requesting blessed nails be sent from the holy pope himself, all the way from the Vatican in Rome. These monsters *will* be contained."

"Oh." I smiled, feeling sure that our own secrets had not been revealed. "It soothes me, but does not surprise me, to hear you have everything under control, Sister."

I admired the immediate action she took, but I knew not a million prayers, nor a million nails from the papacy, would contain this group of undead.

8th September 1728

I am certain I will never recover from the events I have witnessed today. I hardly know where to begin describing them. Melancholic? Ungodly? Unnatural? Or utterly natural? I so wish you were here, Papa.

The door was ajar when I arrived home tonight, and while nothing inside seemed to be awry, there was a disturbance in the air. I wanted to yell for Martine, but the surge of energy tearing through my body, threatening to bolt from my fingers, kept me silent. Instead, I dropped my bundle of flowers and ran through the silent house.

A strange sense of déjà vu dizzied me as I entered the parlor and found her. And *him*.

The vampire Gabriel.

He was bent over Martine, who was splayed on the floor, blood dripping down her neck, as he drank from her. For a split second, I just stood, terrified at the perverse sight.

"Get away from her!" I yelled, running across the room to them, but neither my presence nor my scream distracted him from his meal.

I grabbed his shoulder, attempting to pull him off. "Remove yourself!" But my touch only scorched his clothing before his shove sent me sliding across the slick wooden floor.

As I stood back up, his eyes shifted to me, but his lips remained locked on her neck.

"You monster!" I screamed, all of the metal objects in the room pulling toward me.

He unlatched his teeth from her throat and slurped back the blood. "Oh, my sweet, don't be angry with me," he said, as if his offense had been merely to eat the last macaron. "She begged me for it. You should thank me for putting her out of her misery." He staggered as he tried to stand, nearly falling backward.

"You killed her husband!" I reminded him with fury. "You are the reason for her misery!" With a flick of my wrist, the fireplace poker whipped through the air, heading straight for his heart. But he caught it just before it stabbed his chest and sent it straight back at me ten times as quickly. Had I moved even an inch, it would have pierced my head.

"Actually that was my sister, but I see your point," he slurred, stumbling back to her body. "Adeline, this is not a good time for me to play with sharp objects. *Madonna mia*, how much does this woman drink? Opium too. There are more toxins in her blood than in a Parisian gutter."

My eyes welled as guilt clutched my throat. It was obvious she was dead. My words came out no more than a choked whisper: "You monster . . ."

Gabriel bit his own wrist, just as he had with the island boy, giving me hope that he was somehow going to heal her. I dropped down to her side.

"Adeline," he said in a very serious tone, "you should leave now."

"I am *not* leaving. Help her . . . I beg you!"

He paid no attention to my plea, but simply focused ceremoniously on his task, drizzling the blood from his wrist until her tongue moved, lapping up the sticky red liquid.

In disbelief, I began to stutter thanks, but then she screamed as if in great pain, her torso thrust upward, and, with an indescribable desperation, her jaw clamped around Gabriel's wrist. Dumbfounded, I yelled her name, unable to turn away from the vulgar act. She sucked on his wrist faster, harder, with the glee of an infant attached to its mother's teat, and then her eyes rolled back in her head, as if she were possessed.

I continued to call her name until I sounded hysterical, but she was lost. Nothing was going to distract her from drinking.

"What is she doing? What did you do to her?"

"Adeline," he said again, "you should really leave now. You are worth more to me alive than dead."

I shuddered violently as Martine slumped to the floor. My voice warbled with fear as I yelled, "I am not leaving her!"

The absurdity only increased from there, Papa. Just thinking about it gives me the urge to loosen my corset so I can breathe easier.

"Don't say I didn't warn you," the vampire said, licking his own wounds.

As the punctures healed, Gabriel's eyes became fixed on me, as if we were now alone. He wanted something.

"Where is he, Adeline?" he asked.

My heart raced with the innate feeling he meant you, Papa.

"Where is *who*?" I responded coyly.

"Do not tease me, *bella*." He slowly licked his lips. "I promise you will not like where it leads you . . . but I will like it very much."

Before any more threats could be made, Martine's eyes flew open—red and insane like a rabid animal's—and Gabriel yelled, with a hunter's smile, "*Run*, Adeline. Now!"

Every shred of my instinct told me to obey him.

Martine's disorientation allowed me a few more seconds to dash for the nearest exit. Still worried, I glanced back, but she was gone. When I turned back to the door—there she was, blocking my escape. I was barely able to stop myself from hurling into her.

Gabriel teased, "You could have had a head start, had you listened to me . . . but listening isn't a strong suit of the Saint-Germains, now, is it?"

Martine grabbed my throat with her cold, dead fingers and lifted my entire body with the strength of just one arm. My fingers clawed at hers, and my legs flailed in the air as she walked me back into the room.

"Marti—" I choked out, and that was when I saw her fangs: pointed and lethal as a snake's. My sympathy drained as I gasped for air. On the verge of unconsciousness, I cursed myself and, for the first time, truly regretted not allowing the captain to toss the vampires overboard.

The house became cold and dark—I thought it was Death coming to take me. A howling wind blew through the room, extinguishing the fire in the hearth along with every candle and lamp. Martine dropped me to the floor, covering her ears.

As I tried to stand, my hair whipped around my face, and the layers of my petticoats blew around me. The gusts became so strong I could barely see. Shielding my eyes with my hands, I saw the sudden squall launch Martine into the air—the window shattering into thousands of tiny shards as she went through it and plummeted three stories to the street.

I whipped my hand, and a fire exploded into the hearth. Gabriel was sneering at a girl standing in the rear doorway. Her long red curls swirled around her pale arms, which were raised to the moon. Susannah.

She brought her arms down slowly, and the strong gale tapered to a slight breeze, until we were left with nothing but the soggy summer air.

I hurried to the broken window.

Instantly, Gabriel was by my side. I leaned over the sharp glass jutting from the frame to look down. *"Sacrebleu!"* I whispered as Gabriel leaned over me to see for himself.

Martine had landed on her back with such impact the bones in her legs were protruding from her skin. A circle of blood was pooling in the street around her. And then—I swear to you, Papa—despite her splintered limbs, Martine began to stand up.

Above my head, Gabriel cursed, *"Maledetto!* Now I have to go and fetch her before she causes a scene." He pulled me away from the broken glass and exited the room in a flash.

Susannah's stare lingered on the spot where he had touched my waist.

Still in shock, I approached her, already feeling disappointed in my own failure to take control of the situation.

"I'm sorry for Martine, Adeline!" she said before I had the chance to speak.

I looked up at the red-haired girl and whispered, "That was incredible."

"We can no longer stand idly by," she said with vehemence. "We must take action against the vampires."

"You know about them?" I asked her.

"We all know, Adeline. This vampire trio is no longer just your burden."

"Trio?"

"I have done my own bit of investigating in the night . . . They are siblings from Florence, each one more deadly than the last: Gabriel, Giovanna, and Emilio Medici."

CHAPTER 34
Carpe noctem

"Oh my God!" I said as I translated the last line.

For two hours straight, I'd been scouring Adeline's diary, the grimoire, and even the painting for clues on coven descendants.

"What?" Désirée asked, looking up from her curse research. "Did you finally find a new witch?"

"A new witch, a new vampire, a new Medici sibling—it's like a gothic telenovela—coven member number six threw Martine DuFrense out a third-story window!"

"Whoa—"

"After *Gabe* killed Martine and turned her into a freaking vampire!"

"Whoa."

We both hopped up to the painting, eying the two still-unidentified girls.

"My money's on the redhead. She looks like a total badass," Désirée said, pointing to the girl in the simple, dark dress, with wild red curls, bonnet and apron in hand.

"*Oui.* Susannah Bowen, from Bermuda. She was a servant in the convent. Liked plants. Used magic right in front of Adeline, so the others let her into the coven. And when undead Martine went for Adeline's throat, Susannah sent her packing."

I handed Désirée my journal with the translation and rubbed my eyes. "That's all I've really gotten so far."

I stared at the remaining girl as Désirée scanned the first few pages. The girl had long braids, so black they shined blue. The sleeves of her simple dress were too short—I guessed it wasn't her usual fare—her copper-toned skin and her accessories indicated she was likely from one of the indigenous tribes that had predated French colonization.

"Do you think Gabe and Adeline had a thing?" Désirée asked.

"Really? Out of everything happening in those pages, *that's* what you're taking away?"

"It's a totally valid question . . . Wait . . . Susannah?" She grabbed Marassa's grimoire and began scanning the earlier pages with her finger. "Susannah . . . Susannah. Here." She laid the book in front of me and pointed to a phrase that had been underlined twice:

Les enchantements de Susannah de protection

Across the fold, the two pages were covered in sketches of plants, with lists in the margins that looked like recipes.

"What are these?" I asked.

"Spells. Really old protection spells." She paused, thinking. "I wonder if these are the spells the coven used when they started to feel threatened?" She began scribbling a list. "Only one way to find out . . ."

"You can cast them?"

"Herbalism is kind of my specialty," she said nonchalantly. "Spells, potions, elixirs . . . anything plant based." Without looking up from the page, she raised her hand, and a jar of dried white flower petals flew into her palm.

"Protection sounds like a good idea, considering the vampire count keeps rising. That woman earlier with Gabe . . . she must have been Martine or Giovanna."

"Giovanna?"

"The fourth Medici sibling."

"Oooh, a sister. I bet she's nuts."

"The woman with Gabe was French . . . which means Martine DuFrense, vampire diva." I anxiously twirled my hair. "She said she wanted to go 'back to Paris,' which means she must have been trapped in the attic too. *Shit*. The three guys, the crazy blonde, Martine, and now a possible sister—all antique vampires—against two prep school juniors?"

"Witches," Désirée said.

My fingers strummed my knees. *Mémé and Pépé. The Wolfman. The man with the blue eyes.* Gabriel *killed* Martine. And Claude, and the other casquette girls on the ship. Emilio and Nicco killed God knows how many people as the Carter brothers . . . *The legends are all true.* They're all connected to the Medici—except for the one about the dead documentarians.

Dead.

Anxiety crept over me like a hundred spiders. *Are we going to die tomorrow night?*

The third legend must be connected . . . I jumped up, suddenly wanting to do some real-life investigating of my own.

"I need a break from the books too," I said to Désirée, who was carefully measuring something that looked like pink salt. "I think there might be some answers out there in the real world."

"Uh-huh."

And so we split up. Désirée stayed back, brewing up protection spells, while I went out into the night to beat the street.

Outside, a chill hung in the heavy night air. I hurried down the streets, through the shadows of gas lamp flames. Ren lived in the Marigny, even closer than Brooke, but my father's rule about not leaving the neighborhood argued with my steps. Little did he know how much more dangerous the streets *within* the Quarter were—the inside of the bullring.

When I crossed Esplanade and felt a slight warble, I now recognized the supernatural sensation—the trapping spell.

The sound of breaking glass cracked through the night air.

Probably just looters. Jesus, Adele, comforted by the thought of criminals?

I found myself wondering whether Isaac was lurking in a nearby tree. It was annoying, but I'd grown accustomed to the crow's constant presence. I wouldn't have admitted it out loud, but knowing he was there might have had something to do with my ballsiness of late.

Five blocks later, I arrived on Frenchmen Street, at a Creole cottage that was painted at least six different colors, next to the Spotted Cat. Frenchmen was famous for its jazz clubs, but tonight it was a strange sight to behold. Laundry lines were strung everywhere, as if everyone had decided to wash their linens at the same time. The sheets rippled in the cold night air. Despite the temperature, people were out on their porches, with BBQ pits fired up to cook dinner, while others stood around open flames burning in old tin garbage cans. My guilt sank deeper because at home we had working fireplaces, a gas oven, *and* a generator.

"Miss Adele?" Ren called out from his porch as I approached. "To what do I owe this pleasure?" He set his book and reading candle down at the base of the rickety rocking chair.

"Bonsoir!" I hopped the steps, kissed him on the cheek, and blurted out: "I want to know more about vampires."

"Oh . . . and here I was hoping you needed advice on fabric choices for a new winter dress."

The severe stare I gave him squashed any further joking.

"Well, shoot. Kommon in, *bébé.*"

He looked both ways down the street before shutting the door behind us.

To say Ren and Theis's house was a reflection of their personalities was an understatement. A large oil painting of Madame Delphine, their white Persian cat, hung on the dark-purple living room wall beside a particularly gothic-looking M. C. Escher print of a skull and eyeball. Dozens of candles had dripped wax onto the windowsills, and a large cast-iron pot hung over a low flame in the fireplace. The smell of its peppery contents meshed with the smoky scent that I now knew to be sage, a bundle of which was burning on the mantel.

Theis was stretched out on a cerulean velvet couch. He looked like he was sleeping, except for his fingers gently petting Madame Delphine, who was lounging on his flat stomach. A harsh cacophony billowed from his headphones.

"Make yourself at home!" Ren yelled as he hurried into the kitchen.

I followed him to the doorway and watched as he threw a plastic tarp over a metal apparatus in the kitchen. Copper pipes coiled into three big barrels. It looked like some kind of homemade chem lab. Various dried herbs, flower petals, and berries were separated into loose piles on the counter.

"No need to try to cover up Operation Bathtub Gin, Ren; the cat's out of the bag."

"Your pa is gonna kill me," he mumbled.

I turned back to the living room and sank into a paisley armchair across from Theis.

His eyelids slid open. He hit a button on his phone, and the music died. "Want to see my new tattoo?"

"Uh, sure." I think it was the first time he'd ever acknowledged my existence.

Madame Delphine jumped down as Theis lifted up his tight black tee to reveal simple black symbols inked across his bony ribs.

"Cool," I said. "Nordic runes?"

"Yeah, it means 'protection during battle' in Old Norse."

"Cool," I repeated. My mind spiraled, thinking about whether or not I was going to need more protection for my own coming battle, or feud . . . , or whatever it was.

"Leftover hurricane gruel?" he offered, pointing to the pot.

"No, thanks."

Ren sat in the chair next to me and snuck a sip from his flask. Theis hit the play button, and his eyes slid shut.

"Will you tell me the vampire story again—the one about the documentarians, *s'il te plaît*?"

"That ole story . . ." He took a larger swig. "Haven't I already told it to you twice this week?"

"*Oui*. I . . . I just have this feeling that I am missing something."

"Missing something? Do you mean about your mother?"

"*What*?" I yelled.

"Oh Jesus. Isn't this a conversation better suited for your daddy, *bébé*?"

"What conversation? Ren, what do you know about my mother? Is it why she left?"

"Oh, sweetheart . . ."

"I'm not a child anymore, Ren! Plus, I can't ask my dad . . . a little piece of him dies every time I mention her name. You have to tell me!" I gave him a look that said I wasn't backing down.

He sighed. "*D'accord, d'accord*. What do you wanna know?"

"Everything!"

He stroked his mustache. "I don't know everything. I'm not sure anyone does . . . Certainly not your father. But this is what I remember:

"Those two students had the bright idea of capturing our urban legends on video. Back then, locals used to spook tourists by telling them vampires lived in the attic and came out at night to feed."

My back stiffened.

"As you know, those kids didn't make it through the first night of filming. Their bodies were found in front of the church, drained—"

"Ren, what does this have to do with my mother?"

"Are you sure you're ready to hear this?"

"*Oui!*"

He scooped up Madame Delphine to use as a buffer, and the chains around my stomach tightened.

"Their cameras were still rolling when they were attacked. A friend at the precinct told me that all the tape showed was a clear shot of the convent attic, then you could hear a voice—a woman who'd approached the students. Several minutes later, you could only hear their screams as the camera crashed to the ground. Blood splattered across the lens before it cut to static."

Giovanna Medici was the first name that came to mind. *Emilio had been in La Nouvelle-Orleans and managed not to get locked up. Didn't Nicco say his sister hadn't been trapped in the attic with the others?*

"An elderly couple who lived across the street told the police they'd seen your mother talking to the documentarians. Then a group of college kids identified her from a lineup. They claimed they'd seen her leaving the crime scene—covered in blood."

"*What?*"

He slowly smoothed the cat's fur. "Brigitte Dupré Le Moyne was the only suspect the police ever had. It was the most heartbreaking thing I've ever seen. When they came for her arrest, she was in such a state of trauma that she almost seemed indifferent to it all. She simply went along with them. Needless to say, your father was outraged. The entire French Quarter was."

"*Ma mère* went to jail? Madame Perfect?"

"*Oui.* Well, she wasn't in lockup for very long. I don't know all the details, but the story I heard was that after they rounded up the witnesses to build the case for the bail hearing, every one of them retracted their statements. It was as if every single witness suddenly had amnesia."

"Sounds so mafioso."

"I suspect there might have been Italians involved, but members of organized crime? I think not."

My mind reeled, reading between the lines.

"Perhaps the strangest thing of all was that when the cops went to release your mother . . . she wasn't there. Her cell was empty. At least, that was the word on the street. The police were never going to admit publicly a murder suspect had escaped from jail, and since she'd been cleared anyway, it was all swept under the rug. She was never seen in town again, and the file was dumped into the bin of unsolved cases. Mac told close friends she'd gone back home to Paris, too disgraced by the scandal to stay in New Orleans. It was a plausible explanation, so no one dug."

"How is this possible?" I whispered. *My mother deserted us because she was a suspect in a double homicide? I mean, I knew she was callous . . . but capable of murder?*

"Adele, your ma was the sweetest, most charismatic lady I've ever met. The whole scandal nearly killed your pa. He was never the same, understandably so."

"He went after her," I said, a latent memory starting to make more sense. "I was only four. He said he was going on vacation with *Maman*, and that she wanted me to stay with Jeanne and Sébastien and speak only French until they got back. Then he left me with the Michels. I was young, but I knew something bad had happened. He came back alone and told me she'd gone to live with *ma grand-mère*, because *grand-mère* was sick. I hated my grandmother for taking her away from us. Of course, when I got older and realized she'd just been the cover, my misplaced anger moved to my mother for abandoning us. Over time, I nearly forgot what she looked like . . . Brigitte Dupré became a figment of my imagination, buried with my earliest memories."

"Mo chagren, bébé. I'm so, so sorry."

Does that make my mother a fugitive? But then what could be so important she'd risk coming back to New Orleans? And what the hell is Emilio doing with her? I'd always thought she'd had such a dominating way with her assistant, but was she actually the one under *his* spell? Guilt hit me. Then anger. Tingles carried through my shoulders. *He* killed those students and let her take the fall. *He's* the reason I grew up without a mother. And why I grew up hating her. I imagined myself engulfing Emilio Medici in flames. The tingling sensation intensified like fire across my back. I winced. Madame Delphine sprang away.

"I knew it'd be too much . . . Your pa really is gonna kill me."

"Ça va, Ren. Merci beaucoup."

The rage continued to build as I walked back to the Quarter. This time, I didn't skip a step when I crossed Esplanade and felt the warble.

Refocus on the curse, Adele. The coven. Finding descendants.

I had two options: go back to translating Adeline's dairy, or go talk to someone who was alive in 1728. I stuffed my cold hands into my jacket pockets and opted for the latter, retracing the path of Ren's tour back to the corner of Royal and St. Ann—my only guess as to where the Medici were now staying—the home of the infamous Carter brothers.

On the way, I replied to my mother's text message.

Adele	**6:47 a.m.**	What do you need to talk to me about?

I'm sure she won't respond. But Ren's story had me ever curious . . .

As I approached the three-story town house, my senses sharpened and my fingers burned, telling me I was close to something, although I wasn't sure what. *Danger? Nicco? The ghosts of the poor souls he and Emilio tortured?* I still had a hard time believing Nicco would do something so vile, despite his admission of guilt. Some stupid part of me was holding out for a reasonable explanation. *He's been stalking you since the Waffle House, Adele—don't be a doormat!*

With a wave of my hand, the front door's gate swung open, and before I could think any more about it, my hand was on the doorknob. The metal clicked once, twice, unlocking, and the door creaked in agony as it let me pass.

I am seriously beginning to doubt my ability to make good choices, I thought as the door swung shut behind me.

And there I stood, frozen, in the pitch-black vestibule of the vampire den.

The silence invited fear.

A small flame sprang out of my palm.

Breathe, I told myself and focused on the shadows the flame cast on the black-and-white marble floor rather than on the fact that fire had just magically appeared in my hand.

The once-splendid foyer was now smothered in dust so thick I left footprints. A chandelier quilted so thick in cobwebs that it looked more like a giant paper lantern hung over a wide staircase that curved up to the second floor. Multiple sets of footprints had unsettled the dust on the stairs—my intuition told me to follow them.

The first stair creaked loudly, as did every step after, and just as I cursed all of those old slasher movies, in which any girl who goes up a dark staircase never comes back down, a step gave way beneath my weight, and I fell forward, banging my knee and wrists.

"Shit!"

My blood pressure skyrocketed as I wondered who I'd just alerted to my presence.

I pulled my leg from the rotting floorboard, cursing the termites who'd long since moved on, and carefully edged up the remaining stairs without further mishap.

Holding out my lit palm, I crept from room to room. Each had the same heavy brocade drapes covering the long windows, cutting off the outside world and the current year. It was easy to imagine lines of corset-clad ladies dancing with wigged gentlemen in the ballroom, or the ghosts of flappers in fringed dresses dancing the Charleston around the piano in the old parlor.

A warm glow shone from a door left ajar farther in the house. I extinguished my palm and quietly approached.

Flames blazed in an opulent marble fireplace, and on a sofa, soaking in the warmth, was the back of a bright-blond head—my attacker. The girl Nicco had called Liz.

"Your boyfriend is not here," she said without moving.

"He's not my boyfriend," I stammered, cheeks burning. "Besides, I'm not here to see him. I'm here to see you."

Her head turned, and she nodded permissively to admit me. My rational inner voice screamed, *Abort!* so loudly I worried she could hear it as I sat nervously next to her on the tufted couch.

"*Je m'appelle Adele.*"

"*Je suis Lise.*"

"*Enchanté, Lise.*" As soon as her name rolled off my tongue with a French accent, I realized who she was. "Lise? You're Lisette Monvoisin?"

A smile spread across her pale lips.

"Someone who can pronounce my name correctly . . ."

"You're—You are one of the original coven members." I was hit with a twisted version of starstruck.

"*Was.* That was a long time ago. Another lifetime. Quite literally." She rose from the couch and walked to an antique serving cart. "Would you like something to drink? We have bourbon, or I could make you some tea."

"Thé, s'il vous plaît."

She removed a small kettle from a hook on the fireplace, not seeming to care that the iron handle singed her skin as she poured the water over the tea strainer.

As soon as she put the kettle down, the burn began to dissipate.

I had to try even harder to control my stare when she splashed a generous amount of dark liquid into a snifter, and then, just as I heard the sugar cubes *tink* against the saucer, she was back on the couch next to me, placing the dainty cup into my shaky hands.

I blew on the water as the tea steeped, and then, with no patience, took a sip, welcoming the warmth.

"Just like her," she said flatly. "Adeline was never able to eat a lump of sugar after that stopover in Saint-Domingue. Blood sugar, she called it."

I desperately wanted to hear more about Adeline, but my attention was fixed on the snifter she was swirling under her nose. The thick, sticky liquid coated the inside of the glass red as she swished it, enjoying the rising notes. My stomach churned. *Where had it come from?* Who *had it come from?*

"Could you not drink that in front of me?"

"Would you prefer for me to drink *from* you?" she purred, lifting slightly from the sofa cushion.

"Where are the boys?" I asked, remembering what Nicco had said about her being volatile on a good day.

"Out."

"Out where?"

"Don't ask a question if you don't really want the answer." She smiled. I tried not to visibly cringe.

Meeting a figure I'd come to know so well from Adeline's diary was like meeting a character from a fairy tale—a fairy tale of the Grimm variety. Lisette didn't look exactly the same as the girl in the painting, and it wasn't just because her peasant dress had been traded for vintage Pucci. On one hand, she was somehow more beautiful, more perfect, but the sparkle was gone from her golden eyes. I don't know if it was the loss of her innocence, or her pulse, or her soul, but she had an edge now. She seemed consumed by bitterness. Pain.

"Shouldn't you be . . . *dead*?"

"Someone has explained the whole vampire thing to you, right?"

"I mean—"

"I did die that night."

"What night?"

"The night the coven cursed the convent attic—so did my sister. Then I evolved and went to sleep for a very long time, and she went to sleep forever."

I pulled out my phone, tapped open a photo of the painting, and handed it to Lise.

"What is this?" She set the glass down as she looked. Her voice dropped to a whisper. "I never thought I'd see them again." Her finger lingered next to Minette. "It was all my fault."

"What was?"

She paused and closed her eyes to compose herself before she began again in French, forcing my brain into overdrive to understand her old dialect.

"Our plan was going perfectly. I'll never forget the magic the coven's power brought us, how three Monvoisin sisters were able to lure the three Medici siblings, and Martine DuFrense, into the attic. It was exciting, terrifying, and mystifying all at once. Dancing down the street with them, not knowing if our magic would hold for the walk all the way from the river. But, through the gardens, up the convent stairs, and into the attic we went. Once we were through the door, there was just one more task to complete, and then the rest was up to Adeline to seal the exits.

"Cosette began our spell," she said, then dreamily repeated it:

Before we close the final seal

Your partner's memories you will steal.

From dawn to dusk are for your reaping,

And all they make until they're sleeping.

A memory spell. My pulse began to thump.

"Emilio turned to Gabriel, and Giovanna to Martine, as if it were a perfectly choreographed opera, and the magic made the vampires use their own powers against each other."

"I thought vampires couldn't alter each other's memories?"

"The influence of magic can change almost anything," she said with near pride. "But I can't take credit—it was Cosette's idea—an addition to the curse that would ensure the coven's safety, should the vampires ever escape. It was brilliant in theory, but in execution it was terrifying. With every word that came out of my mouth, I could feel the vampires fighting it. The look of horror on their faces as they spoke the words to each other that they couldn't take back . . . the look in Gabriel's eyes . . . I knew he'd hunt us to the end of the earth if the spell ever broke.

"As we chanted, the first, second, and third windows snapped shut. The vampires fought through the spell as Minette and I inched toward the door, and as Cosette danced to the last window. When the fourth window banged shut, Cosette nodded to us.

"I can still remember the bang of the fifth window behind my back as we turned to leave—the feeling of elation—as I assumed Adeline had shut it because Cosette was safely out and on the roof. But just as I crossed the threshold behind Minette, Gabriel yelled, 'Gotcha, Cosette!'

"Even though I'd heard no scream from my sister, even though I *knew* Cosette wasn't still in the attic, I turned back around, just for a second. A lethal second . . . Gabriel grabbed me."

She drained her glass.

"I screamed for Minette, begging for help instead of telling her to run. I was weak. It all happened so fast. She lunged back in just before the door slammed shut.

"We'd all cast our parts of the curse perfectly, but Minette and I ended up on the wrong side of the door, and Emilio and Giovanna ended up on the wrong side of the window. They'd escaped with Cosette."

When she used the word "we," I realized I was thinking of her as one of *us* instead of one of *them*. She was no longer the unpredictable blond stalker, but Lisette Monvoisin, triplet witch—the girl who'd been so excited about her engagement, the one Cosette had saved from a pirate, the one who would have followed her sisters to the ends of the earth.

"Minette pulled me down to the ground, wrapped both of her arms around me, and screamed incantations at him, but Gabriel was too strong. Without Cosette, we stood no chance against a Medici and his newborn. Cosette had always been the powerful one.

"He jerked me away from Minette, snapping my arm as he pulled me directly to his mouth. His fangs plunged into my neck without hesitation. With each suck, I could feel his fury grow. As I screamed, blood spurted from the bites more quickly than he could drink in his fit of rage, which drove Martine mad.

"My pulse slowed. I knew my life was ending. Gabriel pulled his fangs from my vein and, with his long fingers still wrapped around my throat, whispered against my ear, 'Do you want to die?'

"When I pathetically whimpered 'No,' he growled, 'That's what I thought,' and bit into his own wrist. I didn't think about the consequences of that one little word, not like Minette or Cosette would have, before he forced my head back and rammed his wrist against my pinched lips.

"Soon, my sister's screams became faint, everything became bright, and I gave into the numbness brought on by the venom coursing through my veins. I can remember that first drip as if it were yesterday . . ."

I tried to imagine Gabe doing something so barbaric. I wanted to hold Lisette's hand, but my own survival instinct drove me to take another sip of tea and wait patiently instead.

"When the first drop of Maker blood melts onto your tongue, it tastes repulsive, like some kind of noxious rust. It courses through your system, mixing with your human essence, suffocating the oxygen from your system, mutating the matter that comprises your existence. Your magic. Then, as you drink, each drop becomes sweeter, like candy. You want more. The evolutionary process is immediate, as is the addiction. The craving flips from desire to dire—the blood no longer like candy but like opium. Your existence depends on it. Your new life. A life that feels stronger, sexier, superior to anything you've ever known.

"The venom seduces you until you are totally unable to make decisions with logic and reason. Lingering in this demonic purgatory—no longer a human but not yet a vampire—your body defaults into survival mode, and your instincts take over. Of course, the only way to complete the transition is to drink. Drink the blood of another human."

Lisette became so still it was difficult to tell whether she was even alive, until she began to speak again.

"Every hour my hunger became more excruciating. I was dying, and not just my human death, the clock was ticking on my evolution.

"Gabriel wouldn't let Martine near my sister. He was saving her . . . As Minette cowered in the corner, watching me in horror, I wanted to bite her. Taste her. I wanted to rip my own triplet limb from limb and feed. I wanted to kill her. And he was saving her for *me*.

"Afterward, knowing I had caused my sister's death, I wanted only to die. Ironic, the way things turn out. Now I must live with it forever."

"What do you mean?" But I understood as soon as the question came out of my mouth. *No.*

"'Do you still want to save your sister?' Gabriel asked Minette. Without fear, she stood and said, *'Oui,'* then reached for a jagged nail on the floor. I screamed out for her to stop, but I was so weak. I was dying. She sliced open her own wrists—"

A gasp squeezed through my lips, but Lisette continued, looking straight ahead.

"'Drink,' she said. Tears streamed down her face, but she told me to drink. Her voice was like an angel from heaven, coming to save me. She sacrificed her human life for my immortal life."

Her gaze dropped to the floor.

"And now, I don't know which is the worst part: that he does not remember any of it . . . or that he completes me."

"Gabriel? *Completes* you?"

"When you opened the seal, I ran as far away from the convent as the spell would permit—away from him—I hid in an abandoned shop on Canal Street. I was scared. Alone. Being so close to death, the need to feed dominated everything else. I had no idea what I was, how to be a predator. I don't know how to explain it, but even after I fed, and I fed, I still felt this utter despair. There were too many explanations to count: being a vampire, losing my magic, the death of my sisters and the coven, the unfamiliar new time and world in which I lived. But the night of the tour, I realized none of these were the reason the emptiness terrorized me . . . When he found me that night, the emptiness went away.

"It's impossible to describe what I felt: love compounded by forever. When we went to bed that night, he confessed to feeling the same, despite not even remembering how I came to be—"

"Gabe doesn't remember *turning you into a vampire?*" My words slipped out louder than I'd intended.

"He said that all he remembers is holding me in his arms for the last three hundred years as we slept . . . and that after he escaped, he was desperate to find me."

"I guess your memory spell worked . . ."

"Which means the Monvoisin witch line is still alive, and so, for now, he doesn't remember killing my sister, or me."

"He should have to live with what he did to you, Lisette!"

"Don't you understand? He might not remember becoming my Maker, but he also doesn't remember that I am one of those who cursed him."

"If you don't want him to remember, why did you demand that I finish breaking the curse?"

"Because that is what *he* desires."

"That is *so twisted*—"

"I don't expect you to understand. The emotional composition of the Maker relationship is beyond human comprehension. Gabriel is like my father, my brother, my best friend. My lover. I would do anything for him." Her eyes narrowed, and she turned directly to me, speaking in English. "Do you understand that? *Anything.*"

Clunky footsteps and voices of merriment approached from down the hall.

I dropped my voice to a whisper. "Lisette, how can you stay with him after what he did? He's a monster!"

There was a blur of motion, and my teacup flew from my hand as she pushed me to the floor; her fingers wrapped around my throat, squeezing with no mercy. I gasped for air, feet kicking. The more I panicked, the less I was able to focus on magic.

Gabe and Emilio entered the room, arm in arm, singing in drunken glee.

I clawed at her hands, desperate not to become a dinner course for three, but then, to my surprise, Emilio whipped over and knocked Lisette across the room into a tall grandfather clock.

"Maledetto, Emilio!" Gabe yelled, rushing to her side.

Her fangs pointed in Emilio's direction, but she didn't retaliate.

"I know that it's tempting," Emilio said to her, "but we told Adele she had until tomorrow night." He pulled me up from the floor. "Medici are men of our word . . . so we will wait till then for our supper."

He licked his lips. I rolled my eyes.

Nicco trailed in, looking sullen as ever. Immediately, his eyes went to Lisette and then to my neck.

Emilio rambled on in French, pulling me onto the couch with him. Too close. As if we were still in France. As if he hadn't threatened my existence mere hours before. "Don't take everything so personally, *ma chérie*. I really did cherish our time together in Paris."

When I heard the word "Paris," all I could think about was my mother.

I pushed myself away. "You disgust me."

His ear lowered closer to my mouth. *"Répéter?"*

"You're a monster!" I yelled, my entire body shaking. "You killed the Michels. And the Wolfman. And those two filmmaker students twelve years ago."

Everyone in the room stopped and stared in silence, waiting for Emilio's reaction.

"Oui." He stood, towering above me, and then bent over until our noses were even. *"Oui. Et, non.* I might have killed the disc jockey and the old French couple"—he wagged his finger in my face—"but it wasn't me who killed those students."

"Stop it, Emilio," Nicco warned from the doorway.

"But you *do* know the killer, Adele." His eyes wandered to his younger brother. "In fact, I think the two of you are quite close."

"Stai zitto!" Nicco flew across the room and knocked his brother to the floor again, shutting him up.

Instead of getting up and fighting, Emilio just rolled over and started laughing. "Oh, Brother, you have got it bad. What's the big deal? She's going to find out eventually."

"It's not your story to tell," Nicco spat. "We're done here," he said to me, grabbing my arm and pulling me out of the room.

"Nicco. Arm!" I yelled, but he didn't loosen his grip until we were down the stairs and out the front door.

I yanked my limb back.

"I'm sorry, Adele."

Just as I was about to yell at him again, I realized he wasn't apologizing about my arm. His eyes were filled with pain.

"No . . . *No*."

"Adele—"

"No, don't tell me!" I shouted, shaking my head. "Don't tell me it was you who kil—"

His hand quickly muffled my voice, and I yelled the rest of the sentence into his palm. Nicco could *not* be the killer who ruined my mother. My family.

He dragged his fingers from my lips and rested them at the back of my neck. My voice rushed out in a desperate whisper. "You're the one who killed those students?"

His face twisted, and his hands dropped to my shoulders. "No, it—" He stopped as my eyes welled.

"Nicco. Did *you*. Kill those students?"

His lips remained closed as he watched the tears in my eyes threaten to spill over. The silence was torture.

"Did you do it?" I screamed and pushed him in the chest. He didn't move, but I teetered.

He reached for my elbow, and once I was steady, the words slipped from his mouth: "I did it. I killed those people."

I jerked away, stumbling a few steps backward. Despite near hyperventilation, I pulled my coat tighter around my chest.

Hearing that someone is a killer never gets easier.

Despite his confession, I still did not want to believe him.

Stop rationalizing his repulsive actions. Actions that destroyed your own mother!

I felt like I was going to explode as I looked coldly at his stoic face.

"I told you to never trust a vampire," he said.

I turned on my heels and walked away before the tears could fall. In a way, I wished I could be more like him, less emotional, always in control.

"Adele, wait!"

I never turned back, and when he didn't follow, it felt as if my heart were ripping in two.

That's when I realized Nicco somehow had a hold of it.

My heart.

CHAPTER 35

Birds of a Feather

My pace quickened until I had to consciously keep myself from breaking into a run. *How could I have been so wrong about Nicco?* My lungs burned, and just as two pathetically loud sniffles escaped me, everything became blurry.

"No," I whispered angrily. "No. No. No. Pull it together, Adele. No crying." *There's no time to worry about boys.*

I took a deep breath, stowed my feelings, and hoped they'd stay put for the duration of my next stop: the one I'd saved for last because I knew I'd have to apologize to Isaac and inevitably admit I was wrong about Nicco. I stormed down the street to Jackson Square. That's when I realized I didn't even know where Isaac and his father were staying. It wasn't like there were any hotels open. I'd never had to find Isaac before; he'd always just been around—just like I had the feeling he was now.

I crossed the cathedral and hopped up the three stairs to the Place d'Armes. The iron fence surrounding the small park in the center of the square had been closed since the Storm, but at this point the lock was child's play.

The formerly manicured garden now better resembled an overgrown swamp. I walked to the middle and just waited.

"Brilliant idea, Adele," I said to myself with a sigh.

I whistled, as if I knew some kind of magical birdcall.

Nothing. I stomped on a Coke can and sent it skidding.

Exasperated, I flung my arms up in defeat. "Hello? I know you're there!"

Wings flapped, and then, sure enough, Isaac walked through the gate. Even though he had already admitted this insane ability, the proof still made me struggle for words.

"Hi," I said meekly.

"Jesus, Adele! What the hell do you see in that guy?"

"Ugh! Why do you have to do that?" My teeth gritted as embarrassment flooded me. "I came to apologize!"

"You did?"

"Why do you always have to ruin everything?"

"I don't know!" he yelled back. "Probably because I'm eighteen and not four hundred years old?"

I paused for a moment, biting my lip, but couldn't help it: a giggle burst out. "I bet that's not something you ever thought'd come out of your mouth?"

He cracked a smile. "That's for sure. But I never thought I'd pull feathers from my hair when I woke up in the morning either." He brushed a small black tuft from his shoulder, and we both watched it float away.

"About that . . ." I said. "We have a lot to talk about and very little time."

"Yeah, and you don't have to apologize. I'm the one who slashed your face open. I'm so sorr—"

"You already apologized—"

"And I'll apologize a hundred more times and still feel horrible!"

"Apology accepted! It was an *accident*, right?"

"I swear."

"Then let's just stop apologizing and move forward, okay?"

"Okay," he said, looking slightly shocked. Then he stood taller, as if a massive weight had been lifted from his shoulders.

"But that doesn't mean I don't have, like, eight thousand questions," I added, walking out of the park toward the river. He followed.

"Yeah, I figured."

As we exited onto the street, he dipped his hand into the water that filled one of the long cement boxes on the sidewalk. "What are these things?"

"Troughs."

"Troughs? For what?"

"For the horses to drink out of."

"Horses?"

"Normally there are horse-drawn carriages lining this block."

"Really?"

"Really."

"That's so weird."

"Yeah, I guess it is." I laughed as we crossed Decatur Street to the concrete amphitheater.

Side by side, we jogged to the top of the stadium-like seats and then sat down on one of the cold rows.

"This used to be the most picturesque view in the city," I said.

The carriages, the iron-fenced park, and the cathedral donned millions of postcards, but now, in the darkness, the backlit steeples looked Hitchcockian and creepy. Behind us, we could hear the river, thanks to the curfew-imposed silence. There were no trains, no barges, no cars, no music to muffle the sloshing tide.

Isaac leaned back on his elbows, seeming perfectly at ease. I leaned back too. As we stared at the empty stage, it felt like a lifetime ago that my father would bring me here and give me dollar bills to tip the street performers, all of whom I knew by name when I was a kid.

"I don't even know where to start . . ." I said.

"What do you want to know the most?"

"Why were you in my house the night we returned home? How do you turn into a bird? Why do you have so many drawings of my ancestor Adeline Saint-Germain—?"

"Whoa." He laughed. "I am completely content spending the entire night with you, but you're the one who said we're on a time constraint."

I blushed.

"You're right. Give me the abridged version, *s'il vous plaît*."

"Whatever you want." He took a long pause. "I suppose it started before we came down to New Orleans. Before the Storm. The dreams started just after my great-grandmother died."

"I'm sorry."

"Thanks." He smiled. "My dad and I were upstate, helping my grandpa take care of her affairs—"

"Wait, upstate? I thought you were from New York *City*."

"I am. My parents moved to the city before I was born—when my mom got her first role on Broadway."

"Your mom's an actress?"

"Before she died."

"I'm so sorry, Isaac." My hand went to his leg as I tried to recall if I'd ever said anything horrible about my own mother in front of him.

"Thanks." His gaze flicked to my hand, which I promptly removed. "We were clearing out my great-grandmother's estate, which wasn't worth much, but . . ." He took a breath and looked at me.

"But?"

"That's where I found this." He pulled out a large leather-bound sketchbook from his knapsack and handed it to me. It wasn't the one I'd previously wanted to hit him with; this one was old. *Very old.* My hands instantly felt alive, holding it.

"Open it."

The delicate pages were filled with beautifully depicted watercolors of a tropical island: cliffs over water, sunrises, fields of dandelions, exotic birds, and sketch after sketch of the same suntanned teenage boy. Then the images gradually became darker. Billows of smoke. Metal bars. Large plumes of feathers. Flames. Waves. A woman swimming underwater—no, drowning. The page margins were full of gibberish.

"This is amazing, Isaac. Your great-grandmother was an artist?"

"No, that book's way older than my great-grandmother. It must have belonged to one of her ancestors. For a couple of weeks, up until she died, I'd been having these crazy dreams about flying," he said. "It's hard to explain, but when I found the book, it was like I couldn't put it down. It felt almost painful to leave it." His hand brushed mine as he gently closed the book to show me the cover. At a first glance I didn't see anything, but as I focused, a carving in the leather came into view: in the lower right corner, there was a small triangle with a horizontal line cutting through the peak.

"I looked it up. It's the alchemical symbol for *air*. My grandpa knew I was applying to art schools, so he let me keep the book—"

"You were applying to art schools? Wait, you're in high school?"

"I was a senior, but my dad let me come down here with him, and then I just kinda ended up . . . dropping out, because there were so few people to go on rescue missions those first few weeks. Getting my GED and applying to colleges were part of the deal—I'm supposed to be studying when I'm at the café."

Good Lord, how much do I not know about this boy?

"When we got back to Brooklyn, my dreams changed. They were no longer about flying, or feathers, or birds. They were about fire. And there was always this girl in a long dress, always surrounded by flames. Then the Storm happened, everything got crazy, and suddenly my father and I ended up here."

"*Aaaand* then you were breaking into my house?"

"I *wasn't* breaking and entering. *Maaaybe* trespassing. But it's not my fault . . . It's hers." He pointed to the sketchbook. Before I could ask what my house had to do with his ancestor's sketchbook, he turned to a page he appeared to know well.

"Whoa."

It was a sketch of my house—the iron gate, the long shutters, the attic windows. The Creole cottage looked exactly the same, only there weren't houses on either side of it yet, just trees.

"My first day in town, I got this strange sense of familiarity when I walked past your house, but I just thought it was déjà vu or something. It took me another week or so to realize where I recognized it from—and I *know* this is going to sound weird—but I developed this *obsession* with your house! Well, I didn't know it was *your* house at the time—I'm not some creepy stalker—I just wanted to know why the hell it was in my book. How had my ancestor drawn a cottage in New Orleans? I mean, we're not Mayflower Society old, but we're a pretty old New England family.

"I found myself making any possible excuse to walk past it. Back then, rescue missions were around the clock, and after every single one of my shifts, I'd walk down your street, even if it was out of my way. I knew whoever lived there hadn't returned, and it was as if I had to check on it. Like I needed to protect it. Which is *insane*, because there were so many houses that actually needed protecting. Saving. I started to imagine there might be someone inside who needed rescuing and that I was developing some kind of psychic powers to save them. I felt like I was going *crazy* . . ."

As I carefully turned the pages, the images pulled at my attention: a decrepit ship, a voyage, scene after scene of *La Nouvelle-Orleans*, a convent, nuns. If Adeline's diary was the novel, then these were the illustrations.

Then a page with a familiar-looking girl made me stop.

She wore a floral-print dress with stays that laced up the front. Her long red curls were whipping wildly in the wind, and underneath the sketch were the words:

Self-Portrait, June 1727

It was Susannah Bowen staring back at me.

I could feel my eyes growing big as I looked up at Isaac.

"You think I'm crazy," he said.

"No! I don't. Not at all. What happened next?"

"One night, I was walking home from a recovery site, and, as always, I paused in front of your house. But something was different. Something felt off. I wouldn't have been able to describe the supernatural feeling back then."

I nodded, remembering the compulsive feeling the convent had on me the morning I accidently opened the shutter.

"I heard something inside break, and that was it. *Bam.* An excuse to go inside. I'd already been in a couple scuffles with scavenging gutter-punk looters. I grabbed a piece of broken fence and snuck around the side to investigate. Sure enough, the kitchen door had been broken." He looked at me. "Someone *else* broke and entered."

I nodded.

"I left my bag on your kitchen counter and crept through your house, but I couldn't find anyone. Or, rather, I didn't see anyone . . . but I could *feel* someone there in the dark with me. It was like someone was messing with me, whipping behind my back every time I turned around.

"After I'd cleared the whole house, I ended up back in the kitchen, but I was really uneasy. Every molecule of my being told me something was wrong. Danger. I was getting ready to run when a gust of wind burst through the door and knocked my bag off the counter. The sketchbook spilled out. When I bent to pick it up, I started having these pains in my shoulders and arms, and I fell to the floor. I mean, I get cramps sometimes from all the manual labor, but this was different—my body felt like it was going to *explode*. And there I was, sitting against a cabinet on your kitchen floor, when another gust of wind came in, swirling around like a vortex, whipping the book open to this page."

I looked down. A black crow was painted across the centerfold, and verses in curly script filled what little white space was left.

"When I looked up, that's when I saw the intruder, staring at me from the other side of the vortex, fangs out . . . a blood binger. I think he knew what I was even before I did. I didn't understand why he couldn't get through the wind, but the look in his eyes said he was willing to wait it out. Something compelled me to grab the book—some intuition—and to start reading the words aloud. I sounded ridiculous, like I was reciting poetry in Old English, and the pain got worse and worse, until I thought I was going to crumble. And then, poof, I had wings."

"You did a spell?"

"If you say so. All I know is the vortex dropped, he lunged, and I could fly."

I glanced at the curly penmanship on the page. The spell at the convent hadn't been broken at that point, so the intruder couldn't have been anyone from the attic. That left only two possible male vampire suspects. "Was it Émile—I mean, Emilio?"

Wouldn't Emilio still have been in France?

"Wait a second. Don't tell me that new douche bag in town is the same guy you were all hung up on when you got back from Paris? The one Jeanne and Ren were always teasing you about?"

My face burned, both because it was true and because he knew about my unfortunate lapse in judgment.

"So much for your headphones being on all those days in the café," I snapped.

He jumped up in front of me, laughing. "No wonder you don't like me. You have the worst taste in guys *ever*!"

I told myself to breathe, but no amount of air to my lungs was going to help.

"*Ever*!" he taunted, bouncing backward down the stairs.

That was it. I sprang up, drew my arm back like I was pitching a softball, and whizzed a perfectly round fireball right past his ear. He whipped around and watched it sail another hundred feet and land in one of the troughs with a satisfying sizzle.

"What the ef?" he yelled, twisting back around. "How did . . . ? You just . . . That was *AWESOME*!"

A rush of relief passed through me.

"Do it again!"

"You want me to throw fire at you again?"

"Uh, if it's coming out of your *hands*, then *YES*."

"Don't say I didn't warn you." I lobbed another flame, but this time aimed it across the street, directly into the horses' drinking station. He ran back to me, unable to contain himself.

"You're like Super Mario!"

"You really know how to make a girl feel special."

"You're like Super Mario, but a hot girl." He blushed, realizing the compliment had slipped out.

My gaze dropped to the ground. I didn't deserve any compliments after the events of the last few days. I tried to look back up at him without thinking about our kiss that night in the Tremé.

"Hey," he said gently, taking my hand.

My heart skipped, worrying we were back there. But when I looked up, he smiled, quickly let go, and started jogging backward down the rows to center stage.

"Hit me!"

"No, Isaac, I don't want to burn you."

"You aren't going to burn me," he scoffed. "Just do it."

Without answering, I launched a fireball at him.

Just before the first flame hit his face, he raised his hand, and a small gust of wind redirected it thirty feet upward. He yelled for more. I threw a second, a third.

"Again, again, again!" he yelled, sending each one upward after the next.

I threw two more. As gravity pulled the arc of fireballs down toward him, he popped each ball back up, one by one. A smile spread across his face.

Isaac was juggling my flames. And it was the most amazing thing I'd ever seen.

I walked down the steps, totally mesmerized by the coolest street performance in history. When he raised his arms, the trajectory of the flames lassoed around him. I bounced up and down, as if preparing to double-Dutch, and then, without thinking, ran into the flaming rope. The momentum made me tumble into him, but he hardly wavered and never took his eyes off the ring of fire. With my back turned to his chest, I craned my neck to watch the flames swirl around us, and even shot a few more into the gentle twister.

For the first time, my power seemed beautiful. Isaac had this way of making everything he touched beautiful.

He lowered his head so it was level with mine. "You see, we are better together."

A smile I hoped he couldn't see came from somewhere deep inside—I slowly inhaled and fought the urge to relax into his chest. "You're right."

"I am?" A fireball fell, squelching into a puddle.

I turned around to face him. "We are better together. Stronger. The three of us."

"Three?"

"You, me, and Désirée," I said with a Cheshire-cat grin and began to jog backward toward our stuff. The flames rained down around us as he chased me with his mouth gaping.

"You mean like a threeso—"

I chucked another fireball toward his head. He easily flung it out of the way and caught up with me. I grabbed his knapsack and his wrist and took off running.

"Now *I* have a lot to tell *you*."

CHAPTER 36

Circle of Seven

"They should really lock their doors this late at night," Isaac said as we burst into Vodou Pourvoyeur.

"No one here has to worry about burglars."

"I hope you found some answers," Désirée yelled from the back room.

I followed her voice deeper into the shop. "I did way better than that," I shouted, dragging a suddenly uneasy Isaac through the shelves of esoteric souvenirs. "I found our third!"

"Your what?" he asked as we stopped in the apothecary-like room.

Désirée looked up from the cauldron she was meddling with. The room was a mess, strewn with books and discarded crumpled sheets of paper. Herbs, oils, powders. And a smattering of bones and other fragments I'd rather remain clueless about.

"You've got to be kidding me," she said, scanning Isaac up and down. She extinguished the fire in the hearth so as to not burn whatever she was brewing.

"You two are starting to freak me out," Isaac said. "Can someone tell me what is going on here?"

"Isaac, show Désirée what you can do."

"What?" His eyes widened, and he said my name under his breath.

"Show her. You can trust Dee. I promise."

He looked at Désirée with caution.

She crossed her arms. "This better be good."

His eyes rolled, and then he was gone.

"Shit! Where'd he go?"

My gaze rose to the wall behind her, where he was perched, perfectly still, on the top shelf in between an enormous cow's skull and two taxidermy bats.

Just as Désirée craned her neck backward, he launched down toward us.

"Jesus!" She jumped, grabbing my arm as he swooped over our heads to the shelf behind me.

I spun around, my eyes never moving from him. Unlike our first encounter, the bird wasn't scary to me—his shiny, jet-black feathers, wide wingspan, and animal grace all left me momentarily breathless.

He transformed back to his human form, cracking up at Désirée. "You should have seen the look on your face."

"An anthropomorphic spell. Big whoop."

"Anthro-what?" he asked. "Oh yeah, it was a real big whoop for you that day you accidentally turned me into a cat and couldn't turn me back!"

"Oh my *God*, that was you?" She laughed. "Serves you right for creepin' me."

"I was not *creeping* you! You were being followed by a vampire!"

"Oh."

"That's not all," I said. "Go on, Isaac."

He looked at me one last time before he raised his hand. A slight wind began to blow back our hair, and soon the scattered mess Désirée had made all over the floor was arranged into neat stacks of papers and orderly piles of herbs.

"Excuse me! That mess meant something to me." Désirée raised her hand, and the flowers began to shift across the wooden floor, like pieces of a Rubik's Cube. But it was different than the way Isaac had moved them with the air. Each little flower and herb moved for Désirée on its own. Then the crystals. And then the stones. And then the papers, until all the objects were back to their seemingly chaotic state. Well, almost. Désirée looked annoyed as she stared at a small pyramid-shaped stack of dried purple berries. Her face scrunched as if she were focusing intensely, and the stack suddenly exploded, a berry hitting Isaac in the nose.

I bit my lip, trying not to laugh. "Isaac, show Désirée your sketchbook."

"Not until you tell me what the hell is going on."

"That's what I'm trying to do!" I grabbed the painting of the casquette girls from Désirée's pile on the floor, along with Adeline's diary, and put them both on the counter.

Désirée added Marassa's grimoire, and we both looked at him. He conceded, handing over the sketchbook. I flipped it open to Susannah's self-portrait, moved it next to the painting, and pulled him close so he could see.

"What the hell?" Isaac asked, looking back and forth between the two.

"Goddess help us," Désirée said. "You are legit."

"You're the descendant of Susannah Bowen. You're our third."

"Your third what?"

"Coven member," I answered, trying to make the word sound natural.

"Excuse me, your *what*—?"

"Our coven," said Désirée. "PS, we have about twenty-six hours to find the other four members so we can break a curse our ancestors cast in 1728."

"Or what? We turn into pumpkins at midnight?"

"Or, we get killed by a clan of Italian vampires that Adele released from an attic."

"Hey!" I snapped back. "You're the one who woke them up."

"Yeah, but if you hadn't released them, they would have just starved to death, trapped in the attic."

"It was an *accident*. Just like this *accident*." I turned to Isaac, pointing to his mark on my face. "And we only need to find two more. The original coven had seven witches, but at least two of them died before having any children, so there are only five descendants max."

"You're serious?" Isaac asked, nodding in disbelief.

"And how exactly do you know when two died?" Désirée asked. "Suddenly discover your power for psychometry in the last couple of hours?"

"I know this because I *met* one of the original members of the Casquette Girls Coven."

She raised one eyebrow. "Well, you certainly had a productive walk . . ."

"Wait," said Isaac, "one of the original coven members? How did you meet a three-hundred-year-old witch?"

"Because she's no longer a witch."

Désirée shot me a confused look, and then her eyes widened as it dawned on her. "No!" she said. "By whom?"

I gave her a look back that said, *Who do you think?*

"Gabriel?"

"*Oui,*" I said, ignoring Isaac's openmouthed stare. "Lisette Monvoisin is a Medici now, so she's not so keen on coven cooperation." I unbuttoned my coat and pulled down the collar of my sweater so they could see the fresh bruising. "This is what happened when I tried to talk to her about her 'Maker,' as she called him."

"Damn!" Désirée said.

Isaac stood up, knocking back his chair. "*Stop.* Can someone just start at the beginning?"

"Sure we can," Désirée said a little too innocently. She slid right beside him and reached her hand behind his head.

"Ouch!" he yelled. "What the hell?"

"You'll thank me later." She walked behind the counter with his strand of hair.

"Welcome to the coven," I said, smiling.

While Désirée made him a gris-gris, she briefed him on what we knew about the myths, the monsters, and the magic. He leaned over the counter, listening intensely, but whenever she said something really contentious, I could feel a disturbance in the air. Literally—the air around him trembled.

I opened Adeline's diary and tried to absorb myself in her writing, tuning out Désirée's voice. I didn't want to hear the part about Emilio's ultimatum. It was hard enough grappling with the idea of my own mortality; handing someone else his potential death sentence was too much.

9th September 1728

I lie awake, thinking about the words Gabriel Medici spoke the night he killed Martine—his demands and his threats. He doesn't believe me when I say I don't know your location, Papa. So this is why you were so secretive about your journey? It brings me great sadness that you thought I could not carry this burden with you.

I haven't told the other girls about his threats, for I feel this is a matter of family affairs.

10th September 1728

The guilt over the DuFrenses' deaths lies twice as heavy now, Papa, knowing the Medici's presence here seems to have something to do with me. With us.

My attempts to communicate with Martine have been fruitless. She would not even look at me when I ran into her on the street this evening. Gabriel says this is common with newborn vampires—that they often reject their former human families as part of their transition. I was the closest thing Martine DuFrense had to family.

15th September 1728

Martine's affairs were all left in perfect order, which makes me wonder if she really did beg Gabriel to turn her. In her last will and testament, she named me as her sole beneficiary and left the proper paperwork to declare Marassa a free woman upon her death—the only good thing to come out of this travesty. Gabriel managed to procure Martine's death certificate from the coroner. Considering there was no body to examine, I assume he was able to persuade the man with his vampiric thrall, just as he had with Makandal's memories. This thrall frightens me more than their fangs. Thankfully, it seems that our kind are not so susceptible to their hypnotic stare. Gabriel was already born with more charms fair to one man.

18th September 1728

Sometimes I think Gabriel believes I am teasing him by not telling him the information he desires and that he is drawn to this game of cat and mouse. And sometimes I think I am only safe as long as he assumes I am withholding something.

Or is he simply leading me to believe I have the upper hand?

Tonight, he was ever peculiar, reminding me how quickly his intentions can flip. As usual, the hour was late, as we both sat in my window bench opposite each other. He appeared to have drunk quite a lot, so I attributed his chatty mood to the anise-flavored wine he is so fond of.

"Do you like *La Nouvelle-Orléans*, Adeline?" he asked, as gentle as a man can be.

"There are things I miss about Paris," I told him. "The salons, the intellect, the art . . . but there is an art in everyday life here. The diversity of my friends, the freedom I have compared to back home." I paused so he could add his commentary, but he remained silent, his glassy green eyes burning into my face, and so I continued. "It is raw, untamed, but it is almost sad, watching on every day as society carves, bends, and polishes the people and land into what it deems worthy of a history book, of a report back to the king."

"You are your father's daughter," he said.

I wanted to probe, to ask what he meant by the remark, but instead the next question flew from my lips. "What is it about the Saint-Germains that gets you so bothered?"

He became explosive, grabbing me with force and pulling me close. "Do *not* toy with me, Adeline. And hear this warning: If you haven't revealed your father's hiding place by the time our brother arrives, then you will be going away with us. You will no longer have to worry about the affairs of the Saint-Germains, because I will make you a Medici."

The misplaced comfort I feel around him made me smile and ask, "Is that your twisted way of asking for my hand in marriage?"

To which he smirked and replied, "Well, that would require my asking your father's permission first, wouldn't it? No, I have a much more permanent idea in mind."

20 September 1728

I don't know what to think about anything anymore, Papa. The past day is not much more than a blurry haze.

Yesterday, I was attacked.

In my lucid dreams, the scene plays over and over in my mind: I was out shopping for new ribbons, when someone whipped past me, not at all trying to hide his supernatural speed, despite being out in broad daylight. He pulled me into an alleyway, and, making no demands or threats, he simply said, "I want to leave this hellhole!" And then he tore into my neck like a demonic animal. I tried to fight back, but he drank so quickly, and it was as if the magic was draining from my body with my blood.

If I survive this, things will be different. I swear on everything holy.

21 September 1728

The pain is excruciating. I can feel the infection setting in. Susannah feeds me a strong medicinal concoction that reeks of fennel. I fade in and out of sleep in a hallucinogenic state—I am unsure if this is a symptom of the homeopathy or of the vampire bite.

23rd September 1728

Yesterday, in my state of semiconsciousness, I could hear the girls fluttering around me. There was a heated debate amongst the circle: they seemed to be split on my course of treatment. In the end, Cosette said strongly, "Her temperature is *too* high. I am going to get him! He is the only one who can save her now."

"We're not letting you go alone," her sisters yelled, running after her.

The room fell silent, except for Susannah's pacing footsteps. Marassa squeezed my hand.

Gabriel entered my room several moments before the triplets made it back. "How did this happen?" he growled, hovering over my head.

"Why don't you ask your brother Emilio!" Susannah spat back.

With angered huffs, he wiped my fevered brow. I will never forget the look in his eyes. Fear . . . mixed with a strange glimmer of hope. The touch of his hand sent chills down my chest.

"You bedda not do anything but help her, monsieur," Marassa threatened.

He hissed at her and then cupped my face with his hands. Although I shook violently, his touch immediately began to bring down my body temperature.

I think every girl in the room held her breath as he removed the bandages, exposing the infected puncture wounds.

Susannah frantically asked him questions in English, which I couldn't understand. He replied in her native tongue and then bit the fingernail on his right index finger so that it cracked at a sharp angle.

Ignoring my own words of delirium, he looked into my eyes and said, "This is going to hurt, Adeline, but I will be quick." Then his left hand slid to my shoulder, pinning me to the bed.

Before I could even nod, he slit open the puncture wounds on my neck with one swipe. I screamed as his lips suctioned onto my neck.

"What is he doing?" Lisette yelled in the background.

"He's attempting to extract the vampire venom," Susannah said. "It is causing the infection."

He released me for a moment, spat into the basin next to the bed, and in a flash was reattached to my neck, and I was screaming.

He spat again and yelled, "It's not enough! The venom is coursing too deep in her bloodstream. Why didn't you call for me sooner?"

No one said anything for a moment, and then Cosette said, "Surely there is *something* you can do?"

"Yes, there *is*," he said.

Susannah screamed, "No!" and my eyes opened again just as Gabriel was lowering his wrist to my face.

I clamped my lips shut before his blood could enter my mouth.

"It's the only way!" Gabriel pleaded with me, but I refused.

He looked grimly at Susannah. "If she dies, it will be on your hands."

My head fell sideways, and his blood smeared across my face. All I could think was, if everything that has happened has something to do with our family, Papa, then I deserve to die, but not the others. Not Sophie, or Claude, or Martine, or Morning Star's brother, and none of the nameless souls in *La Nouvelle-Orléans*.

Marassa rubbed my shoulder and said gently, "You gotta do it, Addie."

And then Cosette was by her side, squeezing my hand. "You have to drink it, Adeline! It will only be a few drops." She shot a look at Gabriel. "Just enough to save your life, *ma fifille*."

The tears in her eyes made me tremble.

Gabriel distracted me by wiping the blood from my cheeks with one hand while parting my lips with his other. When his open wrist dripped onto my tongue, I gagged on the vile, metallic taste. Cosette squeezed my jaw, like I was just a babe, so I couldn't shut my lips.

The blood slipped down my throat, and then suddenly, with animalistic impulse, I found myself pushing Cosette out of the way and clutching Gabriel's wrist, pining for him, for his blood.

But no sooner had I started drinking, than he was forcefully detaching himself from my mouth. "No more, *cara mia*."

I looked back to him, panting, begging.

He slipped underneath the blanket next to me and pulled me into his chest. "Go to sleep, little lamb," he said, scooping me so close my entire body pressed tightly against his.

"What do you think you're doing?" cried Cosette. "Get away from her! Get out of the bed."

"Precautionary measure," he told the girls, his sturdy arms wrapping me into his chill. "You are going to want me around if she drank too much." His voice was steady, but I could sense his worry. "Not that I really care if she rips off all of your heads, if that's what she wants, but I don't want her taking *flight* like Martine did." His fangs flashed at Susannah. "I'm here for the night, just in case."

"Just in case?" Cosette said, fuming.

"When it comes to death," he said, "just as in life, there are no guarantees."

"I knew this was a bad idea," Susannah said, jerking the blanket away from him.

Gabriel rolled over me and grabbed her tiny waist. "If you think a blanket is going to keep me from taking *anything* I desire tonight, then you are an even sillier little girl than I thought."

"Remove your hands from her," I heard Cosette say from behind me.

And, just like every other man, Gabriel did as Cosette commanded.

But it was Gabriel who had the final word. "You have two options. Leave . . . or settle in with us." I could tell by his inflection that he was smiling.

Cosette pulled the blanket back over us and crawled in next to me. "You're going to be okay, *ma fifille*," she said, burrowing against my back. "You will always be one of us."

Her close proximity to the vampire made her sisters gasp, but then they too lay down at our feet. Marassa settled onto the sofa at the edge of the bed, and Susannah curled into a chair in the corner, both of them keeping a sharp eye on Gabriel.

"Well, I'm no stranger to the ménage à trois," Gabriel said, "but I can honestly say that seven is a record for me."

In her goddess-disguised, femme fatale voice, Cosette replied sweetly, "Don't make me sew your mouth shut for the night. It would bring me great pleasure."

He stroked my hair. Even through the numbness of the vampire venom and medicinal concoctions, I could feel his blood coursing through my veins, fighting the infection.

"Go to sleep, Adeline, and don't even think about trying to get seconds. If you bite me again, you'll end up stuck with me for the rest of your immortal life."

His words made me shudder.

Pressed up against him, barely lucid, everything about Gabriel Medici made me shudder.

When I awoke this morning, atop his chest, I hesitated before opening my eyes, allowing myself a brief moment to be held in his arms. He knew I was awake—his heart had flickered the moment my consciousness returned. I remained still for just a few more seconds, lingering in his scent. Just a single stolen moment before I sat up, as decorum demands, and insisted he get out of my bed.

To which he replied, "Are you sure you don't want to lie with me a little longer?" His gaze burned straight through my thin gown.

"Get out!" I yelled, pushing him up.

The other girls woke, making a fuss over the status of my health, while Gabriel sat on the edge of the bed, pulling on his boots and stretching his arms into his jacket.

He stood, shielding his eyes from the sunlight that pierced the cracks in the drapery, then he leaned down and took my hand, as if to kiss it good-bye, but instead he pulled me to my knees, just long enough to whisper in my ear, "This doesn't change anything, mademoiselle. I am still going to drain your father." He discreetly kissed the lobe of my ear and was gone.

"I despise him," I said as Cosette pulled me back down to the bed. And I meant it. I despised the way he made me feel about him.

Now, more than ever. I could feel him inside me, rushing through my bloodstream.

Cosette unwrapped the bandages and examined my neck. "It's perfect," she said and kissed my new, smooth skin.

"It's perfect *now*," Susannah said. "What if it happens again? How long will a vampire help a witch?"

"And at what price?" Marassa added.

"Yes," Susannah said. "Why *did* he help you?"

I nearly began to panic, Papa. This is not the way I envisioned ever sharing the one and only secret I keep from the coven—that the vampires are after *you*. But then Lisette, in all of her innocence, saved me from having to do that.

"Because he loves her, of course!" she said, as if it were the most obvious thing in the world.

"A vampire loving a witch?" asked Susannah, nearly laughing. "Now I know the world has gone mad."

"He does! Have you never seen how he sneaks into her bedchamber every night?"

In retrospect, maybe I was holding two secrets, but I would rather my cheeks flush red with scandal than have our private family matters made public before even I understand them.

Cosette had the final word, for when she speaks, everyone listens: "He is in love with her. I can feel it in his heart." She looked at me, and for a moment I could hardly breathe. Was she speaking the truth, or was she just covering for me?

The look of disgust on Susannah's face reminded me of all the killings. And all of the Saint-Germain threats. I regained my senses and remembered the original advice you heeded. *Trust no one on this trip.* "Susannah is right." I told them. "The Medici have killed for weeks. For months. We must stop them."

"But, Adeline, he saved your life," Lisette reminded me as she sat on the bed.

"A life nearly taken by his brother!" I made my position clear. "The Medici are the enemy. We are powerful together. It is time we do something about them."

A smile slowly spread across each girl's face, but I could see the fear in Lisette's eyes.

"We will no longer be preyed upon," I told her, stroking her cheek. "And besides, Gabriel did not save my life . . . Louis did."

"The dog? Adeline, Louis has been missing for weeks. You must still be feeling the effects of Susannah's tea."

"No, it was Louis. I swear to it! If he hadn't attacked Emilio, I would never have escaped!"

Cosette took my hand and gently explained how they had found me, near death, on the curb two blocks away from the DuFrense estate.

I sprang from the bed. "We have to find Louis. He might have been hurt saving me!" As the girls protested, I slid on my boots. They were not even laced before I was running down the stairs to the front door.

"Adeline, come back!" Marassa yelled. "You are not well!"

But she could not have been more wrong. I was never better. The other girls could hardly keep up with me, for I now had Medici vampire blood flowing through my veins. I didn't stop running until we had twisted and turned into the alley where Emilio had dragged me, off the side of the cathedral.

"Louis!" I called over and over again.

The other girls began to poke through the rubbish in the alley, searching for him.

"*Sacrebleu!*" cried Lisette.

"It's badly hurt!" said Minette.

To my surprise, it wasn't Louis, my black-haired companion. This wolf-dog was a shiny silver color, with a silver star tied to a piece of leather around its neck. When I slid the ornament around to show the others, Susannah shouted frantically, "We must bring her back to the house at once!"

It took all six of us to lift the animal, and even then, I'm certain Susannah was supporting its weight with magical assistance. Even so, when a gruff man offered to help, she yelled, *"No!"*

Her frantic behavior made me fear that the animal's injuries were grave.

When we burst in through the door of my bedroom, she yelled, "On the bed!"

"Is the bed really necessary?" I asked, thinking only of the garbage heap the animal had been lying in as I closed the door behind us. Simultaneous gasps answered for me. When I rushed back to the bed, there was no more wolf—only a young native woman.

"Rougarou!" gasped Marassa.

"Loup-garou!" yelled Minette.

"Of course she needs a bed. She's not a dog, Adeline. She's a lycanthrope," Susannah said. "A wolf charmer."

I had not the slightest idea what they were talking about, but when I pushed the girl's hair from her face, I knew exactly who she was: Morning Star, the daughter of the chief and sister to the boy who had vanished without a trace. And that's when I made the connection over my missing dog and the chief's missing son.

I dropped to my knees, in tears. "Louis was her brother . . . She can't be dead too."

"She's breathing, Adeline," Susannah said. "But she's been beaten badly. There are bite marks, but thankfully her animal skin is thick and tough." With Marassa and Minette helping, Susannah went to work packing Morning Star's deep scratches with herbal pulps.

"How did you know, Susannah?" asked Lisette.

Morning Star answered for her, in broken French: "Because she has the power of wind beneath her wings."

We all looked back at Susannah, but she wasn't there. In her place was the pirate captain's beautiful red bird.

"Scarlett!" Cosette yelped in glee. "You were with us, Susannah! You've been with us all along!"

"It's about time you showed your true self," said Marassa.

A smile spread across my face, remembering the moment on board the ship when Marassa, with Scarlett circling around her, had moved the earth below the ocean, allowing the ship to float free.

But then Morning Star interrupted with the question I feared the most.

"Why are they after you?" she asked, staring straight at me. "They stalk you every night. That's why my brother always stayed close to you. He feared for your life. What do they want with you?"

I stammered, "I don't know. Something to do with my family."

"We are your family, Adeline," all three triplets said at the same time. And they are right, Papa. These girls are my family. Emilio's bite put everything in perspective. The Medici will never touch me again, and they will never use me to touch you.

"This madness must end once and for all," I said. "We are six, and they are three—"

"Four if you count Martine," Cosette reminded me.

"They are four," confirmed Morning Star. "Giovanna Medici is the vampire who killed my brother; she is the sister to the one who attacked you. I plan to rip every yellow hair from her head. They are four, but we are seven."

There was no doubt in my mind that with Morning Star, our group was complete. Everyone else agreed, and on this very night we bound our circle and became a *coven*, as Cosette called it.

Despite being seven girls from five very different families of magic, there was never any debate as to method or approach. Everything just aligned, as if Mother Nature herself had brought us together to serve a greater purpose. And I believe she did. She brought us together to rid the world of these predators. To save the people of *La Nouvelle-Orléans*. And to protect our family, Father.

PART 3
The Curse

It's no use going back to yesterday,

because I was a different person then.

Lewis Carroll

CHAPTER 37

Artemisia absinthium

"Morning Star . . ." I said through gritted teeth.

"Excuse me?" asked Désirée. She and Isaac both looked up from their history lesson at the counter.

"Morning Star." Heat rippled down my back. "She was the seventh coven member."

"And that completes the Casquette Girls Coven: Adeline, Marassa, Cosette, Lisette, Minette, Susannah, and Morning Star," Désirée said, pointing down to the Native American girl in the painting. "How the hell are we ever going to find the descendant of someone named Morning Star?"

I trembled as my necklace—*Adeline's necklace*—began to shake.

"What's wrong, Adele?" Isaac asked.

"He bit her."

"He bit Morning Star?"

"He bit Adeline. He came after my ancestor for *no* reason and tried *to kill her*. I *hate* him!"

They both jumped up.

"Who bit her?" Isaac asked.

"Emilio!"

The medallion shot away, popping the chain off my neck, and flew straight into a shelf of salts, clear through one of the jars. I jumped back from the explosion of glass, and a flame shot out of my palm. "Shit!"

Isaac whipped a breeze around so fast the flame dissipated quicker than it had ignited.

"I'm sorry!" I bent down to clean the mess. "I'm so sorry."

"Don't touch it!" Désirée waved her hand over the pile, and the salts began to separate themselves from the glass. "We need to find a new place to convene," she said, giving me the stink eye.

"Yeah," Isaac said. "Let's not set the city on fire. It's already burned down to the ground twice, right?"

"Someone give the boy a beignet," said Désirée.

"Every building except my house, Vodou Pourvoyeur, and the Ursuline Convent."

"And that brothel," he added. "Weren't you paying attention at all on our first date?" He winked. "There are four original French buildings that survived the fires."

"Oh my God," said Désirée.

"You're a genius!" I yelled to Isaac, grabbing my coat.

"I am?"

"Don't you see? Adeline must have lived in my house on Burgundy Street, Marassa at the Voodoo shop, and your ancestor, Susannah, lived at the convent. What if the brothel belonged to one of the other casquette girls? What if her descendant still lives there?"

We all leaped toward the door.

I didn't know if it was the total darkness or the fact that my pulse climbed with every pounding footstep on the pavement, but the brothel's block felt particularly creepy. We slowed to a walk.

A twelve-foot-high iron fence gated the front of the property, with vines twisted so thick, you couldn't see through the bars.

Désirée loosened the flora from around the gate enough for us to peer through, and Isaac shone a weapon-like flashlight onto the mystery residence: a massive Creole plantation-style house, the kind you'd imagine on acres of land in the middle of nowhere rather than just a few feet from the sidewalk in the middle of a city block. The pale-pink paint was peeling, and some of the windows were broken, while others, along with the door, were boarded up—not in a protection-from-the-Storm kind of way, but in a decrepit haunted-house-on-the-hill kind of way.

"Do you guys feel that?" Désirée asked as I unlocked the rusty gate.

"Yes," we both replied.

"It's a protection spell, like the one on the shop."

We hurried up the staircase that led to the sprawling porch. The closer I got to the front door, the warmer I felt, both metaphorically *and* physically.

Isaac flicked his flashlight on the dormant gas lamps, and with a little mental focus from me, flames shone through the mucky glass boxes and the smell of burning grime wafted over us.

Désirée held her palm over the crooked boards on a window, and they popped themselves off, one at a time, into her hands. She placed them on the ground, and we peered through the impossibly opaque glass. It was obvious the building had been abandoned long before the Storm.

"Look at this," said Isaac, shining his flashlight on a plaque next to the front door.

"No!" I moaned, running over. It had an emblem of the Louisiana State Department. "It's property of the state?" There was also a list of board members, along with the museum director. "No! The building is a museum now?"

"Maybe once upon a time," Isaac said. "I don't think it's been anything for a while."

"I know there has to be a clue here somewhere!" I shook the front door's handle frantically, too overwhelmed with disappointment to focus on the metal.

"Adele!" Désirée pulled me away from the door.

"We're so close! I can feel it. We have to find out who the previous owner was!"

"Even if we do," she aggressively whispered, chasing me back down the stairs, "it's not like we'd be able to locate them tonight and then convince them they're a witch who must join our coven to break a three-hundred-year-old curse before some maniac middle-child vampire kills us all!"

I sank to the curb, my arms cradling my head. The gas lamp exploded behind me.

"Chill!" she yelled.

Breathe.

Without opening my eyes, I knew Isaac had sat next to me.

"Hey," he whispered, his hand lightly touching my back, "whoever the descendant is, they're probably not even in town because of the Storm, okay?"

When I didn't freak out on him, he rubbed my back until my breathing normalized, and I nodded in affirmation. "You're both right. We're on our own for this one."

Désirée sat on my other side. "We need a plan."

"It seems to me we have three options," Isaac said. "One, stake all the vampires."

"Right," I said, "the three of us against six eighteenth-century vampires."

"Two, break the curse."

"Which we can't do without our full coven," said Désirée.

"Or three, fix the curse, trapping the vampires back where they should be."

We all sat still for a minute, thinking it over.

"He's right," Désirée said. "With half a coven, it would be a lot easier to recast the broken parts of the spell than to break the remaining threads."

"And if they were all contained," Isaac added, "it'd be a lot easier to eliminate them. For good."

I ignored the last part. "Okay, now we just have to lure a vampire clan back into a convent. Cake."

"How—"

"Shhh!" Isaac grabbed both of our shoulders. His head perked up, listening.

Footsteps. A figure walked out of the total darkness into our dimly lit part of the block. It was Theis. His walk had a nervous air: quick steps and moving his head side to side as if on alert. Despite seeming so attentive, he walked straight past us without so much as a glance.

"You shouldn't be out past curfew!" I yelled, realizing how ridiculous it sounded coming from someone who was also out past curfew. He completely ignored me.

He shouldn't have. A blur of motion I was beginning to recognize blazed down the street and whirled him into a headlock. "Nice fangs," the monster mocked before plunging into his neck.

"Theis!" I screamed, jumping up onto the curb.

Désirée and Isaac both pulled me back. The scream did nothing to distract the vampire from its meal.

I jerked my arms away. "We have to do something!"

Isaac held out his arm toward the vampire and victim. Wind and trash started blowing down the street toward them. The wind got stronger and stronger, but Isaac only managed to push the vampire back a single step. Holding his ground, the monster pushed deeper into Theis's neck.

"You're just making him angrier!" I yelled through the wind.

The air dissipated, and the street became perfectly quiet, until we could hear Theis's whimpers as the vampire fed. Then three sharp electronic beeps interrupted the stillness.

The monster's head turned slowly to look up at us. At me. I nearly choked on my own breath. It was Nicco.

Beep. Beep. Beep.

He licked the wound, and then pulled Theis's frightened face to his. "You're fine. Forget me," he told him. "Go home, *now*." His gaze was fixed back on me before he dropped Theis to the ground.

Theis scrambled up, seemingly okay, and skedaddled, and Nicco began walking toward us.

Beep. Beep. Beep.

He stopped directly in front of me on the street.

Beep. Beep. Beep.

Everyone looked at me, and only then did I realize the beeping was coming from my coat pocket—the alarm I had set on my phone. I quickly silenced it.

"Don't come any closer!" Isaac said.

He couldn't get any closer. Our fingers were only inches apart.

Nicco didn't even appear to register the words.

"This is so weird," Désirée said, "but I don't think he can see us." The sound of her voice didn't make him stir. "Or hear us."

"Nicco?" I stammered.

He didn't answer, but I could swear his eyes flickered when I said his name.

"There must be an invisibility element in this protection spell. Kudos to whichever casquette girl lived here," Désirée said in amazement.

I barely heard her as she rattled on. I couldn't take my eyes off Nicco's bloodstained lips.

He raised his hand to my face, but then stopped right before his fingers touched my cheek. His eyes squinted in confusion. He tried to push his hand forward, but an invisible wall stopped him. He tried again.

"There it is," Désirée said. "I guess the spell doesn't cover our electronics . . . how very eighteenth century. I'll look into updating it."

Nicco pounded his hand flat against the air. Pissed would hardly describe the look on his face as he appeared to register it all at once—he knew someone was on the other side of the magical double-sided mirror, and I was pretty sure he knew that someone was me.

The rage flashed to embarrassment as his gaze flicked back to the street where he'd had his dinner, but the moment was fleeting. He smirked, exposing his bloody fangs, and flung out his arms, as if to say to me, *This is it. This is me. Told you so.*

And then he was gone.

My heart felt like it had actually stopped.

"What was that all about?" Désirée asked.

"I take it back," Isaac said. "I think we should stake all the vamps."

For some reason, I couldn't look at either of them as the words came out of my mouth. "Whatever we do, we officially have twenty-four hours to do it. That's what my alarm was set for."

I deepened my stride to keep up with them.

"We're going to need a *lot* of magic," Désirée said, looking across me to Isaac. "Especially if that, back there, was any indication of what you've got."

He scoffed. "I don't know what happened . . . I just can't *stand* that guy."

"Do you usually get performance anxiety?" she somehow asked with complete seriousness.

Isaac's eyes grew wide. "That has never happened to me before!" His answers were directed at me, even though Dee was the one teasing him.

"Mmm hmmm," she continued. "Isn't that what they all say?"

I struggled to keep a straight face.

"Maybe it had something to do with the invisibility-barrier thing . . ."

Désirée and I burst out in laughter.

"Oh, this is funny to you?" he asked me.

"Mmm hmmm."

And with a flick of his wrist, a vortex blew down Ursuline Street so quickly I didn't even see it take her.

"Holy shit!" Désirée screamed from the balcony of the LaLaurie Mansion. "That was gooooood."

"Good?" Isaac yelled as she twirled around the balcony, reeling from the coven's surge of power.

"That was incredible . . . It was like I was flying!"

And in that moment, I knew the three of us were meant to be together. Everything changed being around them.

"Okay, get me down from this slave-murdering bitch's house! No! Never mind, don't!" She ran to a huge potted ivy, the kind that usually hung beautifully all the way to the sidewalk. The plant was half-dead, but she swung the vines down anyway, and then she tugged it like a rope, testing its strength.

"What is she doing?" I muttered to Isaac. "There's no way that can support her."

"Let's see what ya got!" He crossed his arms like she'd done when I brought him to Vodou Pourvoyeur.

She placed both of her hands on the top of the ivy, bowing her head slightly. The plant shivered and then, from top to bottom, came back to life in a wave of color. But it wasn't just the hue—the vines grew thicker, twisting into each other. I watched on in wonderment as they sprawled out over the sidewalk and into the street, Jack-and-the-Beanstalk-style.

And then her long legs were over the balcony, and she half climbed, half slid down.

"Let's go make some magic," she said to us and took off running down the street.

"Um, Dee!" I yelled, glancing at the magically modified vine. "What are we going to do about *that*?"

She turned back. "Don't worry, the spell will wear off soon!"

It was almost sad, imagining the ivy going back to its post-Storm state.

"Don't worry," Isaac said to me, elbowing my ribs. "I'll get you back too."

"You'll have to catch me first!"

Despite Isaac's enthusiasm for ending immortal lives, at Vodou Pourvoyeur, we went back to our known knowns: the grimoire, the sketchbook, and the diary.

The curse.

Isaac and I settled into a mound of pillows behind the fuchsia curtain in the altar room, Désirée kneeling next to us on the hardwood with her cast iron pot rigged to hang over a huge candle.

Any tension among the three of us eased. The extraordinary circumstances created an immediate bond, but the quickness with which it formed made it feel surreal. The secret, fantastical nature of it all made it hard for me to trust the magic so *completely* . . . It felt so personal and so strange to let them in on something I was still jostling with myself. Not wrong, just new. Unfamiliar.

At the same time, being around Désirée and Isaac calmed me down in a way that I'd never felt around friends before. The contradicting conditions of the coven made me feel simultaneously anxious *and* completely at ease.

For the next two hours, we threw out ideas, each one fundamentally flawed, but each one with the imagination of a Tim Burton movie.

Isaac picked up the medallion resting against my stomach and rubbed the captain's eye. Désirée stirred her concoction with a wooden spoon as she went on about an idea that used the plants in the convent garden. Navy blue smoke began to rise from her pot and swirled around her fingers in perfect loops.

I sat up, mesmerized. "What is that?"

"It's a heightening elixir from Marassa's grimoire, but it's not going to be ready until tonight. I figured since none of us can control their minds, like Cosette Monvoisin could, we're going to need all the strength we can get."

"She controlled their hearts," I said, "not their minds."

"Okay, well, not *all* of us can control vampire hearts." Désirée smirked and wagged her eyebrows, which brought on insta-blush.

"I can't control—" I couldn't even get the rest of the sentence out, with the way Isaac was looking at me—with that overwhelming disappointment he was so good at.

I pulled Susannah's sketchbook from him, so I'd have something to focus on.

"The heightening elixir is a good defensive strategy," Isaac said. "Too bad we can't dose them with some kind of weakening elixir. Even out the playing field a little more."

"That would require getting them to ingest something," Désirée explained. "Just like you're going to have to drink the heightening elixir."

"Getting them to ingest something . . ." I said, laughing. "Do you guys remember how Martine was so messed up when she died it made Gabriel loaded when he drank from her?"

"Don't even think about it, Adele," Isaac quickly said.

"Hmm . . ."

He sat up. "Adele! You are not letting one of them *drink* an elixir from you. There will be *no* martyrs tomorrow night." He looked at each of us. "Accidental or otherwise."

"You don't have to tell me that," said Désirée. "And, technically, you mean tonight. It's way past midnight."

As she went on about creating elixirs, I turned the pages of the sketchbook. Susannah had certainly had an obsession with plants. I could see why, seeing as they were the base of so many spells. I stopped on a page that was covered in drawings of three plants labeled *Green Anise, Sweet Fennel,* and *Artemisia Absinthium.* In the upper-right corner was a tunic-wearing goddess, with a bow in hand and a quiver of arrows on her back.

"Ha! This reminds me of my Halloween costume."

"You're dressing up as a Greek goddess?" Isaac asked.

"No, not Artemis, the plant."

"You're dressing up as a flower?"

"Not exactly . . ." My voice trailed off as I turned the book in different directions, reading the Old English words that scrolled around the illustration. An idea danced into my head. "We can't control their minds . . . but what if *they* couldn't control their minds either?"

"You're doing that thing where you don't make sense," Isaac said.

I pointed to the page. "This isn't just *any* recipe for absinthe. It's instructions for how to enchant the herbs! Some kind of mind-tripping spell."

"Enchanted absinthe?" Isaac asked, laughing. "I wonder what the street value on that would be?"

"Let me see that," said Désirée.

I passed her the sketchbook.

"Fennel and anise we could get, maybe," Isaac said, "but where would we get *Artemisia absinthium*, whatever the hell that is?"

"*Pfft.*" Desiree motioned for us to follow.

Through the curtain, she led us straight to the wall of herbs and pulled a jar off the shelf. "Wormwood," she said, tossing it to me. "As the common folk call it."

"So, can you do the spell?" I asked, examining the contents of the jar.

"I can brew the potion, but that's still the problem: it's a percolation potion."

"Meaning?"

"It still needs to be ingested—"

"Can you make it undetectable?"

"My gran could, easily . . . but me . . . on the first try? Probably not."

"So can we get her to do it?" Isaac asked.

"No," she said, grabbing his wrist. "My gran can't know about any of this. She's going to kill me when she finds out I joined a coven outside the family's." Désirée didn't let it go until we both nodded in agreement.

"Okay, Jesus," Isaac said. "Got it."

"So we'd have to spike something they'd want to drink," I said.

"Something with a really strong flavor. And smell."

"You make the potion, and leave the rest to me—"

"Like hell—" Isaac interrupted.

"Isaac!" I yelled. "I'm not going to dose myself into human bait! Contrary to what you might think, I do not *want* to be eaten by a vampire." I lowered my voice. "The moonshine. We're going to lace the Hurricane Hooch."

Désirée started laughing. "That's kind of brilliant."

"Then why are you laughing?" I asked.

"Because the only way we can guarantee it will hit their lips is if we spike the entire batch."

I started giggling too.

"I don't get it," Isaac said.

"All those curfew breakers drinking at illegal, little Le Chat Noir are going to be extraloaded tonight," I answered.

"That's sounds pretty par for the course in this town, from what I hear."

"Yeah," said Désirée, pulling more jars from the shelves, "I don't think the locals are going to mind one little bit."

"Let's hope the Medici are thirsty," I said.

"They'll be there," Isaac said. "I've seen them at the bar *every* night since Mac reopened."

I couldn't let the statement pass without rolling my eyes, which made him immediately regret his wording.

Désirée handed us each a jar of herbs and two large rocks. I unscrewed the cap and got a giant whiff of medicinally tinged licorice. My face scrunched.

"Anise," she said. "Don't stop grinding until you're left with only powder."

A couple of hours later, our first potion-making lesson was over, and I couldn't stop my hands from shaking as I put the last stopper in the last little bottle. My nerves were starting to fry. The bottles looked like little perfume samplers, but the clear contents were nothing so innocent.

Are we really doing this? Drugging vampires to get the upper hand in a battle?

"Let's go over the plan one more time," I said before deciding that I would definitely sleep in my own bed tonight. *What if it is my last chance?*

It was nearly dawn when we arrived at my house. This time I hadn't argued with Isaac when he insisted on walking me home, but I almost regretted it when I saw the DVD on my stoop: *La Dolce Vita*. I quickly looked around, but I didn't see any other sign of Nicco.

Isaac scooped it up and handed it to me. Luckily, the alleged "cinematic masterpiece" meant nothing to him, so I was spared any further lectures on my choices in men.

Or maybe he was just preoccupied?

His fingers were anxiously turning the little vials around and around in the front pocket of his jeans.

"Are you sure you don't want me to come with you to the bar?" I asked.

"There's no reason to risk it. I can just fly in and out."

"*D'accord*. But no perching after, okay? Go straight home and get some sleep. We'll need all our strength tomorrow. I mean, today."

"All right," he said, but didn't move. "It's so weird."

"What?"

"That you know all of my secrets now."

"And you know all of mine . . . It's kinda nice. I hate secrets."

"I just wish I'd told you sooner."

"You tried. But I wouldn't listen."

"Well, I don't want you to listen to guys who break into your house and attack you . . . even if it was an *accident* . . . Jesus, I still can't believe I—"

"Stop," I said.

"I promise I won't keep anything from you anymore."

My heart gave a thump. The Medici gift suddenly felt traitorous in my hand.

"No more secrets," I said and quickly kissed him on the cheek before I slipped inside, worried that I might melt the plastic DVD box.

My jacket hit the bedroom floor, next to my unlaced boots, and that was all the undressing I bothered with before I flopped onto my bed and slipped under the covers. For hours, I'd fought thinking about Niccolò Medici. Now the film, still clutched in my right hand, taunted me.

I contemplated watching it. Then I contemplated going to find Nicco so I could throw it at his feet while saying something cutting about his family's fascist behavior.

I shoved it under my pillow, unopened.

Do not think about him, Adele.

The plan was set. There was nothing left to do but try to relax, and for that Désirée had given me a thermos of something she called "sleepy tea." *Who knows?* I took a giant swig and sank back into the mattress with Adeline's dairy.

30 September 1728

There is no time to waste. We've spent seven days and seven nights devising a plan. It is hurried and risky, but it makes good use of each girl's unique skills. We outnumber them, but they are physically superior and more experienced in the art of deception. We can only hope they will dismiss us—a group of silly girls, barely able to communicate with each other. What they don't know is that we each have a story, a destiny, a *raison d'être*.

10th October 1728

I wish I could say our plan was perfect and the execution was flawless, but tales of battle are never so sweet.

Late last night—or early this morning might be more accurate—I sat perched in a tree under the full moon, the ideal vantage point to see through the attic windows. And even though I couldn't see my sisters tucked away on the roof, I could feel them: Marassa casting protection spells, and Morning Star and Susannah casting a trapping spell, which would work in tandem with my enchanted seals to keep the vampires in the attic. Together with the coven, everything was different—even my own magic courses through my veins differently now.

There were five windows to seal and then the door, which I'd have to pull closed blindly. *Child's play*, I remember thinking. I'd practiced closing every door in the DuFrense estate in position from my bed. There were six stakes tucked into my dress, five for the windows and one for good luck.

A lullaby attracted my attention—the triplets entering the attic, in a dance with the vampires. My pulse raced, knowing the lives of others would soon be in my hands. I launched a stake into the air, and the first set of shutters snapped closed, secured forever by the bewitched metal. I can hardly even remember throwing the next three, for it went so fast.

Marassa appeared in position above the window, waiting to help Cosette escape up to the roof. My heart pounded deeper every second.

Cosette's head popped through the last window, her arms reaching for Marassa. There was still quite a gap between their hands—too much distance. I nearly panicked. But then Marassa called for Susannah, who must have given Cosette a little boost, because she quickly flew up just enough to grasp Marassa's hands, who pulled her out and up toward the roof. But just as my arm raised to throw the next stake and close the final set of shutters, Emilio Medici launched himself out the window and grabbed on to Cosette.

Rage distracted me just long enough for Giovanna to jump out too and hook on to her brother. I hurled the stake in the air before any more of our plan could be ruined, but found no joy in closing the final seal as Emilio Medici climbed up to Cosette's waist, pulling Marassa farther over the edge of the roof.

Emilio and Giovanna began to swing Cosette back and forth, not seeming to care whether they fell. Immortality—a sure advantage in battle. The Medici taunted us all in Italian, laughing sadistically and singing as if we were all children playing a game.

My biggest fear, as I climbed down the tree, however, was not the Medici. It was that Cosette would let go of Marassa's hands and martyr herself in an attempt to kill the vampires. I was sure that if they all dropped, only one would die.

By the time I reached the ground, Morning Star was tearing out the front door of the convent. All I could do was jump out of her way as she changed into wolf form and charged by. With a deep-throated growl, she leaped through the air and clamped her jaws onto the waist of the dangling Giovanna Medici.

"Sister!" Emilio yelled, but instead of letting go and helping her, he shook Cosette even harder.

Both vampire and wolf tumbled to the garden with a roll, Giovanna screaming for her brother as she attempted to land on top, despite half of her bodice turning crimson from the wolf's bite.

Baring her teeth dangerously close to Morning Star's neck, Giovanna managed to flip the wolf around, slamming her into the ground. Rage engulfed me as Morning Star transformed back to her human self, and I jumped onto Giovanna's back. She had already killed Morning Star's brother; she could *not* take the chief's daughter too.

Beautiful and blond, just like her brother Gabriel, Giovanna sprang up, laughing, twirling around her gown made of finest lavender silk. "I am done with this place," she said, smashing me into the tree, but I held on tightly as she spewed their plans: "I am done with the precious Adeline Saint-Germain and the traitorous conjurer you call a father. I don't care what Gabriel says. Emilio and I will join Brother Niccolò in Europe and go after your father directly. You are of no use to—"

I pulled the final stake from the belt of my dress and plunged it between her shoulder and neck. Blood sprayed across my face, as she flung me to the ground. She twisted around to me in retaliation, but a gust of wind snatched me up and tossed me gently across the garden.

Despite having the stake lodged in her throat, Giovanna screamed again for her brother. "Emilio, I've been injured! I need you!"

Without skipping a beat, she pulled the stake from her shoulder, squirting a geyser of blood into the air, and then launched it at my chest—but the metal was under *my* control—midflight, I whipped it straight back at her.

The stake plunged directly into her heart before she even realized it had changed direction. Her high-pitched laugh screeched through the air as she spun around, allowing more blood to spew from her neck. She was showing me it was still the Medici who were at advantage. Her bloody hands went to remove the stake once more, and for a moment I believed she really was invincible, but this time when she tugged the stake in her chest, it didn't budge.

"Witch!" she yelled at me.

I held the metal tightly in place with my mind. I could feel the desperate thumps of her heart against the iron tip, and I pushed it harder. I could feel her power as she pulled and pulled. And then I could feel her immortal life draining, along with her blood, as she fell to the ground, gasping for air.

"Emilio . . ." she cried.

He jumped down to the ground, but instead of coming to aid his sister, as I assumed he would, he took off in one quick whip, leaving his sister to fend for herself at the hands of a witch.

A Saint-Germain.

When I looked down, I found the flames in my hands.

As for Giovanna, even as blood trickled from the corners of her lips and her heart pumped its last beat, the sparkle never left her dead green Medici eyes.

I don't regret my action, not even for a breath, Papa, but that image will haunt me forever.

Susannah flew down from the roof in a single swoop, landing at my feet, and instantly turned back to human form. "Emilio escaped just as I was finishing the trapping spell. I think his sprint pulled the spell to the edge of town."

"The rest are trapped in the attic," I told her, looking at Giovanna. "Those who survived, that is. Don't worry, the seals will hold."

We ran to tend to Morning Star.

"I've been bit," she said to us, her eyes as wide as moons. Marassa and Cosette came running from the convent.

"Where are my sisters?" asked a breathless Cosette.

The rest of the story, Papa, will have to wait until tomorrow, because I cannot bear to pen the words.

I could feel Désirée's tea fighting the wave of anxiety trying to wash over me. I took an extradeep breath through my nose, letting my lungs fill until the air moved into my diaphragm, just like my drama teacher at NOSA had taught us to do. As the air slowly began to leak out of my mouth, I felt big droplets rolling down my cheeks to land on the pillow.

Finally alone.

I thought about death. Our plan was either going to work or it wasn't; there were no other possible outcomes. Tonight, someone was going down. The vampires or the witches. The Medici or the Saint-Germains.

Me.

Or Nicco.

CHAPTER 38

Toil and Trouble

October 31st

Shaking. Shaking.

"Adele, sweetheart, wake up."

"Hmm . . . what?" I mumbled, barely able to understand the presence of another person. "Wait, what happened?" I sprang up, nearly smacking heads with my father. "He said I had until tonight!"

A very tired Mac Le Moyne was sitting on the edge of my bed, holding a white paper bag. "Shhh. Nothing bad happened, sweetheart." He squeezed my hand. "You must have been dreaming. I'm sorry. I shouldn't have woken you up like that after the other night."

"No one died?" I stammered.

"No, baby. No one died."

"Did you just get off work?" I looked at the clock: 9:03 a.m.

Ugh. Two hours of sleep.

"Yeah, Halloween pregamers. Some of your friends, the European ones, closed the place. Apparently one of them works for your mother." Then he quickly added, "But she wasn't there."

"Was Niccolò there?" I asked, not wanting to care.

He hesitated before saying yes. I could tell he wished it had been otherwise. "Although, he was brooding, while the others seemed to be celebrating something."

"He was upset?" My eyes must have lit up too much, because he frowned.

"I guess so. He wasn't taking part in the libations nearly as much as the others, but I couldn't understand anything they were saying. Hardly any of them were speaking English." He chuckled. "At one point, I thought they were going to get into a fight with Ren's band of misfits. Can you imagine?"

My back tensed. Only then did I realize what I was doing: tonight I'd make my unsuspecting father the poisoner. I tried not to look panicked, but the little brass alarm clock dove off my nightstand.

He picked it up off the floor and examined it. "Weird. Must be broken." His face twisted into a yawn.

"Dad, you have bartenders, you know."

"Not many since the Storm. Anyway, if the place gets raided, I need to be there to take the heat."

"Like you're going to get raided," I grumbled, rubbing my eyes. Désirée's sleepy tea definitely hadn't worn off yet.

"You'll want to stay awake for this surprise."

"Surprise?"

"Please accept this token as a modification of our usual Halloween tradition." He extended the white bag, out of which wafted the heavenly combination of sugar and fry.

"Oh my God!" I uncrumpled the paper.

"One of the kitchen managers at Café du Monde refused to toss out their pantry inventory since it didn't get water. He brought these by an hour ago."

I shoved one of the warm beignets into my mouth and took a large bite, blowing confectioners' sugar all over my bed.

"I know they aren't sugar cookies in the shapes of ghosts, but—"

"This is way better than sugar cookies, Dad!" I said through a stuffed mouth, inadvertently blowing more powdered sugar on him. He laughed.

My mother used to bake sugar cookies every Halloween. It was a task my father had taken over after she left, because Halloween has always been my favorite holiday. With all the chaos, I hadn't even realized the day had arrived, and I certainly wouldn't have expected us to uphold our traditional baking session.

"Thanks, Dad." I strategically pressed the beignet into the bottom of the bag so it absorbed as much of the loose powdered sugar as possible.

"My pleasure. All right, I'm gonna try to sleep all day. Tonight's sure to be crazy—word on the street is that everyone back in town in a three-parish radius will be downtown for the parade. What are your plans?"

I looked over at the costume I'd cherished not so long ago in Paris, which had been collecting dust ever since I arrived home.

"Um . . . I'm gonna hang out with Désirée." *Although our plans hardly involve trick-or-treating.*

"You've been hanging out with her a lot lately," he said with a little trepidation.

"Well, she's the only person at Sacred Heart with any kind of tolerance for downtown . . ." I added, "and we invited Isaac."

"Oh good. What about that boy from the bar?"

The vague reference to Nicco felt like a squeeze to my heart. "Um, probably not."

"Costume?" he asked, changing the subject, but I caught the look of relief.

"You know it's a surprise, Dad!"

"Okay, okay. Stop by Le Chat Noir on your way to the parade."

"Will do. *Merci beaucoup pour les beignets, Papa.*"

"Anything for you, baby doll." He kissed the top of my head.

I took advantage of his close proximity and wrapped my arms around his neck. The moment he began to shift away, I hugged tighter. He pulled me in with a gentle rock until I was ready to let go.

"Everything's going to get better, Adele."

"I know it is, Dad." *Especially if everything goes according to plan tonight.*

He kissed my head again, snagged a beignet for himself, and closed the door on his way out.

I squirmed under the covers, eager to get back to sleep. A hard edge, protruding from under my pillow, poked my arm. The DVD. I pulled it out and then aggressively stuffed another beignet into my mouth.

Do not open it, Adele.

I popped open the plastic case, and a thrice-folded piece of paper landed on my chest. For a minute I just stared at it, trying to convince myself everyone would be better off if I set the note on fire.

Then I conceded to curiosity and ripped it open. In otherworldly handwriting was a long Italian quote, presumably from the film. I grabbed my phone and prayed to the network gods for a strong enough signal to run my translator app. When the circular icon began to spin, the effect was hypnotic, and for a moment I didn't even realize I was staring down at the English words.

> *Sometimes at night the darkness and silence weigh upon me . . . We need to live in a state of suspended animation like a work of art, in a state of enchantment. We have to succeed in loving so greatly that we live outside of time, detached.*

"Oh, how perfectly *à propos . . .*" I read the quote three more times, then suddenly had the urge to spring out of bed and watch the movie. Instead, I chucked the DVD across the room to prevent any such romantic downward spiral. I fell back into the bed and smashed my still-damp pillow over my face.

What kind of twisted trick is this? Love? Is this his ploy to rattle me on D-day?

If it was . . .

It was working.

I awoke a few hours later with the energy usually summoned by my favorite holiday. But soon enough even the simplest thoughts turned morbid. *Should I even bother making my bed?*

Yes. If I died tonight, I didn't want someone else cleaning up my mess.

I flipped on the radio and nervously hummed along as I picked up dirty laundry, imagining my father tomorrow morning, sitting on my bed, crying. *Would my mother cry? Would she even care?* I grabbed my phone and checked my messages. All I saw were my own words staring back at me. No response from her. I rolled my eyes. *Shocker.*

"Whatever."

I threw the phone back on the bed. My expectations of my mother were so low a stupid text message, or lack thereof, was nothing to get disappointed over.

I debated calling Désirée and Isaac and telling them exactly how bloodily things went down for the Casquette Girls Coven in 1728. *But why make the night even more foreboding?*

As it was, it'd already be a miracle if we pulled off our plan, which was simple: Désirée on spells, Isaac on vampires, me on seals. There were only three of us; there wasn't a lot of room for complexity. *Do three even count as a coven?*

I groaned. "Why did I open that shutter?"

I. I. I.

I couldn't shake the feeling that *I* was responsible for our current situation. *Am I unnecessarily putting Désirée's and Isaac's lives at risk?*

Minette and Lisette had *died* getting those vampires into the attic. Not to mention Morning Star being bit.

Was my family responsible for this mess to begin with? Why were the Medici after the Count? What were they really after?

I snatched up a fresh towel and walked toward the bathroom.

Eighteenth-century grudges?

Feuds?

Curses.

UGH!

With a loud pop, the lightbulb in the floor lamp spontaneously combusted, spraying shards of glass all over the floor.

"Dammit, Adele, *chill out!*"

My phone buzzed as I walked out of the steaming bathroom.

| **Annabelle** | **3:40 p.m.** | D + A, where have u bitches been hiding? Everyone's going downtown tonight to this Halloween homecoming parade. Guess I'll see u there, since it's ur stomping ground. |

Oh joy.

There were also a couple of group texts from Désirée and Isaac.

Désirée	3:32 p.m.	I "mended" the attic shutter you destroyed. Isaac is going to rehang it at the convent.

Isaac	3:34 p.m.	I already hung it, but one of the stakes for the hinge is missing, so it's not very secure. Going to the salvage yard to try to find a replacement. Fingers crossed they have something.

My fingers flew over the screen.

Adele	3:51 p.m.	Don't bother, I have the missing stake. I'll bring it tonight. Meet y'all at Le Chat. 6 p.m.?

Isaac	3:52 p.m.	Word.

Désirée	3:53 p.m.	Don't be late.

I typed something snarky, but before I could press send, I caught sight of a paper airplane lying on my bed. *That definitely wasn't there preshower.* I tightened the towel around my chest as my eyes darted around the room.

Nothing.

Regardless, I hurried to the window and slammed it shut. The airplane was made from a page ripped from a sketch pad. *Isaac.* I could see the pencil lines peeking through as I slowly unfolded the plane. The sharp lines made it seem like he'd been in a hurry, but there was enough detail to capture my expression perfectly. The attic window was behind me, shutters closed. The words "*Last Night's Dreams*" had been scribbled in an entanglement of vines, flames, and feathers, which covered the rest of the page.

Me, Désirée, and Isaac. Who'd have thunk it? This power—magic, whatever it was—had made me feel electric before, but practicing my abilities with those two created far more ecstasy. Fourteen hours later, I was still basking in the euphoric high.

Smiling, I rested the drawing on top of Nicco's note and sat down at the vanity. I lingered under the warmth of the blow-dryer, slowly twisting my waves.

Poor Isaac, getting the crash course.

I soon found myself wondering if he'd also made a drawing for Désirée.

I hoped not.

There was something ceremonial about getting ready, as if I were getting into character. The rage of butterflies in my stomach subsided to a steady flutter as I retrieved my costume for the final act from the garment rack.

My magnum opus.

The base structure of the dress was a vintage burlesque costume I'd found at an antique shop in Le Marais, near *ma grand-mère's* house in Paris. The shop owner had told me the costume once belonged to some famous vaudeville dancer. I had no idea if that was true, but I felt no remorse handing him my grandmother's credit card. Every weekend thereafter, Émile drove me to the atelier, where I took a master class on couture beading. I didn't even want to know how many hours I'd spent hand-stitching the thousands of beads and sequins that now adorned the corset. Émile had constantly teased me about wanting to view my masterpiece—never in my wildest dreams did I think he'd actually get to see me wear it.

I slipped into the bodice.

It took a yoga-like contortion for me to tie the laces up my back, but it fit perfectly. The weight from the beads made it feel a bit like armor. Next came the short skirt, which was made of layers of ostrich feathers and dangling strands of beads—it fit high on my waist and showed off my legs, which shimmered, thanks to sparkly nude hose.

Despite my buzzing nerves, I did a slow turn in the mirror, examining my craftsmanship. A prideful smile slipped from my lips.

The radio flicked on as I sat at the vanity and opened one of my father's art history books to Viktor Oliva's painting *Absinthe Drinker*. The DJ played "Iko Iko," and my feet tapped to the drumsticks, as, one by one, all the candles in the room lit up.

I swept a large makeup brush over my body, leaving a trail of sparkles down my chest, shoulders, and arms, until my skin reflected light like a disco ball. Black mascara. Shiny peach lip gloss. Finally, I twisted my waves on top of my head and inserted a large green plume into the crown of hair. I couldn't help but think of Isaac as I gave the silky feather a quick stroke.

Now, for the pièce de résistance.

The wings were simple cuts of iridescent chiffon that attached to a choker around my neck and hung down my back like a shimmering cape. The ends attached to my wrists, so they blew open when I raised my arms.

I stood in front of the mirror and blinked a few times, barely recognizing myself. I felt beautiful.

I hoped the lavish costume wasn't my death shroud.

My heart thumped, realizing I was about to play the most dangerous role of my life.

The clear, plastic, Barbie-esque shoes I'd bought in Paris certainly weren't going to work for tonight, so I wriggled on my worn hi-tops.

"Désirée is not going to approve," I said to my reflection, laughing. *"C'est la vie."*

I tucked the gris-gris and Adeline's necklace into my cleavage and blew out the candles, ready to leave.

"The stake!" I yelped, running to my nightstand. A surge of strength traveled through my arms to my shoulders as soon as I retrieved the metal object from the drawer.

Again, its weight felt powerful in my hand, but this time I recognized something else. A familiarity.

The enchantment.

Saint-Germain magic.

With nowhere else to put it, I tucked the magic seal through the laces of my corset, making sure I could easily grab it through my wings.

For what might be the last time, my keys flew into my hand. I paused and then set them back into the bowl. I didn't need them anymore.

Instead of going straight to the courtyard gate at Le Chat Noir, I walked through the old bar. So many of my childhood memories were set here: an eight-year-old me doing my French lessons, with my legs dangling from a bar stool; ole Madame Villere telling me about the birds and the bees when I was nine (and my father subsequently freaking out); listening to Ren's tales from Cajun plantations and occult shop owners telling me about the healing powers of quartz crystals; Caulfield Mooney sneaking me sips of Scotch to cure my junior-high coughs.

Could tonight really be my last night at Le Chat Noir? I suddenly felt all grown up.

In the third-floor ballroom, I found my father standing behind the makeshift bar, transferring clear liquid from plastic jugs into empty gin bottles.

"I'm not even going to ask," I said as I approached.

"It's really best you don't." He smiled and shook his head without looking up.

I supposed it was unfair to hold my father to telling me everything when I was keeping so much from him—but I was just trying to protect him.

I guessed he was just trying to protect me too.

He secured the large jug to a funnel and finally turned to me. His eyes bulged like a cartoon's. "What are you wearing?!"

"My costume! *La Fée Verte!*" I whirled around. "I'm the Green Faerie!"

"I know what you are; I'm a bar owner, for Christ's sake!" He held his head. "My sixteen-year-old daughter is dressed up as a hallucinogenic."

I took that as a compliment and twirled around a few more times with exaggerated glee. "Well, you did raise me in a bar and ship me off to Paris at fifteen."

"Why does it have to be so short? You look twenty-five!"

"Stop, Dad! You're going to make me self-conscious."

"Good, then maybe you'll put some pants on."

"Dad!"

Before he could protest further, the door opened, and Désirée walked in with an even-shorter plaid skirt, braided pigtails, and a white button-down shirt tied at her waist, cropping her stomach.

"Oh Lord," my father said with a slap to the head. "I know *your* father didn't let you leave the house in that."

Before she could answer, Isaac walked through the door, carrying a tangle of black curls. "Macalister!"

"I don't envy you tonight, son," my father said, shaking his head. "You're gonna have your hands full."

"You have no idea," I murmured.

Isaac didn't say anything.

"Pick your jaw up off the floor, Isaac," my father said sternly.

"Sorry, Mac." With rosy cheeks, he greeted me and Désirée.

"Is the bathroom locked?" she asked, patting a tiny backpack. "I need to do finishing touches."

"I'll show you the one downstairs," my father answered. "The one up here is officially hazardous, thanks to termites." They walked off, my father pleading with her to unroll her skirt, and I was left alone with Isaac.

Something deep within the pit of my stomach pricked.

Again, and again.

Not that I'd have admitted it to him, but he looked hot in his simple getup: black leather pants, with a matching vest over a fitted white V-neck. A few strands of hair fell to his chin from his usual nub of a ponytail. We looked at each other awkwardly, but neither of us said anything.

He pulled a long red silk scarf from his pocket and hung it around his neck. I opened my mouth to guess who he was, but he held up his hand. "Wait." He bent over, flipped the wig onto his head, then tied back the long, synthetic curls with the scarf.

"Oh my God, you're *REN*!"

"*Laissez les bons temps rouler!*" he attempted to say, but couldn't stop laughing.

"It's amazing!" I yelped, throwing my arms around his neck, catching us both off guard.

"No, you're amazing." He said the words with the utmost sincerity as he lifted me off the ground.

I loosened my grip around his shoulders, but he didn't let go, and I dangled against his chest for a moment. "You look beautiful," he whispered, slowly putting me down.

"Merci beaucoup." I felt every inch from my neck up blush. "I made it while I was in Paris."

"It's sick. You're insanely talented."

My father cleared his throat as he walked back into the room. "Too talented."

We jumped apart.

"Dad, Isaac is Ren!"

"I spent all morning trying to find the wig, so I didn't have time to hunt down a ruffly shirt."

"Where did you get leather pants?" I asked, casually trying to create a little more distance between us by leaning on the bar.

"They're mine!" my dad said, laughing as he walked behind the counter.

I groaned. "You have leather pants? That is something I could have lived without knowing."

"What do you think I wore to all of those Bowie concerts back in the day?"

"Who are you supposed to be?" Isaac asked, leaning on the bar next to me. "Tinker Bell?"

"Not exactly."

My father reluctantly grabbed a bottle of green liquid from his secret hiding place and slid it across the bar to Isaac.

"Whoa, absinthe." He shot a smile at me, now understanding last night's comment about my costume. "Is this the real stuff?"

My father leaned over and grabbed it back, giving us both a stern look. "Don't even think about it."

Little does he know . . .

"You do realize no one's going to get your costume?" Désirée said to me, walking back into the room with a compact mirror in front of her face.

"Oh, I think everyone in the Quarter is going to get it," my father said.

Besides, that's the least of my concerns at this point . . . My nerves started to fire up.

"Who are you supposed to be, Dee?" asked Isaac. "Catholic schoolgirl? Very original."

The look of death she shot him was way scarier than normal. Red contact lenses. "*Sexy* Catholic schoolgirl." She slowly opened her mouth into a sly smile, revealing two pointy canines.

"Isaac!" I screamed as she lunged at him, hissing.

They crashed to the floor, and Désirée buried her face in his neck. I grabbed her shoulders, pulling her back, and she burst out laughing. I fell to the floor as she spit the two fake teeth into her palm.

"Désirée Borges, cracking a joke," I said in between deep breaths. "Maybe today really is the day of reckoning."

"I am *so* gonna get you back for that, witch," Isaac warned as he took a deep breath of his own and gently pushed her off.

"I'd like to see you try." She smoothed out her costume and carefully reinserted her fangs. "I hope you're more ready than that tonight, feather boy."

My father just shook his head at us, trying not to laugh at Isaac, who was now adjusting his wig.

"Please be careful tonight, honey. All the loons will be out with a vengeance."

"Oui . . ." *We're counting on it.*

"Isaac, I'm holding you responsible. I'm tempted to give you my baseball bat so you can keep the boys away from these two."

"DAD!"

"I'm serious. Be safe." He kissed my temple, grabbed the empty jugs, and walked out of the room with a glittered mouth.

I led the way out through the corridor. "Y'all ready for this?" I asked over my shoulder as we descended the stairs.

"Can we get some food first?" Isaac answered.

I turned to him. "How could you possibly eat before—?"

"How could you *not*?"

"Actually, food is probably not a bad idea." Désirée patted her potion-clanking bag with a fangy grin as we stepped into the courtyard. "These are going to be pretty strong."

"Bonsoir, Adele."

The three of us whipped around to find Sébastien and Jeanne standing near the old dormant fountain. Our anxiety-ridden laughs quickly faded.

"Bonsoir!" I barely choked out. The twins were the last people I'd expected to see tonight. I ran over and kissed both of Sébastien's cheeks.

"You look *magnifique*." He turned to Désirée. "And so do you. Dead Britney Spears?"

"Undead," she said, flashing her fangs.

I was shocked Sébastien got the pop-culture reference.

When I moved toward Jeanne, she refused to even look me in the eyes, creating an incredibly awkward silence.

"Yeah, watch out," Isaac covered. "She's leaving a trail of glitter behind." He raised his sparkling arm.

"We're here to see your father," Jeanne said in a way that sliced right through me.

"Oh . . . *d'accord.*"

"He's helping us organize the funeral arrangements," Sébastien explained.

Jeanne looked at my two new friends and then back to me, as if confused by the kindred vibe. "Double, double toil and trouble." Only Jeanne Michel could insult someone by quoting Shakespeare.

"Fire burn, and caldron bubble," I finished with a meek smile, not knowing a better way to comfort her.

"Maybe the three of you can go as *Macbeth*'s witches next year?" she said sharply. I suddenly wished I had told her everything. "Where have you been, Adele? Too busy making Halloween costumes?"

"S'il te plaît sois gentille," Sébastien pleaded with her to be nice.

"It's okay, Bastien," I said. I deserved it. I hadn't been there for her *at all*. For either of them.

Even though Jeanne's expression remained cold, fast streams of tears came pouring down her cheeks, rolling off her chin.

"Désolée!" I whispered, my own eyes welling.

She pushed past me and ran up the stairs. Before I could go after her, Sébastien grabbed my arm and whispered in French, "Don't listen to her. She's still in shock—"

"Elle a raison," I said. "You have no idea how right she is."

"What do you mean?"

"Nothing. *Rien.*"

Sébastien looked to Isaac and Désirée and then back to me. He might not have been the beat-someone-up, big-brother type, but he was way too intelligent *not* to know something was up. Jeanne would have too if she'd been thinking clearly.

"Have fun at the parade," he said to the three of us.

"You should come out later tonight," I told him. "Maybe it will take your mind off things for a little while."

But what I meant was, "Can you please stay in a very public, very crowded place for the rest of the night?"

CHAPTER 39

Fight or Flight

We headed over to Bourbon Street and only had to wait in line for ten minutes before snagging the corner booth at the candlelit Clover Grill. I never thought I'd be happy to wait in line for a table, but it was a sign of life coming back to the city.

A waiter I hadn't seen since before the Storm greeted us loudly as Isaac and I slid into the booth across from Désirée. It was always a letdown to miss Blanche's shift, but this guy had that infectious, happy-to-no-longer-be-displaced glow. For tonight's festivities, he wore a teased beehive wig, with a fake, bloodied nutria rat nestled into it.

"Is Blanche off?" I asked.

"She's gettin' into character, baby. You'll find her on the royal float tonight. Queen of this Hallows' Eve."

"Rat's nest." Isaac laughed. "Nice one."

Our waiter posed for a second, with the je ne sais quoi that occurs in New Orleans when someone *gets* your costume. This moment could happen on Halloween, Mardi Gras, any of the two dozen other holidays that require masquerading, or really just any Saturday night in the French Quarter.

"And what can I get the Green Faerie?"

I didn't miss the opportunity to shoot Désirée a gloating smile.

"I'm not really hungry." Giant crawfish pinchers seemed to have taken hold of my stomach.

Désirée took a small vial from her bag and waved it around, reminding me that I'd shortly have to consume something nasty. Our waiter gave us a *those-crazy-kids-and-their-drugs* headshake.

"It's part of the costume," I explained, grabbing the vial. The last thing I needed was for gossip about me taking drugs to get back to my father—gossip that would falsely explain my erratic behavior as of late and get me grounded for life.

"Mmm hmm," he hummed. "Addie, you aren't gonna wanna take a pass today. We got two boxes of frozen patties this morning."

"What? Actual meat!"

"You can beat our prices, but you can't beat our meat!"

"I'll take the lot!" I yelled. Everyone laughed. "Okay. I'll take a patty melt."

"We don't got all that. How 'bout patty, wit' egg, on toast?"

"We'll take three," Désirée said, eager to get on with it.

"Four," corrected Isaac.

We all looked at him.

"What? I said I was hungry."

Once our waiter was back behind the counter, performing with the spatula (a common theme here), Dee started with the instructions: "Drink that now. I have no idea how long it'll take to kick in."

"So, this is the heightening elixir?" I asked, examining the small bottle of midnight blue liquid. Little flecks of silver dotted the viscous substance, creating the effect of a star-swept sky.

"Yep," she replied, as if no further explanation were necessary.

"So it's going to make her grow?" Isaac joked.

She rolled her eyes. "No. It's going to heighten all of her senses. And ours." She slid a duplicate bottle to Isaac and turned back to me. "Please be careful, Adele. I'm hesitant to dose you, because you're already *so* emotional."

I ignored the dig. "What do you mean, *heighten our senses?*"

"The spell is going to increase all of your natural abilities: your strength, your speed, and whatever else it is you . . . *do*. But it will also increase the strength of your emotions: happiness, hate, whatever—you'll be extra susceptible to it all." Her eyes bopped between me and Isaac.

"So, that's how you knocked me to the floor earlier!"

"Ha, you wish." She smirked at him and pulled a third serving out for herself. "Bottoms up!"

We said "Cheers" as our tiny bottles clinked together.

I tilted the little glass back and waited for the contents to slowly seep out and coat the back of my throat. My hand slapped my mouth as I forced myself to gulp the bitterness.

"Gross," Isaac said, shaking his head like he had just done a shot of tequila.

Other than the acidic taste lingering on my tongue, I didn't feel any different.

"So, that's it?" I asked. "We just hope the elixir heightens our senses right as the *special* moonshine disrupts theirs?"

"Pretty much. But a symmetric balance would be a dream scenario. Don't get overconfident because of the elixir. It's going to give you a boost, but you won't have anywhere near the strength or speed of a vampire—not even if they're completely out of it."

"So no arm-wrestling contests?" Isaac joked.

Désirée looked at him blankly.

My mind lingered on the vampires' strength as Désirée contin-ued. "Wormwood is totally unpredictable. Assuming they *all* drink the moonshine, the spell will affect each of them differently, depending on how much they drink and their natural tolerance for magic. At a minimum, they'll start hallucinating and find their strength and speed muted because the connection between their minds and bodies has been compromised. In the best-case scenario, the ones who drink a lot will experience a kind of berserk effect on their immune systems."

"I wonder how long it's been since any of those bloodsuckers have felt real pain," Isaac asked, with a little glee. "I don't mind taking a hit or two if it means I get to see the shock on their faces when I hit back."

I hesitated before asking the next question. "But . . . the potion's not going to *hurt* them, right?"

They both gave me a funny look.

"I'm . . . I'm just worried about my dad. Since he's inadvertently become the potion dealer."

"It won't hurt them," Désirée said. "It'll just give them the trip of a lifetime."

"Don't stress," said Isaac. "Mac's going to be fine. I'll have them in the attic long before they even make the connection between their hallucinations and the moonshine."

I didn't even like hearing the words "Mac's going to be fine," because it meant there was a possibility that he might *not be*.

"Clear the table," Désirée said, rummaging through her bag. She pulled out five candles. This might have seemed weird anywhere else, but carrying candles in your purse was a normal thing around these parts, post-Storm. "Don't light them," she instructed as I moved our coffee mugs to the side.

She strategically placed the candles around the table—forming a five-pointed star. Then she pushed a full glass of water to the center and continued to pull more things out of her bag: a black feather, a large piece of quartz, a vine of ivy.

"What else ya got in there, Mary Poppins?" I joked nervously.

Isaac tried not to snicker.

She ignored us. "We need something metal."

Isaac passed her a fork.

"Ugh, this is so dinky," she said, bending the cheap utensil without exerting much force. *Or maybe the elixir is kicking in?*

"How's this?" I asked, removing the stake from my corset. Despite my attempt to be gentle, the iron hit the table with a bang.

"That'll work," she said, examining it the same way I had the day I first obtained it—looking for some hidden detail.

"The final seal," Isaac said, taking a turn.

Désirée unscrewed the cap on the saltshaker and carefully circled it around her head, allowing the salt to pour out behind the booth, and then handed it to Isaac.

I shrugged when he looked to me.

He mimicked Désirée's motion, and then I emptied out the remaining grains, completing the circle.

Désirée opened both of her hands to us. My pulse picked up.

Is this really the most appropriate place to be doing this? I looked around: the old diner was dimly lit with candles, patrons were yelling over the blaring music, and everyone in the place looked like freaks in costume. There was less of a chance of being noticed here than in Vodou Pourvoyeur.

"What are we doing?" Isaac asked.

"Casting a circle for protection, to pool our magic, activate the elixir, and, more importantly, bind us. We'll be stronger together," Désirée said as I placed my right hand in hers. "Hang on to your broomsticks, kids; we're about to become a legit coven."

Isaac conceded and took my left hand.

"Close your eyes and concentrate, just like we practiced last night." She took a deep breath and began to murmur indecipherable words. Through one cracked eyelid, I watched the candles spark until all the wicks burned bright. "Repeat after me," she said and began to chant:

Papa Legba, ouvrez la porte.

Papa Legba, ouvrez la porte, open the door.

Papa Legba, open the door to the other side.

Warmth swelled from our hands. We repeated the verse with her again and again, until her words turned back into gibberish. Energy radiated through my veins, causing the beads on my costume to ripple as the warmth spread to my chest, all the way up to the top of my head.

Open the door and be our guide; we come to you in perfect love and perfect trust.

Together as one, with the Earth, Air, and Fire inside us, guide us.

From our ancestors we seek protection. Guide us.

Our decisions. Our actions. Our powers. Guide us.

We come to you in perfect love and perfect trust.

Bind us.

Static broke up the radio waves. Isaac squeezed my hand.

I felt all the flames in the room flicker as we repeated the last lines of the incantation faster and faster. The coffee mugs on top of the espresso machine rattled, and the booth trembled. I tried to contain myself, but a small gasp escaped my lips as I absorbed the supernatural essence. My eyes popped open.

"Wahoo! I love bein' home!" came a cry from the grill, which, in turn, got a receptive roar from the room of patrons.

Around us, everything looked as normal as normal got on Bourbon Street.

And so the Casquette Girls Coven was reawakened at the Clover Grill, on All Hallows' Eve, the year of the Storm. The three of us exchanged smiles, and my nerves slowly began to subside. *I can do this. We can do this together.*

Or maybe it's just the elixir talking?

"Don't remove your gris-gris," Désirée continued, as if we hadn't just caused something totally freaky to happen. "My gran might look old and quiet, but she's, like, as high up as high priestesses go, so those protective amulets are as good as they get in this town."

My hand rested on my chest, where the little satchel lay beneath the glitz of sequins.

"Four patties," said Rat's Nest, setting the plates onto the table.

The glorious smell of grill-marked beef encased us, and I was immediately grateful Désirée had changed my mind about ordering. The very first swallow of previously frozen protein felt like a sponge absorbing the tidal wave of anxiety crashing in my stomach. I eagerly took a second mouthful. Dee spit out her fangs and munched her sandwich with the small, controlled bites of a supermodel, and Isaac grabbed his second patty before he'd even finished his first, making us both laugh. Then, for a few minutes, the only sounds coming from our table were the rustles of napkins wiping grease-dripped lips.

But, as the last bits of crust disappeared, the vibe became heavier, and I knew the same question weighed on all of our minds: *Is this our Last Supper?*

"*Merci beaucoup*, Dee, for everything." The words rushed out of my mouth in a garble.

She pushed my coffee cup away. "I don't think you need any more stimulants."

I grabbed one more sip of my café au (powdered) lait before relinquishing my mug to her.

"You ready?" she asked me.

"Laissez les bons temps rouler."

The door dinged as we exited onto a sunset-pink-hued Bourbon Street.

Despite the confrontation to come, I couldn't help but feel happiness at the sight of people lollygagging. The post-Storm haze was enlivened by the brewing energy from folks in brightly colored costumes.

"I wonder if they're going to try to enforce the curfew tonight?" Isaac asked.

Désirée and I laughed in response. He raised one eyebrow.

"You've never been to a parade in New Orleans," I explained. "The cops are going to have many a thing to enforce tonight before they get around to the curfew."

Désirée smiled in agreement. "If everything goes according to plan, they can count on *extra* mayhem tonight."

"Magic and mayhem," Isaac said. "Let's give them a Halloween like none other."

"And send these vampires back to their graves," Désirée added, further riling him up. "All right, I'm heading back to the shop—my magic will be stronger there—but I'll hold off as long as possible activating the wormwood, so they don't suspect anything too soon."

My pulse began to race as Désirée continued, "Until then, I'll focus on casting protection spells. But keep in mind there is only one of me. The older coven's protection spells would have been much stronger because there were so many of them bound together."

"Focus your energy on Isaac," I said.

"Why?" he asked. "No, split it equally."

I turned to Isaac. "No, you're going to need it more." I was suddenly not okay with him having the most life-threatening part of this plan, considering Dee and I were the ones who broke the curse. "Are you sure you're okay with this? It's so dangerous."

"Maybe the leather pants were a bad idea?" he joked, pretending to stretch his leg.

An image of Gabriel ripping into Lisette's throat flashed through my mind.

"Hey," he said, looking at me. "Me pissing off the Medici clan so they chase me into the attic is the only part of this plan that's *guaranteed* to work."

Désirée scoffed, but then conceded, "True. You do have that effect on people."

"All right, I'll be waiting on the convent roof," I said. "You'd better fly out of that window fast."

I tried to give him a smile so he couldn't tell how nervous I was to have his life in my hands.

Breathe.

Désirée strapped on her miniature backpack of witchy goodies. "I'll see you at the rendezvous point when it's done," she said, just as sure about our victory as she was that the entire senior class wanted to take her to the homecoming dance. "And, Adele, if you see Gabriel tonight, kick him in the balls for me."

"Will do."

Isaac cringed. And with a cock of her hip, Désirée took off before we could have any kind of coven-bonding good-bye.

"She looks like such a badass," I said.

"She does look like she was born to slay vampires."

I tensed up. He noticed. Another awkward silence crept over us as we realized we'd been left alone. Possibly for the last time.

"Oh, I have something for you!" I pulled the chain from my bodice and started to unlatch the silver feather. "I think you dropped it on our steps that day we were figh—"

He wrapped his fingers around my hand. "No need."

"Why?"

"Because I made it for you."

"You did? Why?"

"Adele, are you kidding me? You're the girl of my dreams. *Literally.* I almost had a heart attack the first time I saw you through the window of Café Orléans. Then, watching you make coffee all those days . . . I thought I'd entered some kind of alternate universe in New Orleans."

My cheeks burned, but my eyes didn't move from his. "I think you kind of did."

"Plus, I like seeing you donned in feathers." He dragged his fingers across my ostrich skirt, sending shivers up my spine. "Even if it's just for tonight," he quickly added.

The plume atop my head swayed as I nodded, unable to get even a thank-you out.

He brushed the glitter on my cheek. "You ready?"

I nodded again.

"Make sure to stay out of sight on the roof."

"I will . . . Promise me you won't do anything too stupid?"

"That I can't promise." He smiled. "I'll see you when it's over." And with that, we both turned in opposite directions, slipping into the thin crowd.

I got four steps away before my arm was tugged back; Isaac pulled me into his chest, wrapping his arms around me. His forehead gently knocked into mine, and I committed his warmth to memory. My heart pounded wildly, reminding me that I was still alive.

"I really, really want to kiss you, Miss Adele Le Moyne. One of those epic, just-in-case-it's-our-last-chance kisses."

"I don't want this to be our last chance."

"Exactly."

"So, then let's get out of this alive, okay?"

"We will, I promise."

Isaac tilted my head and pressed his lips against my forehead. Sparks nearly flew from my fingers as the kiss lingered. *Is it the effect of the elixir?*

We parted a second time, both wearing my glitter.

A surge of confusion hit me as I feverishly walked toward my post. *Am I going to die tonight? As a sixteen-year-old virgin with only one passport stamp?* My breathing picked up, and I was shocked to find myself wishing I had kissed Isaac. *What if that really was our last chance?*

I spun around. There was still time. He couldn't have gotten that far. My neck craned as I rushed back through the thickening crowd to find him, but I abruptly halted when he came into my sight line. He was shaking hands with . . .

Niccolò.

"What the hell?"

Isaac didn't seem happy about their agreement, whatever it was.

I quickly walked away. All morning, I had wanted nothing more than to hunt down Nicco so we could watch his stupid art house film, limbs intertwined. *If I had to restrain myself from fraternizing with the enemy, then what was Isaac doing with him?*

My wings whipped behind me as I gained speed. *What could they possibly have been agreeing on? They hate each other! And tonight of all nights?*

When I got to my turn on Ursuline Street, I just kept walking straight, all the way down to Esplanade, and then continued straight out of the French Quarter.

I didn't stop until I got to NOSA. No progress had been made on the campus since the last time I'd been there, but the familiarity brought a slight sense of calm. It was too difficult to sit in my costume, so I lay on a patch of grass underneath the ballerina.

Deep breaths went through my nose and rushed out of my mouth. After a few more tries, I felt more in control.

I wondered what would happen if I just kept walking . . . out of the Marigny, through the Bywater, out of Orleans Parish. *Surely someone would pick up a sparkling hitchhiker?* I opened my eyes and stared up at the changing sky. The sun was almost completely gone, which meant the vampires would soon come out to play. One of them already had. Goose bumps invaded my flesh.

I stood, brushing grass from my skirt.

Who am I kidding? My heart and soul are in this place. They need to leave. The vampires.

The monsters.

A flame rose from my hand, so I could take one last look at the Mardi Gras–masked statue. I envied her anonymity.

I hovered the flame over the ends of her thin metal mask, heating it just enough to pop it off.

"I'll return it later, promise."

I pulled one of the extra laces from my corset's bow and used it to tie the disguise over my eyes.

When I looked up through the mask, I found my mother staring back at me, perfectly re-created in bronze.

What?

She had been hidden by the mask.

Frozen in time.

With me all of these years.

Could anyone ever love someone as much as my father loved my mother?

CHAPTER 40

Night of La Fée Verte

I ran back toward the Quarter. And when I say ran, I mean *ran*.

Like all magic, the elixir felt wholly natural and utterly unnatural at the same time. The effects were physically instinctual but shocking to my psyche: the amount of weight my muscles could handle, the speed at which my legs could carry me, the depth of my vision. Every sidewalk-splitting tree root became an obstacle as my mind struggled to keep up with the supercharge.

I paused from the sprint, bending over my knees to give my lungs a minute to catch up. The head rush was exhilarating. When I waved my hand in front of my face, my eyes had trouble following the blur of motion.

As I continued the trek back through the Marigny, that all changed too. My vision became sharper in the fresh dark of the night, and the pounding of the distant bass drums felt like it was deep in the pit of my stomach instead of half a mile away.

Is being a vampire like this? Times ten?

My internal systems began to sync: my coordination became more natural, and my confidence grew. The music pulsed louder, and the scenery whipped by as if someone had hit the fast-forward button. A soft, billowy material rustled my face, and I stopped midstride, nearly wiping out.

"What the . . . ?"

I was surrounded by hanging fabric.

I waved my hand, with the intention of bringing a small flicker of light from my finger, but a giant flame shot out instead, setting one of the flowing linens ablaze. A sea of ghosts were illuminated around me. *So, this is what everyone in Ren's hood was prepping their sheets for.* I strained my neck, looking up at the floating heads, which had been crudely made by stuffing tufts of newsprint in the center of the linens and tying them off with twine. They were strung across the useless power lines, creaking, dancing in the breeze.

The fire quickly flamed out, and the ashes of the singed ghost blew away into the damp night. I carried on my way.

The closer I got to the Quarter, the more of them there were: hundreds, thousands of ghosts, casting oblong shadows, backlit by tin-can fires in the street, tiki torches on lawns, and altars of candles on porches. Weaving in between them, faster and faster. As the shadows shifted, I became paranoid that someone was tailing me. I pushed one sheet away, only for another to fall in my face. Drowning in a river of ghosts, I broke into a sprint again.

At the end of the street, I halted under a large spray-painted banner made from a molding quilt.

Blessed are the unnamed souls lost in the Storm.
You will never be forgotten.
Rest in peace.

I choked back tears, turning to the army of ghouls floating under the moon. There were so many of them.

Death.

The dead were everywhere.

My own mortality was suddenly very comprehensible. *Am I really prepared to die tonight?* My chest tightened, and I started to wheeze. I remembered Désirée's warning and threw my arms over my head, telling myself that the anxiety attack was just an effect of the elixir.

Breathe.

My chest loosened.

I began to move again, through more ghosts, but this new batch was painted bright colors and adorned with scarves, Spanish moss, and photos, like life-size Voodoo dolls. They had descriptions and birth dates and death dates.

They were no longer unnamed.

I could feel a crying fit coming on, so I sped through the open-air homage, promising to come back later to pay my respects.

When I crossed Elysian Fields, I stumbled upon the parade lining up—the Krewe de Boo—dressed in what might have been the most shocking costumes I'd ever seen in my years of parading: every single man, woman, and child was sporting his or her Sunday best. I'd gone from a river of ghosts to a sea of suits.

What planet am I on?

I tapped the back of a man in a tawny tweed. "Sir, what exactly is this year's theme?"

When he turned around, a short scream escaped my lips at the sight of his milky white eyeballs and rotting flesh. He buckled over with laughter, and I was back to breathing exercises.

"We're marching on Washington tonight," he said, holding out his zombie arms and pointing to his float: a giant papier-mâché Capitol Hill, which peaked in a very, er, mocking manner. I gave him two thumbs-up for their satirical response to the government's recovery efforts and moved on.

The marching crowd might have looked unusually corporate, but the noises of revelry reeled with familiarity. My soul soaked in the trumpets, trombones, and resonant tones of the tuba as if this were the last time I would hear them. Instead of mule-hitched wagons, each float had been constructed from a Storm-destroyed car, truck, or boat whose top had been chopped off. Two long poles protruded from the sides of every vehicle, with drones of stiff-limbed zombies standing by to push them manually down the parade route. A short line of horse 'n' buggies waited to carry the local celebrities who had made it back. Partially returned dance troupes clicked their fringed tap boots and flipped batons to entertain the crowds. There was a tinge of lighter fluid in the air. I'd never seen the Flambeaux out for any occasion other than Mardi Gras, but tonight the torchbearers were dancing wildly in the streets with their heavy, flaming poles and not accepting so much as a penny from the crowd for lighting the way.

The only thing missing was the tourists, of which there were none. This was truly a night of celebration for locals, who were starting to pack the street, singing, dancing, and shouting for the parade to start.

Through the mask, I watched the costumes become more crass and less existent, until they were not much more than fishnets, pasties, neckties, and gobs of ghoulish makeup. I paused, seeing a kissing couple dressed as a witch and a vampire. *Ugh—*

A hand grabbed my shoulder. I tried to jerk away, but a second hand grabbed my arm, and they hoisted me into the air. I was back on my feet, on top of the royal float before I could protest.

"Your chariot, mademoiselle," yelled Blanche, holding her hand out to the converted swamp boat.

"At your service, *ma chérie.*" The king took a deep bow.

"Ren! Is that you?" His hair was slicked back. And with fake glasses, loafers, and a pocket square, he looked weirdly normal. I smiled, hoping he'd get a chance to see Isaac later. *If there is a later.*

"Watch this!" he said and pointed a large gold scepter toward the sky. A blast of funny money and doubloons whooshed out over the crowd, who instantly roared, scavenging the treasure in melodramatic style.

"My king," said Blanche, duGovernor, Queen of the Dead, as she placed a gold-sprayed crown made out of banged-up soup cans and chicken wire on top of Ren's head. Her own tiara of spoons was nestled in a tall bouffant wig that mocked the governor's outdated hairdo. Blanche was also nearly unrecognizable in pumps and a bulging fake ass underneath a red skirt suit. Only her signature glitter-swept eyelids remained in her usual style. "My little Addie," she shrieked, "I could just eat you up!"

"Or drink 'er up!" chimed Ren, laughing at his own joke.

"Hold this, baby," Blanche yelled, handing me a roll of wide red ribbon. She held the other end and twirled around. The crowd began to cheer as she became mummified.

"Ha!" I yelled. "Amazing!"

"I'm gonna die caught up in this red tape, baby!"

Behind the royal couple was a giant papier-mâché bobblehead of the president, whose approval rating was nonresuscitable after the way he'd handled the national emergency.

"How do you like our krewe of stiffs?" asked Ren.

"Pun intended?" I asked.

"Triple pun!" he yelled, looking at the giant phallic symbols capping the pushing poles.

"Everything is awesome!" I yelled, trying not to blush. "How did you know it was me?" I gave my mask a quick flip.

"Honey, I've known you since you were born."

"Besides, who else would be running around the Marigny in couture and those nasty sneakers?" replied Blanche.

"Ha!"

"*Bébé*, you're all grown up! I'm getting a little teary." Ren gave me another twirl. A breeze kicked up my wispy wings.

The float jerked forward.

"Ren, I need to get down! The parade is starting!" The words stunned me, knowing this might be the last time I ever saw him.

"You aren't going anywhere," Blanche yelled, pulling me back. "You're our little princess! Princess of the French Quarter Rats!"

Police sirens blared, and the drum major's whistle shrilled out the tempo for the marching band.

The crowd roared, and the wheels jolted forward as the zombie krewe pushed the old swamp boat onward.

"Wave to your constituents," Blanche instructed, maneuvering one of her forearms from the tape to do her best impression of the Queen of England.

The mask gave me enough anonymity to stand tall before the debaucherous throng. High on the madness, I felt strangely like a princess.

The bleak populace of New Orleans squealed with childish delight as the crowd of corporate zombie drones pushed through them. I'd never stood in a parade before, nor had I imagined how fun throwing Tootsie Rolls at familiar faces would be. Annabelle. Tyrelle. Everyone was out. Maybe it was the times, or maybe Désirée had activated the wormwood, but everyone seemed extracrazy, or extraloaded, as they staggered about, pointing at things in the air.

Pointing at me.

Something knocked me off balance, and I nearly fell backward. Without the boost of the elixir, I would have. We were at Esplanade Avenue, but this time it wasn't just a warble as we crossed the neutral ground to those old streets of the Vieux Carré; the trapping ward was significantly stronger than before. *Way to go, Dee.*

Ren wavered in place, mumbling, "I knew I shouldn't have sampled any of that moonshine."

"It's going to be a wild night," I said.

"Laissez les bons temps rouler!" he cried, as if we were riding into battle.

And we kind of were. At least, I was.

As he continued to hoot and holler, I caught sight of a lonely figure on the street corner. Sébastien.

When the float passed, I reached down, clasped his hand, and yanked him on board. The momentum nearly knocked us to the bottom of the boat, but I managed to hold us both steady as the crowd cheered.

"Adele, how did you do that?" he asked, pushing his black glasses up the bridge of his nose.

"Do what?" I yelled, overjoyed to see him.

"You just lifted me into the air!"

"Adrenaline!" I scrambled to explain, but I could tell he was already mentally calculating weight, leverage, and torque.

One look into his baby-blues and a swell of happiness filled my chest. Before I knew it, my arms were wrapped around him, awkwardly smashing his elbows against his sides. *"Je t'aime!"* I yelled. I couldn't help it—it was as if love were actually radiating from my arms.

"Moi aussi," he said, turning pink and forgetting about the illogical occurrence. *"Je t'aime, mon chou."* He squeezed his left arm out from underneath mine and rubbed my shoulder.

Then my emotions swung, and I felt overwhelmingly sad. *I killed his grandparents. Jeanne is going to hate me forever. And forever might only be the next few hours . . .*

"Adele, are you okay? Are you high?"

Adele, get a grip! It's just the elixir.

When I didn't respond right away, he shook my shoulders and yelled, "Did someone give you something? I think you've been drugged."

My heart pounded at the thought of getting caught. We'd come so far. "I'm not high, silly!" I slipped my hand into his and turned him outward. "Wave to the crowd!"

His shy smile crept back with the warm reception, and soon he was lost, observing the chaos of the streets. That was when I saw Gabriel walking through the crowd, keeping up with the float. Our gazes locked, and he eyed me like a predator who enjoyed the hunt more than the prize. My head swung to the other side of the street: Lisette was pushing through the crowd with annoyance.

I twisted around.

About fifty feet behind Gabe, Martine Dufrense was somehow making a skip look deadly. I assumed the others weren't far away.

So much for giving me until midnight.

My pulse thumped.

Not only was I surrounded, but I'd pulled Sébastien into the bull's-eye.

Jackson Square was in sight. The high school band that filled the amphitheater went into an encore. The crowd chanted out the next ominous verse as the royal court came into the final stretch:

And when the moon turns red with blood,

Lord, how I want to be in that number . . .

I leaped off the float and made a run for it.

When the saints go marching in!

Less than twenty-four hours ago, the square had belonged to Isaac and me: a private stage to juggle fireballs. Now, pushing my way through groups of drag queens, gutter punks, and suburban invaders, it seemed like a distant memory. I was suddenly desperate to get to my post— I couldn't screw everything up for the coven—but every person who stopped to pet my costume or yell, "It's the Green Faerie!" slowed me down.

Then one caused me to come to a complete halt: Annabelle Lee Drake in the guise of Jessica Rabbit—a knockout in the sparkly, formfitting red gown, with her deep auburn locks swept across her right eye.

"Well, aren't you just the belle of the ball?" she said sweetly.

The compliment, combined with her ear-to-ear grin, set my nerves on edge.

She must want something.

Thurston looked less than pleased to be dressed as Roger Rabbit. It still blew my mind how Annabelle so easily controlled everyone and every situation she came into contact with. The world just bowed down to her.

A sexy cop stood on her right and a sexy robber on her left. Most of the lacrosse team was sneaking beers behind them, and the freshmen Little Sisters (a gamut of sexy costumes) completed the group.

Everyone was looking at me, waiting for a response.

"Don't you think Tinker Bell is a little childish?" Dixie asked, her blond ringlets bouncing out of her cowgirl hat. The urge to claw her eyes out overwhelmed me.

Breathe.

"Have you seen Désirée?" I asked Anabelle. "I'm going to look for her."

"No way. We're going to Le Chat Noir."

Voilà. Troy must have cracked down on fake IDs, and now she needed me to get them in. And she was not happy about needing me.

"And *you're* coming with us." She forced a smile, which made me want to vomit on her Louboutins.

"Umm . . . I kind of have plans with—"

"Bring your friends!" Bri yelped, sending all the minions into fits of giggles.

Annabelle's jaw clenched. She floundered for only a second, confused, and then looked straight into my eyes and repeated her proposition. "We're *going* to Le Chat Noir, you're *going* to bring your friends, and we're all *going* to have a good time."

For a split second I almost found myself agreeing.

"Sorry, Annabelle, next time."

She looked baffled, but more by her own faulty power of persuasion than by my defiance. "I guess you really are the Queen of Downtown."

"It's not about controlling their minds, *ma fifille*," a familiar French voice interrupted, speaking directly to Anabelle. "It's about controlling their hearts."

I nearly jumped out of my skin when I saw Lisette's face only inches from mine.

"Freak," Annabelle whispered.

"Voilà, Lise! I've been looking all over for you," I said, my jaw clenched.

Her usual hostile expression had dissipated, and she was staring intently at Annabelle Lee. I feared it meant she was hungry. Not that I would have minded Annabelle getting taken down a notch. Or ten.

"We're totally going to be late for *that thing* everyone has been waiting *so* patiently for." I put my arm on her chilly shoulder. "Let's go," I said, turning her away from my classmates. *"Toute de suite."*

"Bye, Adele! I hope we see you later!" yelled a freshman dressed as a cat (just the regular calico kind). My Little Sis—she no longer had the scarf around her neck. *Thank God.* I attempted to throw her a smile over my shoulder as I pushed Lisette away from the beehive. *Tonight, I have to do a better job of protecting people.*

———

"What are you doing?" I yelled, dragging Lise alongside the cathedral, into Pirate's Alley.

"*Moi!* What are *you* doing? I thought you would be a little more concerned with breaking the curse and saving the lives of those you love, rather than hanging out with your schoolmates? Maybe you really are a Saint-Germain after all?"

"What is that supposed to mean?"

"Adeline put all of our lives at risk!"

"*Je ne comprends pas!* What have they told you, Lise? You're supposed to be on our side . . . the coven's side!"

She opened her mouth to reply and then quickly shut it.

"I know this isn't just about a curse, Lisette. Tell me what the Medici are really after!"

She looked past me. "*Je ne sais pas.* Gabriel won't tell me."

I squinted in suspicion.

"*Adeline* never told us either. We never knew the vampires were after anything other than blood."

"Adeline wanted to protect the casquette girls . . . and the people of *La Nouvelle-Orléans!*"

"Adeline Saint-Germain wanted to protect herself! And the Count. Her *family.*"

"Her coven was her family!" My instinct was to rush to Adeline's defense, but I didn't want to lose Lise—not that we really had her on our side. "Would it have changed anything? Would you have refused to join the coven, even after the vampires tossed your dowry, smuggled on board the ship, and fed upon the other filles aux cassettes? Even after they killed Martine?"

She looked at me with surprise, and her eyes glistened with tears.

"*Non.*"

"Adeline would never have betrayed the trust of her sisters by using the coven's powers for personal gains. She loved the coven more than anything other than her father." But inside I wondered. *Had Adeline really used the coven to do her own bidding?*

"Adeline was never able to give up *le Comte*," Lise said.

"Of course she wasn't! He's her father!

Her slow-spreading smile felt like a noose tightening around my neck. "That's what I thought you would say, *ma fifille*. Just like her."

Then she was gone.

What does that even mean?

I tried to forget her words, but I couldn't. The deeper I got into this sadistic soap opera, the more I felt like it was *my* family's problem, and that I was putting Désirée and Isaac in unwarranted danger. And then, as if my feet had minds of their own, they rerouted themselves once again. My rational side instructed them to go to my post on the roof, but it was like the connection between my brain and feet had gone awry. Deep inside, I knew there was only one way to ensure we got *all* of the vampires into the attic, and it didn't involve me sitting in a cozy post or using passive magic.

There was only *one* reason Nicco would ever enter that attic.

I turned onto Royal Street, into a web of yellow police tape. The two crime scenes were only fifty feet apart. I sped up, imagining Emilio sucking the life out of Mémé and Pépé and then defiantly hanging the Wolfman over the statue in the garden after gouging his eyes out. As I passed St. Ann Street, my fingers began to tingle—someone or some*thing* was near. I moved into a defensive position just as Nicco sped out of the alley behind the Carter brothers' house. He grabbed my hand, while still in motion, with the intent of pulling me along, but my feet didn't move as easily as usual, and he ended up aggressively jerking my arm.

He stopped and let my hand drop. "I'm sorry, I didn't mean to . . ."

"I know."

He looked at my legs and then back to my face.

"I know, they're shimmery," I said, trying not to smile. His surprised expression made me want to do something else to show off my newfound strength, but I refrained. I needed to keep *some* element of surprise.

He didn't laugh. Instead, he circled me slowly.

My back stiffened. *Note to self—enemy.*

Suddenly, I felt very exposed in my scanty costume. I tried to appear confident, although I didn't know why I bothered. Never in my wildest dreams had I thought I'd meet someone who'd be harder to lie to than my father, but Niccolò Medici managed to be that person. His constant, not-so-innocent smile made me want to melt into the floor.

And it scared the hell out of me.

I closed my eyes and tried to visualize the two innocent students he'd killed and *not* to think about the note in the DVD. *Enemy. Enemy. Enemy.*

When I opened my eyes, he was looking at me with pleading concern, and I knew my feet had made the right decision for me. *There's no way Nicco's going to set foot in that attic unless I'm there too.*

"What are you doing, *bella*?"

"What do you mean?"

"You are changing your plans."

"What?" I stammered. "I haven't changed any plans."

"You're lying." He took a step closer.

"How could you possibly know my plans—old or new?"

"I don't know your plans. All I know is that you are lying, and you are choosing a new course."

"I thought you said vampires couldn't read minds, only bend them?" I yelled, suddenly nervous about some, er, inappropriate thoughts I may have previously had about him. About us.

"Calm down, *bella*. I can't read your mind." He moved a rock with his boot, trying not to smile at the ground. "Just the arrhythmia of your heart."

I aggressively twirled a lock of hair that had escaped my updo.

"You see, heartbeats are like fingerprints. No two are alike, but the differences are so delicate no human ear can hear them, no matter how powerful an instrument one uses. And you . . . just made a decision that is making your heart shudder. And I don't like it."

"Great, so my own heart is giving me away to all of you?"

"Not to all of us." He took another step closer and moved the mask from my face, letting it slip down around my shoulders. "Just to me."

I took a loud, calming breath and reminded myself to bottle my emotions, since they were not fully under my control. "And why is that?"

"Do you really not know why I can hear the cadence of your heart, *bella*?" He touched my fingers. His not-so-innocent smile escalated to most definitely *not* innocent. "Can you really not *feel* our connection?"

"We have a connection?" *At least there's one thing I'm not delusional about.*

"What does your intuition tell you?" He moved my hand to his chest. I thought my pulse might burst out of my wrist as he pressed tighter.

I could feel his heartbeat pounding against my hand. And then, I could hear it.

"Why don't you know that we're . . . magical together?"

Again, my eyes slipped shut. I could *hear* his heartbeat—for a split second it was all I could hear.

Thump. Thump.

My fingers drew his shirt into a fist, clutching it tightly as I listened.

Thump. Thump.

How can I hear his heartbeat?

I jumped backward, out of fear I might start ripping his clothes off. "You were right: my intuition is going to get me killed." Mentally cursing the elixir, I rubbed away a fresh glaze of sweat from my hairline, and my mood quickly swung. "Besides," I spat, "none of that really matters now, seeing how I'll likely be *dead* in a couple of hours."

"Adele, just break the curse. I know you can figure it out!"

"It's not that easy, Nicco! Especially when there are giant holes in the story. Which, by the way, you could readily fill—"

"I'm *trying* to protect you." He grabbed my hands. When I pulled them back, his grip tightened. "I am sorry if it hurts," he said, pulling me closer to him. "I really am, but I would rather you be mad at me than dead. And . . ."

"And what?"

"And, it's complicated. I cannot betray my family—"

"Bertrand and Sabine Michel were *my* family!"

"I know."

Each of us refused to look away from the other during the silence that followed.

"Well, isn't this just a fairy tale," I whispered.

"And I am sorry this has become your battle." His fingers twisted into mine. "I tried to stop them—I *am* going to figure everything out. You just have to give me time."

"Ha! Time? The other thing your family stole from me." I ripped my hands away. "Tell me what you were looking for in my house the night Isaac caught you breaking and entering."

He scowled at the mention of Isaac's name.

"What did you want from Adeline? Why were you after *le Comte Saint-Germain*?"

"You should really concentrate on breaking the curse instead of digging up skeletons from days gone by. Your ignorance of the past is the only thing you have going for you."

"Oh really?" A tall flame rose from my hand, lighting up his pale face like a ghost.

He curled my fingers closed, trying not to wince as the fire touched his hand.

"That's not what I meant. They are going to kill you if you don't break the curse, Adele. We can figure out the rest later. Just let the skeletons lie—"

"If the skeletons weren't sticking out of the ground, trying to attack me, I wouldn't be trying to pull them out!" I shoved angrily at his chest, and he staggered one step back.

We looked at each other, both stunned.

His baffled gaze shifted from his chest to my hands. "How did you . . . ?" he whispered. "Magic."

I oscillated between a total meltdown and wanting to jump him. I bolted before I could crack.

"Whatever you're planning," he yelled, "I'm not going to let you martyr yourself, Adele!"

I didn't look back.

This time he caught up with me. I buried my smile when I heard his footsteps behind me and swatted away his hand as it brushed my fingers. He linked his arm through mine.

"What are you going to do?" I said. "Lock me up in chains?"

"Don't tempt me."

"You're worse than my dad," I yelled, making us both come to a halt.

"No. Just from a different time." His eyes dropped to my lips. "When things were far more simple."

My heart leaped into my throat . . . but then his gaze moved up and around my head, as if monitoring a circling fly. He blinked twice and shook his head before looking at me with momentary skepticism.

"What the . . . ?"

The moonshine. Just as I wondered how much he had drank, Gabe came crashing into us from behind, breaking us apart.

"What are you crazy kids up to tonight?" He boxed his arms around our necks. I immediately scooted away. His freed arm resulted in a head tousle for his brother. They wrestled for a minute, and then Nicco wriggled away, annoyed. He ran his hands through his hair a few times, and it fell perfectly back into place.

"Damn, I love this city!" Gabe yelled into the night. "It really hasn't changed all that much in three hundred years."

"Yet you're so eager to leave." My words dripped with disdain.

His head rolled to me. "I'll admit, if there was ever a city to get trapped in, this is definitely the one. There's just one little problem." Suddenly, he was smack in my face, fangs out. "I take issue with the whole being *trapped* part—"

Nicco knocked him to the ground, and they rolled around, just like idiotic human brothers.

"How long are you going to keep up this heroic act, *fratello*?" Gabriel asked, landing on top.

Nicco flipped him over. "As long as it takes."

"Ha!" Gabe yelled, throwing his younger sibling to his feet. "You'll cave in the end. You always were Father's little pet." He sprang up next to Nicco with the grace of a gazelle.

I turned and walked away, fuming. I couldn't listen to them argue any longer as if they weren't referring to my *life*.

They quickly caught up, brushing themselves off.

"I wouldn't have thought you'd be so drunk already on a night so important to you, Brother," Nicco accused.

"Drunk? Who's drunk? Just a few more rounds after you left."

My pace quickened. Knowing they'd all drunk the moonshine, even his threat couldn't quell my smile, which I could tell made Nicco nervous.

"Where are we going, *bella*?"

"You want the curse broken?" I teased. "Then to the attic, of course."

Nicco's catlike eyes surveyed my face for the truth. When I gave him nothing, he sighed and extended his arm in the direction of the convent, letting me play it out.

"Back to where it all began. How poetic!" Gabriel shouted and danced and pulled us along with the exuberance of a recently flowered Titania.

CHAPTER 41

Plight of La Fée Verte

"The Three Musketeers!" Gabe yelled, dancing down the street.

Nicco looked at me, and I did my best to shrug in innocent confusion before we went after him. Gabe's erratic behavior escalated the tone from crazy to dangerous; suddenly, the thought of vengeful vampires not being in control of their minds seemed like a *very* bad idea.

"Isn't it amazing?" Gabe asked, with his neck craned toward the sky.

"Isn't what amazing?" I replied.

"The stars. The universe!"

Nicco smacked his brother's arm and yelled something in Italian. Gabe ignored him, took my hand, and spun me around. My wings flitted up. I finished the twirl, but he didn't let go. His eyes continued to circle around my head. I wondered what kind of tracer he was seeing.

"I think you really are *La Fée Verte*!" he said with a goofy expression. Then he yanked me close to his chest, exposed fangs inches from my face. His grip became painful as he whispered, "What did you do to me, Faerie?"

"Stop being such a freak, Gabe," I muttered, trying to hide my fear as I pushed him aside. He was too loaded to think it strange that I was able to send him staggering, but his flash of fangs had focused my mind on our mission. I continued on to the convent.

Gabriel flanked my left side and Niccolò my right, playing their respective roles of the Fool and the Knight, but whether they were blinded by arrogance or worry, neither saw me as anything more than the doe-eyed Ingénue.

That was my first card to play.

Adeline or Cosette, with their feminine charms, could have more easily slid into the role, but even without their talents, it wasn't too difficult for me—my doe eyes were partially real. Even now, my fingers twitched because I wished Nicco would hold my hand, and I loathed myself for it. I might not know his moves based on the cadence of his heart, but I knew deep within my soul that he was on my side. I didn't know if it was instinct or intuition, but the thought made me blush at the slate-stoned sidewalk. Then I lifted my head, put on an expression as stoic as his, and quietly played my real role: the Pied Piper.

The sounds of revelry faded as we marched farther away from Jackson Square and Bourbon Street, until it was just ambient noise. A mild undercurrent of energy flowed through my body: a subdued state of electricity, as if I'd been continually licking a battery. Between the elixir, the magical wards, the close proximity of vamps, and the constant reality of impending death, I knew the feeling was not going away anytime soon.

You still have two witches on your side.

Witches.

Even though I couldn't see them, I could feel their presence. The closer we got to the attic, the more overwhelming the sense of togetherness, strength, and power became. Even the medallion radiated warmth beneath my costume, making me believe that Adeline and the original casquette girls were with me in spirit too.

When we arrived at the Ursuline property, the wrought iron gate swung open before I had the chance to hide the magical action. Gabe moved ahead, unable to contain his excitement.

I hesitated, staring at the attic window that had started it all. The mended shutter hung loose, and the stake burned through the fabric of my bodice—the enchanted metal longing to be back where it belonged.

Nicco's gaze followed mine to the roof. I knew he was trying to figure out my plan, but he didn't ask any more questions.

His hand went to the small of my back. "You can do this, *bella*," he whispered, lips brushing my ear.

I was too worried about whether he had felt the hidden stake to be encouraged by his unbridled optimism. I stepped away and weaved through the labyrinth of overgrown hedges. He silently followed.

The convent door creaked open. No more time to think. No turning back.

"After you, *signorina*," Gabriel said, waving his arm toward a wide, wrapping staircase.

Breathe, I told myself and stepped ahead of them, once again trying to suppress that girl-runs-to-the-attic horror-movie image.

You are the predator, not the prey.

The mantra turned over and over in my mind, forcing out any lame scenarios I'd gained from years of reading tales of unrequited love.

I passed the second floor and hurried up to the third, afraid I might turn back. Not that turning back would have been easy with two vampires at my heels. The staircase became less grand and eventually dead-ended at a simple wooden door with a rusty, old padlock.

"Step aside," said Gabe. "Let's get this party started." He gave the wood a shove, but the door didn't budge—Gabe did. His misjudgment sent him teetering on the top stair.

Nicco caught him before he could take a tumble. "What the hell, Gabriel?"

As they exchanged foreign words, presumably about Gabe's failed strength, I mentally opened the padlock and attempted to move the door, but there was little metal in the old wooden joinery, and that wood was severely swollen in the post-Storm door frame.

Nicco moved past me and pressed his hand against the door. It slammed open.

Gabe looked at his own hands with curiosity and then at Nicco, who was rubbing his wrist and looking at me as if for answers. The ripple of suspicion was soon lost when Gabe took off down the hallway, singing what sounded like an Italian folk song.

The floorboards howled as I made my way down the stretch of doors. The thin slats of wood that formed the old walls barely hung on, the cracks between them revealing small rooms that must have served as simple living quarters at one point in time. I wondered who'd rested so close to the sleeping vampires. *Orphans? Slaves? Ursuline postulates?*

The hallway led us to a room, where I bumped into the keys of a pipe organ. I was tempted to raise a flame to keep from further injuring myself before we even got going, but instead I visualized being able to see everything in the room. I felt the heightening elixir pulse, and my eyesight became stronger.

The floor planks wobbled as I meandered through the sea of dusty objects stacked high upon Victorian furniture and salvaged church pews: ornately framed oil paintings of generations of priests, boxes of Bibles and rosary beads, racks of holy vestments in clear protective bags that had long since yellowed. French maps. Modern Christmas decorations. Statues of the Virgin Mary in different styles from different centuries.

The deeper we walked into the cave of holy artifacts, the thinner the air became, until the smells of dust and mothballs poked at my brain. Nicco and Gabe were both waiting for me at the far end of the room. Generally their dispositions couldn't be any more opposite, but now they both seemed equally anxious—for different reasons, I hoped. As I approached, they parted, making room for me in front of a short door with a mélange of locks from a different era. The attic door. Adeline's seal.

I exhaled loudly. *This is it.*

I didn't know how I'd opened the seal on the window, and I didn't know what to do now, but my intuition guided my hand to what looked like a normal, albeit antique, door chain.

The lock pulled me, just like the stake had. No incantations, no spells or charms. I slid my finger over the first rusty chain. Gabriel practically vibrated with excitement. The lock released with a pop, and I almost fell against the door—taking an invisible punch to the gut.

Nicco pulled me closer to him. I shook him away and moved on to the next lock. And then the next, and the next, opening the intricate metal mechanisms, and each time, I felt an energy suck as I loosened Adeline Saint-Germain's three-century-old spells. It was as if the enchantment had a built-in self-defense mechanism, asking me each time if I was sure about unlocking it. I focused on the medallion beneath my dress. *You have to trust me, Adeline.*

I wanted her enchantments to linger in the metal, weakened just enough to allow us passage but not to disappear entirely. In my peripheral vision, Nicco's fists balled with anticipation. Then the sound of the final lock dropping sent a ripple of fear through my body.

With a lift of my hand, I tried to open the door, but the hinges, rusty from centuries of humidity, fought back, or maybe it was Adeline?

Nicco slowly pushed the door open. An unpleasant creak warned, *This door has been kept shut for a reason. Enter at your own risk, fool.*

Once again, Gabe went ahead while Nicco and I took a beat, knowing that whatever was going to happen on the other side wasn't going to be good.

I stepped into the dark room, and flames burst around the walls in one quick whip, until all of the sconces were ablaze.

So much for the element of surprise.

Suddenly, everything felt right. I knew I'd made the right decision. I couldn't let any more lives be put at risk. Now I just needed to stay alive until all the vampires were contained.

No problem, Adele. Just stay alive.

"I can almost smell the freedom!" Gabe boasted, which I found ironic, given we were now in the room where he'd been imprisoned for so long.

I scanned the battleground-to-be. The room was gigantic, with an angular ceiling that peaked in the center. There were six dormer windows on one side and the asymmetric five on the other. The fifth window was bricked up. That was my target: the lid to Pandora's box.

Thick floor-to-ceiling beams rendered the large room useless for anything but storage space. Across the room, there was an antique oak writing desk. A few more statues of saints and a pile of crude, eighteenth-century gardening tools. And . . . there they were.

"The infamous cassettes," I whispered, approaching the first of a couple dozen long wooden boxes that resembled caskets.

Some were stacked high on top of each other, and others were alone on the floor. My foot nudged a heavy chain from the lid of the nearest one, sending squeaking mice scattering across the room and a rush of supernatural energy through me. A vision flashed through my mind: *The open sea. A cassette about to go overboard. The sound of a scream.*

Mine?

No. Adeline's.

I was seeing the scene through her eyes. I felt the rush of her heart-beat and her fear that it might be Gabriel in the box. She'd been scared *for* Gabe just as much as she'd been scared *of* him. But I could sense she hadn't entirely trusted him—the slave driver in the sugarcane field, the pirate massacre, saving her life after the lethal vampire bite: it was impossible to know whether his actions were selfless or entirely self-serving. *Was he just protecting his food supply? Using her to get to her father?*

The image vanished, and I realized Gabe was waiting on me. He'd asked me a question, and my blank expression seemed to be frightening Nicco.

"Come on, Adele. Do it," Gabe said, his tone now serious. It made me wonder if he had somehow felt the memory too. *How close had the two of them been exactly?*

"Do what?" I asked coyly, trying my best to invoke some of Adeline's allure. "Tell me something, Gabriel . . . something I've been wondering all this time. What did you do to Adeline for her to ban you to this attic for eternity? It must have been pretty awful."

He answered with a heavy backhand that sent me sailing across the room. I hit the northern wall with a thud, landing hard on the metal stake hidden in my corset.

Inhaling sharply, I rolled to the side in pain, but when I saw Nicco's fangs come out, I forced myself to jump up.

"I'm fine, Nicco!"

Walk it off, I told myself.

"Don't bother trying to help your little girlfriend, Niccolò," Gabe yelled. "It will only make things more painful for her in the end."

He launched at me again, but I quickly sidestepped, and he crashed into the wall. He fell back in a drunken stupor.

"Looks like she doesn't need my help." A little laugh slipped from Nicco's lips as he jumped on top of the large, shaky desk and crouched in a pseudo-referee stance.

I'm glad this is humorous to him.

Unfazed, Gabe picked himself up and began to circle me. "There is something about you that looks a little like Adeline, I'll admit."

His eyes seemed to have trouble focusing on me, so I bounced away like a boxer.

He blinked and shook his head. "But you're nothing alike," he spat and took a swat, missing me completely. Baffled, he forced himself to refocus. "You're so innocent, so sweet . . ."

It was just the provocation I needed to plant my feet. With a flick of my wrists, I pulled one of the chains from a cassette and sent it whacking across his chest, throwing him against the wall. The sound of his cracking bones made me want to rush to help him, but I forced myself still.

He slumped down to the floor.

Nicco stood on the desk, knowing my actions would cause an aggressive counterattack.

"Nice shot," Gabe said, with an almost genuine flair. He attempted to stand but stopped, holding his rib cage. His strength and speed weren't his only failing attributes: his bones were taking their sweet time to regenerate. "*What* did you do to me, *witch*?" He lunged, but the chain popped up, and he tripped and fell back down, landing face-first.

"Are you still bored of this feud?" I yelled, taking a few steps backward, shocked by my own attack and still uncertain of the extent of my powers.

He looked up from the ground, seething, and then charged, yelling through the pain. The look in his eyes made me gasp, but then, just before he grabbed me, the chain jerked up and lassoed him.

I watched in astonishment as he was hurled back across the room into the wall.

Holy shit, I thought, trying to hide the fact that I was visibly shaking.

Before guilt could set in, I remembered that in this very room, he had forced Lisette Monvoisin to murder her own triplet, to literally suck the life out of her.

My fingers slowly twirled. The lasso tightened, and the chain wrapped itself around him three more times as he yelled obscenities at me, in shock that his perfect body was failing. I forged the ends of the chain together, trapping him.

Confidence grew inside me with the defeat of one vampire. *Thank you, Désirée.* The absinthe potion had definitely been activated. Without it, I wouldn't have stood a chance.

Now I just had to pray I could take on his pair of volatile progeny . . . and, of course, his psycho brother.

I walked back to Nicco, who sat down on the desk, making us nearly eye level. "What are you doing, *bella*? How can I help you if I don't know the plan?"

"It really is better this way." I did my best to keep a wily smile from forming. "I'm just trying to protect you." My hidden grin transferred to his lips as he heard his own words used against him.

I took a deep breath. "And now we wait."

He gritted his teeth, knowing I wasn't willing to divulge the plan any more than he was willing to give up the past. I rested my hand on his leg, and his jaw relaxed. At this point, I *was* trying to protect him. The less he knew, the better, because things were about to get *beaucoup* awkward for him. The only way for him not to betray his family was for me to fall—a reality both of us kept pushing to the back of our minds.

"Little girl," Gabriel said with a strange mix of ecstasy and threat. "You are really, *really* going to regret this in about ninety seconds. And, Brother, when I get free, you'd better run."

"Chill out," Nicco said, pushing himself off the table, seeming to enjoy the humility forced upon his older sibling. He traipsed over to

Gabriel and bent to his face. "She locked you in a chain, Bro. It's not like she set you on fire." He tousled his brother's hair.

"And how do you think this is going to end for you, little *Bro*? The two of you are going to ride off in the moonlight together?"

"Something like that," Nicco grumbled with a swift kick to his brother's foot.

He walked back to the table in discontent. We tried not to let the question cripple us, but how quickly the energy in the room had changed.

"Ticktock," Gabe said. "Ticktock. Ticktock."

At first, the childish words went in one ear and then out the other, but soon I had to hold myself back from kicking him in the face to shut him up.

"Ticktock," he taunted like a broken record.

A spark buzzed from my finger.

"That's it, *bella*. Stay angry!" Nicco yelled, just as Lisette burst through the door.

"Where is he?" she shrieked and then rushed to Gabe's side, frantically trying to release him from the magical chains.

"Kill her now, Lise!" Gabe ordered.

Lisette whipped around the room and came straight for me.

I underestimated her speed, and in a second her open palms smashed against my chest, and I was sliding across the floor, not stopping until I smacked into an upright cassette.

My head knocked a board loose, and I caught a glimpse of what was inside. I hesitated, horrified.

"Adele!" Nicco yelled, as Lisette grabbed my hair and spun me around.

"I'm fine!"

I had an idea—an idea so horrible I almost felt bad, but then Lisette's pale hand clutched my throat.

"Have you no sense, girl?" she screamed in my face as she lifted me from the ground, her sharp fingernails digging into my skin. "Do you not remember what I told you about Gabriel?"

Kicking the air and clawing at her wrists, I choked: "Do you not remember why your sister *died* for you?"

Screaming, she shoved me back into the dry-rotted cassette. I felt the corpse's rib cage crack against my back. Rage filled Lisette's eyes as the dusty remains of her dead sister crumbled onto both of us. She instantly dropped me, screaming in French, trying to catch Minette's skull before it tumbled to the floor.

"Whose family name are you trying to protect, Lisette?" I yelled, scurrying away as she caught the skull. Her own tears muffled her screams, as she dashed from piece to piece, grabbing the bones. "Medici or Monvoisin?"

Her fangs snapped out, and the bones spilled from her arms, all except the skull.

"Gabriel!" I yelled. "Why don't you get *Lisette* to break the curse . . . after all, she's the one—" Suddenly my vision fogged, and I couldn't breathe.

I doubled over—clutching the skull that Lisette had hurled into my stomach—and fell on the floor. She wasted no time coming after me, but this time Nicco intercepted and threw her across the room. Gabe shouted at him in the background.

Minette's poor skull rolled away as I scurried to the nearest beam, desperately needing a breather. Lisette began sparring with Nicco, and I relished the pause from the fight as my lungs sucked in gulps of air.

They were both wavering, although Lisette wavered far more than Nicco. I guessed they'd drank less of the moonshine than Gabe, as they both seemed merely tipsy, whereas Gabe seemed more like a drunk flopping down Bourbon Street at dawn.

Lisette hurled a ceramic statue of an unknown saint at Nicco. It split over his head into large chunks. My shoulders tensed up, although

I got the feeling that, for vampires, they were hardly roughhousing. Nicco shook off the broken pieces with a dangerous smirk and then cracked his neck twice, ready to pounce.

"Niccolò!" Gabriel yelled, growling beneath his chains.

Nicco looked back at his brother and then rolled his eyes and stepped away from Lisette, as if deciding not to assert himself over a drunk girl who was acting crazy. My chest swelled with some bizarre sense of pride.

Gabriel yelled provocative things at both of them, easily switching back and forth between Italian and French. Between the languages and his slurred speech, I could only understand a fraction of his banter, but it didn't take a genius to fill in the blanks.

"You disgust me," Lisette sneered at Nicco. "How could you betray your brother?"

Despite Nicco's gentlemanly showmanship only a moment ago, she snatched up another statue and lifted it over her head.

Nicco dodged the flying saint. His jaw tightened as the statue smashed against the wall behind him. My own teeth clenched, but it was more than that: a lethal, protective instinct flared inside me. I moved from behind the beam, toward her, and one of the thick, rusty chains slid off a cassette and slithered to my feet like a snake.

"How could *you* betray your *sisters*?" I yelled back with what was left of my voice. The chain slid from my ankles to hers. "You are making Minette's death in vain!"

Her face darkened with rage. She jumped toward me, but the chain tightened and yanked her to the ground with a crack.

No longer hearing the words that came out of my bruised windpipe, I raised both hands and pulled the chain into the air, along with her. As the metal carried her past me, screaming, she swiped me with her razor-sharp fingernails, slicing the skin from my clavicle to my ear. I winced but remained focused on driving the chain into the rafters, until Lisette Monvoisin—*la petite-fille de La Voisin Magnifique*, founding member of the Casquette Girls Coven, and eighteenth-century Medici-made vampire—was left hanging upside down like a bat.

The hissing sounds coming from Gabe brought my mind back to reality. I removed my hand from my burning neck, and blood dripped from my fingers to the floor.

Gabriel violently thrashed about in his chains, hissing louder.

Breathe. Fight the pain.

I looked up at the ceiling and sucked air through my nose. *You're fine.* Liquid dribbled down my chest. Muscles in my back spasmed.

One more down. Two to go. Three, if you count Niccolò.

Lisette spat extra lewd indecencies about the smell of my blood. The warmth that rose to my cheeks alerted me to Nicco's presence—or, rather, the sudden lack thereof.

I scanned the room again. *Where the hell did he go?*

Then the vibrations of a trembling voice directly behind me sent shivers down my neck. "Get . . . away from me," he growled. *"Now!"*

I darted across the room, behind the desk.

When I whipped back toward him, he was leaning over the table-top, fangs out, biting his bottom lip hard enough to draw blood.

"Just stay over there, Nicco!" I yelled, my voice cracking.

His knuckles were white from clutching the table, and I could see the trance state coming on.

"I'll put you in chains, Niccolò. I swear!"

"You absolutely will not!" His eyes were threatening. "Do not even *think* about it, Adele."

The idea of Nicco being chained when Emilio and Martine showed up was not exactly ideal, but I reminded myself of my number-one priority: *survive.*

"Then stay on that side of the room!" I frantically ripped the bobby pins out of my hair, allowing the waves to cascade around my neck and mask the bloody wounds.

He blinked.

Gabe began to laugh hysterically. "Oh, this is too good, Brother. How the irony of this tale will be remembered for years to come, when you end up being the one to kill your *bella*! It's almost too sweet." His laugh faded. *"Almost,"* he added, exposing his fangs to me.

In a flash, Nicco was in his face. *"Silenzio!"*

The aggression in his voice reverberated through my bones.

CHAPTER 42

Flight of La Fée Verte

Nicco exiled himself to a dark corner to cool down while I pressed my hair into the gashes and prayed to the coagulation gods. Never in my life had I thought I'd look forward to the onset of scabs.

"Tiiiiiiiicktock. Tiiiiiiiicktock." Gabriel synched his taunts with Lisette's swings from the rafters.

I had banked on Lisette and Martine flocking to aid their troubled Maker, but it was up to Isaac to play a serious game of cat and mouse to get Emilio here.

And where the hell is Martine? Why hasn't she come yet to help Gabe?

In the soft voice of a child, Lisette slowly began to echo Gabe: "Ticktock. Ticktock."

My foot twitched. Désirée just might get her wish after all. Just as I was contemplating whether a kick to the crotch was worth risking the physical contact with Gabe, in sauntered the middle child, fangs protruding.

His nonchalance made my pulse skip. He'd arrived on his own accord. No wind.

No wind.

Emilio stopped in the middle of the room. "*La Fée Verte* . . . my, my, aren't you just stunning tonight? Did you wear that blood just for me?" He retracted his fangs and ran his tongue over his bright-red lips. His gums and teeth were also stained crimson.

A chill passed down my spine. *What if the cat caught the mouse?*

Emilio ended his dramatic cleansing process and then paused, looking my way. His teeth rested on his bottom lip, similar to the way Nicco's did, as if he were forcing some kind of self-control.

"That redheaded bombshell friend of yours is so feisty," he said, and Lisette began to thrash about above us. "But I had to settle for that blonde again." He rolled his head in annoyance. "She never *shuts up.*"

As horrible as it was, I let out a sigh of relief.

"They *really* should stay out of the bars . . . You never know what kind of seedy characters you'll come across in this town." His eyes dropped to my bloody cleavage, and he smiled. "Now, what kind of trouble have you been getting yourself into?"

He took a slow spin on his heel, assessing the attic situation. My heart pounded rapidly, as I realized the trap was completely busted.

I eyed the door.

If I close the seal now, Désirée and Isaac can figure out what to do with Martine, right?

But there was no way I could get around Emilio, even with all of the elixirs—it was too risky. He shook his head at Gabe, who was stewing. The only thing I could count on was Emilio running his mouth for a few minutes.

"*Bravissima, signorina,*" he said to me, looking up at Lisette. "*Impressionnant, ma chérie.*" When he switched to French, back to the Émile I knew in Paris, it made me want to gag.

I tried to focus on the door and the mélange of locks and not on him.

Metal. Metal. Handles. Hinges. I pushed and pushed until it felt like my brain was going to pop, but the door didn't budge.

"I'll admit, I had you pegged more as the Damsel in Distress . . ." He took a deep bow in hyperbolic admiration. I wanted to drop-kick his head.

"So everyone keeps telling me . . ." I said, stalling. I spotted an antique rake resting against the wall near Gabe. *That* would be easy.

I grunted as I lifted it in the air and hurled it into the door.

But the swollen door scraped forward only a few inches, and the rake clanged to the floor.

"Dammit!" I whispered.

Emilio whipped to the door, to the wall where the rake had been, and then back to the door. "How did you do that?"

"Do what?"

"Move that quickly?"

"Um . . . I haven't moved, Emilio."

But he didn't spin toward my voice. He looked for me up in the rafters. I wondered if Dixie had also been drinking the moonshine—now he was being just as weird as the others, and I wasn't the only one who'd noticed. Nicco lurked in the nearest shadow, his eyes fixed on his brother.

Emilio spun around again and even swatted at the air.

"I'm over here, E." I whistled.

"Wormwood," I heard Nicco mutter. "But how . . . ?"

The word lit a fire in Emilio's eyes, and suddenly he was right in front of me, and he did *not* like whatever was going on in his head. But he sucked in a couple of deep, loud breaths through his nose and calmed himself almost as quickly as he'd been set off, which scared me even more.

"I don't know what you think you did," he said, "but I can drink my weight in absinthe, *ma chérie. Merci beaucoup* for the trip."

"You're welcome . . . I hope you find this one to be especially *magnifique.*" My smile was genuine.

"My, how quickly humans grow up," he said, shooting Nicco a meaningful glance before running his finger over my left cheekbone. His cool touch sent a chill through my burning, magic-saturated shoulders. Lisette giggled in delight at my forced submissive position. I pinched her restraints tighter.

I took a few steps backward. He followed.

"It seems like just yesterday you were that little, lost duck in Paris." He brushed my face again. "Now you're poised to be the Heroine. But it really wasn't the brightest plan . . . trapping yourself in an attic with the most brutal vampire I've ever known . . . and me."

What?

His gaze went back to Nicco, and I realized this was just the pre-show—Emilio was just rousing his little brother. And now, backed up against the wall, I was exactly where he wanted me.

Focus on the door, Adele, not on him.

He looked back at me through his thick lashes, and his face came closer to mine, until his cool breath tickled my flushed skin. *"Paris. La cité de l'amour . . ."*

Nicco snorted from the corner.

Emilio stole another glance at his brother as his fingers traced my jaw. I focused all of my energy on the hinges of the door. I could feel them wanting to move. I could feel them start to shake. My body began to tremble with the locks. *Come on . . .*

Emilio's other hand swept the side of my leg through the flimsy feathers of my skirt. My whole body stiffened. My fists squeezed, containing the sparks. *Ignore him. He's just trying to piss off Nicco.*

And it was working. Nicco was inching out from the shadows, fangs exposed. My eyes begged him to stay back. I focused again on the metal.

What use is this power if I can't even shut a door?!

"We did have some good times, didn't we, *ma chérie?*" Emilio smiled salaciously as his hand crept through the fringe and grabbed my ass.

My arm reflexively twisted, and I slapped him across the face, releasing all the stored-up energy.

He spewed profanities in my direction as he fell to the ground, yelling, his arms covering his face, in what seemed to be an exorbitant amount of pain.

"You wish," I scoffed, breathing heavily, satisfied with my impulsive move . . . even if it was a death sentence.

The room lapsed into silent confusion as Emilio writhed on the floor. And then I saw the bright red peeking from between his fingers.

My hand burned with a sticky wetness.

I looked down to find bloody chunks dripping from my palm. I shook my hand, flinging his molten skin from my fingers, and a tsunami of nausea crashed into my stomach.

Horror flooded Niccolò's face, and hoots from the peanut gallery encouraged retaliation.

Emilio jumped to his feet, panting—sneering. A smear of skin from his left eye socket, stretching across his nose and right cheek, down to his chin, was missing. The wound, in the shape of my hand, left his facial muscles exposed, and the bone protruded where the ball of my hand had made contact with his cheek. Every time he blinked, it looked like his left eyeball might fall out.

My knees buckled, and I hit the splintered floor, forcing myself to choke back my own vomit. "Why . . . why couldn't you have just given me more time?" I stammered, pushing myself backward on the floor.

"Emilio, it's just skin," Nicco yelled. I could tell he was nervous—unsure of what role to play. "It will grow back."

But Emilio was no longer concerned with his baby brother. He was only concerned with me.

I froze, repulsed by the bloody mess of veins and tissue I'd exposed. I didn't move fast enough when he came straight for me.

A silent scream escaped my wounded throat as he slammed me into a stack of cassettes, crushing the wooden tower and bringing a round of cheers from Gabriel and his hanging progeny. Pain shot from my torso to all of my extremities.

Lying in the pile of broken wood, I attempted to pull the rake back into my hands, but Emilio had straddled my chest and was kneeling on my elbows. I could barely feel my fingers, much less cast magic.

"I am starting to think draining you might be more satisfying than this whole curse-breaking business." He slowly licked the bridge of my nose, reminding me that I might actually die tonight. Then Nicco pummeled him from the side. I rolled in the opposite direction, groaning.

"Let's go, Brother!" Emilio screamed, blood flinging from his face. "I just fed, so let me know if I hurt you."

I crawled to a dark corner as they tumbled across the room.

The floor shook as they pounded each other into the ground. Each gripped the other so viciously I wondered if we'd officially entered the fight-to-the-death portion of the night.

Nicco landed on top and slammed his brother's shoulders down, cracking the floorboard beneath. "The only part of you stronger than me after you feed, Emilio, is your mouth."

As they spewed more sibling rivalry at one another, the sound of creaking metal distracted me. I looked at the ceiling. Lisette was swaying in the breeze. *A breeze?*

My eyes shifted to Gabriel, who was smirking at his younger brothers with nostalgia. The blond locks that hung in his face gently lifted, but he was too engrossed in the fight to notice the inconspicuous whoosh of air filling the attic.

At first I thought my ears were ringing, but when I strained, I heard a faint whistle. It rapidly grew louder until it howled like a derailed train.

The boys stopped scuffling, and everyone's attention turned to the door as a giant force of wind blew in, extinguishing all the wall sconces. In the pitch-black, someone landed in the room with a series of loud thuds, simultaneously shouting in angry French and squealing in delight.

Martine DuFrense.

This was the moment—and even better, Isaac had managed to *push* her in rather than leading her in. *Nice one, bird boy.*

The last vamp was at the party. I knew what I had to do.

No one else would die.

I took off toward the door, arms pumping, ignoring the pain shooting from multiple points. Even in the darkness, I felt all eyes shift to me as I hurled myself against the door, slamming it shut from the inside.

The building quaked as the hexed door joined the circuit of spells cast upon the building.

I stumbled behind a wooden pillar in the pitch-black attic and leaned over my knees, sucking air into my lungs and relishing the knowledge that Désirée and Isaac would now be safe.

I braced myself for Medici retaliation, but no one attacked me for sealing the exit.

Well, this is anticlimactic.

The waiting caused a squeak of nervous laughter. *Oh God, I'm losing my mind.*

When I stood up, I realized there was a distinctly fresh tension in the air. The kind of tension that only resulted from silence.

"Lise! You're flying!" Martine squealed. "We were flying too, in the wind!"

Jesus, no wonder she and Gabe get along. So freaking dramatic.

"Martine," Emilio yelled with urgency, "what is *she* doing here?"

She? Something is wrong.

"You were supposed to be guarding her!"

"I was!" She giggled into the dark void. "No one touched a precious hair on her head!"

Had Martine rolled in with a hostage?

"You were supposed to stay home!"

"Home was booooooooring. We just went to the bar. That's where the wind lifted us up into the sky and we flew!" Martine squealed in drunken, gleeful French. *"Il était merrrrveilleux!"*

We? The high I'd just felt after sealing the exit crashed as my self-sacrificial plan atrophied. The entire point of me deviating from the coven's plan had been to *avoid* putting any other lives at risk. I bolted into the darkness toward them but was immediately blocked by someone. Nicco.

"Adele . . ." He nudged me backward, his hands on my shoulders.

"What's going on?" I asked, trying to move around him, but I froze when I heard a dainty voice ask, "You're hurt, Emilio?"

Not Martine's voice.

"What happened to your face?" the very sophisticated, very French voice continued.

I know that voice.

"It's nothing . . ." The tender change in Emilio's tone was alarming.

"Why aren't you healing?"

My chest heaved, and all of the sconces exploded with flames. I moved to get a closer look, but Nicco moved with me, purposefully obstructing my view. "Nicco!"

"I guess it's time for a family reunion," Gabriel teased.

Sighing, Nicco finally let me push him out of the way, revealing a scene that absolutely nothing could have prepared me for.

My heart seized, refusing to believe I'd just trapped my mother in an attic with a clan of vengeful vampires. With a slim-to-zero chance of getting her back out alive.

"This ends now!" Emilio yelled violently.

Hot tears began to stream down my face, blurring my vision. I was too paralyzed to wipe them away. *Did I just sacrifice my mother for the safety of the coven? For the other innocent people in New Orleans? For my father?* I didn't even notice that Emilio was lunging toward me until I heard *ma mère* scream my name.

Maybe she does care—

I got only a couple steps away before Emilio roughly grabbed hold of my hips and swung me in the air. I crashed back-first against a wooden beam. The hidden stake in my corset felt like it had become permanently lodged in my spine. Before I could fall to the ground, Emilio smashed my palms together and pushed me back against the pillar. I gasped as his other hand wrapped around my throat.

Nicco stormed toward us, only to be tackled to the ground by Martine, who clung on to his waist like a prizefighter.

"Niccolò's right," Emilio jeered at me. "You don't know anything about the Count. You're *useless* to us."

I tried desperately to move my hands, but he crushed them tighter. *Breathe. Focus. Get. Hands. Free.*

I willed my vocal cords to work. "I know you don't care about the curse, *Émile*."

His eyebrows rose with suspicious interest. "Aw, *ma chérie, je t'aime zhat* you know me so well." His faux sexy French accent had suddenly returned.

"You don't care about Gabriel's freedom, just like you didn't care about leaving your sister behind . . . poor Giovanna Medici."

His face drained white.

"Still think I don't know anything?"

"Where is she?" he asked, slamming me back into the pillar.

"Does her ghost torment you while you sleep?"

"What is she talking about?" Gabe asked in the background.

Emilio squeezed my throat tighter. "Don't break the curse, then," he said. "There are other ways to break a witch's curse." Blood spattered from his wound onto my face, making me gag.

You don't know what they want, so focus on the things you do know: they're looking for something . . . something to do with Adeline's father.

And then it came to me: Gabriel's desperate fake-out, which had cost Lisette her life—the thing a Medici would do in my situation. My second card to play was a bluff.

"What if I could do something better than break the curse?" I tried hard to keep my poker face, despite the lack of oxygen flowing to my brain. "What if I gave you *him*?"

All movement in the room stopped in a wave of shock.

Emilio leaned so close I could see the curls of his torn skin slowly beginning to regenerate. Excitement flickered in his Medici-green eyes. "And how can you be so certain *le Comte de Saint-Germain* will flock to a little, fledgling witch like you, *chérie*?"

I strained my neck forward until my lips swept his ear and whispered, "Because he's right behind you."

He released me as he spun around.

That second was all I needed: when he turned back to me, an enormous pair of sparkling spheres pulsed in the palms of my hands.

"Move the hell away if you want the other half of your face to stay pretty, Emilio!" I pushed the flames toward him and pulled them back again.

"Adele, stay away from him!" my mother screamed. "You'll only get hurt!"

Martine restrained her, but my mother fought her like a lunatic.

Normally it would have felt completely unnatural to listen to my mother, but hearing her voice brought an unfamiliar yet welcome comfort. My intuition listened, and I backed away, never taking my eyes off Emilio.

I'd almost reached the other side of the room when he snorted like a bull and charged me. I had no choice but to release the perfectly aimed orbs in self-defense.

I didn't even contemplate *not* killing him.

The rest happened so quickly.

My mother broke away from Martine, tore across the room in a blur, and leaped directly into the line of fire. The flames engulfed *her* instead of her assistant.

Exorcism-like screams expelled from my raw throat as I ran to extinguish *ma mère*, but Nicco caught me midleap and dragged me away, kicking and screaming. With my back to the room, he held me tightly against a beam, until my muscles could no longer fight him and wisps of nothing came from between my lips. I sucked in air that reeked of burned hair.

"Je ne comprends pas." I wiped my tears with the back of my hands. "I don't understand . . . I don't—"

With a heavy sigh, Nicco moved me to the other side of the beam, so I could see my mother lying on the ground. "I'm sorry, *bella.*"

The flames were gone, and smoke now rose from her charred body, but what sent me into complete shock was seeing Emilio hovering over her with desperate affection.

Nicco caught me as I sank toward the floor in what felt like a million shattering pieces. "I don't understand," I repeated over and over.

The world as I knew it ceased to exist.

"I'm so sorry you had to find out this way, Adele," he said.

I couldn't take in enough air. I began hyperventilating as my entire psyche unraveled.

Emilio was cradling my mother's shoulders, petting her arms. Below his hands, her skin was charred and blistered . . . but as I watched, it began to shift back to perfect porcelain. It was regenerating.

I didn't know which was worse: thinking I'd just killed my mother or realizing what she really was. I sank the rest of the way to the floor as the explanations hit me like bullets from a firing squad:

Why she wouldn't let me live with her in Paris.

Why she preferred to see me at night.

Her finicky eating.

Her unusual relationship with her "assistant."

Her mysterious disappearance twelve years ago, when she abandoned my father. Abandoned me.

It was all there in front of me, and most of it had been for a while. My mother hadn't deserted us.

She had *died.*

My mother was a vampire.

I couldn't breathe. I couldn't talk. I couldn't hear. She screamed something to me in French, but it was like I suddenly didn't understand the language.

Nicco shook my shoulders, also yelling. Everyone in the room was yelling.

My head became very light, and dizziness overwhelmed me. Heat radiated from every part of my body. I felt like I was going to spontaneously combust, like the lightbulb in my bedroom.

But I couldn't stop gaping. The way Emilio held my mother's head, as if she were his child, made my stomach lurch.

Is she his child? His lover? Has she killed people? Did she kill the man with the blue eyes?

Then it dawned on me.

"Nicco?"

"Sì, bella?"

"You didn't kill those students."

He looked down at me and gently shook his head.

My heart ached as I looked back at him. For a split second, the chaos in the room seemed to freeze around us, and I regretted all of this. I didn't want to die. I wanted *him.* And for longer than the next five minutes.

What have I done?

Emilio yelled a command to Martine, and she twisted Nicco around, straight into her fist, cracking his nose, then she burst out laughing, running away. Enraged, Nicco went after her.

Now that I was alone, Emilio rose from my mother's side, snarling.

I didn't care. I didn't care about anything anymore. I didn't understand anything anymore. I wanted this all to go away.

No. I wanted to kill him.

My half-broiled mother leaped toward Emilio's feet, and he spun around in confusion.

"Stop it, Emilio! She's my daughter! *Arrête!*"

He bent down and yelled something to her in French about killing me.

She knocked him to the floor and jumped on top, pinning him down. *Ma mère* had apparently not partaken in the moonshine.

Emilio dug his hands into her charred chest. Flesh that I had burned.

She screamed in agony, but didn't budge. She looked directly at me. "Get out of here, now, Adele! I'm so sorry."

Then my mother turned back to Emilio and apologized to *him* despite still straddling him and baring her fangs in his face. *"Je suis désolée."*

"Mom! I'm not leaving you with him!"

"Échapper-toi maintenant!" she screamed to me. *"GO!"*

"You're a monster, Emilio!" I cried and sprang for the last gardening tool, an old spade. Martine beat me to it, snatching it up, but instead of attacking me with it, she took a dramatic spin, as if performing onstage, and began humming a French lullaby.

I lifted my hand to the heavy iron tool. It jerked to and fro, but she grasped it like a tango partner. I spun her around, faster and faster. She squealed in delight and began singing the lyrics operatically, louder and louder.

In her rapturous state, she didn't even notice the handle twisting around her wrists into a makeshift pair of cuffs. The spade floated upward, spinning the singing diva into the air, until it plunged itself into one of the wooden ceiling beams.

"Look, Lise! We're flying!" Martine yelled as she swung around in delusional glee, singing something about breaking the curse and finally going back to Paris. Gabe's commentary became more and more profane, while Martine sang louder and louder, with intermittent shrieks of laughter.

I ran toward the door. If there was a chance of surviving this pit of predators, then I wanted it. If I could get the door open, I knew Nicco, my mother, and I could defeat Emilio and escape. It wasn't the original plan, but I didn't care.

"Niccolò Giovanni Battista Medici, you'd better stop her," Emilio commanded from across the room. "You shame our family's name!"

I looked back over my shoulder at Nicco, who was standing in the middle of the room, breathing heavily, like he might implode. He was the only one left unrestrained. Gabriel echoed Emilio's command as I turned back to the escape route.

My hand touched the doorknob, and suddenly Nicco was pressed up against my back.

"Do you trust me, *bella*?" he whispered into my ear.

My nervous system felt like it was short-circuiting. Every primal instinct told me to fry him, but my intuition consumed me. There was only one thing I was sure of in this supernatural world where nothing made sense.

"Yes," I gasped, turning around.

Before the syllable was out, his hands wrapped around mine, and I knew something was wrong.

His grip was too tight.

A sharp edge pressed into my palm as he pulled me from the door.

"I knew you would crack in the end!" yelled Gabe. "You are a Medici after all!"

"Whhh . . . what are you doing?" I dug my heels into the ground, but Nicco squeezed my hands and pulled, forcing me to stumble.

His eyes begged me for forgiveness, but I was unable to accept that I'd made the wrong decision.

"What are you doing, Niccolò? Stop."

We were back to the middle of the room. He began to turn on his heel and spin me around.

This is not happening.

This is not happening.

"How could you?"

"Adele, please stop resisting. It will hurt so much less if you stop."

"What?"

"I'm so sorry, *bella*," his voice cracked. "But there is no other way." He gained momentum, and my feet left the ground.

"No, Nicco!" I screamed as he let go of my hands and flung me toward the ceiling.

Never trust a vampire.

My shoulder crashed directly into the fifth window, and I went straight through the bricks. His pitch was so fierce I continued to soar upward.

My last glimpse showed my mother attacking Nicco. He didn't resist.

Higher and I higher I flew.

I yanked the stake from my corset and hurled it back toward the window—my death was imminent, but I'd be damned if it would be in vain—Adeline's spirit stayed with me as the metal zipped through the air and snapped the shutter closed, just as it had been for the last three centuries.

The entire building trembled, and I knew the curse was restored.

But the moment of solace didn't last long. Nicco's pitch peaked.

The stars held my heart as gravity plunged my body back down to Earth, twisting, turning, faster and faster. Images from my subconscious flooded like waves crashing ashore: all those times I had used magic as a kid, every metals lesson my father had taught me, every story Ren had told me, every clue that my mother was a vampire.

The signs had always been there. I just hadn't been open to them.

I told myself I was getting what I deserved for being so naïve.

Knowing it would all be over in a few seconds didn't make my broken heart ache any less.

Nicco let go of my hands.

Nicco let go of me.

CHAPTER 43

La fin de La Fée Verte

The sensation was strange—the impact not as painful as one would expect. But then again, maybe my mind was so numb with shock that my body was impervious to pain.

Or maybe the impact killed me and I'm already dead?

Everything was peaceful and serene. Sleepy. So, so sleepy.

When my eyes fluttered, all I saw were thousands of stars in the pitch-black sky. That's the nice thing about no electricity. Stars.

I heard noises in the distance.

People.

Celebration.

Trumpets.

The deep brass tones had always brought me such comfort in the past, but now I worried they were being blown from Gabriel's horn—the angel Gabriel, not the vampire.

Ugh, vampires.

My heavy eyes slowly blinked open, making me very aware of the weight of my own eyelids. I struggled to focus on a new shape coming into view.

A big triangle.

No, a cone.

A big ice-cream cone.

Maybe I am in heaven?

I squinted to sharpen my focus on the giant ice-cream cone, and the outline of another object appeared. I stared at the lines that separated the negative and positive space until a church came into focus.

Something was wrong.

It was upside down.

Why is there an upside-down church on top of a giant ice-cream cone?

The church looked like the cathedral. Once more, I tried to refocus my eyes. Pressure flooded my head. My neck fell slightly to the side, and the ice-cream cone suddenly reminded me of the bell tower.

Our bell tower.

Nicco let go of my hands.

Nicco tried to kill me.

Maybe Nicco did kill me?

I gasped for air and was struck with a wave of vertigo. My hand slapped for something solid, to ease the spinning, but I just ended up swatting air—the pressure was building in my head because I was upside down.

I was not, in fact, splattered on the concrete.

A focused stream of wind was pushing into the arch of my back, lifting me up toward the sky, like a geyser. I was no longer falling but floating upward. Up, up, up toward the looming crescent moon that hung low over the Crescent City.

My city.

The jet of air morphed, and I dropped.

The gust caught me again, this time like a mitt. I wheezed as the wind flipped me around. Right side up, the vertigo eased, and I extended my left arm to help navigate. My wings whipped up to the celestial sky, and I felt like I was flying up to the heavens.

Is this the way to heaven?

My blood-caked hair blew behind me, and the night air began to cool my dangerously feverish body temperature, sending ripples of tickles to the tips of my toes. The strength of the gust held me tight, and the thickness of the wet air wrapped a comforting familiarity around me that almost made me smile.

Fear abandoned me as the gale carried me closer to the glistening Mississippi and back down to the Vieux Carré.

The rendezvous point came within my line of sight, and the gentle twister lowered me onto the cupola of the Presbytère, the historic building adjacent to the ice-cream-cone steeples of the St. Louis Cathedral. The wind dissipated, and I fell the last six feet without much grace, but Isaac moved underneath me to break my fall.

He helped me stand, holding me steady by my left elbow while examining my other arm.

I tapped my foot on the stone roof, reveling in the sensation of stability. Solid ground.

"Are you okay?"

"He tried to kill me," I choked out, not quite able to look Isaac in the eyes. I was overridden by the need for some kind of confession. An admission of guilt. "You were right all along."

"What?" he asked, pulling me closer. "Who? What the hell happened, Adele? You're covered in blood."

My wild eyes locked with his, which were filled with worry. "He let go of my hands."

Isaac went to hold my hand, but hesitated briefly to pry something out of my palm. I felt instant relief, not having the sharp points pressed into my skin anymore. "He threw me into the bricks."

Isaac laced his fingers with mine, and his touch brought immediate comfort.

"Actually," he said, "we kind of pla—"

Rising on my toes, I tried to slide my bloodstained arms around his neck, but only my left arm obeyed. My right hung limp, its wing drooping on the stone roof, but the aid of his arm slipping around my waist was enough to hoist my face close to his.

"Adele, you're blee—"

My mouth brushed against his.

Just inches away from mine, his heart pounded, but he didn't stop talking. He asked questions my ears didn't hear, forcing my kisses into birdlike pecks.

"You're hurt, Adele," he said sternly, imploring me to stop.

Ignoring his concerns became futile, so I refrained from kissing him and leaned my forehead into his; his nose nuzzled against mine. He didn't really want me to stop.

"What happened in there?" he asked me again.

It all rushed back. My mother. Emilio. Nicco. Each flashback made me want to melt into him more.

"We won," was all I whispered as my eyes fell shut.

His lips swept the thin skin of my eyelids, sending shivers through my shoulders. I didn't have to see to know he was smiling. He kissed my cheekbone and jawline and then pushed my hair aside to continue down my neck.

"What the hell?" he said, suddenly alarmed. "Adele, you need a hospital."

"No! It's too overcrowded. They would just turn us away." The truth was I was scared to leave this moment. I quickly pressed my lips to his cheek, letting them linger. His body responded to my touch, and I felt him let the thought go.

I knew that every part of him wanted me. Wanted to protect me.

And I wanted to drown in that feeling.

The heightened sensory experience caused the rest of my aching body to press into his, and with that, his lips pushed onto mine, finally giving in to me.

Giving in to the elixir.

My hand moved to his face; I'd never wanted anything so badly. His arms circled tighter around me, until I could barely tell where I ended and he began. Dizziness overwhelmed me again.

I could feel his heart race faster. This time it was me who broke our embrace. He didn't release me so easily, but I held his jaw at bay.

"You're shaking," I whispered.

His eyes searched for something else to focus on.

"I . . ." He pushed his face back to mine and roughly pecked my lips, then took a deep breath and looked me in the eyes.

"I was so scared I was going to drop you." The shaking caused a slight vibration in his voice.

"But you didn't." The scratchy stubble of his otherwise baby face scraped across my cheeks, and my lips parted his. His vulnerability sent me into another manic tizzy.

My pulse raced.

Too fast.

The electric feeling expelled from my body as a breeze rushed around us, but this time it wasn't from the wind-wielding witch in my arms. It was simply Mother Nature.

Although, there's nothing simple about Mother Nature.

Her knowledge. Her beauty. Her power.

Cold.

My arm wrapped around Isaac until it wasn't possible to hold him any tighter.

And that was it. Everything I had left inside me.

I was drained.

Blackness.

CHAPTER 44
Mourning of the Casquette Girls

Orbs of color flashed beneath my eyelids. Blindness only exacerbated the pain searing every inch of my body. My muscles cramped and convulsed. Someone was hovering above me, aggressively cursing . . . panicking.

Isaac.

I tried to raise my hand to comfort him.

"Jesus, what's wrong with her arm, Isaac?" came a female voice. Maybe Dee's? "Keep trying to wake her up."

"Adele, wake up." He frantically shook my dead weight.

I winced.

"Isaac, watch her shoulder!"

Definitely Désirée.

"Sorry. Adele, it's time to wake up. Please," he added, as if it might have been his lack of manners keeping me in a semiconscious state.

"What happened?" Désirée demanded with a hint of accusation. Her pitch was a little higher than usual.

If Désirée's worried, should I be worried?

"I don't know . . . we were just . . . and she . . . she just blacked out." His voice warbled.

Through the slits of my lashes, I saw Désirée leaning over me, dragging her hands down my torso, lips moving quickly. My body burned as if I'd been struck by lightning.

I blinked slowly. Everything was fuzzy, but I could tell we were still on the roof of the Presbytère. The stars were gone. A dense fog now bridged the gap between the clouds and the small cupola. Chills swept over me.

Isaac yelled something to Désirée.

I tried to move my mouth, but nothing came out.

"Adele, can you hear me? Please, say something."

I had a strong desire to answer him but couldn't seem to remember how to do that . . . how to make words. I blinked again, willing my eyes to stay open this time, but they drooped shut.

"She's alive."

"Of course she's alive, birdbrain, she's breathing!" Totally unsatisfied with Isaac's efforts, Désirée commanded, "Adele, open your eyes, *NOW.* Tell me who I am."

My eyes popped open as if attached to marionette strings. "You're Voodoo Queen Dee."

The puppet master leaned back and breathed a sigh of relief. "Jesus, Adele."

I tried to sit up on my own but fell back. Isaac caught me.

"What happened?" I asked. My throat felt like it had been clawed raw, inside and out.

"You passed out," Isaac said from above me. His upside-down head hovered so close to mine his eyes looked giant, like a prehistoric bug's.

"I was about to take you to the hospital, but Désirée rolled up with her juju. For the record, I still think we should go to the hospital."

"There's only one open hospital," Désirée told him. "Unless you want to put a bullet in her, she'll never be seen. We're better off waking up Gran if we need help."

"Thaaaaanks, Dee. No hospital. My dad'll freak." I smiled, not recognizing my own voice.

Désirée was rubbing something cool and minty into my shoulder.

"Wait, why might we need Gran?"

"We don't, Adele. I can handle it."

"Are you sure you know what you are doing?" Isaac asked.

"All Voodoo is based on the art of healing."

"I'm a little inclined toward science at the moment. No offense."

"Well, then, it's a good thing Adele has me."

The minty rub soothed my feverish skin. "I'mmmm gonna go back to sleep now."

"No!" Désirée yelled. "Isaac, switch places with me."

Suddenly she was gone from my sight. My eyes drooped closed.

"Hey! No sleeping, Tinker Bell."

My eyes flew open again. Isaac was straddling me on all fours. His outline was blurry, but I could sense his frazzled nerves. I focused on him until I could finally make out his expression—intense concern. Despite the pain, my stomach did a small somersault.

"I'm not Tinker Bell."

"I know. I know. *La Fée Verte.*"

"Haha. Your accent is terrrrrrrible."

Désirée snickered. Isaac leaned over my head to whisper to her. His black leather vest hung open, and his bare chest hovered over my face.

"Where's your shirt?" I slurred.

My words brought his face back, and he shot me a short, nervous smile. He didn't answer, but his eyes fell to my neck, and I realized there was something tight and damp wrapped around it.

"Isaac, you have to hold her down!"

"I *am*."

"Don't be a wuss. Sit on top of her. If she tries to fry me, I'm using you as a human shield." Désirée pushed the hair from my shoulder.

I cried out as Isaac's knee moved into my open palm, pressing it against the stone roof.

"Do it, Désirée!" he yelled.

"Do what?" my loopy voice asked. I stared at his chest. "You're hot . . ."

He let his hair fall in front of his face to hide his blushing cheeks.

Désirée snickered again. "Don't flatter yourself, Isaac; it's just the elixir talking."

He leaned in, crushing my left shoulder and right hip. "Agh—!"

"Do it!"

A bolt of pain surged.

The scream that came out of my mouth sounded like that of a dying animal. My body tried to lurch into a sitting position as Désirée rammed my arm back into the socket, but Isaac kept me pinned down. My eyelids fluttered in shock as my brain registered that my arm was now reattached and the pain was actually a good thing.

Isaac shifted off, and they were both silent for a minute while I wheezed.

I curled the fingers on my right hand, and Désirée let out a loud sigh.

"Breathe," Isaac whispered, brushing my hair off of my face.

I nodded and inhaled deeply, and the convulsions slowed.

"Merci beaucoup, Dee." I sucked in a few more breaths, utterly exhausted. "Now can I take a nap?"

"Not if you want to avoid the hospital," she snapped.

"*Ça va! Non hôpital!*"

"We still need to torch the convent, Désirée," Isaac said. "If she's too weak to light the fire from here, I can go down and do it the old-fashioned way."

"No fire!" I rasped. Suddenly, consciousness was not an issue.

He squeezed my hand. "Don't worry . . . we can handle it. We're almost mission complete."

"We are *not* burning the attic!" I yelled, jerking my hand away.

They both stared back at me with wide eyes. The surprise on Isaac's face slowly morphed as he drew his own conclusion about why I didn't want to burn the attic.

He was only half-right.

I didn't want to kill Nicco, even if he had tried to *kill me*. But, more importantly, my mother was trapped in that attic, thanks to me. I'd already nearly burned her to death by accident, but I definitely couldn't do it on purpose—even if she was a vampire. Even if she had killed those two students twelve years ago.

"We are not burning the attic," I repeated and looked at Isaac, expecting him to cave and take my side.

He didn't.

There was no way I could tell him about my mother. He hated vampires. There was no way I could tell *anyone*.

"Arson *is* a little seventeenth-century witch hunty . . ." said Désirée.

Thank you, Dee.

"This is *not* the same as Dark Ages witch hunts," Isaac said. "Those witches were innocent. These are cold-blooded *killers*. Vampires!"

I gave Isaac a look, letting him know there would be no forgiveness if he took matters into his own hands.

"Fine," he said, jaw clenched. "But we have to do something. It's not safe, leaving them like this."

"He's right," I said. "They'll die, not being able to feed—"

"That is *not* what I meant."

"We can recast the same slumbering spell," Désirée suggested.

"Do you think we're strong enough?"

"We're only three, and they're now six," Isaac said. It seemed to take all of his strength not to gloat. "That's *three* additions to the original bloodsucking attic crew."

"Three?" Désirée asked. "Emilio, Niccolò, and who?"

"I don't know for sure," Isaac said. "I'm assuming the sister. She was with Martine, but I got them both in one swoop."

Isaac saw my mother. And he thinks she's Giovanna Medici.

"Nice," Désirée said. "Well, there's only one way to test a spell." She grabbed our hands, forming a circle.

My fingers slid around Isaac's. I rubbed his thumb, begging him not to be mad at me. He barely glanced at me but attempted to crack a smile.

"Focus on the attic," Désirée said, and then she began to chant the French words of Marassa Makandal. Soon Isaac and I joined her, repeating the ethereal phrases over and over again, until they felt as natural as saying our own names.

The pain in my body began to subside as the wind swirled around us in a swell of paranormal excitement. I didn't know if it was the elixir, or the delirium, or the magic, but I could have sworn a harmony of girlish voices began to sing a lullaby from the sky. I smiled, knowing that *les filles aux cassettes* were with us in spirit.

Then the air stilled, and everything felt totally at peace.

"How do we know if it worked?" I asked.

"We don't," Désirée said. "Unless you want to open the attic door and—"

"Not happening," Isaac said, just in case she wasn't joking.

She smiled a deviant smile, causing his chest to puff, and then she started laughing.

I unwrapped Isaac's bloodstained shirt from my neck and let it drop to my feet, then ripped a strip of fabric from my wings and tied it into a bow around my neck.

Jackson Square had emptied; the streets below were totally desolate, making the moon feel extra bright.

"Where did everyone go?" Isaac asked, looking over the rail while putting his wig back on. Désirée inserted her fangs.

"I have a hunch," I said, fluffing my hair to further conceal the poultice-covered slashes on my neck, which were numb thanks to Désirée's juju. "Let's go."

Frenchmen Street was filled with zombies, squealing children, and revelers of all levels of intoxication, drinking and laughing under the sea of ghosts. Horns tooted as musicians warmed up the Second Line.

"So this is where everyone ran off to," Isaac said as two old geezers chased past us with sparklers, shouting with delight.

"Looks like the wormwood is still active," Désirée murmured. We all let out a short laugh.

"Dead Green Faerie?" a placid voice said. "Awesome costume."

I turned to find Theis approaching, with Ren on his heels.

"Merci beauc—"

"Oh, thank God, *bébé*, you scared me when you jumped off the float!" Ren cried, bending over me, but Isaac intervened.

"No hugs."

I chuckled.

Ren understood and made a crack about Isaac's chest being almost as hunky as his own. Theis wolf-whistled as Isaac quickly fastened the two buttons on his vest. I couldn't help wondering about the leather collar around Theis's neck. The weapon-like four-inch studs rivaled the punk-spikes on his head. *Is it a regular part of his ensemble, or is he wearing it because of . . . Nicco?* Either way, he seemed okay.

I spotted the twins passing out small white candles in red Solo cups.

"I'll be right back," I said and walked over to them.

"Adele!" Sébastien yelped, his lit candle fumbling to the street. "You disappeared again! You scared me half to death."

I picked up his candle and sniffed away a tear. "Sorry about that."

"Why are you covered in blood?" Jeanne asked, with genuine concern.

"Oh . . . this stupid girl from school thought it would be funny to have a *Carrie* moment and dumped corn syrup on me."

Did I really just lie to a chemist about blood?

She looked at me with doubt and opened her mouth to protest, but then let it slide.

I beamed in gratitude. Despite being covered in actual dried blood, I wrapped my good arm around her. *"Je t'aime,"* I whispered.

"Moi aussi."

"Can I get three candles, *s'il te plaît*?" I asked Sébastien, wiping my eyes.

"Oui, mon chou."

"Merci beaucoup. Come find us when you're done."

They smiled in agreement.

I walked back to Désirée and Isaac, who were both mesmerized by the linen-strung tribute, and handed them each a candle-poked cup. We all watched a flame magically grow from my candle, and then I kissed it to each of their wicks, lighting theirs the old-fashioned way.

Other than the specks of a thousand candle flames, the street was totally dark. A solo accordion squeezed out a chord, and then a woman in the middle of the block began to belt the first phrase of "Cryin' in the Streets." The horns followed, and the crowd started moving together, back toward the Quarter.

As I listened to the beautiful alto voice, fresh tears rolled down my face. I thought of Brooke, Klara, and Alphonse Jones. I closed my eyes and wished for them to come home soon.

At least my mother is home, I thought, surprising myself. In a weird, twisted way, I really *was* glad she came back. I finally knew the truth.

I looked at Désirée and found her crying too. Everyone was.

We all linked hands and walked down the street. Our voices, singing together, gave me the confidence that my city was going to get better.

Our city.

When we crossed Esplanade Avenue, both the warble and the close proximity of the convent made my pulse climb. Désirée signaled to me, and our trio peeled off as the crowd continued its procession to St. Louis Cemetery No. 1.

For the second time that night, I entered the iron gate and walked through the overgrown hedges, this time flanked by two witches. Nestled in a weed-covered hedge was a large metal bucket, filled to the brim with the long carpenter nails that had rained down on that strange morning when everything went haywire: the original Vatican nails the Ursuline sisters had used to seal the shutters.

The convent's front door was wide open, but all that mattered was that the attic was secure. Both Isaac and Désirée breathed sighs of relief to see the windows still sealed, but I would have sworn that *one* shutter had a slight vibration. As I stared at it, my heartbeat echoed in my chest until it felt like my whole body was reverberating to the beat.

I could still feel the elixir coursing through my veins.

I closed my eyes. All I saw was Nicco and his not-so-innocent smile. *I am such an idiot.* My heart pounded. *Why? Why? Why?* Despite all the fires, all the hurricanes, the crimes, the hauntings, and the magic in this city, somehow that shutter had stayed shut tight over the centuries, until right before I got to it. I felt the metal stake rattling high above us.

Breathe.

"Are you okay?" Isaac asked.

I nodded, sucking in a big breath through my nose.

"Are you sure?"

I opened my eyes to find him standing right in front of me. All the chaos stopped.

"I locked the front door," said Désirée, walking back to us. "We all good over here?"

"*Oui. Tout va bien.* All good," I replied.

I smiled at Isaac, and his hand went to my face. "Just don't go opening any more shutters, okay?"

"*Oui. Oui.*" I knew he was only half-joking. I glanced back at the attic. Emilio's torn face flashed in my head—

"*Il ne faut rien laisser au hasard!*" I yelled, and with a flick of my wrist, the old nails rose from the rusty pail and hammered themselves back into the wooden shutters.

They both stared at me.

"Why leave anything to chance?" I asked, looking straight at Isaac.

He smiled at me without worry for the first time since we'd parted ways on Bourbon Street, and then he fell in beside me as I walked away.

And I knew he would always be there. Beside me.

In a subdued state, the three of us crossed the railroad tracks to the Moonwalk and kept going to the river's edge, where we sat under the star-swept sky. Now that everything along the riverfront had been obliterated by the Storm, I wondered if our view was closer to how the landscape had looked for Adeline, Marassa, and Susannah three centuries ago.

I wondered if Adeline ever left *La Nouvelle-Orléans. Did her father ever make it to the city?* The number of unanswered questions was maddening, but the one that bothered me the most was about my mother: *Was she just a casualty in the magical ripples set in motion by my father's family so long ago? Had I been wrong about her my entire life?* I'd just locked up the only people who could answer those questions for eternity. And now I had a family secret from the coven—just as Adeline had.

Désirée finally broke the silence.

"I'm glad we didn't torch them." She paused, rolling her eyes. "I think I'm going to miss Gabriel."

Isaac groaned, leaning back on a small tuft of weeds.

I tried my best to contain my giggles as I lay back next to him. "I miss ice cream."

"Mmm . . . pralines and cream," Désirée agreed, lying back.

"These other two descendants better be dudes," Isaac said, and we all burst into delirious laughter.

"All right." Désirée leaned toward me, propped on her elbow. "Time to spill it, sister. What the hell happened in the attic?"

"Yeah." Isaac mirrored her propped elbow on my other side. He fiddled with the silver feather resting on my stomach.

I took a deep breath and thought about where to begin. "Well, in essence, *le Comte de Saint-Germain* saved me."

"Your dead great-great-great-something-grandfather *saved* you?" Isaac asked.

"Yeah . . . although, I'm not so sure anymore that he's dead."

"Oh Lord." Désirée sighed.

After I finished telling my version of the night, Désirée told hers and then Isaac his. And when all was done and all was said, we sat silently staring at the moon's reflection on the rippling river, soaking it all in: the differences between people, cultures, and times. The similarities.

The monsters. The myths.

The heroes.

The victims.

The love and loss.

Loss and love.

EPILOGUE

La toussaint

November 1st

"Well, Dad . . . your wife is locked in an enchanted attic a few blocks away, on the property of the Catholic archdiocese, forever or until further notice," I explained to my reflection in the toaster. "Last night, I nearly killed her by way of fireballs exploding from the palms of my hands. Also, she has a strange, familial relationship with this eighteenth-century psychopath, whom I used to have a massive schoolgirl crush on. That was before he tried to kill me, by the way. Oh, and those murders that Mom was accused of twelve years ago? Totally guilty. So, in a nutshell, you sent me away to Paris to live with a bloodsucking vampire. At least Mom had enough sense to send me away to boarding school. Oh, and did I mention this is all because of *your* magical lineage?"

The toast popped, startling me.

"You're right," I told the toaster. "That's not gonna work."

Too bad Hallmark didn't make a "Sorry, your wife is undead" card. It was hard not to wonder if he really knew *nothing* about his insane ancestry.

I sipped my lukewarm café *sans* au lait, wishing I could magically turn stale bread into beignets, and buried the idea of broaching the subject. Instead, I opened up Adeline's diary and began to think in French.

13th October 1728

The feeling is indescribable, Papa. The whole world feels like it is slightly off balance, like I have drunk too deeply of the bubbly wine . . .

I still cannot believe we have lost Lisette and Minette. I visit Morning Star each morning and evening to check on the status of her recovery.

So, I now know the answer to the dilemma I posed to myself on the SS *Gironde*: Am I capable of taking one life to save the lives of others? *Yes.*

And I would kill one hundred more of them if it meant I could bring back Lisette and Minette. It should not have been those two who found eternal slumber.

I worry constantly about you being out there with Emilio Medici on the loose. And then, of course, there is the mysterious Monsieur Jean-Antoine Cartier, whom I can only assume is the brother Giovanna Medici referred to as Niccolò.

Even though Martine is a vampire, Marassa could not stand to harm the woman who bought her freedom—so she led us in casting a slumbering spell. One more layer to the curse. One more layer of protection for the people of *La Nouvelle-Orléans*. One more layer of protection for the Saint-Germains.

Now Gabriel Medici can dream about catching us for eternity.

30th October 1728

It took weeks, but Morning Star's tribe was finally able to heal her bite—her shaman, as she calls him, extracted the venom every day until she was able to row across the river. The chief was so happy he even invited me, "the warrior witch," who hunted his son's murderer, to a ceremony on their tribe's land. It is incredible how open and accepting her people are when it comes to our *nature*.

We worry most about Cosette. She hasn't been the same since that night in the attic—understandably so. She wanders the streets after dark, lamenting her sisters and blaming herself for their deaths. Every night she ends her wandering by seeking solace in the arms of another man. She lures them in with her looks and her lullabies. It's as if she is trying to use up all of her powers so she can forget who she is. Her salacious behavior got her banned from the convent, after which she refused to stay with me, so as not to tarnish my reputation. Marassa and I watch over her silently from afar. My heart breaks for her, though I know she will end up on top; after all, she is the granddaughter of La Voisin Magnifique, one of the greatest, most scandalous sorceresses in the history of Paris.

As for the rest of *les filles aux cassettes*, I replaced their dowries with gold turned from lead. I know I am supposed to do this only under grave circumstances, Father, but this is the only chance these girls have to be married. If it wasn't for me, the vampires wouldn't have used their royally bestowed cassettes as coffins to rest in. Everyone in the town knows of your wealth, so there was not one eyebrow raised when the gold was suddenly procured.

Every day, Marassa and I stroll to the port to see if the arriving ships are carrying either her brother or you, Father. They never are.

17th December 1728

Weeks have gone by, the season has finally changed, and I am afraid this is the end of a chapter for our little coven of casquette girls. I am devastated to report that Morning Star is moving farther out with her tribe, as the strife between the French and the Indians worsens. As a parting gift, she presented me with a silver, eight-pointed charm and said, "As long as we live under the same blanket of stars, we will be sisters." I will cherish it forever and carry her spirit with me always.

If this news wasn't bad enough, Susannah received a marriage proposal from a merchant. Of course, I am overjoyed for their pending union, but they plan to leave for the port of New York next week! I suspect they met prior to *La Nouvelle-Orléans*, for I have never seen two people so happy to have found each other. I have rather adamantly insisted that they allow me to host the celebration for their nuptials, which I am trying to persuade them would be best after carnival season. If the coven is going to be split up by thousands of miles, it is only right that we have one last night together. Although, I firmly believe that this celebration will *not* be our ending. And, of course, Papa, I know that this is not *our* ending. I have never been more certain that *our* story has just begun, for I have just received my final maleficium. I patiently await news.

Love and affection always,
Your daughter, Adeline Saint-Germain

Next to her name was a tiny triangle. My phone buzzed.

Brooke	**9:17 a.m.**	Adele!!! Sorry I've been MIA. I can't tell u why. Seriously. I'm under contract

not to. HINT HINT! This message will self-destruct in 5... 4... 3... 2... BOOM. XOXOXOXOXOX

"What?!" I quickly pecked,

Adele   **9:18 a.m.**   BROOKE JONES, DID YOU GET A RECORD DEAL?!? You're going to be famous!

The front door heaved open.

"Adele?"

"Kitchen!"

My father's boots clunked on the wooden floor, and a few seconds later, he threw his keys on the table, hurrying to the chair next to me. His hair was messy, a blue-and-red lightning bolt was painted down the right side of his face, and his eyes were slightly bloodshot.

"Dad, Brooke's going—"

"Why didn't you call me? Are you okay?"

My heart skipped. *How does he know?*

"Ren just came by the bar and told me about a cat attack knocking you off the king's float, nearly getting you run over by a drunk on a mule?" he said with a smidgen of disbelief.

"Wha—? Oh yeah, um. I'm kinda banged up." I stretched the collar of my black turtleneck to show him the bandage.

"Do you need a doctor?"

"No, Désirée's mom patched me up and gave me some kind of herbal tea for the bruising on my back." It was a little more than herbal tea, but whatever—it was a little more than bruising.

"Well, let me know if anything gets worse," he said, not thrilled with my choice of treatment.

I nodded. If he'd bought that load of bull from Ren, he must have thought I was an even bigger spaz than I realized.

"What's with the lightning bolt?"

"Oh, sweetheart, we still have so much David Bowie immersion to do." He kissed my cheek, then reached for my coffee mug and took a sip. "No school today?"

"Nope. It's a Catholic holiday. All Saints' Day, not to be confused with All Souls' Day, which is tomorrow." I took back my mug.

"Speaking of miracles, I have good news."

"Hmm?"

"Once this semester is complete, you won't have to return to Sacred Heart in the spring."

"What!" I shrieked, sloshing coffee onto the table. "NOSA is reopening?"

"Not exactly." He extracted a newspaper from his interior jacket pocket. "This, by the way, is the first post-Storm issue of the *Times-Picayune*."

"Fancy."

I unfolded the thin newsprint and found a photo of Morgan Borges standing in front of the convent. I read the headline and quickly set down the mug so I wouldn't drop it on the floor.

OLD URSULINE ACADEMY
TO REOPEN HISTORIC FRENCH QUARTER CAMPUS

Mayor Morgan Borges and Ursuline Prioress Sister Angela Rouen are pleased to announce the reopening of the Ursuline Academy's historic French Quarter location, which miraculously received little damage from the Storm.

"I am so proud to make this announcement. The Ursuline Academy is almost as old as New Orleans herself. I look forward to the Ursuline sisters carrying on the traditions of the school and its mission to provide education for students of all walks of life in the French Quarter area," says the mayor.

"What the . . . ?"

My pulse started to crawl back toward the danger zone as I thought about attending class inside a vampire catacomb. A loud buzz erupted, and the lights flickered. We both jumped from the table, clutching our chests before we started laughing, realizing it was just the air conditioner revving up after being dormant for so long.

"Damn, we're back on the grid!" He smashed a kiss against my cheek. "See, sweetheart? I told you things are gonna be all right."

A light rap at the door interrupted the celebration. My stomach cartwheeled when I saw Isaac's silhouette through the white curtain.

"I hope he doesn't think we're working the day after Halloween," my father said, going to the door. "Morning, Isaac."

"Good morning, Mr. Le Moyne."

The switch in formality made my father immediately suspicious. He looked at me, then back to Isaac, and then stood his ground, barricading the entrance. "Just remember I have a gun, okay, son?"

"Dad!" I cringed.

"I'm just putting it out there, that's all." He grabbed the paper and my mug of coffee and exited the kitchen.

"Does your dad really own a gun?" Isaac asked as I took my father's place in the doorway.

"Yeah. I know, it's surprising."

"I also have half the Parish Precinct on speed dial!" my father yelled from the other room.

"Dad!"

"And don't forget that everyone in this town owes me a favor. Or ten. I've got dirt on everyone!"

Isaac's confidence was wavering, so I stepped outside, shutting the door behind me.

He hopped down the stairs, but I leaned against the door, suddenly nervous.

"Hey," was all I managed to get out.

He repeated the greeting back, but then just stood there.

"What are you doing up so early?" I asked.

"Early? I'm usually knee-deep in mold by now. What are you doing up? I just dropped you off a few hours ago."

"I don't know. Couldn't sleep. I guess it was the excitement, or the elixir." I left out the part about the severe anxiety brought on from locking Nicco and my mother in an attic to rot for eternity. Then there was, of course, our mini make-out sesh.

"Yeah, I know what you mean." He spun something in the front pocket of his jeans over and over.

"So . . . what's up?" I asked, with the feeling we were teetering on a no-going-back moment.

"Oh, I just wanted to see if you were okay . . . and, uh, to tell you something."

"Well, if by 'okay' you mean 'feel like I got hit by a truck'"—a truck called Niccolò Medici—"then, yes, I'm okay."

He frowned.

Nicco let go of your hands, Adele.

Nicco let go of you.

My feet moved out of the doorway, as if they knew my mind was about to downward-spiral, stopping on the last step to make up for the gap in our heights. I was surprised to feel my best ingénue eyes peering at him in admiration.

All I got back was awkward silence. It felt, strangely, as if it were the first time we'd ever been alone.

"I still really think you should see a doctor . . ."

I groaned internally. Maybe everything between us last night had just been due to the elixir-and-adrenaline cocktail?

"I'm fine." *I'm an idiot.*

Just as I began to feel mortified over my aggressive rooftop behavior, his two index fingers hooked the front belt loops of my jeans.

My head stopped spinning.

"Did you just come here to lecture me?"

He tugged the denim loops, making it difficult to balance on the edge of the step. My eyelashes batted nervously as I looked into his golden eyes.

"Oh, I am never kissing you again, if that's what you are wondering," he said.

I bit my lip to keep the shock from sprawling all over my face.

He did his best not to crack a smile. "Do you realize that after the first time I kissed you, you started crying, and then after the second time I kissed you, you blacked out?"

"Third time's a charm. Maybe I'll burst into flames next?"

"Oh, so this is funny to you?" He struggled to keep his serious demeanor, but didn't budge on his statement.

"Fine," I said, lightly sweeping my fingers over his cheekbone.

His eyes followed my fingers. I could feel his pulse accelerating.

"Glitter," I whispered, showing him my finger.

"Wonder where that came from?"

I tried not to smile. "So, what were you going to tell me?"

"Nothing . . ." he whispered. Then he repeated it with more authority. "Nothing."

I pulled back. "If you have something to say, you'd better just spit it out."

"Forget it," he reassured me, gripping my hips.

I didn't totally buy it.

"It's just that . . ." His fingers crawled together at the small of my back, and he pulled me close again. "It's just that I can't believe after everything we've been through, you ended up with me."

"Oh, did I?"

His head bobbed as it came closer to mine.

"*Oui*, you definitely did."

It became difficult to hide my smile.

"Isaac . . ."

"Hmm?"

"*Merci beaucoup* for catching me."

"I'll always catch you, Adele, I promise." His lips gently touched mine, breaking his short-lived vow.

No wind. No fire. No magic. No elixir. Just the warmth of his hot-blooded heart. When he pulled a tiny bit away, he took my breath with him.

"I can't believe it either," I said, trying to contain a giggle.

"Oh really? Is this still funny to you?"

"Mmm hmm," I said angelically, which he returned with devilish eyes that could only mean one thing.

"No. No!" I tried to leap back to the kitchen door, but there was no chance of escape. He easily pulled me back and attacked my ribs first. "No, stop, please!"

"I told you I'd get you back," he said, laughing.

I deserved it, but still, I hated being tickled. Although, it was impossible to really hate his touch.

Buckled over, I did my best to wriggle away, but the attempts were futile, because I was laughing so hard I could barely breathe.

"Isaac, stop it!" I screamed between gasps.

A scream that brought on another kiss. And a scream that resonated for six blocks and slipped into the slumbering subconscious of the Knight, whose trust in the Heroine trumped all.

ACKNOWLEDGMENTS

I want to thank all the people who believe in magic. Most of all I want to thank the people who believe in New Orleans—the people who've had to eat Hurricane gruel for months, who've suffered the smell of Bourbon Street on a late August afternoon. To the coffee slingers, beignet fryers, and omelet beaters. To the street artists, jazz boys, and Coke-bottle-top-tap-shoed dancers. To the Cajuns, to the Creoles, and to all those who have dreamed and suffered on our rocky streets. I want to thank the drag queens who raised me to think wearing costumes is a nightly affair. I want to thank the tarot-card readers and Nosferatu-ring-wearing blood drinkers. I want to thank every person who has cleaned mold, bailed water, or seen a nutria on the neutral ground. I want to thank the people who've rebuilt after every fire and every flood.

My journey into writing started out in total solitude, veiled by the shroud of Internet anonymity, but as I stumbled around in the void of my imagination, meeting Adele and Mac and Ren and Isaac and Désirée and Nicco, I found myself on a rainbow, sliding through the sky, through sun and rain and hurricanes (literally) and moonbeams and Milky Ways, collecting stars along the way. Never in my wildest dreams could I have imagined that so many brilliant, talented people would touch this book. In particular, and in no special order, I would like to express beaming gratitude to the following individuals:

Marissa Van Uden, my original editor, whose voice of reason is able to rescue me when I am drowning in my own world and who has reset my bar for creative collaborators; Marita Crandle, proprietress of Boutique du Vampyre, who has believed in me and Nicco since the very first day I walked into her shop, book in hand; Lucy Silag, of Book Country, who has been my unofficial mentor and who convinced me there was space for me in the traditional publishing world too.

I'd like to thank all of these amazing folks who have dedicated their time and artistry to my world: Hellvis and Christina Deare, for the original map and cover photo; Jim Havercamp, for finishing my world-class videos; Ann Horton; Ashlee Nell Rivalto; Dominique Ellis; Charlotte Ashley; and Laura Perry. To the Ogden Museum of Southern Art, the New Orleans Pharmacy Museum, and the entire team that worked on the book trailer.

Breaking into any industry is a frightening experience. Many people held beams of light on my path as I stumbled around in the dark. I want to thank these people for taking a chance on a first timer: Sue Quiroz, for inviting me on my first conference panel; Monica S. Kuebler, for being the first magazine editor to feature the book; Russell Desmond, proprietor of Arcadian, for being the first bookstore in New Orleans to carry the book and for nearly making me sick when he actually read it; Garden District Book Shop, for being the second; Candice Detillier Huber of Tubby and Coos Mid-City Bookshop; Justin Shiels of Invade; and Rachel Muller Rivera of ParaJunkee.

To Sister Carla Dolce of the New Orleans Ursulines and Emilie Gagnet Leumas, archivist of the Archdiocese of New Orleans, you have my undying gratitude. To all of the eighteenth-century Ursulines who traveled in woolen habits to the relentless swelter of *La Nouvelle-Orléans*, thank you.

The list of friends is impossible, but without these people, I might have actually thrown my manuscript into the Gulf of Mexico. My bestie, Jennifer Thurnau, who always listened attentively as I explained complicated threads about French triplets as we ran along the Hudson day after day. Lucas Stoffel, who hopped around New Orleans with my manuscript to read all of the scenes "on location." Thank you, Alex Rosa, for diving into both independent publishing *and* traditional publishing with me. Amanda deLeon, for inspiring me to be a better artist every single day. Emma Leech, for helping me not lose my mind. Jamie Gandy, for turning my hair magical colors even when it fights back. Thank you to everyone at Fifi Mahoney's and all the baristas in the French Quarter for being the only people that I spoke to for days at a time while writing and editing. Lisa Gillis, Lindsay Clarke, and Melissa Lucas, thank you for believing in this book from the very first page of the very first draft. And special thanks to my sister and my parents for supporting me in the plunge into this new phase of my life.

To my golden team of agents at ICM Partners, Alexandra Machinist, Zoë Sandler, and Katrina Escudero, thank you for diving headfirst into this ever-changing publishing landscape with me.

To Miriam Juskowicz, thank you for loving my vampires in a time when loving vampires was going against the grain and for bringing me into the Skyscape family. Robin Benjamin, for gently guiding me through the new draft, and Galen Dara, for the beautifully macabre cover illustration.

Last and most certainly not least, I want to thank everyone on the Internet! I'd like to thank the twenty-five thousand of you who followed me on Wattpad while I wrote the original draft in real time online. To the Book Country Community. To all of you who inspire me every day on Facebook and Instagram and Twitter and every other dark corner of the Internet. To those who have stuck by me through all of the iterations—David, Dan, Zeena, Wendy, Zee, Keevs, JB, Rebecca, Natalie, Varsi, Renée, Dan, Sarah, Melanie, and Melissa, to name a few . . .

Merci beaucoup.

ABOUT THE AUTHOR

Photo © Lucas Stoffel

Alys Arden was raised by the street performers, tea-leaf readers, and glittering drag queens of the New Orleans French Quarter. She cut her teeth on the streets of New York, has worked all around the world since, and still dreams of running away with the circus one star-swept night. Follow her adventures on Twitter or Instagram: @alysarden.

ABOUT THE AUTHOR